Karen Rose fell in love with books from the moment she learned to read, with Jo from *Little Women* and Nancy Drew becoming close childhood friends. She started writing stories of her own when the characters started talking in her head and just wouldn't be silenced. When she's not writing stories for readers, Karen writes stories for computers – programming keeps the other side of her brain out of trouble. She lives in sunny Florida with her fantastic husband, an avid fisherman, and two wonderful daughters who also love to read – and write! Karen would love to receive your e-mail at *karen@karenrosebooks.com*, and be sure to check out her Web site at *www.karenrosebooks.com*.

ALSO BY KAREN ROSE

Don't Tell

HAVE YOU SEEN HER?

KAREN ROSE

WARNER

FOREVER

A *Warner Forever* Book
First published by Warner Forever US in 2004
This edition published by Warner Forever, an imprint of
Time Warner Book Group UK, in 2004

Cover design by Diane Luger
Cover illustration by Danilo

A CIP catalogue record for this book is
available from the British Library.

ISBN 0 7515 3669 5

Printed and bound in Great Britain by
Clays Ltd, St Ives plc

Warner Forever
An imprint of
Time Warner Book Group UK
Brettenham House
Lancaster Place
London WC2E 7EN

www.twbg.co.uk

To the KARENS—Solem and Kosztolnyik—for believing in me and for making dreams come true.

To TERRI BOLYARD—for your openhearted generosity and constant, priceless friendship.

To SARAH and HANNAH—you are the lights of my life.

And as always to my husband MARTIN—for loving me just the way that I am. I love you, too.

Acknowledgments

DR. MARC CONTERATO and KAY CONTERATO for medical advice on this book and for all the wisdom and support they've provided over the years—they are remarkable people and incredible friends.

MARTIN HAFER for his hard-won insight into the mind of evil perpetrators, gained through years of counseling families shattered and broken through insidious crime.

MARY and MIKE KOENIG and NEIL BLUNT for their insight into the Catholic faith.

HAVE YOU
SEEN HER?

PROLOGUE

Seattle, three years earlier

"I WISHED THEY'D FRIED HIS MURDERIN' ASS," declared the first man bitterly, breaking the silence that had become explosive in its intensity.

Murmurs of heated agreement rippled through the small crowd that had gathered to watch the moving van being loaded. God only knew why they had. There really wasn't anything to see. Sofas, chairs, antiques of all shapes and sizes. Vases that probably cost a year's salary of an average workingman. A grand piano. Simply the belongings of an opulent family forced to flee the rage of an incensed community.

And the guards the family had hired to keep the crowds at bay. That was all.

The off-duty cop dressed in old jeans and a Seahawks sweatshirt wasn't sure why he himself was there, standing in the cold Seattle drizzle. Perhaps to prove to himself that the murdering sonofabitch was really leaving town. Perhaps to get one last look at his face before he did.

Perhaps.

But more than likely it was to torture himself over the one

who got away. The cruel, demonic, sadistic brute who got away. On a goddamn technicality.

There would be no justice for the grieving community, still in shock. *Not today, anyway,* he thought.

An elderly woman shook her plastic-rainhat-covered head as the movers loaded more boxes into the unmarked truck. "The chair wouldn't have been good enough, not after what he did."

Another old man squared his once-robust shoulders, staring at the darkened house with contempt. "Shoulda done to him what he done to those poor girls."

His wife made a soft clucking sound in her throat from under the umbrella she held over them both. "But what decent person could they get to do it?"

"How about the girls' fathers?" her husband returned, helpless fury making his voice tremble.

Again murmurs of agreement.

"What I can't believe is that they just let him go," a younger man wearing a Mariners baseball cap said in a bold, angry voice.

"On a technicality," added the first man who had spoken, just as bitterly as before.

On a mistake. An error. A goddamn technicality.

"Cops arrest 'em, damn lawyers let 'em go," said the man sharing the umbrella with his wife.

"Oh, no," said the man in the Mariners cap. "This technicality was the fault of the police. It was all over the front page. The cops fucked up and this monster goes free."

It was true. But he knew it wasn't "cops." It was only one cop.

"Richard," shushed the younger woman at Baseball-cap's side, grabbing his arm. "There's no need to be vulgar."

Richard Baseball-cap shook off the woman's restraining

hand. "*He* rapes and butchers four girls and *I'm* vulgar?" he declared in loud disbelief. "Don't be an idiot, Sheila."

Sheila looked down at the pavement, her cheeks crimson. "I'm sorry, Richard."

"Yeah, whatever," Richard muttered, looking up at the house. "It just pisses me off that rich people hire rich lawyers and get away with bloody murder."

Agreement again passed through the group and the conversation turned to the inequities of the modern legal system until the movers loaded the last box and sealed the truck's back doors. The truck pulled away to a cacophony of jeers and name-calling that did absolutely no real good at all, unless it made the crowd feel better. But how could it?

Then the small crowd hushed as one of the doors of the three-car garage slid open and a black Mercedes sedan emerged. No one said a word until the Mercedes was upon them, gliding by on the wet street. Then Richard Baseball-cap yelled, "Murderer!" and the cry was taken up by the others.

Except for the off-duty cop in old blue jeans and a now-soaked Seahawks sweatshirt who said not a word, even when the Mercedes rolled to a stop next to where he silently stood.

The crowd hushed again as the heavily tinted window rolled down, revealing the face that haunted his dreams, asleep and awake. Cold dark eyes narrowed, filled with unleashed fury. It was subhuman, the face and the eyes and the mouth that curved in a smug smile that he wanted to slice right off the subhuman face. Then the smug mouth spoke. "Go to hell, Davies," it said.

It's no less than I deserve. "I'll meet you there," Davies returned through clenched teeth.

The woman in the Mercedes's front passenger seat murmured something and the subhuman raised the window. The engine gunned and the tires squealed against the wet asphalt as the Mercedes leapt forward, sending up a fine cloud of charred steam that burned his nose.

And off they go, Davies thought. *Off to have a life.* Unfair. Inequitable. A vicious, sadistic murderer robbed four teenaged girls of their lives and was set free to have a life of his own. *For now.*

Because soon enough the blood lust would rise up again and more girls would be at the murderer's mercy. More girls would die, because the murdering sonofabitch had no mercy.

More girls would die. *But the next time I'll be ready.* The next time there would be no technicality. The next time the murdering, sadistic monster would pay.

Neil Davies watched the Mercedes turn the corner at the end of the street and then it was out of view. *Next time,* he vowed to the four girls. To himself. *I'll get him. He'll pay. I promise.*

ONE

THE FACT THAT HE'D SEEN MORE HORRIFIC SCENES over the course of his career should have made this one easier to mentally process.

Should have.

It didn't.

Special Agent Steven Thatcher loosened his tie, but it didn't do a thing to help the flow of air to his lungs. It didn't do a thing to change what he'd found in the clearing after the North Carolina State Bureau of Investigation received an anonymous tip leading them to this place.

It certainly didn't do a thing to bring the poor dead woman back to life.

So Steven centered the knot of his tie right over the lump in his throat. He stepped forward carefully, earning him a glare from the rookie Forensics had sent because the rookie's boss had picked the week they discovered a gruesome, brutal murder to take a cruise to the Caribbean.

Now, looking at the mangled corpse, heavily scavenged by

whatever creatures lived in these woods, Steven couldn't help wishing he were on a boat far from civilization, too.

"Watch your feet," the rookie cautioned from his hands-and-knees position on the grass next to the body, irritation in his voice. Kent Thompson was reputed to be quite good, but Steven would hold his judgment. However, the fact Kent hadn't thrown up yet was a stroke in his favor.

"Thank you for the lesson in crime-scene investigation," Steven replied dryly and Kent's cheeks went redder than chili peppers.

Kent sat back on his heels and looked away. "I'm sorry," he said quietly. "I'm frustrated. I've checked this entire area three times. Whoever left her here didn't leave anything else behind."

"Maybe the ME will find something on the body," Steven said.

Kent sighed. "What's left of it." He looked back at the corpse, clinical detachment on his face. But Steven also noted the flicker of controlled compassion in the young man's eyes and was satisfied. Kent would do his job, but still remember the victim. Another stroke in the newbie's favor.

"Sorry, Steven," said a ragged voice behind him and Steven turned to find Agent Harry Grimes taking labored breaths as he slipped a handkerchief in his pocket. Harry's face was pale, although the green tinge had passed along with the Egg McMuffin Harry had downed on his way to the scene.

New to the SBI, Harry had been assigned to Steven for training. Harry showed a lot of promise, except for his very weak stomach. But Steven couldn't blame him too much. He might have lost his own breakfast had he taken the time to eat any. "It's okay, Harry. It happens."

"Have we found anything?" Harry asked.

"Not yet." Steven crouched down next to the body, a pen

in his gloved hand. "Nude, no ID or clothing anywhere around. There's enough left of her to know she was female."

"Adolescent female," Kent added and Steven's head shot up.

"What?"

"Adolescent female is my guess," Kent said, pointing to the corpse's torso. "Pierced navel."

Harry's gulp was audible. "How can you tell?"

Kent's mouth quirked up. "You could see if you put your face a bit closer."

"I don't think so," said Harry in a strangled voice.

Steven balanced himself on the balls of his feet, still crouched. "Okay, an adolescent female. She's been here at least a week. We'll need to run a check through missing persons." He gently rolled the body over and felt his heart skip a beat at the same time Harry cursed softly.

"What?" Kent asked, looking from Steven up to Harry and back at Steven. "What?"

A grimness settled over Steven and he pointed his pen at the remains of the young girl's left buttock. "She had a tattoo."

Kent leaned closer, then looked up, still squinting. "Looks like a peace symbol."

Steven looked up at Harry who wore a look of the same grim acknowledgment. "Lorraine Rush," Steven said and Harry nodded.

"Who was Lorraine Rush?" Kent asked.

"Lorraine was reported missing about two weeks ago," Harry said quietly. "Her parents went in to wake her up for school and found her bed slept in but empty."

"No evidence of forced entry," Steven added, looking at the corpse with new concern. "We had to assume she'd run away. Her parents insisted she never would run, that she'd been kidnapped."

"Parents always insist their kids would never run away," Harry said. "You still don't know that she didn't and just met up with some rough character along the way."

Steven could see in his mind's eye the picture of Lorraine as she'd been, the smiling girl in the photograph on the Rushes' fireplace mantel. "She was sixteen. A year younger than my oldest son." Steven let his thoughts briefly linger on his troubled son who'd undergone such a radical change in personality in the last month. But that was another worry. He'd dwell on his very personal problem of Brad when he'd put Lorraine Rush out of his mind. Whenever that would be.

"Damn shame," said Kent.

Steven pushed himself to his feet and stared down at what was left of what had once been a beautiful, vibrant young woman. Pushed back the primal rage at the monster who could take the life of another so brutally. "We'll need to inform her parents." He didn't look forward to that task.

Breaking the tragic news of a loved one's murder should have been easier after all these years.

Should have been.

It wasn't.

TWO

Thursday, September 29, 8:55 A.M.

"HOW ARE YOU, STEVEN?"

Steven looked up to find his boss, Special Agent in Charge

Lennie Farrell, looking down at him with that troubled expression that made Steven want to groan. When most people said *how are you,* they meant *how are you?* but when Lennie Farrell said *how are you,* it meant they were going to have a chat, which in Steven's case would almost certainly include a discussion of "the incident" from six months before. Which Steven didn't have the emotional energy to go through. Not now.

Not after yet another argument with seventeen-year-old Brad last night over his oldest son's month-old attitude that gave "sullen teenager" new meaning. They'd fought, screamed at each other, and Steven still didn't know why or who had won.

Not after yet another over-breakfast argument with his aunt Helen over the "nice young woman" she'd lined up for him to meet this weekend. Helen never understood that he was determined to remain a widower for the foreseeable future, at least until all his boys were grown.

Steven pressed his fingertips to his throbbing temple. And especially after trying to hug his youngest son before leaving the house and once again having seven-year-old Nicky push him away. Nicky and "the incident" were inextricably intertwined.

Steven would rather date one of Helen's debutantes than talk about it again.

But Lennie's expression said that's what he'd come to talk about and although Steven had learned from experience that Lennie would not be deterred, he did know his boss could be distracted. So to his boss's *how are you,* Steven replied, "About like you'd think after looking at pictures of a mutilated, animal-scavenged corpse." He pushed the folder to the edge of his desk.

Lennie took the bait, flipping through the pictures of the

body in the clearing, his seasoned cop's face showing no sign of emotion. But he swallowed hard before closing the folder.

"And our suspects?" Lennie asked, his eyes still on the folder cover.

"Not many," Steven said. "Lorraine Rush was a well-liked girl, a cheerleader at High Point High School. Sixteen, no boyfriends her parents knew about. Her friends are stunned."

"And her teachers?"

"Nothing there either. We've checked her whereabouts every day for three weeks before she was reported missing and nothing stands out. Lorraine was a clean-cut all-American girl."

"With a tattoo on her buttock," Lennie said.

Steven shrugged. "She was a teenager, Lennie. They paint and pierce themselves, God knows why. In my day it was dyeing your hair green and sticking safety pins in your nose. We ran a tox screen on what was left and didn't find any evidence of the usual teenage party scene."

"So, in other words, no suspects," Lennie said, frowning.

"Nope."

"And the Forensics report?"

"She was killed there in the clearing. Her blood was found soaked three inches into the soil."

"It's been so dry lately," Lennie murmured. "The ground just drank her up."

Steven eyed his half-drunk coffee with new distaste. "Yeah. Cause of death may have been stabbing, but the ME wouldn't swear to it. There just wasn't enough of her body left. She'd been there five days based on the larval state of the maggots that were busy eating what the animals left behind. She was probably raped, although the ME wouldn't swear to that either."

Lennie's mouth tightened. "What *will* the ME swear to?"

"That she's dead."

Lennie's lip twitched. Once. Through all the horror, they had to find ways to lighten the stress. Humor normally sufficed, as long as they kept it to themselves. But the humor was a trapping, a cover that just hid the horror for a moment or two. Then it was there again, staring them in the face.

Steven sighed and opened the folder. "Kent also found what looks like a new tattoo on the Rush girl's scalp. Whoever killed her shaved her bald and left his mark on her."

Lennie bent down and squinted at the picture. "What is it?"

"Not enough left to say. Kent's investigating. Whoever shaved her head didn't do it there in the clearing or if he did, he's one meticulous sonofabitch. We picked at the grass with tweezers for two days and didn't find a single hair. Nothing," Steven added irritably.

It was Lennie's turn to sigh. "Well, now you've got another place to look."

Steven straightened in his chair. "What are you talking about, Lennie?"

Lennie pulled a folded sheet from his pocket. "We got a call from Sheriff Braden over in Pineville. His sister went in to wake his sixteen-year-old niece for school this morning and—"

Dread settled in the pit of Steven's stomach. Two of them. Two meant the "s" word. *Serial killer.* "And the girl was gone," he said woodenly.

"Bed slept in, no evidence of forced entry, window left unlocked."

"Could be unrelated," Steven said.

Lennie nodded soberly. "Pray they are. This one's yours. I have to ask if you can handle it."

Irritation bubbled and Steven let just a little of it show. "Of course I can, Lennie. I wish you'd just leave it the hell alone."

Lennie shook his head. "I can't, you know that. I don't want one of my lead agents cracking in the middle of what could turn out to be a high-profile serial murder case. I also don't want you to have to go through another case where children are stolen out of their beds."

Like Nicky had been, six months before when a wife-beating, murdering cop took his littlest boy hostage to make Steven back down. Nicky was returned, physically unharmed, in large part due to the heroics of the cop's abused wife, but his baby had not been the same. Gone was his infectious laughter, the way he'd hugged them for no reason at all. Nicky had allowed no hugs since that day six months ago. He hadn't slept in his own bed, either, and he hadn't slept through the night.

Steven knew this because he sure as hell hadn't slept through the night either.

Lennie broke into his thoughts. "Steven, can you handle this or not?"

Steven looked at the picture of the mutilated body of Lorraine Rush and thought about the newest girl, missing from her bed. These girls deserved justice, above all else. He looked up at Lennie, his smile a mere baring of teeth. "Yes, Lennie. I can handle it."

Lennie handed him the report, concern still evident in his eyes. "Her name is Samantha Eggleston. Her parents are waiting for your call."

Thursday, September 29, 11:00 P.M.

Thunder rolled off to the east. Or was it west? It really didn't matter, he thought, scratching the back of his neck with the flat of the blade. With his very sharp blade. He grinned to himself. One slip would be the end of him. He glanced down at the ground and raised a brow thoughtfully. One slip would be the end of her, too. But never stop with just one slip. Not when he'd gone to so much trouble. Every movement must be planned. And savored. He rolled up his left sleeve, then transferred the blade from one gloved hand to the other and methodically rolled up the right while she watched, her blue eyes wide and terrified.

Terrified was good. Just looking at her lying there tied, and scared—and nude—made his skin tingle with anticipation. She was completely under his control.

It was like . . . electricity. Pure electricity. And he'd made it. He'd created it. What a rush.

Rush. As in Lorraine Rush. No pun intended. Lorraine had been a good practice run. A good way to return to the game after so long on the sidelines. He'd forgotten just how damn good it felt.

This new one, she hadn't made a sound yet. Well, she was wearing a thick strip of duct tape over her mouth to be perfectly fair. But he'd take the tape off eventually and she would. She'd try not to. She'd bite her lip and cry. But in the end she'd scream her head off. They always did. And it wouldn't make one lousy bit of difference. That was one good thing about Hicksville. There were places you could go and scream bloody murder and nobody would ever hear a single word.

Another roll of thunder rattled the dry ground under his feet and this time he looked up to the night sky, totally annoyed. It could actually rain. How irritating was that? "The best laid plans," he muttered, then had to grin as he punned once again. *Laid.* That was the operative word. One of 'em anyway. Then the wind changed and his grin faded. Of all the sonofabitch nights to rain.

He crossed his arms over his chest, holding the ten-inch blade out to one side, and frowned. He could just get it over with, but that seemed anticlimactic. He'd planned for quite a while to bag this little doll. She'd been so unsure. "I just don't know," she'd whispered into the phone, trying not to wake her parents and sound breathy at the same time. In his mind he mocked her maidenly refusals. If her parents only knew their little darling was a real little slut, meeting a stranger after they'd gone to sleep. No brainiac here. They'd raised a slut *and* an idiot.

He closed his eyes and brought the image of another to mind. He could see *her* face in his mind. So incredibly beautiful, so . . . pure. He'd have her someday. Soon. But until then . . . He looked down at the huddled form at his feet. Until then, this one would have to do.

Thunder rolled again. He needed to make up his mind. Either hurry up and finish before the rain closed in or pack her up and store her until the storm passed through. Either way he was taking a chance being out here in the rain. A hard rain would leave the ground soft. Soft ground left footprints and tire prints and cops were pretty good about tracking those kind of clues these days. Damn forensics. No matter. He was as smart as they were. Smarter.

Hell, a baboon was smarter than the cops. If he'd waited until the cops had discovered little Lorraine's body on their own, there wouldn't have been enough left of it to identify.

And he wanted little Lorraine's body identified. He wanted everyone to know. *To fear.*

Fear me. Your daughters aren't safe even in their own beds. Fear me.

He'd wait, he decided. He'd rushed the last one and it was over too fast. Like an amusement park ride you stand in line for two hours to ride and the damn ride only lasts three and a half minutes. He'd gone longer than three and a half minutes with the last one, for sure. But it was still over too fast. He wouldn't make the same mistake again. It had been his only mistake, he thought, rushing the grand finale. Everything else he'd done to perfection. Not a single thread of evidence left behind. No surprise there. He was thinking much more clearly now.

Carefully he sheathed his blade and slipped it under the front seat of his car, popping the trunk latch on his way back to where she lay, eyes still wide with terror.

"C'mon, sugar," he drawled, scooping her up and tossing her over his shoulder. "Let's go for a ride." He dropped her in the trunk with a loud thud, then patted her bare butt fondly. She whimpered and he nodded. "Don't worry, we'll come back tomorrow. Until then, sit tight and entertain yourself. You could think about me," he suggested brightly. "You *do* know who I am." She shook her newly bald head hard, denying the inevitable, and he laughed. "Oh, come *on,* Samantha. You *have* to know who I am. Don't you watch the news?" He leaned a little closer and whispered, "Don't you have a good imagination?"

Her eyes shut tight, she pulled her nude body into a fetal position, shaking like a leaf. Two tears seeped from her eyes and slid down her cheeks.

He nodded again and slammed down the trunk. "Good girl. I guess you do."

THREE

Friday, September 30, 12:30 P.M.

TWENTY-SEVEN DOWN, THREE TO GO. And Brad Thatcher's
would be one of the three.

You're a coward, Jenna Marshall told herself. Afraid of a
sheet of paper. Actually five sheets of paper stapled precisely
in the upper left corner. Times the three students whose tests
she'd yet to grade. She stared hard at the purple folder con-
taining the ungraded organic chemistry tests.

You're a coward and a procrastinator, she told herself,
then sighed quietly. She looked across the scarred old table
that dominated the faculty lounge, a wall of haphazardly
stacked folders meeting her eye. Casey Ryan was back there
somewhere, behind the folders, busily grading the junior English class's thoughtful analyses of Dostoyevsky. Jenna shuddered. Poor kids. Not only did they have to read *Crime and
Punishment,* but they had to write a theme on it, too. She
rolled her eyes.

*Get to work, Jen. Stop procrastinating and grade Brad's
test.* She picked up her red pen, stared hard at the purple
folder, thought about Brad Thatcher and the test he'd more
than likely failed, then desperately looked around for anything else to do. The only other occupant of the faculty lounge
was Lucas Bondioli, guidance counselor by day, pro golfer in
his dreams. Lucas was intensely focused on sinking a putt into
an overturned plastic cup. Lucas tended to become very unhappy when his putting was disturbed so Jenna turned her attention back to Casey.

Casey's hand appeared over the top of the leaning stacks

of folders and grabbed another theme paper, sending the stack swaying. Standing, Jenna grabbed the closest stack to avert certain disaster.

"Don't even think about it," Casey snapped, not even looking up from her grading.

"Dammit!" Lucas bit out.

"Just put them back and nobody gets hurt," Casey continued, as if Lucas hadn't spoken.

Jenna looked up in time to see Lucas's putt go wide, winced, meekly put Casey's folders back, and sat down. "Sorry, Lucas."

"It's okay," Lucas responded glumly. "I wasn't going to make it anyway."

"What about me?" Casey demanded from behind the wall of folders.

"I didn't do anything to you," Jenna shot back. "I was just trying to bring some order into chaos." She waved her hand at Casey's leaning stacks. "You are a disorderly person."

"And *you* are a procrastinator," Lucas said mildly, sitting down next to Jenna.

Casey's hand appeared to grab another theme. "Why are you procrastinating, Jen? That's not like you."

Lucas slid down in his chair. "Because she doesn't want to grade Brad Thatcher's chemistry test, because she knows he probably failed it, and she knows contacting his father about his sudden personality changes is the right thing to do, but she's scared to call any more parents because Rudy Lutz's father cussed her out on Wednesday"—he drew a deep breath—"for failing Rudy in remedial science and getting him suspended from the football team," he finished. And exhaled.

Jenna looked at him in annoyed admiration. "How do you do that?"

Lucas grinned. "I have a wife and four daughters. If I don't talk fast, I'd never get anything out."

Casey's chair scraped against the tile floor and her blond head poked up from behind the paper wall. Five feet tall on her tiptoes, she was only visible from the chin up. "Brad Thatcher failed his chemistry test?" Her brows scrunched, making her look like a profoundly perplexed disembodied elf. "Are we talking about *the* Brad Thatcher, Wonderboy?"

Jenna looked down at the purple folder, sobering. "Yes, only he's not the same Brad. Not anymore. He got a *D* on his last test. I'm afraid to grade this one."

"Jenna." Lucas shook his head, taking on the quiet, thoughtful persona that made him a wonderful mentor to new teachers like herself. "Just do it. Then we'll talk about what to do next."

So Jenna grasped her red pen firmly, opened the purple folder, and found Brad's test at the bottom of the thin pile. Her heart sank as she marked an "x" next to every question, feeling hopelessness mount with each one. Brad had been her most promising student. Bright, articulate, a veritable shoo-in for a prestigious scholarship sponsored by a group of Raleigh companies. He'd all but thrown that opportunity away. One more test like this and he'd fail her class, jeopardizing his chances at admission to the top colleges he'd chosen. And she had no idea why. With another sigh she wrote *F* on the first page, top and center. She looked up to find Lucas and Casey quietly waiting.

"I didn't think I'd ever put an *F* on anything Brad Thatcher did," Jenna said, putting down her pen. "What's happened to him, Lucas?"

Lucas picked up Brad's test and flipped through the pages, her concern mirrored in his dark eyes. "I don't know, Jen. Sometimes kids have problems with girlfriends. Sometimes their problems are at home. But you're right. I never would have expected Brad to change like this."

"You think he's into drugs?" Casey asked soberly, voicing their collective fear.

"We all know it can happen to kids from good homes," Jenna answered, slipping Brad's test back into the purple folder. "I guess I need to call his father, but I'm not looking forward to it, not after breaking the news to Rudy Lutz's dad that his son flunked his last test and is on the bench until he pulls up his grade."

Casey came around the table and half sat against the edge closest to Jenna's chair. "Mr. Lutz let you have it, huh?"

Jenna felt her gut churn just remembering. "I learned some new words during that phone call." She managed a weak grin. "It was certainly educational. I just feel so helpless with Brad, watching him throw his life away like this. There's got to be something I can do."

Casey's eyes narrowed. Quick as a flash her small hand shot out and grabbed Jenna's chin. "There is. You call his parents, offer your support, then you step back, Jen. You aren't the savior of the world. He's not one of your pound puppies you can save from the needle. He's a high school senior with enough brains to make his own choices. There's nothing you can do to force him to make the right ones. That's just a cold reality of life. Understand?"

Casey had always assumed the role of Jenna's protector, ever since their college days at Duke. It was really quite comical as Jenna towered over Casey's petite frame. Mutt and Jeff they'd been called in college and it was a fair description. Jenna tall and dark, Casey small and blond. Casey, the perennial cheerleader and social butterfly; Jenna, much more quiet and reserved. Now, pushing thirty, Casey still played the mama tiger to perfection. Jenna had long since given up trying to dissuade her from it. "Yes, ma'am. You can let go now."

Casey let go, still eyeing her uncertainly. "Let me know how the talk goes with his parents."

Jenna found her list of students' parent or guardian contacts. "Brad only has a father."

"His mother died about four years ago," Lucas offered. "Car wreck."

Casey pushed her mouth into a thoughtful frown. "That alone's enough to impact a kid on top of what he went through last spring with his brother getting kidnapped and all. Look, I need to go. My fourth period's doing *Macbeth* and I need to set up the cauldron." She made her way to the faculty lounge door, then turned suddenly, her expression intense. "Don't let her get too involved in Brad Thatcher's problems, Lucas. She has a control problem, you know."

Lucas's lips twitched. "I know," he said soberly. "I won't, Casey."

When the door closed, Jenna rolled her eyes. "*I* have a control problem?"

"Yes, you do," Lucas said affably. "So does she. Are you sure you're not related?"

"Positive. Casey's mother didn't eat her own young." Jenna turned her focus back to the parent contact information. "Brad's dad works for the State Bureau of Investigation. I bet contacting him is going to be difficult."

"Probably."

"He'll probably say he's not available, that he doesn't have time."

"Possibly."

Jenna glared over at him. He just stared back, smiling.

"You are maddening, Lucas."

"Marianne's told me that every day for twenty-five years."

Jenna crossed her arms over her chest and sucked in one side of her cheek. "You know, as a mentor you really suck. Obi Wan told Luke Skywalker what to do."

Lucas's salt-and-pepper mustache quivered. "Listen to the

Force," he said in a deep voice, then raised a challenging brow. "So what will you do, young Jedi?"

Jenna sighed. "I'm going to call his father," she answered irritably. "Then if his dad yells at me like Rudy Lutz's father did, I'll come and cry on your shoulder."

Lucas stood up and patted her head. "My box of Kleenex has your name on it."

It actually did. *Dr. Jenna Marshall, Ph.D.*, written across the box in Lucas's even hand. She smiled, a little sadly. Marianne was lucky to have shared her lifetime with such a kind man.

Her smile faded as inevitably her mind wandered. If only she and Adam had been lucky enough . . . But they hadn't been. She sat still, trying to remember the days when Adam was healthy, instead remembering those last days of his life she wished she could forget. She stiffened her back and shook her head, as if the memories could be shaken loose that way. Hardly.

She made herself stand up. She only had a few more minutes left on her lunch break and she needed to call Brad Thatcher's father. Today. Before Brad slipped even further away.

Friday, September 30, 2:45 P.M.

Two of them, Steven thought as he watched Kent Thompson comb the grass inside the twenty-square-foot area they'd cordoned off with bright yellow tape.

A second young girl stolen. A second family crushed.

They'd caught a break in the case of Samantha Eggleston's disappearance, thanks to a four-year-old Lab named Pal, his eighty-year-old owner, and Sheriff Braden who'd secured the crime scene and called the SBI posthaste. Steven watched Kent search the ground once again on his hands and knees, this time wearing a contraption over his head that made him look half welder and half German spy, complete with monocle. In Kent's hands were tweezers and carefully labeled plastic evidence bags. Harry Grimes canvassed the outer perimeter next to the woods, just as carefully. No one wanted any evidence lost. They might not get another chance to catch their prey.

Steven studied the scene with a clinical eye. It was a clearing, identical to the one where they'd found Lorraine Rush, surrounded by the pine trees that had given this suburb of Raleigh its name: Pineville, North Carolina. Soon this pretty little town would be known for a hell of a lot more than its Christmas tree farms. Soon it would be known as the hunting ground for a new serial killer.

Lorraine Rush found four days ago. Samantha Eggleston reported missing yesterday morning. Both pretty high school girls. Both missing from their beds in the middle of the night. No sign of forced entry or evidence of an intruder in either case. With the current facts in hand it seemed they were related. Steven couldn't afford to think anything else until he proved otherwise.

The clearing was deserted now, but something had happened here within the last few hours. There was a patch of flattened grass, roughly five by three, which could have held a body at one point. It didn't now. The area to one side of the flattened grass was spattered with blood—presumably from the dog that belonged to the owner of this land, although Kent would thoroughly check to make sure none of the blood was human—belonging to either the missing girl or her abductor. The blood trail went from the clearing back to the owner's house, about a mile away on the other side of the trees, where the dog had shown up an hour before, stabbed and bleeding.

The old man had acted quickly, following the trail of blood from his house to the clearing. The man's old eyes were sharp—he'd noticed the scrap of white that fluttered beneath the graceful limbs of one of the pine trees. It was a pair of women's underwear, size four with delicate little flowers— the same size and pattern worn by Samantha Eggleston. The old man had immediately called the sheriff, who'd immediately called Steven.

Kent sat back on his heels and pushed the monocle up and out of his line of sight. He glanced up briefly. "I found a hair," he announced, deeply satisfied. "Dark. Very straight."

Steven's pulse spiked and he gingerly approached the area of flattened grass Kent was still inspecting, avoiding the areas that were spattered with blood. Samantha Eggleston's hair was dark but very long and curly. That the single hair belonged to their perp was almost more than he would dare to hope. "Unbelievable. I can't believe you found anything in all this mess."

Kent grinned before lowering the monocle and dropping back down to his hands and knees. "I'm good."

Steven shook his head. "And humble. Don't forget about humble."

"And humble," Kent added, now talking to the ground.

"Bullshit," Steven said mildly. "Tell me that hair has a follicle and I'll buy that you're good. Otherwise you're just one more geek in a welder's mask."

Kent chuckled. "I wish I were a welder. I'd probably make a hell of a lot more money."

Steven crossed his arms over his chest. "Stick with me, welder-boy. Follicle or not?"

Kent's smile dimmed. "No. Sorry."

"Dammit," Steven hissed. Without the follicle they'd have no DNA analysis.

"Hold your horses," Kent said patiently. "I still may be able to get you a DNA print."

"How many days?" Steven asked, gritting his teeth.

"Seven to ten." Kent sat back on his heels again. "Where's the dog?"

Steven looked over to one side where the sheriff stood with his arm around the shoulders of the dog's owner. "Probably back at the owner's house. The vet should be on his way to patch him up." He hoped the dog was treatable, for the old man's sake, but the Lab had lost a lot of blood during whatever altercation had occurred here in this clearing. "Why?"

"I want to swab the dog's teeth."

Steven's brows went up. "Why?"

"If the dog bit your perp, there might be some skin cells lodged in his teeth."

Steven reconsidered the young man who'd joined the SBI only a few months before. "Okay, I stand corrected. You are good. I wouldn't have thought to check the dog's teeth."

Kent grinned again. "Can't take credit for that one. Saw it on *Law and Order*."

Steven rolled his eyes. "Of course. We should bypass the academy and just make all our recruits watch *Law and Order* reruns."

"It'd save the taxpayers money," Kent said with another chuckle, his eyes glued to the grass.

Steven smiled in spite of himself. He was finding he liked the young man's easy manner a whole lot more than Kent's boss's waspish edge. Kent's boss would have normally supervised an investigation of this magnitude, but Diane was currently sunning herself on a cruise ship. It gave Kent a chance to show his stuff and gave the rest of them a much-needed break from Diane. "I'll make sure the vet doesn't do anything that would compromise the dog's teeth."

"Thanks. Tell the old man I won't hurt his dog," Kent added, dropping his head back down to search.

Steven looked over to where Sheriff Braden and the old man stood silently watching on the other side of the yellow tape. "Any more than he's already hurt," Steven murmured. Sheriff Braden's eyes met Steven's and in them Steven saw a wild mixture of abject anguish and terrified helplessness. Samantha Eggleston was Sheriff Braden's sixteen-year-old niece.

Looking now at Braden's shoulders bowed in grief and terror, Steven felt a connection with the man that went past the polite but inadequate empathy law enforcement felt for the victim, past the kinship for a fellow cop. Steven knew how Braden felt. Knew how Braden's sister felt. Knew how it felt to live with the terror that a madman held your child.

Steven carefully made his way to where Braden and the old farmer stood watching his approach. "We may have something," Steven said and Braden nodded, tight-lipped. "You did a good job in securing the crime scene. Mother Nature helped by holding off the rain," he added when Braden said nothing. Steven wasn't sure Braden could speak and Steven couldn't blame him. Braden had seen the dog's wounds, and undoubtedly his mind was conjuring every possible outcome while his heart broke at the mental picture of his niece at the mercy of a vicious abductor with a knife. Steven reached out and briefly clasped Braden's shoulder, meeting his eyes. "I'm sorry," he murmured. "I really do know how you feel."

Braden swallowed hard. Cleared his throat. "Thanks," he managed. Then he straightened his back, lifted his chin, and dropped his arm from the old man's shoulders. "My men are chompin' at the bit for something to do here. Anything you guys need, just name it."

Steven looked over his shoulder. Kent was still on his

hands and knees while Harry was searching the woods. "I think the best thing would be to limit the number of feet trampling the crime scene at this point, but they could reassemble the search party. How many acres are here?"

Braden deferred to the old man. "Bud?"

"Three hunnerd and sixty-two," the old man answered without hesitation. His voice was stronger than Steven would have expected given the old man's whole body shook in constant trembles. One gnarled old hand gripped a cane. The other he stuck out in greeting. "Name's Bud Clary. I own this land."

Steven shook the old man's hand. "I wish we were meeting under other circumstances, Mr. Clary. I do have a special request. Your dog, sir."

One gray brow went up. "Pal?" Mr. Clary asked.

"Yessir. We want to check his teeth when the vet is finished sewing him up. There might be some evidence there if Pal bit the person who stabbed him."

"Hope he did," Clary muttered. "Hope he took a chunk outa the sonofabitch."

"Me, too," Steven agreed grimly. "Sheriff, can you tell the vet not to touch Pal's mouth?"

Braden was already moving toward his cruiser. "Will do."

Steven turned back to Mr. Clary. "Do you need to sit down, Mr. Clary?" Steven gestured toward his car. "I have a folding chair in my trunk."

Clary nodded and Steven quickly retrieved the chair and set it up. He'd sat in it next to every stream between Raleigh and William's Sound, fishing for whatever would take his bait. "It might smell a bit fishy," he said as Mr. Clary lowered himself into the chair.

"It's okay, boy," Clary replied, attempting a tired smile. "So do I." He settled himself, then drew a deep breath. "I have Parkinson's and the shakes get worse when I'm stressed." He looked over his shoulder at Kent, still on his hands and knees in the middle of the bloody grass, then back at Steven, his old eyes clear and piercing. "Will you find Samantha, Agent Thatcher?"

Probably not, Steven thought, considering the vicious attack on the dog and the fate of the first victim. *Not alive anyway.* Still, he forced optimism into his voice. "I hope so, Mr. Clary."

Clary shook his head. "Call me Bud. Callin' me Mr. makes me feel old."

Steven smiled down at the old man. "Bud it is, then." He sobered and watched Bud Clary do the same. "Can you tell me what happened, sir?"

Bud sighed. "Pal's always takin' off after a bird or a rabbit or somethin'. Sometimes he'll be gone for a couple hours at a stretch, so I didn't think anything about it when he took off about ten this mornin'."

"You're sure about the time, sir?"

Bud nodded. "I had to take my wife into town for some sundries. We left about ten and Pal followed us out of the house, then took off after a squirrel." He looked up, the midafternoon sun making his eyes squint. "You need to know where we went in town?"

"Not right now, sir. What time did you get back?"

"It was around twelve-fifteen. Pal was lying on the back porch, bloody and all tore up. The missus saw the trail of blood and right off thought to call the sheriff."

Steven's lips curved at the obvious pride in Bud's voice. "Mrs. Clary's a sharp thinker."

"Always has been," Bud answered with a satisfied nod. He thumbed over his shoulder. "I took the tractor across the field, following the blood trail until I got to the trees, then I walked the rest of the way till I got to this clearing. Took me twenty minutes or so from the house." He shrugged his thin shoulders. "Then I hightailed it back and called Sheriff Braden again and I guess he called you."

Then they'd all driven to this clearing, accessing it from an unpaved dirt road that forked off the main highway. Which was how Samantha's abductor had brought her here. And taken her away.

"What exactly did you see when you first got to the clearing?" Steven asked gently.

Bud swallowed. "I knew I'd see some blood—Pal bleedin' like he was. I guess I didn't expect to see so much blood. I got off the tractor to see if there was anything else, then I saw somethin' white when I got closer."

"Samantha's underwear?" They were in an evidence bag, on their way to the lab.

The old man's jaw clenched. "Yeah. Her underthings were off to the side, blown under the limbs of one of those pine trees."

"Did you touch anything, Bud?"

Bud frowned up at him. "No, I did not," he replied indignantly. "I may be old, young man, but I'm far from stupid."

"Sorry. I'm supposed to ask."

Bud settled back into the chair, arms crossed over his chest, slightly mollified. "All right, then."

"When you came close to the bloody area of grass, did you notice anything else?"

Bud nodded, his ire suddenly cooled. "Yeah. The blood was still warm."

Steven's brows came together. "I thought you said you didn't touch anything."

"I didn't. I could smell it. I slaughtered pigs on this farm for fifty years, boy. I know the smell of warm blood."

Steven drew in a breath and let it out. So close. Bud Clary must have stumbled on this clearing less than an hour after Pal was stabbed. At least they could pinpoint the time. Given twenty minutes from his house to the clearing, Bud would have arrived at twelve-thirty-five. That meant Samantha had still been here at eleven-thirty. "That's helpful, Bud." He pulled a business card from his pocket. "If you remember anything else, can you give me a call?"

Soberly Bud took the card. "I will. Please find Samantha, Agent Thatcher. This is a small town. There's not a soul around that doesn't love Samantha Eggleston or her family. She baby-sits my great-grandbabies." Then he bitterly added the phrase Steven heard far too often. "This kind of thing just doesn't happen in Pineville. We're a peaceful town."

Too bad evil people sometimes live in peaceful towns, Steven thought. His job would be so much more uneventful if all the evil people congregated together, killing one another instead of innocent people.

Steven was walking back to the grassy area when his cell phone jangled. One glance at the caller ID told him it was his assistant. "Nancy, what's up?"

Nancy Patterson had been his assistant since he'd been at his post. She'd been secretary to the special agent before him and the one before that. She was a computer whiz with invaluable experience and Steven trusted her as much as he trusted any woman.

"You've had several calls from one of Brad's teachers."

Her tone and his own growing worry over his oldest son made Steven stand straighter. About a month before, almost overnight, Brad had changed from a warm, happy boy to a sullen stranger. Any attempt to breach the wall Brad had built was met with sarcasm and anger. They'd been through teenage rebellion, years before. This was different. And now his teachers were seeing it, too. He forced his heart to calm. "What's wrong?"

"She wouldn't tell me. She insists on speaking with you in

person. She's called twice already since lunch. She's very . . . insistent."

Steven looked around him. They were still gathering evidence and he needed to stay. But his son needed him more. "Did she leave a number where I can call her back?"

"Just the school's main number. The first time she called on her lunch break, the second time between classes. She said she wouldn't be free again until four o'clock."

Steven glanced at his watch. He could just about finish up here and make it to Brad's school by four. "Can you call the school and leave her the message that I'll meet her in the lobby at four?"

"Cutting it a bit close, aren't you, Steven?"

"Story of my life," he responded grimly.

"Steven!" Harry yelled. "Come here!"

Steven looked over to where Harry stood next to the road.

"Nancy, I have to go. Tell Brad's teacher I'll meet her at four o'clock. Call me back if she says no. Oh, and, Nancy? Which teacher is this?"

"Dr. Marshall. She's his chemistry teacher. Steven, are you okay?"

Steven's mouth flattened. "Tell Lennie I'm fine," he said grimly. "I'm not planning to freak out and blow the investigation."

"He doesn't think you will, Steven," Nancy admonished gently, making him feel like a truculent child. "He's worried about you. So am I."

Steven sighed. "Tell him I'm fine. But if I feel stressed I'll go to Meg. Okay?" Meg was the staff psychologist who had continually pestered him to meet with her after Nicky. He'd finally gone, just to get the infernal woman off his back. But she'd helped. A bit. Offering to see her at this point should make Lennie Farrell a happy supervisor.

"Okay. I'll call Brad's teacher. Dr. Marshall," she added, reminding him. She knew him well.

"Thanks." Committing the name to memory, Steven slipped the phone into his pocket and carefully made his way to where Harry impatiently waited, holding a syringe in his gloved hand. "Damn," Steven muttered and looked back to the flattened grass, the shape of its perimeter clean. "That would explain no evidence of a struggle."

"We'll get it back to the lab along with the hair." Harry gestured to where Kent was examining the trail of blood leading back to the house. "Kent wants to watch the vet swab the dog's teeth."

Steven sighed. "I just hope we find a lead in a hurry. We're running out of time."

Friday, September 30, 3:50 P.M.

"So, did you call Brad's dad?"

Jenna looked up from cleaning lab tabletops to find Casey standing in the doorway of her classroom. "Kind of. He was out in the field, so I talked to his secretary. He's coming to meet me in"—Jenna checked her watch—"ten minutes."

Casey's brows scrunched. "Out in the field?"

"He's a cop."

"Hmm."

Jenna paused mid-scrub and looked up. Casey looked thoughtful and that was always a dangerous sign. "What?"

Casey smiled and sent a chill down Jenna's spine. "I don't know. Cop, widower. Brad's a pretty good-looking kid, so Dad's got to have some good genes . . ." She shrugged. "Possibilities."

Jenna shook her head, feeling a familiar tightening behind

her eyes. Casey considered finding Jenna a mate one of her personal goals. Jenna walked to where Casey stood, deliberately towering over her. "Don't go there, Casey," she warned. "Promise me you won't do anything stupid."

Casey stared up defiantly. "You're taller today."

Jenna's eyes narrowed. "Because I'm wearing these damn shoes you convinced me would be perfect with this suit. My feet hurt and I don't have time for this right now. Promise. No contact with Mr. Thatcher. That includes telephone, telegraph, fax, sticky note, and smoke signals."

Casey sulked. "I promise. Dammit."

Jenna backed away. "Good." Gathering her papers into her briefcase, Jenna glanced over her shoulder to find Casey looking thoughtful again. Seeing Jenna's stare, Casey brightened.

"I almost forgot. I have a date tomorrow night with Ned and he has a friend. I—"

"No." Jenna cut her off with a shudder. Ned was adolescent on his best behavior, but his friends were worse.

Casey frowned. "Why not?"

"I'm having dinner at Allison's tomorrow night."

Casey made a grumbly sound. "Blow her off. Ned's friend is really cute."

"I can't just cancel on her. She'd be hurt."

"She has the hide of a rhino," Casey muttered. "You couldn't hurt her with an elephant gun."

Jenna huffed a chuckle. "She's a lot more tender than she looks." Then she remembered the purpose of Allison's dinner and grew serious. "I can't cancel on her. Next week is the eighth of October."

Casey put her small hand on Jenna's arm and squeezed gently. "I know what month it is," she said softly. "That's why I don't want you staying home by yourself. It's been two years since . . ."

Jenna pulled her arm free, suddenly irritable. "Since Adam

died. You can say the word. D-i-e-d. As you've pointed out, it's been two years. *I'm* over it. I wish everyone else would be, too."

"I don't think you are, but there's nothing I can do about your being stuck in denial."

Jenna shoved her desk drawer closed with far more force than was necessary. "I'm not in denial," she hissed. "Adam's dead. I was there holding his hand when he breathed his last, two years ago October eighth. I am not in denial."

Casey set her lips in a firm line. "You're only thirty. You need to start living your life again."

Jenna drew a careful breath. Counted to ten. Casey meant well. In fact, every one of her friends and family that told her to start living her life again meant well. "I have a very full life, Casey," she said evenly. "I don't need a steady stream of men on my arm to fill it any further."

"No, you don't need a stream of men," Casey agreed quietly. "One would be enough."

Jenna laughed, a hollow sound. "And I suppose you're going to find him for me?"

Casey just looked at her in that way that cut through every defensive layer Jenna possessed. "So how about dinner on Sunday night? Or Monday or Tuesday?"

Jenna sighed. "You're not going to give up, are you?"

Casey's smile was triumphant. "Nope."

"Where are we going?"

"Italian. New place off Capitol. Be there at seven on Sunday?"

Jenna didn't need to check her calendar to know she was free. Sunday nights normally found her in bed by nine with a good suspense novel, her two dogs curled up beside her. Who knew? Maybe this friend of Ned's would provide a pleasant evening of company. "Okay. But I'll drive myself so I can leave when I want to." Jenna glanced at her watch and gri-

maced. "Shit. Now I'm late. You go ahead and if you see anyone remotely resembling a parent in the lobby, pass by without a smile or a nod. Understand?"

"Yeah. Spoilsport." Casey started out the door, then turned
around, an uncertain expression on her pixie face. "Hey, Jen?
Did you say Brad's dad is a cop?"

Something in Casey's face made Jenna's hands still.
"Yeah? Why?"

"Ask him if he knows anything about the missing girls."

A feeling of dread settled in the pit of Jenna's stomach.
"What missing girls? Last I heard there was only one missing
girl—the one from High Point High that they found dead on
Tuesday."

"There's another," Casey murmured. "This one from
DuVal High. It's been all over the news since last night."

Jenna bit her lip. "I had karate last night and went right to
bed when I came home. I didn't see the news. God, Casey,
two girls? We need to warn our kids."

"Lucas says he'll make an announcement on Monday
telling all the girls to be careful," Casey said. "So ask Brad's
dad if he knows anything more, okay? Anything we can do to
keep our girls safe."

"I will." Jenna glanced at her watch again. "But I can't if I
don't meet him in three minutes. Go on now. I'll call you if I
learn anything new."

Now subdued, Jenna checked the lock on the chemical
closet, locked the door of her classroom, adjusted the straps of
both her purse and her packed-full briefcase, and set out for
the front lobby at the fastest pace her high heels would allow.

"Dr. Marshall, can I talk to you?"

Jenna looked over as eleventh-grader Kelly Templeton fell
in step beside her as she hurried down the stairs. "If you can
run with me, you can."

Kelly hastened her step. "It's about my test. I should get partial credit on four problems."

Kelly Templeton always thought she should get partial credit. Rarely did Jenna agree. "Tell you what, Kelly. You come by Monday morning and we'll talk. Right now, I'm in a rush."

"But Monday morning I have a cheerleading meeting."

"I can talk at lunch on Monday, then. Just not now." She softened her refusal with a smile. "You got a ninety-two, Kelly. How much more partial credit can you expect?"

"Eight more points," Kelly muttered, then tossed her long dark hair over her shoulder. "All right, Dr. Marshall. Monday at lunch." She veered off toward the lockers without a good-bye.

"Kelly?" Jenna called and Kelly looked back, impatience on her young face. "Be careful, okay? Miss Ryan just told me there's a second missing girl."

Kelly's eyes grew large. "Oh, wow. Which school?"

"DuVal."

Kelly bit her lip. "That's close. I know kids at DuVal." Then a beat later her expression brightened as she shook off the worry as only a teenager could. "See ya, Dr. Marshall."

And watching her flounce away, Jenna turned for the lobby at a quick clip on aching feet, wishing she had a tenth of the sixteen-year-old girl's energy.

"Dr. Marshall, may I speak with you for a moment?"

Jenna skidded to a stop, this time at the sound of the principal's voice, wincing when her ankle wobbled in her damn high heels. Last time she'd go shopping with Casey, she thought irritably, resisting the urge to hop on one foot and massage her ankle. Drawing in a breath to slow her racing pulse, she turned to find Dr. Blackman standing near the office door, his expression grim. Distaste instantly bubbled up at the sight of him. He was an overtly political man and . . . sleazy.

"I'm late for a parent conference, Dr. Blackman. Can I meet you when I'm finished?" By that point it would be after five on a Friday. Blackman would be long gone by then, sitting on the front bleacher of the football game scheduled to begin in less than an hour.

"This can't wait, Dr. Marshall," he answered, his voice glacial. "Come with me, please." And without waiting for her response, he turned crisply on his heel.

Jenna searched the front lobby. No one resembling a parent waited, so she bit back her annoyance and followed Blackman into his office, hoping whatever was so cataclysmically important would also be short.

A man waited in Blackman's office, staring out the window with his back to them. He was huge, his shoulders at least two feet wide. A black fedora covered his head, a black overcoat draped over one arm. Jenna raised a brow at the sight of the coat. It was brisk for fall in North Carolina, but the coat was surely overkill. Then he turned and Jenna's heart stopped for the briefest of instants at the expression in his narrowed black eyes, the clench of his square jaw. His very body seemed to vibrate although he stood perfectly still.

He was angry. He was angry with *her*. And she was sure she'd never met the man before.

Dr. Blackman closed the door. "Dr. Marshall, this is Mr. Lutz. I take it you've met before?"

Oh, God, Jenna thought, her pulse scrambling now. Lutz. The father of the star quarterback of the high school team. The star quarterback who'd be warming the bench until he brought his grade in her science class up to at least a *C*. It was school policy, she thought a little frantically as her brain reacted to her last conversation with Mr. Lutz. He'd been furious that she'd given his son's last test a failing grade. He'd called her foul names. She'd shaken for a full hour after hanging up the phone. He was staring at her now from beneath the brim of the fedora, his eyes oddly gleaming.

He thinks he's won, Jenna thought, a spurt of anger supplanting the fear. *He thinks he's got me cowed. He'll think again.* "We've spoken on the telephone, briefly," she said, gratified her voice was cool and steady. Grimly satisfied that at just over six feet tall in her four-inch heels she didn't have to look up to meet the arrogant you-know-what eye to eye. "Mr. Lutz's son, Rudy, is in my second period science class." Remedial science, she added mentally, then aloud, "When he chooses to come to class, that is. He is currently failing."

Lutz's dark eyes flashed and his nostrils flared. "My son has been suspended from the team."

"As dictated by school policy," Jenna supplied smoothly. And waited for Blackman to back her.

And waited. The silence became stifling as she and Lutz continued to lock glares.

"Perhaps young Rudy's test could be given another look," Blackman suggested from behind her, his tone artificially mild. "Perhaps his answers might have been . . . misinterpreted."

Jenna slowly turned her head and stared at Blackman, for a moment too appalled for words. "It was a multiple choice and true-false test," she said coldly. "You know, *true* or *false*. A, B, C, or none of the above. Misinterpretation would be difficult especially since Rudy wrote nothing but his name on the paper. He didn't even try to guess. Rudy failed the test, Dr. Blackman. Just like he failed the one before it. He failed because he never comes to class and when he does he sits in the back and flirts." With any girl whose self-esteem is low enough to be impressed, she added to herself, then drew a careful breath. "His grade stands."

Dr. Blackman's thin face became beet red. She noted his

trembling hands just before he shoved them in his pockets. "Dr. Marshall, I don't think you fully appreciate the severity of this suspension, to both Rudy and the team."

Oh, for God's sake, she thought, feeling the surface of her skin begin to tingle. "What I appreciate is my responsibility to ensure Mr. Lutz's son gets an education." She turned to Lutz, then felt a spurt of alarm at the cold expression in his eyes. She pushed the alarm away, focusing on the boy, on his future. "I hope you agree that your son's education is more important at this stage of his life than his extracurricular activities."

Lutz's square jaw tightened. He deliberately removed his hat, revealing well-tended dark hair, with the hint of silver at his temples. *A distinguished thug,* Jenna thought, fighting the shrill warning bells going off in her head. His eyes ran the length of her. His expression was one of cultured disdain, of blatant sexual disrespect. It made Jenna feel as if she were wearing a thong bikini instead of the tailored suit that came modestly to her knees. Again she waited for Blackman to intervene. Again she waited in vain.

Lutz took a step forward and smiled. Chills ran up and down Jenna's arms. It was not a pleasant smile. This was intimidation, in its purest form.

Jenna cleared her throat. "You do agree, don't you, Mr. Lutz?" she asked pleasantly.

Lutz smiled again, a mere baring of teeth. "Miss Marshall—"

"*Dr.* Marshall," Jenna corrected with a brittle smile. A muscle quivered in his cheek.

"*Miss* Marshall," he repeated from behind gritted teeth and Jenna lifted one shoulder in a halfhearted shrug.

"Now I see where your son has learned such impressive disrespect," she murmured, not breaking her gaze. Mr. Thug would look away first, because she sure as hell wasn't going to.

Lutz took a step closer, the toes of his black wing tips even with her open-toed sandals. Now she was looking straight up as Lutz had a good five inches on her, even in her heels. "You don't seem to understand who I am, *Miss* Marshall. I could buy and sell the school like this." He snapped his fingers next to her ear and Jenna managed not to flinch. "I could have you fired like this." He snapped his fingers again, his hand closer this time. "You have caused me a great deal of inconvenience, *Miss* Marshall. I was conducting an important business meeting in Boston when my son called to tell me he'd been suspended from the team. I had to leave my business unfinished to fly home and reassure my wife that the scout her father arranged to see our son play would indeed see Rudy play."

"The scout will not see him play today." Jenna met his anger with what she hoped was cool firmness, because her heart was knocking like an unbalanced piston. "The scout can see your son play as soon as he brings up his grade in my class." She stepped back and drew a breath. Decided to be the only grown-up in the room. Grace under pressure, her father used to say.

"You may be able to buy and sell this school, Mr. Lutz, but you can't buy and sell me. If money were important to me, I can assure you I wouldn't be here. I am here, however, and I'm here to see children learn. I can't do that without parental support. If we can't find a way to work together for Rudy's benefit, then you'll get the opportunity to attempt to intimidate Rudy's next remedial science teacher next year, when he repeats the class. Good day, sir." Jenna turned and found Dr. Blackman's face pale, mottled with red splotches of rage. She inclined her head, fighting the urge to smack him. "And thank you for *your* support, Dr. Blackman."

Shouldering her briefcase, Jenna walked out of the office and let the trembles take over.

Four

Friday, September 30, 4:20 P.M.

"DAMMIT," STEVEN MUTTERED, APPROACHING the front of Brad's high school at a fast jog. He was late for his meeting with Dr. Marshall by twenty minutes. He was lucky she'd agreed to stay at all on a Friday afternoon. That she'd stand around waiting for him was a virtual impossibility. If only he hadn't stopped by the Egglestons' house on his way from Pineville. No, he thought, taking the steps in three giant leaps, that had been the right thing to do. Samantha's parents needed to know he was working to find their daughter. They needed the consideration of human contact when he asked if they knew anyone with a propensity to mutilate animals. They'd needed his quiet strength when they fell apart, clinging to each other while silent sobs shook them until Steven wasn't sure they were even aware of his presence anymore. Seeing the Egglestons had been the right thing to do.

But now he was late for an appointment critical to his own son's life. Dammit. Someday he'd find a way to juggle it all. Yeah, right.

Steven searched the school lobby, but no one resembling a chemistry teacher waited. She'd probably gone home. Steven sighed, feeling the weariness of the day overtake him. He'd have to call Dr. Marshall on Monday and reschedule. And in the meantime worry himself senseless over what she would have told him about Brad, although Steven wasn't certain it was possible to worry any more than he already was. He knew better than most parents what kids could get involved in these days. He knew better than most how dangerous it was. Too bad his knowledge hadn't saved Brad from whatever had changed his boy to a sullen stranger in four short weeks.

"Couldn't she have waited a lousy twenty minutes?" he muttered, and made his way to the office to leave her a message for Monday, simultaneously turning his body to scan the lobby, hoping to catch a glimpse of her. He'd walked a grand total of three steps backward when he slammed into something that cried out and fell to the tiled floor like a brick.

Years of habit had him reaching for his weapon even as he spun around and looked down to find a woman sprawled on the floor, her face hidden behind a curtain of shiny black hair, her lavender skirt hiked high on her thighs, exposing the top edge of silk stockings, the bottom edge of an honest-to-goodness garter, and a set of legs that seemed to go on forever. He heard the hiss of his own indrawn breath, felt his heart thump hard, his fists clench, felt every drop of blood drain from his head.

Oh, my God, was all he could think. *Oh, my God.*

Then she looked up and pushed her long hair from her face with both hands, revealing dark blue eyes that snapped with fury and full red lips that frowned with authority. Twin flags of color stained high cheekbones. Mesmerized, he could only stare.

Until she opened her mouth. "You incompetent idiot."

Steven blinked. Opened his mouth. Closed it. Opened it again. "Excuse me?"

In response she rolled her eyes and blew out an explosive

sigh, throwing one arm wide. "Just *look* at what you've done."

Steven's eyes looked around the school lobby, seeing at least a hundred papers strewn across the lobby floor, her soft leather briefcase turned on its side. Lipstick and pens and keys had dumped out of her purse. Then he saw her massage her ankle and her face tightened, her eyes sliding shut as dismay gave way to pain.

He dropped to one knee. "I'm sorry, ma'am. I didn't see you."

"You weren't looking," she snapped back, her lips quickly returning to a firm line.

"No. No, I wasn't." He laid his fingertips against her ankle and her eyes flew open, alarm mixing with the pain. Quickly he pulled his hand back.

"What do you think you're doing?" she demanded, her voice gone low and shaky. She scooted back a foot on her bottom, her eyes dropping to her thighs. Her face flushed dark red. "Shit." She struggled with her skirt, pulling it down to cover most of her thighs.

Damn. Gone were the garters and the tops of the silk stockings. He should feel guilty for having looked, but somehow couldn't find it in him. He did, however, regret that he'd frightened her, on top of knocking her down. He held up a hand meant to soothe. "I didn't mean to scare you, miss. I was just trying to see if you'd broken your ankle." He moved his hand to her ankle, stopping an inch away to look for permission. "Okay?"

She nodded, her eyes now wary, and he went still. This close he could see her eyes weren't blue, but a deep purple. Violet. The combination of violet eyes with her black hair was . . . striking.

"It's okay," she said, bringing his attention back to the matter at hand. Her ankle. Her potentially broken ankle. She frowned again. "I can sign a waiver if you're worried I'll sue you," she added sarcastically when he still didn't move.

Surprised to feel his lips twitch, Steven made himself look away from her violet eyes and concentrate on her ankle that was already starting to swell. As gently as he could he probed the ankle while watching her response from the corner of his eye. He didn't miss the way her arms folded tightly across her chest, the way her breath caught, the way she bit down on her lips. She was in pain, but her ankle was probably not broken. Gently he placed her foot back on the tiled floor, trying not to notice the way her toenails were painted a soft pink, the way the silk stockings clung to her calves. Trying very hard not to remember she wore honest-to-goodness garters under her modest lavender skirt.

God. How many women wore real garters anymore?

He cleared his throat and hoped his voice sounded normal. "I'd say it's just a bad sprain, but you might want to get it looked at," he said, sitting back on his heels, looking away from her legs. He took note of her shoes, both lying off to the side. Black, open-toed, four-inch skinny heels.

Forcefully, he pushed the image of her legs in those heels from his brain, instead going for a tone of mild reproach. "A pair of more sensible shoes might have done a better job at breaking your fall."

Her lips fell open. "Of all the—" Her violet eyes rolled again and she struggled to her knees, smacking his outstretched helping hand out of the way. She stared him in the eye, her hands plunking down on her rounded hips. "You, sir, have one hell of a lot of nerve. You run into me, knock me down, and then have the nerve to criticize my choice of shoes!" She grabbed her purse and started to shove her lipstick, keys, and other sundries back into it. "Like I wanted to buy the damn things anyway," she muttered.

Steven picked up a shiny black compact and she snatched it from his hand with a scowl. "Give me that," she snapped.

"Then why did you?" Steven asked, handing her a plastic bag filled with . . . He narrowed his eyes and stared. *Dog biscuits?* These, too, she snatched from his hand and shoved in her purse.

"Why did I what?"

"Why did you buy those shoes if you didn't want them?"

She stopped, her hand on her palm pilot. When she looked up, her dark hair parted like a waterfall and Steven felt his heart stop. She was smiling. Grinning, even. Frowning, she was striking. But smiling . . . She was absolutely beautiful. And her smile made his own lips curve up. Warmed him, inside and out.

"My friend talked me into buying them," she answered. She reached for one of the shoes, holding it up for a rueful inspection. "I told her I'd probably fall and break my ankle."

Steven laughed out loud, physically feeling the burden lighten from his shoulders. Not forgotten, not by a long shot, but lighter. For the moment. Suddenly uncomfortable, Steven stood up. Her eyes followed him, not looking away as he found himself wishing she would.

"I'm sorry," she said softly. "I wasn't watching where I was going and I ran into you as much as you ran into me. You've been very polite and I've been surly. I've had—" She shrugged. "A bit of an intense day. I know that isn't a good excuse, but it's the best one I've got. I hope you'll forgive my bad manners."

Steven cast his eyes around the school's lobby seeing the papers still strewn about. "It's okay. Let me pick up your papers." He could hear the brusque note in his voice and hated it, just as he hated it every time it came out. But it had become a part of him, part of the shield that kept all nonessential people at bay. Still, he hated the way her violet eyes widened and her dark brows scrunched together, puzzled.

Jenna stayed where she was for a long moment, offensive shoe in her hand. The change in his expression had been abrupt, laughing one moment, then distant the next. She wondered what she'd said. He'd started picking up the strewn papers. As he leaned forward, his golden hair picked up the reflection of the overhead lights, taking on a reddish gleam. He was tall and powerfully built and she found herself mentally comparing him to Mr. Lutz as she set the shoe aside and began gathering papers. Both men were tall, but the similarity ended there. Lutz used his size and physical power to intimidate. The stranger had a gentle touch. After her initial surprise when he'd picked up her foot, she'd felt no fear at all. Lutz's eyes had been cold as ice. This man's were a warm brown and crinkled around the corners when he laughed.

Her hands stilled. Brad Thatcher had dark hair and a slender build. But her student's eyes were brown and crinkled around the corners when he laughed. In fact, Brad's brown eyes and warm smile were a lot like those of the man gathering her scattered papers. She closed her eyes as heat rose in her cheeks and she pressed her hands against her face. Brad's eyes and smile were *exactly* like this man's. Like father . . . like son. *Oh, Lord,* she thought, swallowing the groan that had started in her throat. This man was Brad's father. She'd called him an incompetent idiot. And she'd practically shown him her underwear. Some first impression she'd made.

She looked up, unsurprised when she saw her purple folder in his hands. He was reading a test in the folder, his face a study in helpless, frustrated misery. He looked up and met her eyes and she felt as if she'd taken a rabbit punch to the gut. In his eyes she saw a riot of fear, disappointment, and a weariness that made her heart clench.

"You're Brad's Dr. Marshall," he said quietly.

She nodded. "And you're Special Agent Thatcher."

He slid Brad's test back into the folder. "I'm Brad's father, yes."

"We need to talk, Agent Thatcher."

Friday, September 30, 4:30 P.M.

Leaning one shoulder to the wall, Victor Lutz watched the principal pace the threadbare carpet of his office with growing impatience. "It's quite simple, Dr. Blackman. Overrule her."

Blackman looked up, his scrawny face tight with anxiety. "I can't do that," Blackman said.

Lutz didn't blink. "Why not?"

Blackman paced to the window and, arms crossed, shoulders hunched, looked through the glass to where the Friday night football crowd was beginning to assemble.

Lutz shook his head. Blackman was a fool and Lutz was growing very tired of having to deal with him. He pushed away from the wall. "Blackman."

The principal's head whipped around at the curt address.

"I asked you a question. Why not?"

Blackman swallowed and pushed his glasses up his thin nose. Cleared his throat. "Because technically she's right. Rudy is failing her class. School policy—"

"I don't give a flyin' rat's ass about your school policy," Lutz interrupted with a snarl. "I want Rudy to play. Today."

"I can't do that. Today," Blackman added quickly. "I need time."

"How much time?" Lutz asked, mentally planning to beat the shit out of Rudy for his sheer stupidity. It would have been so easy for him to pass that test. There were ways to manage situations like this. But did his blockhead of a son think? No. He walked into the class, unprepared, and handed in a blank sheet of paper. Idiot. Just like his mother.

"A few weeks."

"Unacceptable," Lutz bit out. "I want Rudy playing next week, Dr. Blackman, or you'll find your plans for the new stadium severely underfunded."

Blackman swallowed. "That stadium is not for my benefit, Mr. Lutz. It's for the school."

"Bullshit." Lutz smiled and watched Blackman's trembles creep up a notch or two. "Your promise to build a new stadium is the only thing keeping your contract negotiations open for next year. You lose your job, you lose everything." He shook his head. "For a man who makes his living administrating, you've done a piss-poor job on your own finances. Here and at home." Blackman's face slackened in shock and Lutz chuckled. "I make my living based on obtaining information and using it most effectively. I know everything about you, down to the color of the boxers covering your pathetic skinny ass." He placed his hat on his head. "You'd be wise to remember that." He held up a finger. "One week. This time next week Rudy is back in the game."

Blackman jerked a nod. "One week."

Satisfied, Lutz took his leave, carefully closing the door behind him.

Friday, September 30, 4:40 P.M.

Steven helped Dr. Marshall to a chair at the worn table that dominated the teachers' lounge and wordlessly pulled up a second chair for her foot. She lifted her foot to the chair, silently grimacing.

"You should ice that ankle," he said.

She met his eyes, visibly smoothing her grimace to a smile, and once again he felt warmth curl around his heart. A man could get used to such a comfort. Unfortunately Steven Thatcher could not be such a man.

"We keep an ice pack in the freezer," she said, gesturing to a refrigerator in the corner.

Easily he found it in the freezer door. Murmuring her thanks, she gestured to an empty chair.

"Please sit, Mr.—I'm sorry. Agent Thatcher."

He shrugged. "It doesn't matter." He sat. And waited.

For a full minute she stared down at her hands before lifting her head. "You saw Brad's test," she said abruptly and Steven could only nod. His voice seemed stuck in his throat. She leaned forward, her expression now earnest. "Brad was in my basic chemistry class last year, Mr. Thatcher. He made it a year I'll never forget. He loved to learn. He was always prepared. He was polite, alert. Now he's not any of those things."

Steven closed his eyes and massaged his temples, a headache pounding behind his eyes. "When did you see him change?"

He felt her fingers close around his wrist and pull his hand from his face. He opened his eyes to find hers narrowed and worried. "Are you okay, Mr. Thatcher? You look pale."

"Just a headache. I'll be fine. It's just stress. Really," he added when she looked unconvinced. "When did you first notice a change in my son?"

She settled in her chair, back to business. "Four weeks ago. When school started in August I was thrilled to have him in my advanced chemistry class this year. Then right after the Labor Day break he was different."

Steven frowned. "Different, how?"

She shrugged her shoulders. "Restless at first. He missed simple questions. We had a test the Friday after Labor Day.

He got a *D*. I was stunned. I thought I'd give it a few weeks, see if he snapped out of it." She shrugged again. "Then today I graded his latest test and he failed it. He's grown more isolated every day. I couldn't wait any longer. I had to call and let you know."

Steven made himself ask the question that had kept him awake most of the nights over the last four weeks. "Dr. Marshall, do you think my son has gotten involved in drugs?"

She pressed her fingertips to her lips and sat quietly for a moment that stretched on and on. He thought she wasn't going to answer at all when she sighed. "Good kids can get involved in drugs, Agent Thatcher." She met his eyes, her gaze sympathetic. "But you knew that already. The truth is I don't know. I hope to heaven he's not, but we can't afford to believe he's not."

Steven watched her bite her lip and felt a strange calm settle around his shoulders. *We*. She'd said *we*. He still didn't have the slightest idea what to do about Brad, but knowing this woman shared his frustration and seemed to genuinely care for his son provided a foothold, a place to rest, if only for the few minutes he sat across from her. "Then where do we go from here?"

She smiled, so gently it made his heart clench. "The guidance counselor would be a good place to start. He's a friend of mine and very experienced." She pulled a sheet of paper from her briefcase and wrote a name and phone number. "Call Dr. Bondioli on Monday. He's expecting you."

Steven folded the paper and slid it into his pocket. "You were sure I'd be willing to talk to him."

"Brad's a good kid. Good kids rarely raise themselves."

"Thank you. Believe it or not, I feel just a little better."

Dr. Marshall stood, balanced her weight on one foot, and extended her hand. "I'm glad."

He pushed himself to his feet and shook her hand, feeling

a reticence to let go that was foreign to him. He abruptly released her hand. Foreign, unwise, and unwanted. "Thank you for agreeing to see me tonight. How's your ankle?"

She put some weight on it and winced. "Better."

Steven hesitated. "Is there someone you can call to get you home?" His eyes dropped to her left hand, quite of their own volition. No ring. No husband. *No way,* he thought. *Don't go there.* But he had. He wondered if his face was as heated as hers had become. Her eyes dropped to her feet.

"No, I'm afraid not," she murmured, almost as if to herself, and he wondered if he'd hurt her feelings. But when she looked up, her smile was firmly back in place. "No significant other. Just my trusty dogs." Briskly she gathered her belongings. "No worries, though. My car's an automatic and my right foot's still good, but I could use some help getting to my car if you don't mind."

"Not at all." He took her briefcase and offered his arm, steeling himself for the warm feel of her touch.

She isn't married. Gritting his teeth, he pushed the thought aside and with it the little spark it lit inside him. He needed to focus on getting her to her car and then getting home to find out what the hell was wrong with his son. That's what he should be focusing on. If he were a good father that's what he'd be focusing on. He must not be, he thought grimly, because what he was focusing on was the way her shoulder barely brushed his as she limped across the tiled lobby floor.

She fit well at his side. She was tall, taller than his wife had been, and the comparison stung as much as the memory. He tried to squelch the memory, to push it down deep where he could pretend it didn't exist, but once begun it continued to roll. There was a time, long ago when the boys were small, when Melissa would nuzzle her cheek to his chest . . . He'd lower his head, smell her hair . . . A sharp pain struck him square in the heart. He couldn't allow himself to remember anymore.

Melissa was gone, taking . . . no, *stealing* everything comfortable with her. *Damn you, Mel,* he thought, anger sweeping away the yearning.

Steven straightened so abruptly that Dr. Marshall looked up in surprise, her sudden movement sending her black hair swinging over her shoulder.

"Did I step on your foot?" she asked. He could see she was in pain. Her lips curved, but the smile was for polite show only.

He shook his head. "No."

Her eyes questioned, then dropped back to her feet when it was clear he would say nothing more. Her head lowered and her hair fell forward to hide her face. Quickly she tucked it behind her ear. Coconut. Her hair smelled like coconut. Beaches and suntan lotion. And bikinis. *God.*

She smelled good. He didn't want to notice it any more than he wanted to notice the curve of her jaw or the straight line of her nose. Or her full lips. Or her legs that went all the way up to her shoulders. He didn't want to notice any of her attributes, but he found them impossible to ignore. He drew an appreciative breath before locking his jaw.

The last thing he needed at this stage of his life was the distraction of a woman. Normally ignoring distracting women was one of the things he did best, much to the dismay of his aunt Helen. But it seemed harder today. Today he was feeling very . . . vulnerable. He grimaced. Just thinking the word left a bad taste in his mouth. But it was true, be it the emotionally taxing experience with Samantha Eggleston's parents or the fact that his son's life was falling apart and there didn't seem to be anything he could do.

Dr. Marshall paused as he opened the front door of the

school for her. Her hand that so gently grasped his arm for support gave a single soft squeeze.

"It will be all right, Mr. Thatcher," she said quietly. "You need to believe that."

He needed to believe that. He almost did. Almost wished he could have someone like her at his side, giving him the same kind of encouragement day in, day out. Almost.

He nodded once. "Do you think you can drive yourself home?"

She tilted her head as if to sharpen her focus and he felt suddenly exposed, as if she could see his most acute fears. He expected more wisdom, but instead she simply answered the question he'd asked. "Yes. As I said before, my right foot's fine and my car's an automatic. I'll be fine."

"If you give me your keys I'll bring your car."

He watched as she fished in her purse, coming up with a set of keys. "It's a red Jag."

He blinked. "You have a Jaguar? On a teacher's salary?"

"I inherited it," she said and pointed to the far corner of the parking lot. "It's over there."

He took the keys from her hand and helped her down the flight of stairs leading from the school. At the bottom she released his arm to grab the iron guardrail. And he felt bereft. He didn't like the feeling.

Distraction. Brad's Dr. Marshall was definitely that. Brad needed to get his act together and fast, both for his own sake and to keep his father from needing to see his teacher again.

FIVE

Friday, September 30, 4:45 P.M.

BRAD THATCHER SAT ON THE EDGE OF HIS BED, his head in his hands. He'd failed his chemistry test. He knew it even though he hadn't stayed in class long enough to get his test back. One look at Dr. Marshall's face told him everything he needed to know. He hated disappointing her after everything she'd done for him. He thought of his last test, the way she'd put the test paper on his desk, facedown. He'd always felt sorry for the kids who slipped their test into their backpacks without turning it over to see the grade because they knew they'd flunked. Because they were losers.

Like me, he thought. "God, I'm such a loser," he muttered, dragging his hands down his unshaven face, the stubble making his palms sting. After that first *D*, his first *D* ever in his life, Dr. Marshall had asked him to stay after class. She'd asked him what was wrong, what she could do to help. Reminded him if his grades continued to slip he'd lose the scholarship he'd wanted so much.

Slip? He hadn't slipped. He'd dived straight off a damn cliff. He clenched his fists. She should have told him to stop fucking up. She should have smacked him upside the head. But she hadn't. She'd just looked at him, her eyes so sad. She'd been so careful not to make him feel dumb. His head dropped back and he stared at his ceiling. She'd been so nice to him. He'd wanted to blurt it all out, to tell her what had been eating him alive. He still did. She'd understand. She wouldn't pat him on the head and tell him not to fret, that everything would be okay.

But what could she do? *What could anyone do?*

Brad stood up, paced, then turned to stare at his unmade bed, knowing it was there, hidden between his mattress and box springs, fighting the need to drag it out, just to look at it again.

He'd become . . . obsessed. Disgusted, he squeezed his eyes shut, made himself turn around, made himself stop looking at the line that separated the mattress from box springs. Tried to stop seeing it in his head. He opened his eyes, chanced a glance in the mirror over his dresser. Shuddered at what he saw. His eyes were red, his hair dirty, uncombed. He hadn't shaved in days.

He was a wreck.

"Brad?"

His nerves crashed and he spun around to find Nicky standing in his doorway, his hand on the doorknob. The kid never knocked. No respect for his privacy, not from anybody in the whole damn house. Rage blazed at the intrusion and he took a step forward.

"What do you want?" he snarled, then immediately regretted his words and his tone when Nicky's eyes widened and his baby brother shrank back, half hiding behind the door. Nicky's lower lip trembled and Brad felt lower than shit. He made himself smile, but Nicky didn't smile back. He stepped forward and Nicky stepped back, not taking his wide brown eyes from Brad's face.

"I'm sorry, Nicky." He reached to ruffle Nicky's red hair and hated himself for Nicky's flinch. His brother was just now getting to the point where he tolerated their touch again. Just now getting over the nightmares of guns and monsters stealing him from his bed. Nicky didn't need any anger, least of all from him.

Brad crouched down until he was level with Nicky's freckled face. He slowly extended his hand and touched the tip of

Nicky's nose. "I'm sorry," he whispered. "I was wrong to yell at you."

Nicky nodded. "Aunt Helen says it's time for dinner," he whispered back, too solemnly for a seven-year-old boy, and Brad hated himself again.

He seemed to be doing that a lot lately.

Hating himself. He thought of it again, still hidden between the mattress and box springs. Wishing it weren't there, that he'd never laid eyes on it. Wishing his life was different. Back to the way it was before, but it never would be the same again. It was a hard truth to swallow.

Brad pulled the corners of Nicky's mouth down in an exaggerated frown and found himself smiling at the soft, almost silent giggle that emerged from his baby brother's lips.

Well, they could still smile, he thought.

That was something.

Friday, September 30, 5:00 P.M.

Jenna gripped the railing of the school's front steps, the iron cold against her palm still warm from Steven Thatcher's arm. She watched him walk across the parking lot, his stride long and strong. Even from here she could see the tight fit of his jacket across the breadth of his shoulders and remembered the way those shoulders had sagged as they'd talked about his son, as if the weight of his worry was simply too heavy to bear. Jenna chewed at her lower lip. She'd told him everything would be all right. She hoped she hadn't told the man a lie.

How she wished she could have said, "Oh, no, Mr. Thatcher—there's no way Brad could be involved in drugs!" in a perky little voice that would make the anguish in his eyes disappear. But that wouldn't have been honest. She'd learned a long time ago it was far better to approach a problem with all the facts, even though the facts were often hard to accept when the fear and hurt were fresh. So she'd told him the truth. Good kids can get into trouble. He knew that already. But somehow the truth had seemed to help, making his shoulders relax just a bit.

"Jenna, you're a fool," she muttered. "An optimistic fool."

But she didn't really think that was the case. She hadn't been what anyone could call optimistic in a very long time. No, on some level, she really did believe Brad Thatcher would be all right. Maybe it was just knowing he had a dad that cared so much about him.

That had to be it.

That also had to be the reason for the urge, one she'd just barely managed to fight, to brush her fingertips across Steven Thatcher's brow, to smooth away the deep lines of worry. Because he was a kind father who cared about his son.

Not because he had warm brown eyes that crinkled at the corners when he smiled.

Or because his shoulders were so broad. Or because his upper arm was solid and strong, yet his hands were gentle. Or because his smile over her stupid shoes had simply taken her breath away.

No, she'd had the urge to comfort him because of Brad.

But the other urges were all hers and, quite frankly, surprised the hell out of her. She hadn't felt any stirrings, not even modest ones, since . . . She sighed, the sound lonely in the quiet night. Not since Adam got sick. Certainly not since he died. *See, Casey,* she thought. *I can say it. Died. D-i-e-d, died. I'm not in denial, for God's sake.*

It had been two years since Adam's death, and in that time she hadn't touched a man—not unless you counted that last friend of Casey's boyfriend Ned, the one whose hand she'd needed to firmly remove from her ass.

She tilted her head, considering her reaction should Steven Thatcher try the same thing—she would not be nearly as annoyed. In fact . . . *Just stop,* she mentally ordered herself. *Just stop that right now.*

"Jenna Marshall," she murmured aloud. "Shame on you." She looked out across the parking lot to where Mr. Thatcher stood next to her car, his hands on what probably were very trim hips.

Casey would be amused, both at her noticing Steven Thatcher was indeed a man and at the way she was scolding herself for noticing. Therefore, Casey must never know. That was simple enough. What wasn't as simple was the knowledge her body had emerged from a two-year deep sleep and her hormones were now active again. *Well, you are human,* she thought. *You had to start looking again sometime. Just look, but don't touch.*

A cool breeze fluttered and Jenna shivered first, then frowned. Minutes had ticked by as she'd stood here balanced on one foot, woolgathering. Mr. Thatcher should have been here with her car already. In fact, where was he? She lifted herself on her toes and stared off to the edge of the parking lot only to see a gray Volvo station wagon approach, Steven Thatcher at the wheel.

He pulled the car up to the curb next to where she stood, got out, and stood inside the open driver's door with his arms folded across the roof of his car.

"Do you have any enemies?" he demanded with a scowl.

Jenna's heart sank. Adam's XK 150. Then her temper surged. "Only about nine hundred," she answered from behind clenched teeth. Word of Rudy's suspension was out and now she was on the hit list of roughly nine hundred hormonally whacked teenagers. She sighed. "How bad is it?"

"Your tires are slashed, all four of them."

Jenna limped a few steps to lean against his passenger door. "Reparable?"

He shook his head. "I don't think so. These aren't just punctures, they're slashes. The tires are ribbons. But that didn't worry me as much as this." He held a sheet of paper across the car's roof. "Don't touch it, except for the corner," he cautioned.

Jenna scanned the page and her heart stilled. "'Put him back on the team or you'll roo the day you were born, you bitch,'" she read in an unsteady voice, then cleared her throat and looked up at Mr. Thatcher. "They misspelled 'rue,'" she said, simply because she couldn't think of anything else to say.

Mr. Thatcher smiled grimly. "I don't think they were too worried about the school spelling bee. Who'd you flunk off the team?"

Jenna stared back down at the paper in her hand. No one had ever threatened her before. Her anger fizzled, numb fear taking its place. "Rudy Lutz," she murmured.

"The QB?" She looked up in time to see him wince. "You're not from around here are you?"

Jenna's temper simmered. First her car was vandalized, then this *person* intimated it was all her fault. Any lingering admiration of his soft brown eyes and trim hips went right out the window. "I've lived in North Carolina for more than ten years."

"Then you should know the risks of interfering with high school football in the South."

Jenna saw red. "What I *know* is that he failed my class and I'm not only within my rights, but my *responsibility* as a teacher to—to—" She stuttered to a stop when Thatcher held up his hand.

"I didn't mean you shouldn't have failed him." He considered her thoughtfully. "In fact, I'd say you have some real guts to do what no other teacher's probably ever done before."

"Well, thank you," Jenna began, calming again.

Thatcher raised his hand again. "However, you should know that your actions are not without risk. Your car needs all new tires and you've been threatened. You shouldn't park at the far end of the parking lot anymore. And ask someone to walk out with you after school—especially if it's dark outside." He looked around at all the cars in the lot. "I'd better take you home. I don't like the idea of you being here all alone when that crowd breaks at halftime. It could get ugly."

Jenna looked down at the threatening note she still held gingerly by two fingers at the upper corner, as instructed. "It already has." She looked up and her heart skipped a beat at the sincerely caring expression in his brown eyes. *Good God, Jenna,* she thought, *when your hormones wake up, they really wake up.* Her throat was suddenly as dry as soda crackers. "I, uh, I hate to keep you from your family."

"My aunt is probably feeding them dinner as we speak and they're used to my odd hours. I'll be home before bath and bedtime for sure."

Jenna drew a breath just as an angry roar came from the direction of the football field. "That didn't sound too cheerful, did it?"

He shook his head. "No." He came around the car and opened the door, taking her briefcase in one hand. He feigned a stagger and the corners of his eyes crinkled. "What are you carrying in here? Bricks?" He put her briefcase in the backseat and pretended to stretch his back.

Jenna smirked as she got in the car. "Yes. I alone have discovered the secret for turning metal into gold bricks. I change a few folding chairs to gold every day in the hopes of early retirement."

He was chuckling when he slid into his seat. "I wouldn't say that too loud. The parents that don't hate you for benching the QB will torment you for your secret." He pulled his door shut with one hand and grabbed his cell phone in the other. "Let's go report the damage to your car and get you home and out of those ridiculous shoes." He winced. "I said that out loud, didn't I?"

Jenna smiled over at him as she buckled her seat belt, comfortable in their banter. "You did. But you're right." She held three fingers in the air, Girl Scout style. "I from here on out promise to put comfort and safety ahead of high fashion."

"My son would ask you to spit in your palm to seal such a serious covenant."

Jenna raised a brow. "Brad?"

A shadow passed over his face. He put the Volvo wagon in gear and headed to the back corner of the parking lot. "No, not Brad." And just that quickly, the crinkles were gone from the corners of his eyes, replaced by the lines of worry across his forehead.

Friday, September 30, 5:45 P.M.

Necessity truly was the mother of invention.

He stood in the middle of the empty room, viewing the bare walls in the dim glow of the electric lights. Probably not a candidate for a Martha Stewart prize, but it was solid, it had a roof, electricity, running water, and best of all, it was unoccupied. Besides, with a couple of Chinese lanterns, a little paint, a bit of cheery wallpaper, perhaps a throw pillow or two—hell, he could turn this barn into a real little home away from home.

He glanced up at the rafter beams and smiled to himself.

He could truly hone his craft in a place like this. He should have thought of this place sooner. To hell with sacrificing his victims under a starry sky. Starry skies clouded and threatened rain. And then didn't deliver. He scowled. He couldn't believe he'd aborted his plan on a false alarm. Not a single drop. He glanced down at the form at his feet. He'd stored her in the trunk of his car all night long on a goddamn false alarm.

His scowl darkened and he flexed his fist. Only to go back again this morning and be derailed by a damn dog. He'd always hated dogs. He wished he'd chased the mutt and finished him off, but if he'd left her unattended in the woods, someone would have come. That was just his luck.

He mentally took inventory of what he'd so stupidly left behind. One of his hypos was gone from his toolbox and her panties were gone from the pile of clothes he'd quickly thrown in the trunk. Damn. He'd planned to keep her dainties as a souvenir. But noooo, that fucking dog had to come sniffing, then had to play Lassie. Now there were damn cops all over the place. Luckily he'd worn his gloves. He smirked. And he'd been sure to gather all *that* before exiting stage left. They wouldn't find anything of a more . . . personal nature he'd left behind.

He scowled again. Damn dog. Spoiled everything. The next time he came across a dog . . . His scowl melted into a smile as he pictured the scene in his mind. Knives and blood and gore. He nodded, satisfied with the picture. He'd take care of the next dog he met in the manner of Bundy or Dahmer. He'd read about their mutilations. First for practice, then for fun. He'd practiced himself. Often. Of course, he didn't need to practice on animals anymore. He looked down at his feet.

Not when he had the real thing.

He nudged her with his toe, then again when she didn't respond, harder this time. Her eyelids fluttered, opened. Her eyes widened. Her tongue slipped out to wet her lips. He'd taken the tape off—no need for her to wear uncomfortable duct tape over her mouth when they were miles away from everywhere. He smiled down at her.

"Wouldn't want you to be uncomfortable, would we, Sammie? That just wouldn't be civilized." He walked across the barn, each step kicking up a cloud of the sawdust that littered the floor. He crouched in front of his toolbox and surveyed the interior with the air of a sommelier choosing the night's fine wine. He chose a syringe, a needle—fully sterilized of course—and a vial. He frowned. He was running low on supplies. He'd need to get more soon.

He stood up and crossed back to where she lay. He drew the precious liquid from the vial and withdrew the needle. He knelt down at her side. "Ready for some more dreams, Sammie?"

She struggled, but there really wasn't much she could do under the situation. She went stiff when the needle penetrated her upper arm, then moaned. "No," she whispered, her voice pathetically weak. "Please."

He tilted his head to one side. "But I do please." And he leaned forward to whisper in her ear, the suggestions as horrific as he could conjure. Her reemergence dreams would be . . . interesting.

"Welcome to the k-zone," he intoned in a deep voice. But she was already too far gone to hear him. He swept the sawdust aside, sat back, and waited for the show to begin.

Six

Friday, September 30, 6:45 P.M.

BRAD'S DR. MARSHALL HAD BEEN QUIET FOR MOST of the ride to her apartment, speaking only to give him the most basic directions. Steven pulled into an empty slot in front of her apartment and turned to study her face. After Raleigh PD took her statement she'd become subdued, as if the import of the threat was finally real. He saw it often. After an incident people tended to behave with excessive bravery or optimism—until the adrenaline wore off and reality sank in. He suspected that's where Dr. Marshall's mind was at this point. Mulling over the possibilities. Who could have written that note? And would they carry through on their threat?

She sat very still, looking down at her hands clasped tightly in her lap, her hair hanging down so that all but the tip of her nose was obscured. Her left hand was bare, as he'd noticed before, but now he noted the thick silver ring she wore on her right thumb. A Celtic design. A man's ring.

He didn't like that. He didn't like that she wore a man's ring or that she worried it. But, of course, it didn't matter what he didn't like as he'd only see her this once.

Only this once.

He didn't like that, either. To his great irritation, he realized he didn't want to leave. Didn't want their time together to come to an end. Hah. As if "they" had "time together." They'd met, talked, and would likely never meet nor talk again. Still, he hesitated. She sat so quietly, staring down at her hands. Miles away. He was almost afraid to break into her thoughts.

He leaned toward her and caught the coconut scent of her hair. Breathed deeply. Then cleared his throat.

"Dr. Marshall?" he said quietly.

Her head jerked up, sending her hair sliding back against her cheeks. Her eyes, wide and startled, met his, blinked, then focused. And her cheeks turned the most becoming shade of rose.

"I'm sorry," she said. "I didn't realize we were here already." Her eyes dropped to her fingers, busily fidgeting with the silver ring. "I guess I just realized that someone hates me enough to slash my tires and threaten me with hate mail." Her lips quirked up. "Without a spell-checker of course."

He smiled back. "Are you ready to go in?"

She reached to the floorboard for her purse. "Sure. Just give me a second to find my keys." She rummaged for a minute, then stopped and looked back at him, her eyes almost black in the shadow of the Volvo's overhead light, her dark brows bunched. "I think you still have them."

"Oh." Without taking his eyes from her face, Steven reached in his coat pocket and pulled out her keys. "Here you go."

She took her keys gingerly, not even brushing his hand in the process. And he felt disappointed. Then felt annoyed at feeling disappointed. He sat back firmly in his seat. "You put the card for the towing company in your purse. They said your car would be ready by tomorrow at noon. And don't forget to call the Raleigh PD for their report for your insurance company."

Her expression went blank for just a moment and she blinked. "I'm sorry, my brain just crashed. What was the name of the officer again?"

"You're feeling the aftereffects of an adrenaline high," Steven explained, reaching for a pen and one of his business cards. He scrawled the officer's name on the back. "His name is Al Pullman and he's with the Investigative Division." Steven hesitated, then blurted, "My office number's on the front. Call me if you need anything else."

She took the card, her lower lip clamped between her teeth. "Do you have another card?"

Silently he gave her one and watched as she wrote on the back in neat block letters. She looked up, still biting her lower lip, and he felt the sizzle of lust head straight down along with the urge to bite her lip himself. But that was crazy. Primal and crazy. In a few minutes, he'd be gone, never to see her again.

She held out the card. "I'm not making a . . . a . . . pass at you, Mr. Thatcher," she said softly. "Truly. I just wanted you to know I care very much about Brad. If you need to talk, here's my home number and my e-mail address." She gave a little shrug. "He's important to me, too."

He slipped the card into his pocket. "Thank you."

"I guess I'll get out of your hair now. Thanks for everything." She got out and waved.

He watched her limp up the sidewalk. The apartment unit had a floor-to-ceiling window, three stories high, and through it he could see the flights of stairs winding to the top. That meant there was probably no elevator. And she'd written Apartment 3-D on the back of his business card. Third floor. He continued to watch as she limped inside and climbed to the first landing, one plodding step at a time. Then stopped to rest. And slip off her ridiculous shoes.

Steven sighed. He was the cause of her injury, even though her shoes were ridiculous. Sitting here while she navigated the stairs alone went against everything his mother had ever taught him. Open doors, hold umbrellas, pull out chairs and assist those you've maimed. Well, Mom had never said the last one, but she would have, had the occasion come up. Helping would be the gentlemanly thing to do. Helping would also give him one last opportunity to feel her brush against him and to smell the soft fragrance that made him wonder if it was any stronger on her bare skin. He drew a deep breath. *Bare skin.* That particular picture was one he should put out of his mind that minute. But once there, the picture stubbornly refused to budge. It was a very nice picture.

If he was perfectly honest, he wanted to see her to her door, whatever his motivation. *So do it, putz,* he told himself. He didn't need to tell himself twice. He was out of his car and at her side by the time she was halfway up the next flight of stairs.

She made a face at his appearance. "Now I'm really going to feel guilty at keeping you from your kids. I'm fine. Go home, Mr. Thatcher."

He took her shoes in his right hand and offered his left arm. "Steven," he said before he realized the correction was coming out of his mouth. Once said, the wall of formality couldn't be rebuilt. Even if he'd wanted to. Which, given the picture still flashing in his mind, he didn't want to.

She took his arm, embarrassed gratitude in her expression. "Jenna. And thanks. You really don't have to." She hopped up a step, leaning on his arm. "But thanks just the same."

By the time they reached her apartment she was flushed and heated and he more so, and very glad he was wearing his suit jacket. It was a good thing he was never seeing her again. His heart couldn't take it.

"Thank you, once again." She smiled and extended her hand. "It was a pleasure meeting you, Steven. Thank you for being there when I needed you."

He took her hand. "Thank you for caring about my son."

Her next words were cut off by a pandemonium of barking. She glanced at her door and gently pulled her hand from his. "I need to go." She gestured at the door. "I have to, um, walk the dog."

"What kind of dogs are they?"

Her eyes darted sideways. "Just one," she said brightly. "Just one dog." She glanced over to her neighbor's door and rolled her eyes. "I'm all *right,* Mrs. Kasselbaum. No need for concern."

Steven looked to his left, just in time to see the neighbor's door close. "Nosy neighbor?"

She rolled her violet eyes again. "You have no idea." The barking continued and she put her key in the door. "Well, um, thanks again."

Steven raised a brow. She was trying to get rid of him and he thought he knew why. "Your *dog* get any media attention, Jenna?"

She looked startled. "Why would you say that?"

He shrugged. "Seems to me a two-headed dog would be the toast of the talk-show circuit." He leaned forward. "That's an awful lot of barking for just one canine," he murmured and watched her cheeks color up and her brows snap together in irritation.

"Oh, for heaven's sake," she snapped and opened the door. "Come in and close the door."

He followed her into her apartment, unsurprised to see two identical German shepherds crouched, teeth bared. Their barks had turned to ominous growls.

"I'm fine," she told them. "No bark. Down." Both dogs dropped to their bellies, barking ceased, but eyes still narrowed and wary. "They're trained," she said defensively.

"Impressive."

"They wouldn't hurt a fly."

Steven shook his head. "I don't know about that."

"They're trained to defend. If they perceive me to be in danger . . ." She shrugged.

He lifted his eyes from the dogs and looked around her living room. It was decorated in warm browns, a large soft-looking sofa dominating one wall. The far wall was covered in a collage of framed photographs. He would have liked to walk over and inspect each one, to learn more about this woman who cared for his son. But the one step he took brought new growls from the defending duo. "Why do you have two dogs trained to defend? And why all the secrecy?"

She limped over to an antique rolltop desk where every piece of paper was tidily filed in the various slots. She opened a drawer and began rummaging. "I'm a woman living alone. I thought it was safer than having a gun. Where is that ace bandage?"

He nodded. "Wise. So why the lie? Why did you say there was only one?"

"Here it is." She pulled out a rolled bandage and sat down on the chair in front of her desk. "Turn around, please."

"Excuse me?"

Her face flushed once again. "You've already seen more of me today than I show at the beach. I want to wrap my ankle and my stocking's in the way. Please, turn around."

Steven's breath caught in his throat even as he turned around obediently. The memory of those long legs with the sheer stockings was enough to suck the air right out of his lungs. He gritted his teeth at the sound of whispering silk, knowing it was sliding across that long expanse of leg. He clenched his hands into hard fists, wishing it were his own hands doing the sliding. He breathed in. Breathed out. It didn't help.

He really shouldn't be here. He should leave. *Just a few more minutes,* he promised himself. He cleared his throat. "Why lie about having two dogs?" he asked.

"Because my lease says I can only have one," she answered. "You can turn back around now. I'm decent."

And to his chagrin, she was, her skirt back in place, her fingers nimbly winding the last few inches of bandage around her ankle. "So why do you have two?"

She secured the end of the bandage before looking up with a grimace. "Because I'm a sucker who can't say no to sad eyes and a wet tongue," she replied, her tone wry. "I used to volunteer at the local shelter and one day somebody brought in a very pregnant female shepherd they'd found abandoned. She had a litter of eight pups and I took one." She pointed to the dog on the left. "Jim, shoes." The dog got up and trotted back to the bedroom. "Jean-Luc here was passed over again and again because he had a bad eye, and he was coming up on his time limit." She sighed. "I couldn't let him die—I'd taken care of him from the day he was born. So I brought him home with me." She snapped her fingers. "Jean-Luc, slippers." The other dog got up and followed the path the first had taken. "Jean-Luc's eye cleared up eventually. I'm only supposed to have one dog here, but I'm on the waiting list for some places that allow two." She shrugged guiltily. "So I walk them one at a time and keep hoping everybody will think they're the same dog until I can get into one of the multi-dog apartments." She frowned. "Mrs. Kasselbaum suspects," she said darkly. "She's just the sort to rat on me to the building manager and get me evicted."

Steven shook his head, unable to hold back the smile. "Today little white lies, tomorrow you'll be robbing banks. It's a slippery slope down the path of moral decline, Dr. Marshall."

"Jenna," she corrected and narrowed her eyes warily. "You won't tell, will you? Because if you plan to, I'll have to kill you and feed you to the boys."

Steven shuddered. "No, I promise your landlord won't hear it from me."

She nodded once. "Well, all right then. So long as we're clear. Oh, good, here they come. What took you guys so long?"

To Steven's amazement both dogs came trotting back, one

holding a pair of running shoes in his mouth, the other a pair of oversized fuzzy slippers with Tweety Bird's head on the toes. "I wouldn't have believed that if I hadn't seen it with my own eyes. They must have spent a lot of time in obedience school."

She grinned and his heart stuttered. "I tried to teach them to fetch pizza and beer from the fridge, but they kept confiscating the goods en route." She scratched each dog behind the ears in turn.

"But you didn't teach them to defend in obedience school."

She shook her head while slipping her wrapped foot into Tweety Bird. "No, there was a rash of robberies near here when I first moved in so I found a training facility out past Pineville." She looked up from tying her running shoe on the uninjured foot. "I hate guns, so I put the boys to work for their kibble."

Pineville. Steven glanced at his watch and grimaced as she got up and limped to her coat closet. He still had hours of paperwork to do before bed tonight and he still hadn't talked to Brad.

"So are you ready to stop procrastinating?" she asked from inside the closet.

Steven frowned. "What are you talking about?"

She reappeared, a golf club in one hand. "You've been putting off talking to Brad." She followed up the accusation with a smile. "It's okay. I procrastinated myself today, grading his test, then calling you. A bit of apprehension is perfectly normal. I don't mind being a temporary distraction under the circumstances. But it's time to go home, Steven." She picked up a leash from her lamp table and clucked her tongue. One of the duo jumped up and she snapped the leash on the dog's collar. "Good boy." She opened the door and waited for him to follow.

"I am not procrastinating."

She shrugged. "Okay." She looked over her shoulder. "Make sure that door closes behind you."

He closed the door and followed her down the stairs, the dog happily behind at her side. Once at the bottom, she stopped on the sidewalk next to his Volvo.

"I'm not procrastinating," he repeated, a bit more weakly this time. "I don't think."

She smiled again. "Well, it's either that or I'm utterly fascinating and a brilliant conversationalist—and I know that's not true." She hesitated, then lifted her hand to his upper arm and squeezed. "Have courage, Steven."

She was standing close enough that he caught the faint scent of coconuts. Without her ridiculous shoes the top of her head was level with his chin. She'd fit perfectly in his arms. He knew it instinctively. Just as he knew she was wrong about one thing. He did find her utterly fascinating. With her face lifted up, her forehead was inches from his mouth. He looked into her eyes and for a brief moment thought about pressing a kiss to her forehead, then took a mental step back. It was crazy. Sheer lunacy. But he still wanted to.

God knew he didn't get everything he wanted.

"Thank you," he said, his voice husky. "For Brad."

She took a few steps backward, leaning on the golf club, the dog matching her step for step. "Go home, Steven. Take care."

Friday, September 30, 7:30 P.M.

Steven pulled into his driveway and simply sat for a moment, trying to quiet the riot in his mind. He was having a devil of a time focusing on anything. His brain would flip from Brad to Samantha Eggleston to Jenna Marshall's violet eyes and her soft voice telling him to have courage. Then back to Brad and the whole damn slide show would begin again, accompanied by the rhythmic throbbing in his head. He rested his forehead on the steering wheel and closed his eyes.

Brad. His son who had changed before his eyes. His son who was the most important person in the world right now. His son who needed him. His son who had responded to every overture in the last month with hostility and a defensive wall Steven had found unscalable.

A knock on his car-door window had him nearly jumping out of his skin. But he had to smile at the little freckled face whose nose was currently smushed against the glass, whose mouth was distorted into a terrible grimace by little fingers. Steven narrowed his eyes, then responded with a horrific face of his own, his eyelids pulled back, every tooth exposed, then stuck out his tongue.

They held their individual poses, each waiting the other out until Nicky folded and pulled back from the window. There had been a long time when Nicky couldn't play. He still rarely laughed and never slept through the night. Steven could only hope soon they'd reach the end of those horrible days, never to return. He climbed from the car and pulled his baby into his arms, hugging him tight. Nicky pushed against him, struggling against the hug and Steven immediately loosened his hold. It had been that way since "the incident" six months ago. Physically unharmed, his son's spirit had been broken. Steven missed Nicky's giggles and spontaneous laughter.

But he missed Nicky's hugs most of all.

Steven hoisted his littlest boy high.

"Sorry, baby."

Nicky pursed his lips. "I'm not a baby."

Steven sighed. "Sorry, I forgot. You keep doing that growing thing, no matter how many times I tell you to stop."

Nicky lifted a brow. "The book didn't work either."

Steven chuckled. It was their favorite parley these days. He'd threaten to stunt Nicky's growth by putting a book on his head and Nicky would grab the heaviest book he could carry. His little arms were growing stronger—last week he'd grabbed the thickest dictionary on Steven's shelf. "I'll just have to get a bigger book."

"Can't. Aren't any bigger in the whole house, Daddy."

"Then we'll have to go to the library." He lifted Nicky to his shoulders and jogged toward the house, bouncing Nicky all the way. "Duck," he said just before they passed through the front door. Inside, Steven drew a deep breath. "Smells good. What was for supper?"

"Pot roast with mashed potatoes." Nicky wiggled until Steven set him on the hardwood floor. "Aunt Helen saved you a plate. She said you were going to get fat from all that fast food."

"And wasn't that just so kind of her," Steven said dryly.

Nicky poked him in the stomach. His still very flat stomach. "She said you'd never be able to catch a pretty wife if you got fat."

Steven rolled his eyes. Catching him a wife was Helen's mission in life. He crouched down and motioned Nicky to come closer. "We guys got to stick together. Warn me true. Does Helen have a new lady lined up?"

Nicky covered his mouth with both hands. And winked.

Steven laughed aloud even as he dreaded this latest battle with his aunt. A tenacious matchmaker, she never gave up. He ruffled Nicky's red hair. "Benedict Arnold."

"Who's that?"

"A traitor." Steven straightened and looked around, seeing neither of his other two sons. "Where are your brothers, honey?"

"Matt's playing video games." His face fell. "Brad's in his room."

Steven looked up the stairs, wishing he knew what to say when he reached the top. "Can you do me a favor, Nicky? Can you tell Aunt Helen I need to take a shower and head back out?"

"But—" Nicky started, then sighed. "Okay, Daddy."

The beleaguered acceptance hurt more than a temper tantrum. He was spending more and more time away from home these days. "Nicky, what do you say we go fishing next weekend?"

His baby's face brightened marginally. "Promise?"

Given the Eggleston case, that might be a hard promise to keep. "I can promise to try."

Nicky looked away. "Okay. I'll go tell Aunt Helen."

Wishing he could make an honest-to-goodness promise that he could keep, Steven watched his youngest drag his feet on the way to the kitchen. Wishing he weren't so bone-tired, he climbed the stairs and knocked on his oldest son's bedroom door. "Brad?"

"What?"

Steven closed his eyes at the belligerent reply. "I need to talk to you, son."

"I don't want to talk to you."

Steven's temper simmered and with an effort he slapped a lid on it. "Tough. You're going to." He pushed open the door and entered, closing the door and leaning back against it. His eyes took a ride around the room, looking for anything that was out of place, not sure what he'd do if he found it. But everything looked normal, with the exception of the unmade bed and his unkempt son sitting against his pillows, his dirty high-tops perched unapologetically on the rumpled blanket. Brad's dark hair was dirty and uncombed, his face heavy with dark stubble, his bloodshot eyes narrowed suspiciously. Clean and kempt, Brad was the spitting image of his mother. At this moment his son looked like an extra from a biker flick.

Steven pulled the chair from Brad's desk and straddled it, resting his chin on the chair's back. Brad's stare had gone from suspicious to hostile. "We need to talk, Brad."

Brad shrugged sarcastically. "Can I stop you?"

"No." He met his son's turbulent gaze and held it until Brad looked away. "What's going on here, Brad?" he asked quietly.

Another shrug. "Nothing. Nothing at all."

Steven swallowed, let his eyes roam the room, taking in the familiar posters from Brad's favorite horror movies. Steven wasn't certain why his son wanted to stare up at Anthony Hopkins sporting a wire muzzle when he woke in the middle of the night, but Brad apparently did. Should he comment on the football that lay idle in the corner, suggest they throw a few? He drew a breath and let it out. No, he'd tried all those things already, in one form or another. He had to confront this head-on and pray for wisdom. And courage. The picture of Jenna Marshall's face filled his mind and this time he held on to it as long as he could. *Courage, Steven.*

"Dr. Marshall called me today."

Brad's head whipped around, a look of unholy rage lighting his eyes. "She had no *right*!"

"She had every right. She cares about you, Brad." Suddenly weary beyond measure, Steven closed his eyes. "So do I."

"Yeah, right," came the muttered response.

Steven opened his eyes abruptly to find his son's arms folded tightly across his broadening chest, his face staring straight ahead, his eyes locked on nothing at all. Steven bit the inside of his jaw, fighting the overwhelming urge to cry. "What's that supposed to mean?"

Brad huffed a mirthless chuckle. "It means . . . yeah . . . right."

"What's happened to you, son? One month ago you were bright, happy, *clean.* Now you're failing chemistry, for God's sake! How many other classes are you failing where the teachers haven't called me? Where they don't care enough to stay an hour late on a Friday afternoon to tell me how low my son has dropped?"

Brad said nothing and Steven felt his frustration building.

"Just tell me the truth, Brad. Are you doing drugs?"

Brad stiffened, then deliberately turned only his head to stare coldly. "No."

"And I can believe you?"

One corner of Brad's mouth turned up in a surly parody of a smile. "Obviously not."

Steven jumped to his feet, staring at Brad, incredulity robbing him of any intelligent response. He turned his back and stared at the wall, unable to stand the virulent anger, the dark hatred in his son's eyes. It was as if Brad blamed *him.* "Why, Brad?" he whispered.

"Why, which?" Brad answered with a sarcastic question of his own.

"Why are you doing this to me, to your brothers? To yourself?" Steven folded his arms across his chest, putting pressure against his heart that felt physically sore. His throat ached, but he managed to contain the emotion, swallowing back the lump he feared would choke him. His son. The fear clawed at his gut. Betrayal ripped so deep it left him numb. "Why?" He could barely hear his own whisper.

Brad simply looked at him, his eyes gone cold. "Because."

Because? *Because?* What the hell kind of answer was that? Steven waited, his heart pounding in his throat. And then he stepped backward toward the door, because it seemed that was the only answer he was going to get. When his back hit the door he cleared his throat.

"I have to go out again. I have a missing girl in Pineville." Was that a flicker in his son's eyes? Some evidence of compassion? "I don't know when I'll be home. Aunt Helen has a canasta game tomorrow night. I need you to be here with your brothers in case I'm not here. Brad?"

Brad jerked a nod, then leaned back against his pillow and closed his eyes. Steven stood for a moment, watching his oldest son effectively ignore him. Dismissed, he opened Brad's bedroom door, waited until he closed the door on the other side, then let his body sag against the wall.

"What should I do?" he whispered hoarsely, his eyes clenched shut. "Please, God, tell me."

But the voice quietly murmuring in his mind was Jenna Marshall's. *Have courage, Steven.* If only it were that simple.

Friday, September 30, 7:30 P.M.

Jenna unsnapped the leash from Jim's collar and straightened her back with a sigh. Her ankle throbbed, but at least both dogs were walked for the evening. There was no way she'd have asked Steven Thatcher to do it for her, although he probably would have welcomed the chance to put off going home another fifteen or twenty minutes. She wondered if he'd talked to Brad.

Wondered if there was anything more she could do.

She put the thought out of her mind. Casey was right. There was truly nothing more she could do other than let the parents know. She needed to tell them, then walk away, even if they had broad shoulders, beautiful eyes, muscular biceps, and smelled really good.

Jenna chuckled at herself. "Hormones," she murmured. It was a good thing she didn't need to see Steven Thatcher again, she thought. She needed a bit of time to bring all those newly awakened hormones under tight control. "Wouldn't want to do anything stupid," she said to Jean-Luc who sat looking up hopefully.

But Jenna Marshall rarely did anything stupid. "I rarely do anything at all," she said to Jean-Luc, who licked her hand. And tonight would be no exception. Tonight she'd snuggle into the corner of her sofa, alone. And watch old movies, alone. And, if she was lucky, she'd have some leftovers in the fridge she could warm up and eat. Alone.

It was rare for her to indulge in self-pity. *So stop it,* she told herself. But once rolling, the pity train was hard to brake. Her thoughts ran to Adam, about the days she hadn't been alone. "Great," she muttered aloud. "Now I feel even worse." She eyed Jim and Jean-Luc balefully. "At least you two can't tell me I've grieved long enough and to get on with my life."

A knock at the door sent both dogs into a snarling crouch.

"Settle," Jenna commanded and limped over to the door to peek through the peephole. And sighed. Adam's father stood there, tapping one foot. She opened the door. "Hi, Dad." Having lost her own parents years before, she'd been instantly adopted by Adam's family. She nodded to the pair of eyes peeking from the darkened apartment across the hall. "Hello, Mrs. Kasselbaum."

Mrs. Kasselbaum appeared, her silver hair perfectly coiffed, her housedress perfectly starched—as usual. She patted her hair, then lightly stroked the ever-present pearls around her neck. Jenna often thought this was how Beaver Cleaver's mother would look, forty years later. "Hello, Jenna. Your young man didn't stay very long."

Adam's father raised his bushy brows. "What young man? Where's your car? It's not outside."

"I don't have a young man. Come in, Dad."

Seth Llewellyn turned to Mrs. Kasselbaum with a frown. "What young man? Where's her car?"

Mrs. Kasselbaum leaned forward conspiratorially. "She came home with a man. Tall, clean-cut, very handsome. Blond hair, size forty-eight long, brown eyes. I know nothing about her car."

Jenna rolled her eyes. "Come *in,* Dad. Good *night,* Mrs. Kasselbaum."

Seth didn't even glance Jenna's way. "How tall? How handsome?"

Mrs. Kasselbaum looked up, batting her eyelashes. Mrs. Kasselbaum had a thing for Adam's father, a widower for as long as Jenna had known him. "About as tall as you," Mrs. Kasselbaum said coyly and Jenna rolled her eyes. Steven Thatcher, although not her young man, was at least three inches taller than Seth. Maybe four. Mrs. Kasselbaum batted her eyes again, with enough power to take off in flight. "But not as handsome as you."

Seth laughed. "Go on with you, now." He leaned a little closer toward Mrs. Kasselbaum, only encouraging her further. "And how long did he stay?"

Jenna hit her head against the door frame. Several times. The two matchmakers ignored her.

"Sixteen minutes," Mrs. Kasselbaum answered, nodding emphatically.

Seth pursed his lips. "Only sixteen minutes?"

Mrs. Kasselbaum shrugged her thin shoulders and sighed dramatically. "I can only tell what I see." She raised a superior gray brow at Jenna. "She'll have to do the rest by herself."

"Oh, for heaven's sake," Jenna said. "Dad, I hurt my ankle and shouldn't be on my feet."

Seth was instantly contrite. "Why didn't you say so, young

lady?" He waved a fast good-bye at the disappointed Mrs. Kasselbaum and hurried inside where he put his hands on his hips. "What happened to your ankle? Who was the young man? And where is your car?"

Jenna rolled her eyes again. She loved Adam's family dearly, but sometimes they could be a bit smothering. She limped to the sofa and sat down. "He's not a young man. He's the father of a high school senior so he's got to be—oh, I don't know—forty at least."

Seth winced. "Forty is ancient."

"You know what I mean."

"Does this forty-year-old father of a high school senior have a name?"

"His name is Steven Thatcher. I called him for a conference and when we met he accidentally knocked me down and I twisted my ankle. He felt badly and brought me home."

Seth looked alarmed. "Your car's still in the school parking lot? We shouldn't leave it there over the weekend—I'll drive over and get it." He turned for the door and Jenna cleared her throat.

"Dad, wait." He stopped and turned, his expression expectant. Jenna had hoped not to have to tell them that her car—Adam's car—had been towed. Adam had restored the old 1960 Jag XK 150 as an undergraduate. It had been his pride and joy, even when he'd become way too sick to drive it. Adam had left her the car in his will and although none of Adam's family had disputed it, the well-being of the car was well monitored by the entire Llewellyn clan.

"The car's fine, Dad." He breathed a sigh of relief. "But the tires were slashed today."

His whole body tensed. "How?"

Jenna shrugged. "I flunked one of the kids on the football team. It was childish retaliation." She would keep the threatening note to herself. "Don't worry, I asked the guys that towed the car to replace the tires with the same kind Adam used." It would cost her a fortune, but . . . Well, it was Adam's car. And hopefully the insurance would cover most of the cost.

Seth sat next to her on the couch. "I'm not worried about the car."

Jenna raised a brow. "You are so full of it."

"Okay," he amended. "I was a little worried about the car."

Jenna nodded. "Just so we're square."

Seth smiled and shook his head. "Such a mouth on you, girl." His smile faltered. "Such grandchildren the two of you would have made."

Jenna's stomach turned upside down. She closed her eyes for a brief moment and reminded herself she was over this. "I'm missing him tonight, Dad," she whispered.

Seth swallowed. "Me, too, Jenna. That's why I came to see you. I always feel a little closer to Adam when I'm with you."

She patted his arm and for the second time that day tried to remember Adam as he'd been when he was healthy. For the second time that day she failed. She pushed herself to her feet, suddenly feeling guilty for having sexual thoughts about Steven Thatcher when she couldn't even remember Adam's face clearly. The guilt was irrational. She knew it in her head. But that made no difference to her heart. There was, of course, one primary solution for guilt. "I was going to have ice cream for dinner. Want some?"

"You really need to have better nutrition, Jenna." Seth stood up. "Butter pecan is my favorite."

"It's Rocky Road."

Seth pushed her hair behind her ear and smiled. Looking into his kind face, so like Adam's, Jenna finally conjured a mental snapshot of a healthy Adam. Somehow that made her feel better, being able to remember the face of the only man she'd ever loved. Seth cleared his throat. "Like I said, Rocky Road is my favorite."

Jenna swallowed hard and leaned her forehead against Seth's shoulder. "I love you, Dad."

Seth's arms came around her, hard and strong. "Love you, too, Jenna." He let go and tilted up her chin. "So tell me about the not-so-young man who's almost as handsome as me. And please don't make me go to Mrs. Kasselbaum for all the details." He leaned forward and whispered, "Don't tell anyone, but that woman is a terrible gossip."

Jenna hiccuped a laugh. "Last one to the kitchen has to eat the top layer with all the ice."

SEVEN

Friday, September 30, 8:30 P.M.

"STEVEN, YOU NEED TO EAT," HELEN SAID FROM the kitchen doorway.

Steven set his briefcase by the front door and followed his aunt to the kitchen where a single hot plate of food waited. Helen poured herself a cup of coffee and sat in the chair across from him.

"Eat."

A ghost of a smile pulled at his mouth at the barked command. "Yes'm." Dutifully he ate while she watched, her eagle eye trained on every bite he put in his mouth.

"You were late tonight," she observed, her voice gone softer.

He nodded, swallowing. "I had an appointment with one of Brad's teachers."

"Oh, dear."

"Yeah." His fork drew an aimless design in his gravy-laden mashed potatoes. He looked up to find Helen patiently waiting. "He's failing chemistry, Helen. His teacher wanted me to know."

Helen closed her eyes and sighed. "What's happening to our boy, Steven?"

He kneaded his browbone. "I don't know. Jenna recommended I see his guidance counselor."

"And will you?"

"I'll call him first thing Monday morning." He shrugged, feeling utterly helpless and hating the feeling. "I tried to talk to Brad, but he shut me out."

"I know." Helen reached across the table to squeeze his hand and they held on quietly until she asked, "So who is Jenna?"

Steven's fingers tightened on his fork. His face was turning red, he could feel it. He damned the involuntary response that was the curse of redheads and he damned the light that came on in his aunt's matchmaking eyes. He pulled his left hand from Helen's. "Brad's teacher," he muttered, dropping his eyes to his potatoes.

"I see."

"No, you don't see anything, Helen," he ground out. "She is a nice woman who cares about my son. She stayed late on a Friday afternoon to tell me he was failing her class. That's all."

"Okay."

He glanced up to find her expression serene. Chills went down his spine. Extreme measures were called for. "She's

married, okay? She's sixty and married with four children."
He'd confess the lie whenever he made it back to church.

Helen sighed in resignation. "Do you really have to go
back out tonight?" she asked, changing the subject.

Steven thought of the Egglestons. "Yes," he answered. "I
do. I should be home before midnight, though. I read Nicky a
story and put him to bed already." Which meant tucking his
baby into a sleeping bag on the floor. Since being abducted
from his bed in the middle of the night six months before,
Nicky had refused to sleep in his own bed. The counselors
said Nicky would return to his bed in his own time. He wondered what the counselors would say about Brad.

"Then eat your dinner, Steven."

He ate the rest of his dinner in silence, trying to ignore his
aunt's watchful stare. Truth be told, he loved her more than
any other woman in the world. He could tell her fifty times a
day he never planned to marry again and it was like talking to
the wind. But Helen loved him and loved all his boys dearly.
At the end of every argument it always came back to that.

He cleaned his plate. "Thanks, Helen. That beats dinner
out of a sack any day of the week."

"Do you want any more? I made plenty."

Steven stood up and pecked her weathered cheek. "No,
ma'am. I wouldn't want to get fat."

Helen had the good grace to look embarrassed before she
laughed aloud. "I'm going to have to teach that son of yours
when to keep his big mouth shut."

He arched a brow. "You can try." He got to the front door
and stopped short. "Shit."

"Steven!" Then she saw it too. "Oh, no. Cindy Lou!" She
ran to the door and pulled the hundred-pound sheepdog away
from Steven's briefcase. "She didn't mean to, Steven."

With a grimace, Steven fetched a towel from the kitchen

and cleaned the dog drool from the handle. "Look at these teeth marks! That dog's a menace."

"She's a sweet dog." Helen's lips twitched. "She just has overactive drool glands."

"So get her a glandectomy." He wiped the bag, then cleaned his hands. "I need to go now."

She followed him to the driveway, the drooling ball of hair from hell in tow. "Drive carefully."

"I always do." He opened the rear passenger door and stopped short again. "Shit," he repeated, this time in a whisper.

"I heard that," Helen said from behind him, then peered around him to peek inside the car. "Whose briefcase is that?"

He could feel his cheeks heating again. "It belongs to Brad's teacher."

Helen was quiet for a half beat. "Jenna?"

Steven rolled his eyes, damning his own slip of the tongue. "Yes, Jenna." He should return it, he thought. He should return it to that comfortable little apartment of hers where she was probably sitting on that soft brown sofa with her two dogs at her feet. *She'd be grateful,* he thought. She'd smile up at him with those violet eyes. And those full lips. He bit down hard on the inside of his cheek, but it was too late. His body had already responded to the image his mind had conjured. He pulled her briefcase from the backseat with a harder jerk than necessary.

He put the bag in Helen's arms and she stumbled a little from the unexpected weight. "Put it in my study. I'll return it to her on Sunday."

"But—"

"I need to get to the office." He put his briefcase in the backseat and slammed the car door.

Helen winced. "But—"

He climbed into the front seat, pulling his seat belt on with one motion. "Don't wait up. I'll see you tomorrow." He pulled out of his driveway and chanced a look back in his rearview mirror. Helen stood in the same place, her mouth slightly open, watching him drive away.

Steven grimaced. He probably could have handled that with more finesse. He shifted his body in the car seat, trying to relieve the pressure against his zipper. It was stupid, just plain foolish. Jenna Marshall had a nice pair of legs. That was all. No, that wasn't nearly all. Her breasts were nice, too. His hands gripped the steering wheel, hard. And her rear end. He cracked his window to let in some of the cool night air. And her eyes. And her smile. He shifted in the seat again, the pressure unabated. Okay, he could admit it to himself. She was a tidy little package. He was . . . attracted to her.

He pulled his car from his subdivision onto the main highway. *Be honest, Thatcher. She makes your mouth water.* He frowned in the darkness. *Be* really *honest, Thatcher. You want to jump that woman's bones.* He shuddered, able to imagine it all too well.

It was just that it had been such a long time. A very, very long time. Maybe he just needed to get it out of his system. A little honest sex, with no expectations for a long-term commitment. No promises made, no regrets when he walked away. Because he *would* walk away.

He'd almost made himself believe casual sex with Jenna Marshall was a feasible solution to his problems when he remembered the way her eyes softened in compassion over his son, then again over saving a puppy about to be put to sleep. A woman like that was not a candidate for a no-strings sexual relationship. She was just not that kind of woman.

Steven sighed. No more than he was that kind of man.

That's why it had been such a very, very long time since he'd been with a woman.

That's why it would continue to be a very, very long time.

Frustrated and alone, he turned his thoughts to the subject of Samantha Eggleston. Her parents would want an update. Hoping Kent was still in the lab, he pulled his cell phone from his pocket.

Friday, September 30, 11:00 P.M.

"So they lost."

Victor Lutz looked over his mostly empty glass with a sneer. His wife stood in the doorway of his study, dressed for bed in the same nightgown she'd worn every night of their miserable marriage. It wasn't really the same nightgown, but one of ten identical gowns that hung in her closet, magically replicating themselves year after year. It had to be magic. No one in their right mind would buy such an ugly garment on purpose, much less ten of them year after year.

After year after year after year.

On top of being hopelessly stupid, Nora Lutz had absolutely no sense of style. Unlike Rudy's teacher. Not that *Miss* Marshall had style either, but with a body like that he'd be willing to turn a blind eye to the prim suit. Unfortunately on top of having a great body, she also had guts.

Victor hated women with guts. Guts, brains—they only served to distract women from their sole purpose on this earth. Sex and servitude. In that order. He glared at Nora over his glass. She was a failure on both counts.

"Of course they lost." *Idiot.* "Rudy sat on the bench the entire goddamn game." He tossed back the last swallow of vodka, stood, and crossed the Aubusson carpet to pour himself another.

Nora pursed her lips, sending deep lines radiating from the corners of her mouth. "I thought you were going to straighten

Karen Rose

that out with the principal before the game started. Daddy isn't going to be happy about this. He had to pull some strings to get that scout to come watch Rudy."

He hated that mistress-of-the-household tone. She'd learned it from *Daddy*, the rich sonofabitch.

He tossed back half the glass. The rich sonofabitch whose money bought the Aubusson carpet under Victor's feet, the roof over his head, the business that paid his salary. He eyed the clear liquid in the now half-empty glass. Whose money bought the hundred-dollar-a-bottle vodka that helped Victor drown out the reality of being married to the rich sono-fabitch's tired, ugly, whiny daughter.

Thank God for mistresses and whores, was all he could say. Of course, not out loud. *Daddy* wouldn't like that. Thank God *Daddy* didn't really know everything.

Nora crossed her arms over her scrawny bosom and leaned back against the wall with an air of superiority that she liked to remind him was born, not bought. The rich dark hair that had been her only notable attribute would once have blended into the black walnut wood that paneled his office. But she'd started to gray and never lifted a finger to halt the change. She, like *Daddy,* was a dried-up old prune. "I thought as much," she said curtly. "Big man going to tell the stupid prin-cipal how to run his school." She shook her head. "You are so full of hot air, Victor. You make me ill."

"That makes two of us," he muttered into his glass.

"Excuse me?"

Victor looked up and focused his eyes on hers, saying nothing until she paled. There was more than one way to deal with Nora when she got too nasty for her own good. He rarely had to carry through on his threats. She usually backed down before he had to rouse himself into enough of a rage to raise his hand to her. Although the satisfaction at seeing her cowed and silenced was always well worth the effort. After the first time, years ago, he'd waited for Daddy to send a couple of thugs to put him in perpetual traction, but the thugs never came. Not that time, nor the times after. Victor guessed there were some things even Nora didn't tell Daddy. He cleared his throat.

"I said, that makes two of us. I did visit the school today for your information. I might have gotten your son reinstated this afternoon if he hadn't been such a fucking idiot."

Nora frowned. "What do you mean?" she asked, her tone now significantly less belligerent.

"I mean, your idiot son pushed the wrong teacher. He handed in a test on which he'd written only his name. That and the smirk on his face are making his teacher dig in her heels. I gave the principal a week to fix this."

"And if he doesn't? What then?"

"Then we pull *Daddy's* funding of Blackman's new stadium."

Nora smoothed her hair away from her face, one of her many nervous gestures. He knew every last one. Every last one drove him nuts. "Not everyone is motivated by money, Victor."

Victor drained his glass. Not motivated by money. *Hah.* Only a person who'd grown up wanting nothing could actually believe that. "Of course they are. They just don't always know it."

Friday, September 30, 11:55 P.M.

The church's old door handle was cool under Steven's sweating hand. They didn't make handles like this anymore. Doors either, Steven thought, feeling the cool night air on his hot face. Both were vintage 1923, as was the rest

of the church. He'd lost track of how long he'd been standing there, telling himself to either go in or go home.

Hours of paperwork hadn't cleared his mind, just served
to stave off the worry gnawing at his gut for just a few more
hours. He'd left his office and driven around aimlessly, not
really surprised when he stopped in the parking lot of the
old parish.

His old parish. He'd grown up here, served as an altar
boy, been confirmed. Taken his first communion and
planned to study the priesthood himself. His grip on the
door handle tightened. Then his life had taken a sharp turn
after a single night of . . . What would he call it, looking
back now? Certainly not passion. They'd been seventeen in
the back of his father's Olds. Passion it certainly was not.
Experimentation? It was that. Folly? In many ways it was
that as well. Melissa had turned out to be the greatest folly
of his life. Brad, on the other hand . . . He could never call
creating his oldest son a folly, no matter how troubled Brad
was at the moment.

Conceiving Brad that night in the back of his father's
Olds made him change his life path. Gone were plans for
the priesthood, which had broken his mother's heart until
she'd held her first grandson in her arms. Steven had gone
to college, become a cop. He and Melissa had two more
beautiful sons. They'd been a happy family for a time.
Melissa may have even been happy . . . for a time.

And look at me now, he thought. Successful career. Dis-
astrous marriage. Unhappy children. A lonely widower.
Lonely and . . . scared.

No, he was terrified. For years after Melissa died he'd
held his family together. But now his family was unravel-
ing and he had no clue what to do about it. The idle promise to confess the lie he'd told Helen pricked at him all
night, bringing back a host of memories about this place,

about the peace he'd always felt here. He tried to remember how long it had been. It hadn't been a watershed moment, but a gradual thing. Week after week he sat in the pew, feeling the priest's eyes on him, his priest's disapproval of what he'd done. Knowing just as clearly there was not one iota he'd change. The cycle of guilt continued until he'd started finding all the reasons he couldn't go to Mass. Then he just stopped going altogether.

So here he stood. "Go in or go home, Thatcher," he said harshly.

God knew he didn't want to go in. Devil of it was, he didn't want to go home even more.

So he yanked at the heavy door and slipped inside. He'd known it would be open. It always was. He hesitated for a moment before pushing himself to the altar. He hesitated even longer before dropping to his knees. Crossing himself.

Opening his heart.

He'd lost track of time, deep inside himself until a noise behind him brought his head up and his hand to the weapon in his holster.

"I wondered when you'd come home, Steven."

Slowly standing, he turned and regarded the man sitting in the pew two rows back. Noted the silver at his temples. He was older now. They both were. They'd been children together, served in this very parish together. Been best friends together. Until four years ago when everything changed.

Four years ago when Melissa died and Steven found himself confessing one of the greatest sins of his life to the only man he knew he could trust to keep it secret. To the man sitting in the pew two rows back whose white collar was a stark contrast to the tanned column of his throat.

Steven swallowed. "Mike."

Mike raised a bushy black brow. "That's Father Mike to you." He smirked. "My son."

Steven felt the smile bending his lips despite the turmoil within him. "Stick it. Father."

Mike shook his head in mock chagrin. "I should order you to say five Hail Marys for that."

"For 'stick it'?"

"No, for the impolite words you really wanted to say."

Steven met his friend's eyes and both sobered. "I should say a whole lot more than five."

"Why are you here, Steven?" Mike asked softly, his voice carrying in the quiet of the church.

Steven looked away, turned around to focus on the statue of the Madonna and Child. Tried to figure out the answer himself as he gazed on the serene countenances, so at odds with how he felt inside. "I don't know," he finally answered. "I guess I couldn't think of anywhere else to go."

"That's as good an answer as any," Mike said. "I've missed you, Steven. I thought I might see you after the trouble with Nicky last spring. I called . . . a number of times, but . . ."

Steven listened as his friend's voice trailed away and Mike wasn't Father Leone anymore, but the best friend of his heart. A friend he'd wounded through neglect. "But I didn't return your calls," Steven finished, dropping his chin to his chest. "I'm sorry, Mike."

"I'm sorry, too. I should have tried harder. I should have come to you."

Steven lifted a shoulder. "I don't know that it would have done any good. You know."

Mike sighed. "I'm sorry about that, too. How are they?"

Steven looked over his shoulder to find Mike in the exact same position. That was one of the things Steven had always admired about his friend—his calm patience that seemed to settle the most anxious parishioner. "I wish I could say they're fine, but they're not. Of the three, Matt is the most normal."

"Matt?" Mike tilted his head. "I find that hard to believe. What happened to Brad?"

The weight suddenly seemed heavier. "I don't know." Steven's shoulders sagged. "I don't know what to do, Mike. Brad changed . . . overnight."

"People rarely change overnight," Mike observed.

"Brad did," Steven insisted. "And I don't know what I or anybody did to trigger it. I thought it would pass, but . . ."

"But it's gotten worse."

"I guess you hear this all the time."

"Unfortunately, yes. Sit down, Steven. Please." Mike leaned forward and patted the pew in front of him. "You're making me nervous. You're wound tighter than a spring."

Steven dropped into the pew, sitting sideways and resting his arm along the wooden back. "I met one of Brad's teachers today. He's failing chemistry."

"Ouch."

Steven nodded. "I asked him about it when I got home and he acted like he . . . hated me," he finished in a shaky whisper. "I don't know what to do." He flinched when Mike covered his hand with his own, but didn't back away. It was so like . . . old times. Emotion welled up in his throat and Steven swallowed hard to force it down before it became overwhelming. He drew a deep breath and waited until he could speak normally. "Like I said, Matt is the normal one now and Nicky's improving every day." He made himself smile. "Helen's the same as ever."

Mike was quiet for a long time, then squeezed his hand. "So Brad is troubled, Matt is maturing, Nicky is improving, and Helen is the same old Helen. But how are *you*, my friend?" he asked softly. "How is your life?"

Again emotion pushed up his throat and again Steven shoved it back. "My life is . . . what it is."

"You can do better than that, Steven," Mike said dryly.

Steven smiled in spite of himself. "It was a bit theatric, wasn't it?"

"A bit." Mike waited, and when Steven said nothing, trudged forward. "And your personal life? Have you changed your mind about taking another wife?"

The corner of Steven's mouth quirked up. "Taking another wife. It sounds so archaic when you say it that way."

"You didn't answer my question, Steven."

"No, I didn't, did I?" Steven squared his shoulders, preparing for the argument he knew was just ahead. "No, I haven't changed my mind. I won't be marrying again. At least not until the boys are grown."

"Nicky won't be grown for ten more years, Steven," Mike said quietly. "That's too long for you to be alone."

Steven narrowed his eyes. "You're alone."

Mike smiled. "That's different and you know it. Besides, I have the Church." Mike lifted a wry brow. "I'd bet it's safe to say you don't even have that."

Steven looked away. "Below the belt, Mike." But he was right. Of course.

"Wherever it does the most good. Ten more years is a long time for you to be alone."

Steven stared at the Madonna and Child, knowing where this conversation was headed. "You said that already."

"And I was right both times. Hasn't Helen found *anyone* you like?"

Steven jerked his gaze back to where Mike still sat patiently. "What do you know about Helen's matchmaking?"

Mike shrugged. "She and I chat from time to time."

Steven rolled his eyes. "I bet she's confessing all the lies she's told to set me up with every Tania, Dorothy, and Henrietta this side of the Mississippi."

"That would be privileged," Mike informed him archly.

"Yeah, yeah," Steven muttered and Mike grinned, then sobered.

"So tell me, Steven. You haven't met anyone? In four years?"

A face flashed before his eyes. Black hair, violet eyes, kind smile. "No. Yes." Steven closed his eyes. "I don't know," he said miserably.

"I like the 'yes' answer the best."

"You would," Steven muttered.

"What's her name?"

Steven stood up. "This is ridicu—"

"Sit down, Steven." It was a soft roar, a command meant to be obeyed.

Steven sat.

Mike nodded and tilted his head. "So . . . Her name is . . . ?"

"Jenna." Steven glared over the pew. "If Helen gets a word of this, I swear I'll . . ."

"It's privileged," Mike said and leaned forward. "And you met her when?"

"Today," Steven snapped and watched Mike's eyes grow round. Looking at his watch Steven added, "Seven and a half hours ago, to be most accurate."

Mike sat back in the pew. "Well, *now* your visit makes sense. So what do you plan to do about this woman? This . . . Jenna?"

Steven clenched his jaw. "Nothing."

Mike pursed one side of his mouth. "Oh, please, Steven. You're here. You're troubled." Mike folded his arms across his chest. "Not all women are Melissa, you know."

"I know. But I refuse to expose my kids to any woman until I'm sure she's not."

Mike waved his hand. "And because you can't afford time away *from* the boys, you don't have the time it would take to get to know a woman well enough to bring her home *to* the boys. I seem to recall having heard this argument before."

Steven shook his head stubbornly. "I can't . . . no, I won't put the boys through that again."

"You didn't put them through it the first time, Steven," Mike reminded him. *As if he could forget.* "You brushed the truth under the rug and let the world believe what you wanted them to believe." Mike frowned, his voice growing stern. "You lied to your children."

Steven squeezed his eyes closed, clenched his fist tight. "I know. Dammit, don't you think I know?" Then Mike covered Steven's clenched fist with his steady hand and just held it there.

"I know you know, Steven," he said softly. "And I know you believe you did the right thing by the boys by not telling them the truth about Melissa's death."

"I *did* do the right thing," Steven hissed, feeling it all come back. Four years of hurt he'd so successfully buried came rushing back. Now he remembered why it had been so long since he'd been to church. "What *good* would it have done them to know she was deserting us? To tell them her *lover* smashed up her car because he was too drunk to walk, much less drive? That she was hurrying to the airport with her married *lover*?" He spat the word, knowing no other way to make it sound as bad as it really was. "What good would it have done to tell them she didn't even intend to say good-bye to her own *children,* that she just left me a *note*?" He squeezed his eyes tighter and tried to swallow the lump in his throat. "What good would it possibly have

done, Mike?" he whispered, his voice shaking. "*Tell me.*
Please, tell me."

Mike sighed heavily. "I don't know, Steven," he murmured. "But I do know that in spite of all you've done to
protect your family, it hasn't made any of you any happier."

There was nothing to say to dispute that so Steven said
nothing and Mike removed his steadying hand and leaned
back in the pew.

"I take it I'm still the only one who knows," Mike said
after another minute of quiet.

Steven opened his eyes, then narrowed them. "You are."

"Hmm. So I'm the only person you could come to when
you finally realized you've painted yourself in a corner
with this ridiculous ban you've put on marriage."

"It's not ridic—"

"Hush, Steven. Save it for yourself because I'm not buying. So tell me about this Jenna."

"There is nothing to tell," Steven insisted through
clenched teeth.

"I sincerely doubt that. What's her last name?"

Steven twisted in the pew so he faced forward, his arms
pulled tightly across his body. "Marshall," he answered.

"And what does she do?"

"She's a teacher." He threw a sour look over his shoulder. "She's Brad's teacher."

"Oh. Well, now the picture's a bit clearer. I bet she's
kind."

"Yes."

"Pretty?"

Steven drew a breath, irritated. "Yes." Let it out. "She's
kind and pretty." Anger started to simmer deep inside him.
"You want to know the truth, *Father* Leone? You want to
know it all? Every last dark thought in my *soul*? Okay, *fine*.
I want her. I haven't had sex in four years and *I want her.*"

He exhaled, the burst of temper leaving him drained. "But I can't have her."

"Because you choose not to marry her."

Steven stiffened at the disapproval in Mike's voice. "That is correct, Father."

"You're a fool, Steven Thatcher."

"Why, because I believe in sex within the sanctity of marriage? I thought that would earn me some brownie points," Steven said bitterly.

"It earns you a hair shirt and a flogging strap," Mike snapped back. "If you want to be a martyr, do it in somebody else's church, because I don't want to hear it anymore."

Steven turned back in the pew to find Mike red-faced and visibly trembling. "What does that mean exactly, Father Leone?" he asked coldly.

Mike's chin came up, challenge in his dark eyes. "It means that you have set up a situation that's a no-win for everyone."

"So what do you recommend, *Father*?"

"If you ask me as Father Leone, I'm not going to recommend anything," Mike said sharply.

Mike was hurt, Steven realized with a shock. He'd always thought Mike impervious to insult, but that was obviously not the case. This man was his best friend. He'd been best man at his wedding, had christened both Matt and Nicky. Softening, he met Mike's flashing eyes and asked, "So what do you recommend, my friend?"

Mike stilled. "Don't swear you'll never marry again, Steven. It's not right for you to be alone. You need help with the boys, someone to support you when life doesn't work out the way you plan."

Steven thought about the support he'd felt just talking to Jenna Marshall. He could easily see her in that role—helping with the boys, supporting him. But still . . . "I don't want her around the boys," he insisted. "They'll get attached to her, and if it doesn't work out . . ."

Mike nodded thoughtfully. "I can see where that is a legitimate concern. So spend time with her away from the boys. Take her to dinner." He lifted a brow. "Take her to church."

Steven smiled. "Yes, Father."

"But also realize you are putting this woman under an enormous level of scrutiny. That's not fair to her. At some point you will know enough. You need to know in advance what that point is."

Steven was considering that advice when the clock in the old tower chimed. One in the morning. Where had the time gone? He stood up. "I have to get up in a few hours for a meeting at the office." He stuck out his hand. "Thanks, Mike."

Mike looked at his hand a moment, then stood and embraced him over the pew. "I've missed you, Steven. Please don't make me wait so long before I see you again."

"You can come see me. They don't lock you up in here, do they?" Steven asked, going for a jaunty grin that felt forced.

"Only on Thursdays." Mike patted his stomach under the black robes. "And that's only because Sal's Pizza has an all-you-can-eat special that night." He walked with Steven toward the doors. "What case are you working now that has you meeting so early on a Saturday?"

Steven sighed. "You've heard about the two girls missing from their beds?"

Mike's face tightened. "I have. Their families are part of this parish."

Steven stopped. "You're kidding."

Mike shook his head and looked back toward the altar.

"That's why I was here so late tonight. Samantha Eggleston's parents were here most of last night praying for her return. I thought they might come back tonight."

"Can you think of anything the two girls had in common?"

Mike frowned. "I've thought of nothing else since the Egglestons called me yesterday morning. Only that they were both cheerleaders. Both were shy, which surprised me. I always thought cheerleaders were outgoing and confident, but neither of these two were. They went to different schools, really didn't hang out with each other while they were here. I can have their youth pastor call you tomorrow, if you like."

Steven's mind was racing again. "Please. Thanks, Mike." He started off toward the door, but Mike caught his sleeve.

"I want to help those families any way I can, Steven, but it's hard to hold out hope. Do you think there's a chance we'll get Sammie back? Alive?"

Steven hesitated. "Between you and me, no. But please don't tell her parents that."

"You have my word."

Steven pushed the door open and felt the cold night air on his face again. "Thanks, Mike." He walked out of the church with more to think about than when he'd gone in. But there was a peace as well, one he hadn't felt in a very long time.

He'd focus on Samantha Eggleston and Brad for now, but the idea of exploring a relationship with Jenna Marshall little by little held incredible appeal. Soon, he promised himself. He'd call her up and ask her out to dinner sometime soon.

EIGHT

Saturday, October 1, 7:45 A.M.

STEVEN STOOD AT THE COFFEEPOT IN THE CORNER of the SBI conference room, his arms crossed, his fingers drumming his upper arm impatiently. The coffee dripped in slow motion, just to annoy him. If he pulled the carafe away now he'd have a mess and he still wouldn't have a full cup of coffee.

Which, when he got it, would be his fourth. Helen, bless her heart, had set up the machine in their kitchen to start brewing at six in the morning. She knew his habits well, knew he'd be calling an early-morning status meeting. So the pot at home had taken care of his first three cups.

Hopefully the fourth would actually wake him up. He dragged his palms down his cheeks, wincing when he touched the razor nick on his jaw. His hands had been unsteady this morning. It was a small wonder he hadn't cut his face to ribbons. He hadn't slept all night, worries about Brad in the front of his mind periodically interrupted by thoughts of Brad's teacher that lurked in the back. He wished he could say another night of worrying had miraculously solved the mystery of his son's problem but that was no more true than his hope that the morning light would dispel Jenna Marshall's soft voice that still echoed in his mind. *Have courage, Steven.* If only it were that easy.

"An IV would be faster."

Steven looked over his shoulder to find Lennie Farrell leaning against the wall behind him, his tie perfectly knotted, not a wrinkle in sight. Special Agent in Charge Lennie Farrell was a Joe Friday cop if there ever was one. His cardboard walk was mimicked by the department, although never with malice. Lennie was a good man. He even laughed when they called him "Joe." As much as Lennie laughed, anyway.

"And probably less painful," Steven responded, looking back at the coffeepot that hadn't speeded its drip one single iota. "When I finally get my cup, it's going to scald on its way down."

"You could wait for it to cool," Lennie said, his tone wry. "But that would require patience."

Steven glanced at him from the corner of his eye. "I *am* patient."

Lennie pushed away from the wall and walked over to the bulletin board Steven had set up the night before. Photos of both young girls were hung with thumbtacks, smiling yearbook photos provided by their terrified parents. Lennie bent down to look at the photo of the mutilated body of Lorraine Rush, the first victim, then straightened as he drew a deep breath. "Steven, if you are patient, I'm a stand-up comic."

"Your point. This time." Steven grabbed a chair and swung it around so he could straddle it. "What are you doing here this morning? I'd planned to call you with an update at the ninth hole."

Lennie sat down at the table. Heavily. "I got a call from the governor last night."

Steven sighed. In a case with the potential to become such a high profile, it was only a matter of time. "We knew it was coming. Well?"

"He's concerned, of course, and wanted to know what we had. I told him I'd call him after this morning's briefing."

"At least we don't have help from the Feds or the press yet."

Lennie lifted a brow. "Let's try to keep it that way."

"I talked to Kent Thompson last night." Steven pulled a folder from his briefcase, conscious of Lennie watching his every move. Steven knew why and it pissed him off. Lennie was looking for signs of strain. Of stress. Of anything that might suggest Steven was ready to blow a gasket because this was his first abduction case since Nicky. He'd felt like a fish in a damn bowl for six months now and Lennie's watchful stare wasn't helping matters. He drew a deep breath. "You know Kent, don't you?"

Lennie nodded. "New guy. Works in Diane's department."

"Yeah. Seems like he knows his stuff. Anyway, he was here until midnight last night, doing some lab tests on the material we found in the hypo at the clearing. Said he needed to let the samples sit overnight before running the chromatography test. He should be here any minute."

"I wish Diane were here," Lennie mused. "This is a big case for a rookie. Maybe I should call in someone from the Charlotte office until Diane gets back from her cruise."

Steven shook his head. "Give the guy a chance, Lennie. Let's see what he's come up with. Coffee's done, finally. Do you want some?"

"Not till Nancy comes. Don't forget I've tasted your coffee."

Steven grimaced. "So have I. Caffeine addictions can be a real bitch."

One corner of Lennie's mouth lifted. "So what time is this meeting scheduled to start, Steven?"

Steven glanced at his watch. "Ten minutes. Everybody will be here."

Within ten minutes the conference room was filled with the team Steven had assembled Thursday morning, a few hours after receiving word of Samantha Eggleston's disappearance. Kent Thompson brought up the rear, carrying an overstuffed folder and looking like he'd slept in his suit. Steven could see Lennie giving him a look that clearly won-

dered if he'd made a mistake in not calling for Charlotte reinforcements sooner.

"Sorry," Kent mumbled and took the last empty chair.

Nancy put a cup of coffee in front of the young man who
stared at it warily. "Did Steven make this?" Kent asked and
Steven rolled his eyes at the chuckles that rippled through the
room.

"You're safe, honey," Nancy said and patted Kent's shoulder in her motherly way. "I dumped Steven's pot and made a
new one."

"And I called the plumber to repair the corrosion to the
pipes," Harry chimed in with a grin.

"Yeah, yeah," Steven muttered. "Are we ready to begin?"
Steven asked loudly and the side conversations abruptly
ceased. "Thanks." He looked around the table at the team
he'd assembled. Seven men and women, including himself.
Solid agents, all of them. Kent Thompson was their forensic
scientist, Harry Grimes and Sandra Kates his fellow investigating agents, Meg Donnelly would profile the killer they
sought, and Nancy Patterson would provide the database support. He'd added Liz Johnson, the assistant DA, to ensure any
move they made would stand up in court.

He knew they'd need every drop of talent the group offered to stop this killer before Samantha Eggleston's battered
body ended up in a clearing like Lorraine's. "I want to start
with results from Forensics, then review the database search
of like perps." He raised his eyes across the room to Meg, the
staff psychologist. "And then, Meg, I'd like you
to give your take on who we're looking for." Steven turned to
Kent, hoping that he had something decent to say or Lennie
would have a more experienced replacement up from Charlotte before lunchtime. "Showtime, Thompson. Let's see what
you've got."

Kent opened his file folder, exposing a two-inch stack of

papers. "I have a number of items to cover this morning. Please stop me if I talk too fast." He gave a funny little smile. "I'm a little nervous, but I'm sure I'll get over it." Everyone smiled back in encouragement, including Lennie.

"Let's begin with the underwear Bud Clary found under the tree in the clearing yesterday morning," Kent said and pulled out a photograph showing two magnified hairs. "They were the same size and brand worn by Samantha and I found these two pubic hairs stuck in the cotton fibers. We can compare the DNA to hairs from her brush and epithelial cells from her toothbrush."

"So we at least can put her underwear at the scene," Sandra Kates commented. She was a seasoned agent with a niche expertise in sexual deviants. Steven didn't envy her dreams. His own were bad enough.

Kent nodded. "Exactly. I searched the flattened grassy area for hair from Samantha's head, but found none which I thought a bit odd."

"Why?" Lennie asked, leaning forward slightly in his chair.

"Because Samantha has very long curly hair." Kent pulled another photograph from his stack, one magnified with a microscope. "Here's a blade of grass from the clearing at fifty-ex. See the way the little thorny structures protrude all up and down the blade? It makes the grass like Velcro."

"Which should have pulled at least one or two hairs if she'd been laid on the grass," Steven finished and Kent nodded again.

"Exactly right, especially with how dry the grass is right now."

Steven glanced over at Meg. "He shaved her head? Just like Lorraine Rush."

Meg shrugged. "That would be my guess."

Steven looked back at Kent. "What about the dark hair you found?"

"The hair was clipped at the edge, almost like it had been shaved with a razor or some other kind of blade. It's not Samantha's, I can tell you that. As for DNA, there was no follicle, like I told you yesterday, so I'll need to use mitochondrial cells for the DNA print instead of cells from the nucleus. It doesn't provide the full range of gene mapping as it only holds genetic material from the mother."

Steven turned to Assistant DA Liz Johnson. "Admissible?"

Liz nodded. "Yes, I've used it before. Not often, but enough."

"What else do you have?" Lennie asked brusquely and Steven knew he was impressed.

Kent's expression hardened. "The hypo had traces of ketamine."

Steven's shoulders slumped as murmurs ran round the table. "Shit. Are you sure?"

"Unfortunately, yes. I ran the GC three times, which is why I was late this morning. All the peaks match up."

Steven looked to Harry. "Did Latent find anything on the hypo itself?"

Harry shook his head. "Not a print. Bastard wore gloves."

Nancy raised her hand. "I'm out of the loop here. What's ketamine?"

"Close relative of PCP," Sandra answered grimly. "Widely used as an anesthetic, especially with vets. Veterinarians," she specified. "Available from most veterinary supply catalogs."

Meg pushed away from the table and walked to the window. "Legally used, it's an effective replacement for general anesthesia, especially outside of hospital environments."

"Doctors on charity missions to Africa will use it when they're operating out in the field," Kent offered. "It completely immobilizes the patient."

Meg nodded. "That's right. And when used correctly it's quite safe."

"But?" Nancy asked.

"But it's one of the fastest-growing illicit drugs out there today," Steven said grimly. "If you take enough you enter what users call the 'k-zone.' Users have out-of-body experiences. Some even say they witness their own death."

"Our perp uses ketamine to immobilize these girls," Nancy murmured. "Like a date-rape drug."

"Something like that," Meg replied. "But unlike rhohypnol where the victim doesn't remember anything, ketamine users have a detached awareness of their surroundings." She turned to the group. "But the worst part is what they call the reemergence dreams. They can be simply horrific."

Steven rubbed the back of his stiffening neck. "Wonderful. Was there anything else, Kent?"

"The dog's teeth were clean. If Pal bit our perp, he didn't bite deep enough to take any flesh. His stab wounds were deep and wide. I took some digital photos before the vet sewed him up."

"Good thinking. Let's compare them to the pictures from Lorraine Rush's autopsy," Steven said, "and let's hope there's something to compare. Also see if they can do any tests for ketamine on Rush's tissue samples. Harry, I want you to focus on finding out where he got the ket."

Harry wrote it in his notebook. "I'll start with the vet supply houses and the local vet clinics."

"Good. Sandra, see if any of your contacts on the street have heard about this."

Sandra nodded. "I've already put out some feelers. I'll see what I can drag in."

Steven turned to Nancy who was busily taking notes of her own. "Nancy, what have you found in your database search?"

Nancy looked up and lifted her half-lensed glasses off the

end of her nose. "I checked for perps charged with sexual assault crimes in a one-hundred-mile radius and popped up more names than we can run through in a month. I'll see about doing a cross-ref with ketamine and perhaps we can narrow it a bit."

Steven mentally ticked off the items he planned to cover in this meeting. "I'm going to work the connection between the two girls. I know they went to the same church. I want to know how well they knew one another and how our perp knew them. Finally, Meg, can you paint a picture of what kind of person we're looking for?"

"It's just a top of head sketch," Meg cautioned. "We're assuming he's killed twice. At least. The savagery with which the first girl was brutalized before and after death indicates he's angry. He probably doesn't communicate well, probably holds his anger in. We'll likely find he's killed animals leading up to this. Most certainly he's committed some lesser sexual crimes in the past, again working up to this. By not burying the Rush girl, it seems like he wanted her to be found. Media exposure will make him very satisfied." She stopped and fixed her stare out the window. "I'm wondering how the ketamine factors in. Does he dope them up before he kills them? During? Does he use it to initially immobilize these girls while he's kidnapping them or as an anesthesia to keep them from feeling anything while he's killing them?"

"A considerate serial killer?" Sandra asked skeptically. "That would be one for the books."

"Bundy volunteered at a suicide hotline," Harry said thoughtfully.

"That's not the same thing and you know it," Sandra shot back. "These guys kill for the thrill of seeing another person in pain."

"You mean our guy is *abnormal*? Perish the thought." Harry recoiled in mock horror and Sandra glared.

Steven lifted his hand. "Boys and girls, please. What else, Meg?"

Meg glanced over her shoulder, then back out the window. "Sandra could very well be right. His use of ketamine could have nothing to do with its anesthetic effect. It could be he's using it for the dream effect. That would indicate a curiosity about psychology or maybe even firsthand experience with some kind of therapy."

"Or he could have a trigger-happy mouse finger," Nancy said, her eyes on her laptop screen. "In the last few minutes I've come across six articles written by chem-heads espousing the awesome trips you can take into the 'k-zone.' Some of these are incredibly well written. It's hard to believe such articulate people are stupid enough to do this drug." She looked up and slid her glasses off her nose. "Sorry, Meg. I didn't mean to interrupt. I was just surprised at the amount of information I was able to get so easily seeing as how I'd never heard of this stuff before."

"It's everywhere, Nancy," Meg murmured. "That's what makes it so scary." Clearing her throat she went on. "I'm also wondering about the timing of this second abduction—it bothers me."

"It's too soon," Sandra supplied.

"It is," Meg agreed. "We found the Rush girl's body five days ago and the autopsy showed she'd been dead less than a week. That's less than two weeks between incidents. Early in their 'career' serial killers may go months or years between incidents. I don't know. Maybe he's done this before—many times that we don't know about—and he's now at the critical escalation point."

Steven sat back in his chair. "But you don't think so."

"No, not really. This feels more . . ." She tightened one side of her face, struggling for the words. "Immature," she said finally. "Especially given the way he was shaken up by the dog yesterday morning. Leaving behind the hypo was . . . unprofessional at best."

"An amateur," Harry said wryly and Meg smiled.

"For lack of a better word, yes." She shrugged wearily. "Summing up, if I had to guess his age I have to say he was younger and I'll bet we find he's well educated. He's probably white, since serial killers tend not to cross ethnic lines. That's all I can offer until I have more information."

Steven closed his notebook and stood up. It wasn't much. But it was the best they had at the moment. "Then let's go get some more information."

Saturday, October 1, 12:30 P.M.

Helen Barnett had been staring at the leather briefcase on her kitchen table for close to half an hour, debating whether she should unzip the front panel in the hope that Brad's chemistry teacher had stored a phone number inside so she could return the briefcase.

Such a stuffed briefcase meant this teacher had brought home a lot of work that, Helen was willing to bet, a busy teacher would be needing to get to earlier than Sunday afternoon.

Jenna. Helen liked the sound of the name. It was pretty without being simpering. Helen knew by now that Steven hated simpering women. Unfortunately Helen wasn't sure what kind of women Steven didn't hate.

It just wasn't natural for a young man Steven's age, with half his life ahead of him, to insist on staying lonely. He was handsome, had a charming disposition when he wanted to, and rarely left his dirty socks on the floor. He didn't snore, usually put the lid down, was financially comfortable, and had three beautiful sons—who needed a mother.

It wasn't natural for those three boys to grow up without a mother when it was so unnecessary. Steven could have had his pick of pretty young things who would have adored his boys. Helen ought to know. She'd handpicked the pretty young things herself.

"But no," she muttered, staring hard at the briefcase, annoyed she was so tempted to snoop. Snooping was what desperate people did. Desperate was what Helen Barnett had become.

She'd agreed to come and live with Steven four years ago when Melissa took such an untimely death, leaving her poor boys motherless. At the time, Helen was sure within a few years Steven would have remarried and she, Helen, would have been on her merry way, resuming the life she'd dropped without a second thought.

Now, four years later, Helen desperately wanted her old life back. She wanted to play canasta whenever the mood struck, every night if she wanted. Without having to get a baby-sitter. She wanted to go on cruises with her friends with a week's notice. She wanted to go on a safari to Africa for a month. Maybe even get a gentleman friend of her own. A woman had needs, too, after all. But until Steven got a wife, none of that could happen. Nicky needed someone here all the time. He was just a baby, after all. And he'd been through so much. And Brad? God only knew what was wrong with that boy, but Helen knew sooner or later he'd come around. So Helen wanted Steven to get himself a wife. For the boys. For Steven. For her own sanity.

And this Jenna was the first woman Steven had even appeared to be interested in. Maybe if Helen asked this Jenna to dinner, gave them a chance to get to know each other better . . . And for that she'd need Jenna's phone number. Which was likely in the briefcase.

"So are you going to open it or not?" a squeaky voice said behind her.

Helen gasped, her hand flying to cover her heart, which, her doctor assured her, was as strong as an ox. Slowly she turned to find Matt lounging against the microwave, an insolent grin on his face, looking just like Steven at thirteen. Brad looked like their mother, but Matt and Nicky were Steven all over again, red hair, freckles, and a smile to make girls swoon. Matt's hair had started to lighten to that strawberry blond color Helen so loved on Steven. In a few years the girls would be lining up outside Matt's door. Hopefully by then the boys would have a real mother with a stick to beat off the undeserving girls. Only the best for her boys, the middle one of whom was a real sneak.

"How long have you been standing there?" Helen demanded, her eyes narrowing.

Matt just grinned wider. "Long enough. Yenta."

Helen bit back a grin of her own. Insolent pup, using *Fiddler* against her at his age. "I am *not* matchmaking." *Not yet,* she thought, *and not without a phone number.* "How did you know?"

Matt shrugged. "I was listening last night when you and Dad were talking about Brad."

"Eavesdropping? Matthew Thatcher, I'm shocked," Helen said, deadpan.

"It's the best way to get information around here. Besides, how could I resist when you're saying something bad about Mr. Perfect?"

Helen frowned. "I can't believe you're taking pleasure in whatever's wrong with your brother," she said severely. "I thought I raised you better than that."

His face fell and he looked down at his feet. "Man, you

know how to take all the fun out of life." He looked up, ducking his head like the little boy he used to be, when, just yesterday? How had he grown so tall and so old . . . so fast? "Look, I'm not happy that Brad's in trouble, but I am happy you're not yelling at *me* for a change."

She put on her imperious face. "News flash, Matthew. I'm a versatile woman, capable of multitasking. I can yell at two boys at the *same time*."

"Now you tell me," he mumbled, then she watched his expression slide from sullen to sly.

"What?" she asked, narrowing her eyes.

Matt leaned forward. "I also heard Dad call Brad's teacher by her first name last night. Very interesting. You want to know what she looks like?"

Helen bit her lip. The boy was incorrigible. Utterly. It was one of the things she loved most about him. "Your dad said she was sixty."

Matt cracked out a laugh. "And you believed him?"

Helen stiffened her back. "Of course not." She tilted her head to one side and crossed her arms over her chest. "You have a picture?"

Matt pressed the lever on the microwave, popping open the door and exposing a bound book sitting on the glass turntable.

Helen glanced up to find his brown eyes dancing. "Brad's yearbook?"

"I'm surprised at you, Aunt Bea. I thought you would have already thought of this yourself."

"I'm old. Cut me some slack. And don't call me Aunt Bea." Helen reached for the book only to have Matt grab it first. She sighed. "What do you want?"

"Lemon meringue, apple, and pumpkin."

"*And* pumpkin?"

"She's a looker. Aunt Bea."

"Okay. *And* pumpkin. You're going to get fat."

"I am a thirteen-year-old growing boy. I won't get fat. Oh, and I want ice cream with the apple pie. Vanilla."

"You're pushing me, boy. *Give it.*"

Matt handed over the yearbook. "Page forty-two."

Helen flipped to the page and stopped short. "Oh, my goodness."

Matt looked over her shoulder and let out a low wolf whistle. "Yeah, mama."

Helen looked up and over her shoulder with a glare. "Matthew!"

He grinned. "Come on, Aunt Bea. I'm thirteen. If I didn't drool a little you'd say I was sick and take me to Doc Theopolis for a shot."

Helen considered and conceded. "Okay, you have a point. This time." She dropped her eyes back down to the photo where a tall, black-haired woman and ten lab-coated teenagers held a test tube in each hand and beamed sunny smiles. "If she's sixty, I want to know what she's been cooking up in her lab to keep her face so smooth. She's beautiful."

"Great legs, too."

"Matthew!"

"Oh, like I'm the first guy to say that. I'll bet every one of those six guys in the science club joined for 'academic stimulation.'" He punctuated the air.

"Matthew!" Helen choked on the laugh she tried to stifle. "Please. That is a picture I don't need in my head. Okay, fine. She's pretty and obviously very smart."

"Probably too smart for Dad."

"Probably," Helen agreed. "But maybe she won't figure that out until it's too late."

"So are you going to open the briefcase or not?"

Helen shook her head. "It's an invasion of privacy. It

would be wrong." Matt shrugged nonchalantly, putting Helen on instant guard. "What do you have, young man?"

"A business card." He grinned. "With her address and phone number."

"Hand it over."

Matt sulked. "I was going to hold out for turkey with trimmings."

"If it's good enough, I'll throw in the turkey for free."

"I love you, Aunt Bea."

"Shut up, Matt."

He grinned. "Check the back."

Helen turned it over and read Jenna's address and phone number. "She has good penmanship."

"And great legs. Hey," he added at her impatient sigh, "at least I stayed at her legs."

"And this is supposed to please me? Don't answer that. Where did you find this card? Or do I not want to hear the answer to that either?"

"In Dad's suit pocket. I was looking for loose change to support my arcade habit."

"Uh-huh. Okay, so I guess the ball's in my court now."

"So you'll call her and invite her for dinner?"

"Was my plan so transparent?"

"Predictable, at least."

Helen looked up at him, suddenly suspicious. "Why are you helping me?"

Matt pulled a glossy brochure from his pocket. "I found this under the cushion on the couch. When I was looking for—"

"Loose change to support your arcade habit," Helen finished and took the brochure from his hands. "Africa, the Dark Continent," she read. "I was wondering where I'd left this."

"And I overheard you talking to your friend Sylvia."

"Quite the little spy, aren't we?" Helen asked, not sure whether to be annoyed or repentant.

"I didn't mean to," he defended himself. "You were right here in the kitchen and I got hungry. I didn't sneak or anything. Anyway, I heard you tell her you couldn't go on the safari because no one could watch the kids for that long. I started to think about all the cool places you went before you came here and . . ." He let the thought trail off with an awkward shrug.

Repentant it would be. "You know I love you guys," she said, relieved when he nodded.

"You just want to have fun. I can buy that." He gently yanked a hank of her hair. "You know you'll have to get a buzz cut when you go to Africa or the tsetse flies will make nests in your hair."

"I'll have to take my chances," Helen returned dryly. "You want mashed potatoes or Stove Top with that turkey tomorrow?"

Matt's eyes lit up. "Which is easier?"

"Which do you think?"

"Then you know which I want." He took the yearbook and sauntered out of the kitchen.

Helen watched him go, wanting to swat his sauntering behind and marveling at his growing maturity at the same time. She'd done a good job raising these boys if she did say so herself. And Brad would come around. "Mashed potatoes, turkey, three pies, and repentance," she said aloud to no one at all. "This Jenna better be worth the trouble."

Saturday, October 1, 2:30 P.M.

Marvin Eggleston surged to his feet, pushing back from his kitchen table so hard the chair fell to the floor with a clatter that made his trembling wife jump in her chair. "So you're telling me you are no closer to finding my daughter than you were two fucking days ago!" he exploded. He leaned on the table, balancing on the knuckles of his clenched fists, his face inches from Steven's. "What the hell have you been doing, sitting with your thumbs stuck up your asses?"

Steven smelled whiskey on the man's breath and said nothing. Eggleston was a grieving father. Steven would have preferred to see the man sober, though, if for no other reason than to answer the questions he needed to ask. But everyone dealt with grief and terror differently. While Marvin Eggleston blustered, his petite wife sat quietly crying.

Anna Eggleston grabbed her husband's arm, holding on for dear life. Her face was haggard, her eyes haunted. Beyond pale, her skin had a translucence, the look of being stretched too thin over her bones that came from forty-eight hours of constant fear and tears. Her voice shook when she spoke and Steven's pity grew. "Marvin, please. Serena will hear you." Steven was grateful Mrs. Eggleston's mother had taken four-year-old Serena upstairs when he arrived. No child needed to see her parents so wildly grieving. More tears welled in Anna's eyes and spilled to her cheeks, unchecked. "You're not helping. Please, sit down." She turned to Steven. "I'm sorry. It's just that we've had no sleep." She bowed her head, her shoulders shaking as a new wave of sobs took over. "We can't sleep. He has my baby," she whispered, her hand still clutching her husband's arm.

Steven placed his hand over hers, feeling the chill of her skin. "It's all right, Mrs. Eggleston. I truly understand. You don't have to apologize to me." He placed his other hand on Marvin's arm, creating a circle, connecting them. "Mr. Eggleston, if I knew where your daughter was, believe me, she'd be with you right now. I know it doesn't help, but we're doing everything we can."

Eggleston slumped, his chin dropping to his chest. "God, I can't believe this," he whispered. "I feel so damn helpless." He looked up and in his eyes Steven recognized the desperate terror he himself felt when that bastard Winters held Nicky.

"Yesterday, the young one from your office . . ." Eggleston shook his head as if trying to clear his thoughts. "The one that took the cast of Sammie's footprint outside her window."

"Agent Thompson?"

Eggleston nodded, not breaking eye contact. "Yes, he's the one. He said it had happened to you. That someone had stolen your child out of his bed."

Steven wasn't sure whether to thank Kent or curse him to eternal perdition. "That's true."

Anna looked up, her face streaked and puffy. "But you got your son back."

Steven nodded. "I did, yes."

She bit her lip. "Was he . . . all right? After you got him back?"

Steven knew what she was asking. Was his baby molested? Was his baby normal? Was his family normal? The answer to every one of those questions was a resounding no. "The man that abducted my son didn't physically hurt him, if that's what you mean, Mrs. Eggleston. But no, my son is not all right. He has nightmares. He refuses to sleep in his own bed. His schoolwork suffers. He doesn't hug anyone and hasn't since that day."

The Egglestons absorbed this information. Finally Marvin Eggleston drew a deep breath. "So even if we get her back, she won't be our daughter anymore, will she?" he asked gruffly.

Steven carefully avoided the "if." These parents were grasping at straws, trying to hold on to hope. "She'd need counseling. You all will."

Anna blinked, sending fresh tears down her stained cheeks. "You did?"

Steven nodded. "I did." He squeezed Anna's hand and Marvin's arm, then let go and sat back in his chair. "I need to ask you all some more questions. Some of them may sound the same as questions I asked yesterday and the day before. Please don't become frustrated with this process, though. Sometimes you remember tidbits today that you didn't think about yesterday."

"And those tidbits could help you find our Sammie," Anna said, very faintly.

"They might."

Marvin Eggleston pulled his chair forward and collapsed into it. "Then ask."

"Please understand I am in no way blaming your daughter for what happened," Steven began. Marvin held out his hand and Anna placed hers in his, the gesture so trusting that Steven found himself wishing he had someone to lean on. *Jenna.* Steven let out the breath he didn't realize he was holding and focused on his notebook. "Can you tell me about Samantha's friends?"

"She was popular," Anna said. "She had lots of friends."

"Did she date?"

Anna shook her head. "She had a boyfriend, but they broke up about six weeks ago."

"What happened?"

Anna lifted a shoulder wearily. "They're sixteen. Nothing lasts forever when you're sixteen."

"Why did they break up, Mrs. Eggleston?"

Anna clearly hesitated and Marvin turned to fully face her. "What, Anna? What happened that you two didn't tell me?"

Anna sighed. "He dropped her for another girl."

Steven watched Marvin's fist deliberately clench and release. "You didn't approve of the boy I take it?" Steven asked and Marvin tightened his jaw.

"No, I didn't. He was a fast boy."

Anna laid her hand on Marvin's arm again, this time gently. "And she said 'no,' Marvin. That's why he dumped her for another girl."

Marvin swallowed hard. "She cried for a week over that sorry piece of shit."

Steven cleared his throat and Marvin looked up, his eyes filled with tears. The sight shook Steven soundly. "Does the sorry piece of shit have a name?" he asked carefully.

"Gerald Porter," Anna said, stroking her husband's arm as Steven scratched the name on his notepad. "She didn't want you to know because she knew you'd give him a piece of your mind."

"And I would have, too," Marvin muttered.

"And she would have been embarrassed," Anna murmured. "She wanted to keep her dignity at school. To hold her head high and pretend Gerald hadn't hurt her so badly."

"So she may have been vulnerable in that respect," Steven said thoughtfully.

"What do you mean by that?" Marvin demanded.

"Not that Samantha did anything wrong, Mr. Eggleston," Steven reminded him and Marvin's body relaxed a notch or two. "Just that if she'd been abandoned by the sorry Gerald, then maybe she would have been more readily accepting of someone new. Who would she have confided in?"

"My wife," Marvin said.

"JoLynn Murphy," Anna said at the same time. "I know

you think my relationship with Samantha is that close, Marvin, but it isn't. She doesn't tell me everything."

"She loves you," Marvin said, desperately.

"Of course she does," Anna murmured, stroking his arm. "She loves you, too. But I was a sixteen-year-old girl once and I didn't tell my mother everything." She looked over at Steven. "I also understand that you found no evidence of forced entry into the house or her bedroom. Wherever she is, she started out, at least, of her own free will."

It was true, Steven thought. No forced entry and Samantha's perfectly formed shoe print outside her window. What could he say? "If not her own free will, at least on her own two feet. JoLynn says she hasn't talked with Samantha in over a week. Did she have any other friends?"

Anna closed her eyes, thinking. "Pamela Droggins," she said finally. "And Emily Robinson. They're all on the cheerleading squad together." She opened her eyes. "And Wanda Pritchard. They knew each other from the drama club. I don't think I gave you Wanda's name the other day."

Steven smiled at her. "No, ma'am, you didn't. Thank you for trying so hard to remember. Now, do you happen to know the name of the girl that Gerald Porter dumped her for?"

Anna shook her head. "No, she wouldn't tell me that. All she would say is that the new girl 'put out.'" She curled her lip distastefully. "Sammie said she was a low-class slut."

Steven looked at his notepad. He had names of one new friend and a sorry piece of shit and an unnamed low-class slut. Progress. He stood up and slid his pen in his pocket. "I want to thank you for your time," he said. "I know how difficult a time this is for your family."

"Agent Thatcher, wait." Anna looked at her husband. "Marvin, CNN called this morning when you were out with Serena. They want an interview."

Steven's heart sank. The last thing he wanted was to give

their perp any more media coverage than he'd already received. If Samantha was still alive, it could force him to kill her. If she was dead, the surge of publicity could incite him to do it again.

"Why didn't you tell me?" Marvin demanded.

"I wanted to hear what Agent Thatcher had to say first," Anna answered. "I'd say we have nothing to lose by talking to them."

"Mrs. Eggleston, I don't think that's a good idea at this point."

Marvin Eggleston looked at Steven with challenge in his eyes. "If you're truly doing all you can, then you won't mind the public seeing you do it."

"That's not it at all. Our team psychologist believes whoever took Samantha may have done it to call attention to himself. If you talk to the media, he will have what he wants."

Anna Eggleston pursed her lips and Steven knew he had underestimated her influence on the couple's decisions. For all his high-volume bluster, Marvin wasn't the decision-maker. Anna was.

"I will consider your position, Agent Thatcher," was all she said.

"I need to talk with the names you've given me," Steven said evenly, controlling his frustration. "Please don't go to the media. In my experience, that would be the wrong thing to do."

"I understand, Agent Thatcher," she said quietly. "I understand."

So did Steven, all too well. He understood she was a desperate mother willing to do anything to get her child back and that even though she'd given him her full cooperation in his investigation this desperate mother needed to feel she was doing something. Something, anything was better than the helpless waiting.

He also understood he'd be seeing the Egglestons on the never-ending CNN loop before midnight.

Dammit.

NINE

Saturday, October 1, 6:00 P.M.

JENNA STOPPED AT THE BASE OF THE STEPS leading to Allison's house, her ankle throbbing from the trek up the steep driveway. Her feet didn't move, even though the foot in the sock was becoming chilled. Shivering, she admitted to herself just how much she'd been dreading this dinner.

Adam's memorial dinner. On the week before the second anniversary of his "passing." She'd never heard the Llewellyns say "dead." They said "passing." Talk about being in denial, especially Allison. But even as she dreaded it, she could never bring herself to tell Allison "no." This dinner was a family tradition, and the Llewellyns were her family.

So move, Jenna. Get up those stairs and get this dinner over with.

But still her feet didn't move. The dread of how it would be overpowered family traditions.

Jenna knew exactly how it would be—exactly as it had been the year before. Allison would set her table with her Noritake china and Waterford crystal. The table would be set for six, although they'd be only five—Allison and her husband Garrett, Charlie, Seth. And herself, sitting next to the chair Adam had always occupied. His now-empty chair. They'd sit and join hands and Garrett would say his solemn grace.

And that would be the first bad moment—having to reach across Adam's place setting to grasp Seth's hand. It was such a physical reminder that Adam was no longer there.

Like she could ever forget. But somehow reaching across his not-to-be-used butter plate made it worse. It was stupid, she knew, but true. The next bad moment would come when they all toasted him. Jenna couldn't even remember what she'd said last year. She had no idea what she'd say this year. The very thought made her nauseous.

Lifting her foot to take the first step, Jenna felt her stomach do a cartwheel so strong she swung around and sat instead. From here she could see Adam's car at the curb. The shop had done a good job finding the old-style tires on short notice, but it had cost her. She'd paid the bill, grateful she had the car to bring tonight. The last thing she wanted was to add anxiety over Adam's car to the family angst on memorial dinner night.

She heard the door open behind her and caught the jingle of bangles—Allison's daughter Charlie—along with a whiff of what was to be dinner. It would be Adam's favorite meal, just like last year. That was another part of the family tradition, preparing the deceased's favorite meal at their memorial dinner. They remembered Adam's mother with liver and onions, Adam with sloppy joes from a can. On top of being the tiniest bit eccentric, the Llewellyns had terrible taste in food.

The bangles jingled louder until eleven-year-old Charlie dropped down to sit on the step beside her. She crossed her arms, creating another jingle from the bracelets that hung from both wrists. "Hi, Aunt Jenna," she said in a dramatically melancholy voice. Charlie had called her Aunt Jenna from the time she was six years old and Jenna wasn't about to ask her to stop.

"Why so glum?" Jenna asked, knowing Charlie needed no real reason. She was a pre-teen girl and that said it all.

"I hate sloppy joes," Charlie grumbled. "Why did Uncle Adam pick that for his favorite?"

Jenna looked down with a fond smile. "You don't know?"

Charlie puckered her lips. "If I knew I wouldn't be asking, would I?"

Jenna ruffled her short hair. "Sarcastic little brat," she said affectionately. "Your uncle picked sloppy joes because your mom's such a terrible cook he figured it was the only thing she couldn't totally ruin." Jenna leaned close and whispered, "He liked spicy Chinese food the best." A memory hit, so clearly it took her breath. The tiny apartment they'd shared after grad school, Adam, hale and hearty, sitting in their bed with a carryout carton in one hand and chopsticks in the other, wearing only his glasses and a broad smile at something she'd said. She remembered thinking she'd be happy with nothing else as long as she had him.

Charlie brought her back to reality with an amused chuckle and the memory slipped away like a wave going back to the sea. *Wait,* Jenna wanted to scream, but knew it was a fruitless waste of energy. Adam was gone. She no longer had him. And she'd learned to be happy anyway. She had.

"He really said that about my mom's cooking?"

Jenna swallowed the sudden lump in her throat. "Really."

"And I thought I was the only one."

She swallowed again, willing away the emotion that threatened to overwhelm. "You're not." She pulled herself to her feet. "But this means a lot to your mom, so let's go."

Saturday, October 1, 7:00 P.M.

"You wanted to see me, Dad?"

Victor Lutz looked up from the ledgers he'd been reviewing. Rudy stood in the doorway of his home office, the breadth of his shoulders completely filling the opening. His son was a handsome boy. Dark hair, bronze skin, strong jaw. Got his looks from *his* side of the family, thank God. "Yes, Rudy, come in and sit down. Did I also hear your friends out in the hall?"

Rudy sat down in one of the rich wine leather chairs and slid into a slouch. "Yeah, we're going down to the Y to lift weights." He winked. "Gotta keep my throwing arm in shape for next week."

"Yes. That's a good idea. Rudy, we need to talk about this problem at the school."

Rudy's smile faded. "I thought you fixed it."

"Blackman promised you'd play next week. But I'm not certain he'll keep his word."

Rudy was frowning by this time. "What are we going to do?"

Victor shrugged. "Depends how highly your teacher values her principles."

Rudy's expression went blank and Victor sighed. Got his looks from his side but unfortunately Rudy's brains came straight from Nora. God help the boy if he ever lost football, because he sure as hell wasn't going anywhere on the force of his intellect.

"Whaddya mean, Dad?"

"Let's be direct, Rudy. I heard her tires got slashed yesterday."

Rudy sat up straighter in the chair. "Now I had nothin' to

do with that," he said quickly. "The boys, they did it all on their own. Kinda like a show of support."

"Of course. That's the 'kinda' thing that may make her change her mind—and your grade."

Rudy's eyes went narrow. "You mean, it's cool?"

"It's cool, Rudy. She's a teacher, for God's sake. How much can she realistically afford to replace? Tell your friends to keep it up, and you stay as far away from them as possible. Tell them to just keep it discreet." He leaned back in his chair with a frown. "You do understand discreet?"

Rudy gracefully rose to his feet, white teeth flashing against his tanned face in a bold grin. "It means don't get caught."

"Exactly." Victor watched his son amble toward the door, the picture of a cocky boy with the world by the tail. "Rudy?"

Rudy paused at the door, his hand on the knob. "What now?" he asked, his expression a familiar mix of teenaged sarcasm and boredom.

"Don't mention this to your mother or Josh." Nora was so unpredictable, it was hard to tell how she'd react to such a plan. Josh, well, he was predictable all right. Predictably slow-witted. Left on his own, Josh would probably lead police right to Rudy and his friends with the tire-slicing knife still in their hands. No one could believe Rudy and Josh were brothers. That they were fraternal twins was a detail Rudy would never even have to bother to deny should it ever come up. It never would, if Victor had anything to do about it. Josh had the misfortune to take his brains *and* his looks *and* his athletic capability from Nora's side of the family. Josh had once shown promise as having some measure of intelligence, but even that seemed to evaporate at the onset of puberty. Now he had trouble remembering his own name most days. It was better to keep him away from anything of any importance whatsoever.

Rudy rolled his eyes in disgust. "Like I'd let that retard anywhere near me. I don't think so." But when he pulled open the door, Josh stumbled in, red-faced and stuttering an apology.

Victor tightened his fists on top of his desk. Well, fuck. He might as well have had Nora in the room, too, because Josh would go straight to her when this conversation was over. Unless Josh somehow became locked in the root cellar . . . for the rest of his life. The idea unfortunately was only a fantasy—a recurring fantasy with immeasurable appeal. "Well, Josh? What do you want?"

Josh straightened and tried for dignity. And of course failed. "It's wrong," he said, haltingly. "She's a nice lady, Dr. Marshall."

Rudy snorted. "So nice she's ruining my chances to be recruited by that college scout."

To Victor's surprise, Josh met his eyes with a full stare. "Rudy failed. He should have to follow the rules like everybody else." Then grunted in pain when Rudy shoved him up against the door frame, one strong hand around Josh's throat, lifting Josh an inch off the ground.

"I don't follow the same rules, turd," Rudy ground out. "Remember that, if you can."

Josh gasped for air and Victor said mildly, "Let him go, Rudy."

Rudy abruptly stepped back, threw Josh a baleful glare, then stalked from the room. Josh sagged back against the door frame, huffing and puffing.

"Don't be stupid, Josh," Victor said softly and went back to his ledgers.

Saturday, October 1, 9:30 P.M.

Steven closed the door to Interview Two behind him and came to a stop next to ADA Liz Johnson who looked like she'd been thoroughly enjoying herself. "Sorry I had to drag you all the way down here for nothing, Liz," he said and she grinned.

"Don't be sorry. Watching you finesse the sorry piece of shit Gerald Porter was worth my gas money. I think the real fireworks will happen when the Porters get young Gerald home tonight."

Steven leaned against the glass, on the other side of which Mr. Porter was ominously promising the sorry piece of shit Gerald that he'd pay for his sins.

"Too bad the only thing we can really get him for is carrying an illegal ID," he said glumly. "The bar where I found him conveniently hadn't noticed their sixteen-year-old patron was carrying the ID of a forty-five-year-old Hispanic man."

Liz patted his shoulder as she had on countless occasions before. "Well, Mrs. Porter seems to have been a mite put off by the fact Gerald dumped Samantha because she wouldn't sleep with him. I think he'll be sufficiently punished."

"But I wanted a murder suspect," Steven grumbled. "Not a candidate for asshole of the year."

"You'll get one, honey. Come on, I'll buy you a beer."

Steven smiled and pecked her cheek. "You're a good woman, Liz. Why hasn't some man snatched you up?"

Liz shrugged into her jacket. "Well for starters, I don't have a fairy god-aunt like Helen to handpick me a man. And for finishers, I work too damn much."

Steven sighed. "Let's make that two beers."

Saturday, October 1, 10:30 P.M.

"Good boy." Jenna slipped the leash off Jim's collar and patted him on the head, grateful she could finally sit down. Her ankle throbbed, her head ached, and her stomach burned. Damn memorial dinners with sloppy joes from a can. She eased her body into the sofa and sighed as her tense muscles relaxed. A hot tub would be better, but that would mean getting up.

The phone jingled and Jenna glared at it. If it was Allison . . . But on the off chance it was only a telemarketer trying to put himself through college she made her voice pleasant.

"Hello?"

"Hey, Jen, how did it go?" It was Casey and she was yelling over the din of a noisy band.

"Okay, I guess. My bottle of Tums is all gone."

Casey chuckled. "Poor baby. So what feast did Allison serve tonight?"

Jenna winced, her stomach remembering all too well. "Sloppy joes. It's a family tradition."

Casey made a rude noise. "That family is weird, Jen. They're like the Munsters and Charlie's the only normal one, like . . . what was her name again? The blond one?"

Jenna smiled, accustomed to Casey's quicksilver topic shifts. "Marilyn."

"Oh, yeah. Well, now that Allison's dinner is done, why don't you come down to Jazzie's? The band is great."

"Can't. My foot is killing me."

"What happened to your foot?" Casey shouted above the din.

Knowing Casey would hear about her tires soon enough, Jenna told her the story, as briefly as possible, again keeping

the threatening note to herself. Casey would have a connip-
tion over that. "Steven brought me home and that was all
there was to it," she finished.

"Steven?" Casey asked and Jenna felt her face heat.
"Who's Steven?"

"Nobody," Jenna said, but it was too late. Casey would
never let it go. "He's Brad's father."

"Hmm."

"What does that mean, hmm?" Jenna gritted, her jaw
clenching.

"It means nothing."

"It *was* nothing," Jenna insisted, but the denial sounded
pathetic even to her own ears.

"Just like your Steven is nobody," Casey added, her tone
one of patronizing amusement.

Your Steven. Too bad the name conjured the face. Too bad
it was such a very nice face. "Go back to your band, Casey,"
Jenna growled.

Casey laughed out loud. "Whatever you say, Jen. I'll be by
tonight after my date and you can tell me all about it."

"That's all there was," Jenna spat, frustrated. "Besides,
later tonight I'm going to be up to my chin in a tub of hot
water. Then I'm going to bed. I'll see you on Monday."

"Monday? Don't you need my truck for hospice day?
Don't tell me you've forgotten?"

Jenna groaned. "I did." She and Jim volunteered one Sunday a month at the hospice where Adam had spent his last
weeks. Jim was a certified therapy dog and wagged his tail to
spread joy. Jenna worked a little harder, reading aloud, reliev-
ing weary family members who needed a few hours to themselves, hugging them when the fatigue and grief became too
much to bear. It was her way of turning Adam's death into
something positive. But every hospice day she had to borrow

Casey's truck since Jim was a tight fit inside Adam's XK 150. "Can't you bring the truck by tomorrow?"

"Oh, I could, but then I'd miss hearing the rest of the story. I'll be by tonight."

"There is no more story."

"I'll bring a pint of Rocky Road."

Jenna sighed. Casey never gave up. "I won't open the door for under a gallon."

"I've got a key."

"Dammit."

Casey chuckled. "See you later, Jen."

Jenna hung up the phone, settled back into the cushions when the phone rang again. *Casey.* "What did you forget?" Jenna asked sourly, then sat up straighter at the silence. "Um, hello?"

"Hello," a female voice said uneasily. "May I speak to Dr. Jenna Marshall?"

"This is she." *Oh, crap.* She'd been rude to a complete stranger.

"Dr. Marshall, this is Brad Thatcher's aunt. Great-aunt actually. I hope it's not too late to call."

"Of course not, Mrs.—I'm sorry, I didn't get your name."

"It's Helen Barnett. I tried to call earlier, but kept getting your machine. I have your briefcase."

"My briefcase?" Jenna asked blankly, then it came flooding back. Steven putting her briefcase in the backseat, the way his eyes crinkled when he laughed, how sweet and supportive he was when he helped her file the police report. The way his arm had felt against her when he helped her up the stairs to her apartment.

"Oh, dear," Mrs. Barnett said, jerking Jenna from her reverie. "This is your briefcase, isn't it?"

"Oh . . . oh, yes, ma'am, it's mine. I'm sorry, it's just been a long day. I'd completely forgotten about leaving my briefcase in Mr. Thatcher's car. Can I come pick it up tomorrow?"

"Why, certainly, dear. Steven would have brought it to you himself, but he's in the middle of a major investigation and it's got him preoccupied, I'm afraid. He's been gone all weekend."

"I know he's a busy man, Mrs. Barnett. If you'll give me directions, I'll swing by and pick it up tomorrow afternoon." She and Jim could go by after they finished at the hospice.

"It's Miss Barnett, actually. Would you mind coming by between five and six?"

She'd be done at the hospice by four-thirty. "That'll work. Thank you. I'll be by tomorrow."

Jenna hung up and stared at the phone for a long minute, acutely aware of the disappointment she felt that one, Steven wasn't bringing her briefcase by himself and two, he'd be gone on his major investigation when she went to his house to pick it up tomorrow. Both were ridiculous, she knew.

But still she was disappointed. Why ever for, she had no clue.

You do so know, Jenna, the little voice inside her whispered. She hated that voice. It was so snide. But usually right.

Casey's teasing has me thinking things that just aren't true.

Whatever you say, Jenna.

"Shut up," she snapped aloud and Jim and Jean-Luc looked up, instantly aware. "Not you," she added and looked at her watch. It would be a good two hours before Casey arrived with the Rocky Road, but she was pretty sure she and Seth had left some in the carton from last night. It would have to do until Casey arrived with the reinforcements.

Saturday, October 1, 10:45 P.M.

"Why didn't you ask her to dinner?" Matt asked when Helen hung up the phone.

"It didn't seem right," Helen answered. "I trust my intuition on this."

"I think you just chickened out," Matt taunted. "Aunt Bea."

"I don't chicken out," Helen maintained with hauteur. Then she scowled. "And stop calling me Aunt Bea. Leave me alone. I have potatoes to peel for tomorrow."

Matt dropped a kiss on her cheek. "Mash 'em so thick you can stand a knife in 'em."

"I know how you like your mashed potatoes, young man." Helen took her peeler from the drawer and shook it at his grinning face. "I've been doing it for four years. Four long years."

"I'll have to ask Brad's teacher if she can make really thick mashed potatoes," Matt said thoughtfully. "I think it's a critical criteria."

Helen swatted him with a hand towel. "Don't even think about it. You make one false move tomorrow and I'll take this potato peeler to your behind."

"You're a scary woman, Aunt Bea."

"And don't you forget it, boy."

TEN

Sunday, October 2, 9:00 A.M.

JENNA STUMBLED OUT OF HER BEDROOM, the smell of freshly brewed coffee drawing her to the kitchen like a magical lodestone. Casey must be awake, she thought. She'd arrived late the night before and stayed over, just likc the old days in the Duke dorm.

Cradling the hot cup between her palms, she walked back to her spare bedroom where Casey lay in bed watching TV, Jim curled up at her feet and Jean-Luc with his head on her pillow.

"What do you want for breakfast?" Jenna asked through a jaw-breaking yawn.

"Sshh!" Casey hissed and it was then Jenna noticed how pale Casey had become.

Alarmed, Jenna sat on the edge of the bed, pushing Jean-Luc aside. "What is it?"

"The police are talking about the second missing girl," Casey murmured.

"Oh, no," Jenna whispered as the weeping parents implored whoever had stolen their daughter to bring her home. "Those poor parents."

Casey said nothing, but the coffee cup she held in her hands trembled. Jenna put Casey's cup on the nightstand and listened to the reporter solemnly finish with a reminder of the first kidnapped girl, whose body had been discovered a few days before, butchered beyond recognition.

"Raleigh law enforcement gave a press conference this morning, but refused to make any comments or speculations at the time," said the reporter. Then the scene switched to the press conference and Jenna drew a startled breath. Steven Thatcher stood on the podium, looking impossibly handsome as he faced a barrage of questions from the media.

"What?" Casey asked. "Who is that?"

"Sshh," Jenna hissed, not taking her eyes from the screen.

"—no comments at this time," Steven was saying.

"Do we have a serial killer stalking young women?" a reporter shouted and Jenna watched Steven's jaw tighten.

"We are not speculating at this time," Steven returned evenly.

"Do you believe the abduction of Samantha Eggleston is related to the murder of Lorraine Rush?" another reporter insisted. Bulbs flashed and Steven frowned.

"We are investigating any and all leads. We can't afford to rule out that possibility at this time." Again he tightened his jaw as if clenching his teeth. He looked exhausted.

Jenna was worried about him and annoyed with the media at the same time. The scene switched back to the CNN anchor. Then there was silence as Casey hit the mute button on the remote. Neither of them said a word for a full minute.

Casey wiped her eyes with the back of her hand. "Dammit, Jen. What if we do have a serial killer out there? That's two girls in the last two weeks. What if one of our girls is next?"

Jenna squeezed Casey's hand. "I don't know. But I do know that if Steven's on the job, he'll make sure everything's being done that can be done."

"Steven?" Casey asked cautiously. "As in Brad's dad? That guy was Brad's dad?"

Jenna abruptly stood, making both dogs look up expectantly. "Yes. Agent Steven Thatcher. Brad's dad."

Casey's eyes instantly focused. "Okay," was all she said.

Perfunctory responses from Casey were never a good thing. "What does that mean?"

Casey shrugged. "It means okay."

"Your okays never just mean okay."

Casey retrieved her coffee cup from the nightstand and took a sip. "Jen, sometimes a cigar is *just* a cigar," she said wryly, then raised a brow. "Isn't it?"

The mental image was too powerful to ignore. "What is that supposed to mean?" Jenna demanded, feeling her cheeks flush.

Casey blinked. "You're blushing!"

"No, I'm not."

"Yes, you are." She shrugged again. "But it's no matter. You'll probably never see him again."

"I'm going to his house today," Jenna blurted before she could stop herself.

Casey's blue eyes grew round as saucers. *"Hello."*

"But it's not what you think," Jenna added hastily.

"Of course not."

"It's not," Jenna insisted.

"Whatever you say," Casey said mildly.

"His aunt called last night and asked me to come to pick up my briefcase. So I'm going to pick up my briefcase." She set her lips together. "Nothing more. He probably won't even be there."

Casey sobered, her eyes flicking back to the television. "If he is there, ask him about the girls."

Seattle, Washington, Sunday, October 2,
10:30 A.M. Eastern Time (7:30 A.M. Pacific)

Seattle Detective Neil Davies came home from work, by-passed the piles of newspapers and dirty, sweaty laundry, and went straight to his kitchen for a beer. It wasn't even breakfast time, but somewhere in the world the sun was setting over the yardarm. That had been his old man's way of justifying alcohol at any hour of the day.

He'd no sooner popped the top when the phone rang. He'd given up hoping it would be Tracey. She'd gotten on with her life. He gave a mirthless chuckle. He guessed he couldn't blame her. It was hard for a woman to live with a man haunted by the ghosts of four dead teenaged girls.

"Yeah?" he barked into the phone.

"It's Barrow." His old partner from the West Precinct. "Turn on CNN."

Immediately Neil grabbed the remote and turned on the TV.

"Do you see?" Barrow asked tersely.

"Sshh," Neil hissed and blindly set the untouched beer on the counter. It was a small town in North Carolina. Two girls missing from their beds. Cheerleaders. One found butchered in a clearing, her head shaved. Terrified parents. Mystified police. He felt a strange settling in his gut, a hum sizzling along his skin. "It's him." Neil was sure of it. "William Parker."

"Maybe," said Barrow, guarded as usual. "You thought the guy in California was him and the guy in New York, too. So what are you going to do?"

"I'm going to Pineville, North Carolina. Wherever that is."

"Outside Raleigh," Barrow said. "And once you've arrived there, what will you do?"

"I don't know," Neil answered grimly. "Maybe get rid of some ghosts. Maybe get on with my life. I'd settle for a decent night's sleep."

Barrow sighed. "You know you can call me if you need me."

Neil almost smiled. "I know."

Raleigh, North Carolina, Sunday, October 2, 10:30 A.M. Eastern Time

"Incompetent bastards," he muttered, turning away from the CNN report to examine his most recent photographic handiwork. Having his own darkroom really gave him the freedom to experiment with color and angle and lighting. Lorraine's body looked even more gruesome in black and white. But, he was still partial to color. All that blood . . . It just didn't get justice in black and white.

"And this was the scene at the headquarters of North Carolina's State Bureau of Investigation early this morning," said the reporter, a woman with short, flippy hair.

He frowned. He hated short, flippy hair. Women should have long hair. He pulled out his most recent photo of *her*. She was perfect. She'd never get her hair cut like a man. In fact, if he were king of the world, all women would be required to grow their hair long and all scissors would be illegal. He smirked, looking at his head shot of bald little Samantha Eggleston. Except for *his* scissors of course.

But then, intelligent men weren't subject to the same rules that bound other men. It was fact.

"We will confirm we have a second girl reported missing."

He jerked his eyes up from his photographs and scowled at the talking face on the screen. Special Agent Steven Thatcher, read the caption below the man's face. Special agent. Hah.

Thatcher knew nothing *he* didn't want him to know. Special Agent Thatcher never would have found poor Lorraine had it not been for his anonymous tip. Thatcher couldn't even find a body if he found a neon sign blinking "*body, body, body.*" Idiots. All of them.

He tilted his head, staring at the flickering visage of Special Agent Steven Thatcher.

"So you think you're hot stuff, huh, *Special Agent* Thatcher? You ain't seen nothin' yet."

The question was—what was the most effective means to up the ante?

Sunday, October 2, 4:45 P.M.

This is really stupid, Jenna thought, bringing Casey's Ford Explorer to a stop in front of the Thatcher home. Nevertheless she pulled her visor mirror down to check her makeup. Of course it was fine. She'd just freshened it up in the Hardee's parking lot three blocks back. She looked over at Jim in the passenger seat. "You have the bridge, Captain."

The Volvo wasn't in the driveway, so Steven was probably still out in the field. Or the car could be in the garage and he could be inside. Her heart fluttered and she cursed it. It didn't matter if he was here or not. She'd only be staying for a minute. Just long enough to get her briefcase.

She looked the house up and down as she calmly walked up the sidewalk even though the butterflies were doing the polka in her stomach. It was a nice house, really nice. Jenna was a little surprised how nice. She hadn't realized special agents of the SBI made such a good living. It was much nicer than the house in which she'd grown up, a place where loud voices and negativity were the rule. A place she rarely thought about.

She rang the bell and the door was opened by a woman with gray hair. "Come in, Dr. Marshall," she welcomed and yanked Jenna inside where a tantalizing aroma tormented her nose.

"Uh, thank you." Jenna looked around, noting the darkened room off to the right, a study perhaps. Jenna strained her peripheral vision to spy inside, but the room appeared empty. Mentally cursing Casey and berating her own suggestibility, she yanked her gaze back to the woman.

"Let me take your coat," Miss Barnett was saying and Jenna shook her head.

"No, really, I can't stay. I'll just get my briefcase and be out of your hair."

"It's all right," said a young boy, walking down the stairs. Jenna looked up to find a younger version of Steven coming toward her. "Aunt Helen won't have all that hair much longer anyway." He came to stand next to his aunt and tugged at her gray hair. "Tsetse flies, you know."

Jenna shook her head again, this time a little wary. "I'm afraid I don't understand."

"Neither does Matthew," Miss Barnett said and glared up at him. "This is Brad's younger brother, Matt." She shooed him. "Go . . . do something useful."

"I could test the turkey," Matt said helpfully. He shot Jenna an engaging grin that had her smiling back. "We wouldn't want to serve an underdone turkey. Family might get worms."

Jenna coughed, trying to hold back a laugh.

"It's done, Matthew," Miss Barnett said, her tone lowering. "The button popped."

"Then I could take Dr. Marshall's coat."

"No, I'm just leaving."

Matt had her jacket off her shoulders before she could blink twice. "Don't be silly. I'd like to get to know Brad's teacher and I'm sure my aunt would as well. Don't you, Aunt Helen?"

Jenna was certain she saw the older woman's lips twitch. "Absolutely." She looked down at Jenna's socked foot. "I heard you took a spill on Friday."

"Just a little one. I'll be fine in a few days. Is Brad here?"

Miss Barnett frowned and glanced over her shoulder up

the stairs. "Upstairs somewhere. He and Steven had a bit of a disagreement this morning."

Jenna grimaced. "Oh."

"He's grounded for life," Matt said cheerfully and Jenna had to truly fight to keep her sober grimace from becoming a snicker. It really wasn't funny, Brad's troubles, but obviously there was sibling rivalry at play.

Jenna couldn't help but feel at ease with the two that seemed a bit eccentric. Like the Llewellyns. Except, judging from the wonderful aroma coming from the kitchen, the Thatchers had better food.

Miss Barnett steered her toward the living room. "Come and sit, Dr. Marshall."

And before Jenna could refuse again, she was seated on a high-backed sofa with Miss Barnett at her side and a small ottoman under her left foot. "For circulation," Matt said and Jenna laughed.

"Can I get you some tea, Dr. Marshall?" Miss Barnett inserted. "Or cola?"

"No, ma'am, I really can't stay."

"Nonsense," Miss Barnett insisted. "Dr. Marshall, may I call you Jenna?"

Jenna blinked. "Yes, of course."

The older lady beamed. "Good, good." She patted Jenna's hand. "And you can call me Helen. I have a huge turkey in the oven. Wouldn't you like to stay for dinner?"

Turkey. After last night's sloppy joes a home-cooked turkey dinner sounded just short of heavenly. And her stomach was growling. And if she stayed longer Steven just might come home and she could see him one last time. But she was Brad's teacher. Having dinner at his house could be considered playing favorites. It might even be against the rules. She'd run it by Lucas in the morning. "I'm sorry, Helen. I'd love to, I really would, but I really need to go." She heard a canine whine from a room beyond the kitchen and remembered poor Jim still out in Casey's truck. "I have my dog out in the truck. He really shouldn't stay alone long."

"Well, bring him in," Helen said brightly. "He can play with Cindy Lou."

Jenna raised a brow. "Cindy Lou? What kind of dog is she? A poodle?"

"I wish," Helen muttered. "No, she's an Old English and she's very friendly. I'm sure Matthew wouldn't mind getting your dog from your truck." She stood up and dusted her palms on her slacks. "Now I simply will not take no for an answer. My nephew must have inconvenienced you this weekend by knocking you down and hurting your ankle. The least we can do is feed you."

The turkey did smell delightful. And she realized she really wanted to stay. "Okay, but I'll get Jim from the truck. He does better with strangers when he's been properly introduced."

Jenna led Jim in through the Thatchers' front door and was greeted by a small boy with a head of carrot red hair and more freckles than his round cheeks could handle. Jenna stopped and Jim automatically halted at her side. "Hello, I'm Jenna and your aunt asked me to dinner."

The little boy looked up, his eyes carefully blank, and she remembered the newspaper accounts of the abduction of Brad's youngest brother the spring before. This would be the child, she thought, and her heart squeezed with compassion at what he'd gone through. And was still going through, if his blank eyes were any indication. Jenna made herself smile. "And you must be Nicky."

Nicky stared at her warily for so long that Jenna felt her face begin to twitch. Then he dropped his eyes to Jim. "Is that your dog?"

Jenna knelt on one knee and put her arm around Jim. Now

she was at eye level with Nicky. "His name is Jim. Do you want to pet him?"

Nicky shuffled forward and tentatively put out his hand. "He looks like a wolf."

"He's a German shepherd and big for his age." Jenna bent down and locked eyes with Jim, earning her a lick on her nose. "I can see where you might think he's a wolf, but he's really a baby."

Nicky softly stroked Jim's head. "How old is he?"

"Almost two." She leaned closer and dropped her voice. "You want to know a secret?"

Nicky nodded, too seriously for a little boy, and Jenna's heart clenched again. "Jim has a brother named Jean-Luc. They're identical twins."

Nicky's brown eyes widened. "Really?"

"Really." She glanced up to see Helen watching with intense interest. Apparently Nicky's conversation was not an everyday occurrence. The thought made her feel a little warmer inside. "Do you have a dog?"

Nicky nodded, visibly relaxing a bit. "Her name is Cindy Lou. I got to name her."

Jenna raised her brows. "Let me guess. Cindy Lou Who who was not quite two?"

Nicky nodded again, still way too solemn for a small boy. He couldn't be more than seven.

"*The Grinch* was my favorite book when I was your age. Especially at Christmas."

Nicky scratched behind Jim's ears. "My daddy doesn't like Cindy Lou very much."

Jenna blinked, startled. Steven had seemed to like her dogs a great deal. "Why not?"

Nicky's mouth wobbled uncertainly, then one corner lifted in an almost smile. "She likes to chew things. Usually Daddy's things. Last week she chewed two shoes."

"And I bet they weren't matching shoes either."

Nicky's mouth curved up. "Nope. One sneaker and one church shoe."

Jenna chuckled. "Well, I guess that would explain your daddy's feelings, huh? I'd have a problem with Jim if he destroyed two pairs of my shoes."

Nicky reached out and tugged Jim's tunic. "Why does he wear this?"

"Jim's a therapy dog. He and I go to visit sick people and Jim helps them feel better."

Nicky's red brows scrunched together. "How can a dog make sick people better?"

Jenna watched him scratching Jim's ears and remembering his ordeal, carefully considered her answer. "Have you ever been afraid, Nicky?"

Nicky's hand went still on Jim's head. Nicky stood frozen and somehow sensing the importance, Jim didn't move a muscle.

Jenna quietly drew a breath. "Well, sometimes sick people are afraid. They're afraid because maybe they hurt, or maybe the doctor is about to poke them with needles. When they pat Jim's head, it helps them forget about being afraid for a little while. And that makes them feel better."

After what seemed like an eternity, Nicky began scratching Jim's head again. "Then he must be a very nice dog."

Jenna let out the breath she held. "He is. Would you mind if I let him off his lead?"

Nicky shook his head. "No, let him go. I'll take him to meet Cindy Lou."

Jenna stood up, watching Jim obediently follow Nicky through the kitchen. She turned to find Helen's eyes glistening and Matt's teasing expression replaced with a seriousness that approached Nicky's. This entire family was hurting, she realized. She cleared her throat, forcing emotion back down. "Jim's well trained. He won't hurt Nicky."

Helen blinked, then brushed the moisture from her face without shame. "I don't doubt that, Jenna." Her eyes brightened. "Come to the kitchen and tell me about therapy dogs while I carve the turkey." She threw a meaningful glance toward Matt. "I will be *carving* the turkey, Matt, with a very sharp instrument. I do not recommend trying to steal a taste."

Matt grinned, shaking off his seriousness. "But I'm very fast."

Helen shrugged. "As long as you don't feel you need those fingers. Come along, Jenna."

"Wait."

Jenna stopped in her tracks and looked up the stairs. Brad stood at the top, his hand massaging the back of his neck, his face grizzled with at least two days' beard. He descended the stairs with a shuffling step and came to a stop in front of her.

"Dr. Marshall."

Jenna studied him up close, seeing the dark circles under his red-rimmed eyes. "Brad," she said softly. "I was hoping I'd see you. I left my briefcase in your dad's car Friday when he gave me a ride home after school."

He looked down at her feet, then back up, his eyes alert and discerning despite the dark circles. "What happened to your car?"

Jenna lifted a shoulder in a half shrug. "Somebody vandalized it. Slashed the tires."

His brown eyes flashed and his jaw hardened. "Rudy Lutz. Lousy scum."

She shrugged again. "Maybe. But it's already fixed." She smiled at him, as gently as she could. "How are you, Brad? I missed you in class on Friday."

He looked away. "I couldn't stay." His voice was harsh

with what sounded like self-rebuke and Jenna's heart softened.

She squeezed his shoulder. "We can talk about it on Monday."

Brad turned his head in the direction Nicky had gone. "I heard you talk to my brother."

"He's a cute little boy."

"Yeah." Brad turned back and met her eyes directly and again Jenna felt his misery, a palpable pressure against her heart. "He doesn't talk often. Thank you."

Jenna swallowed, wishing she could take both boys into her arms for a hug. "Hey, I heard there was turkey for dinner. Are you as hungry as I am?"

Brad looked back to the kitchen where Nicky was earnestly introducing Jim to an enormous gray ball of fluff. No hint of a smile touched his lips. "I could eat."

Jenna made her own lips curve even though she felt more like crying. "Then let's go before Matt 'tastes' all the white meat."

Eleven

Sunday, October 2, 6:15 P.M.

STEVEN PULLED INTO HIS DRIVEWAY, KICKING himself for being late for a family dinner, when his eyes narrowed at the old Ford Explorer parked in front of his house. *Company.* A spurt of anger flared. *That old sneak.* Helen lured him home with the promise of a family dinner, turkey with all the trimmings, only to really set him up with a blind date. He ground his teeth. After dealing with the press all day, he was not in the mood to be blatantly disobeyed by a meddling old woman. He'd told Helen again and again to stop her matchmaking. Today was the day she'd listen.

He got out of the car and slammed the door hard. Helen's matchmaking would be a total failure without half the match—him to be precise. He'd pass on the "family" dinner and barricade himself in his study. He had enough work to keep him busy for the rest of the night, easily. But the aroma that met his nose when he opened the front door made him quickly amend his plan. He drew an appreciative breath. As infuriating as she could be, Helen was a damn good cook and he was starving. He'd make himself a plate, *then* barricade himself in his study. A man had needs after all.

Food. Turkey. And sex. *Jenna Marshall.*

Not necessarily in that order, he thought bitterly. He couldn't even say her picture "flashed" in his mind, because it had been there all damn day. Through his team meeting this morning, the hellish impromptu press conference—she'd been there. Black hair, violet eyes, and all those curves . . . *God.* He had more important things to worry about. Samantha Eggleston. Brad. Nicky.

Yet still, Jenna stayed in his mind. Fantasy and memory switching back and forth until he thought he was going to scream. Jenna offering comfort with her eyes wide and hopeful. Sexy as hell sprawled on the floor of the school lobby, her skirt hiked high above the tops of those silk stockings. Naked in his bed, panting and crying his name as she came around him. He shuddered from the sheer force of the fantasy. *God.*

Jenna sitting at his dining-room table.

Steven stopped in the archway and blinked. This was neither fantasy nor memory. Jenna Marshall sat at his dining-room table. Eating his turkey. Sitting between his youngest sons while his aunt looked on in beaming approval.

Jenna Marshall, party to his aunt's schemes.

He'd been set up. By Helen. By Jenna herself. While he'd been kicking himself for having entirely normal fantasies, *she'd* been scheming with Helen. He felt doubly betrayed. Unholy fury, pent up all day, simmered and burst forth.

"What the hell is going on here?" he asked, his voice menacingly quiet to his own ears.

The buzz of conversation instantly ceased and every head looked up. He watched Jenna slowly put her fork on her plate. She said nothing, just looked up at him with those eyes of hers. But unlike Friday, they weren't full of compassion, but reproach.

Which made him even angrier. On the edge of his vision he saw Helen rise to her feet.

"You were late. We started without you," Helen said coldly.

"I can see that," he gritted from behind clenched teeth.

"And we have a guest," Helen added, her voice dropping to sheer ice.

Steven matched her tone, not taking his eyes from Jenna's face, which had gone still as stone. "I can see that too. I also remember telling you I didn't want any company this weekend and I especially didn't want another of your *damn* blind dates. I didn't know the two of you knew each other, Helen. What exactly are you doing here, Dr. Marshall?" he added, his voice deceptively mild.

"We didn't know each other until today," Helen said, balling her fists at her sides. "And I didn't know my nephew could be so rude."

Jenna stood up abruptly. "I think I should be going now." She looked over at Helen. "May I have my briefcase now?"

Briefcase. Steven drew a breath and felt his fury fizzle into a tiny wisp of smoke. He closed his eyes and swallowed hard. He'd stepped in it. Royally. "You came to get your briefcase."

"She left it in your car, Daddy," Nicky offered soberly and Steven opened his eyes to see his youngest sidle a little closer to Jenna who stood still as a marble statue. He could see she was angry, unspeakably so, but she controlled herself to a hair. "Aunt Helen called her to come get it." Nicky frowned. "So she did."

Steven's gut turned over. *She'd come to get her briefcase.* Dammit. He shot Helen a helpless look. Helen returned it with scorn and looked back to Jenna, her expression softening.

"But you haven't finished your dinner," she said to Jenna.

Jenna met Steven's eyes and he felt an inch tall. "I've had enough, thank you."

Nicky tugged on her sleeve. "But, Jenna, you promised to help me teach Cindy Lou to sit."

Jenna bent down and schooled her features into a gentle smile. "So I did. Well, I tell you what. If it's okay with your dad I'll come by next weekend and you and I can take Cindy Lou to the park for her first lesson. How does that sound?"

Nicky frowned. "But I wanted to start now. Please?"

Jenna ran her finger down Nicky's nose and tapped the freckled end. "But you don't always get everything you want. Besides, once I get my briefcase, I have to go home and grade papers."

"Can you leave Jim here?" Nicky asked plaintively and Steven closed his eyes, his heart sinking. He could have predicted this. Nicky had already formed an attachment thanks to Helen's meddling. An attachment that would bring nothing but grief and disappointment. And who could blame his boy? Who wouldn't develop an attachment to a woman like Jenna Marshall in a single meeting? God only knew he himself had.

"No, Nicky, I can't," she said. "If I left Jim here, Jean-Luc would be lonely. You wouldn't want that to happen would you?"

Steven opened his eyes to find Nicky slowly wagging his head back and forth. "I guess not." Nicky's face brightened a shade. "Can you stay for dessert? Aunt Helen made three kinds of pies."

"Three pies? Goodness." Jenna shook her head. "No, I'm afraid not, darlin'. I have to go now." She straightened and angled a look at Brad. "Tomorrow? I'll see you in class?"

Brad jerked a single nod, which Jenna apparently took as assent.

"My briefcase, Helen? Please? And, Matt, my jacket, if you don't mind. Jim, get your leash."

With a sigh Helen left the room. With a disgusted glare aimed in Steven's direction, Matt followed her. Jim the dog had already padded away, Nicky in close pursuit. Brad stood and turned a dark scowl on his unshaven face. "Good work, Dad," he sneered. "Ruined yet another *family* dinner." He turned to Jenna. "Please excuse my father's rude behavior, Dr. Marshall. And feel free to take home some leftovers. I'm not having any more. I've lost my appetite."

Steven locked his jaw as Brad turned on his heel and raised his hand in a sarcastic salute. He waited until Brad was gone, leaving just the two of them and a table overflowing with turkey and stuffing. Brad was right. He'd ruined dinner and had been insufferably rude. "Jenna, I—"

She held up her hand, stopping him midsentence. "That's not necessary, Mr. Thatcher."

Ouch. So they were back to formalities. "I'm sorry," he said quietly.

Her eyes blazed with the same fire he'd seen when he knocked her down in the school lobby. "It's not me you should be apologizing to, but the boys and Helen. That was inexcusable."

"I'd like to explain."

She shook her head. "I don't want to hear it." Helen appeared with her briefcase and Steven stepped forward to help her carry the heavy monstrosity, but she grabbed it from Helen's hand with what could only be called a polite snarl. "I'll carry it myself," she snapped at him, then drew a breath and turned back to Helen. "Thank you for your hospitality. I'm sorry I have to run."

"I understand," Helen murmured and together Steven and his aunt watched Jenna limp to her Explorer, briefcase slung over one bowing shoulder, Jim at her heels. When she'd driven away, Helen looked at Steven with contempt. "You idiot," she whispered and left him standing alone.

Seattle, Washington, Sunday, October 2,
9:00 P.M. Eastern Time (6:00 P.M. Pacific)

"I hope you know what you're doing," Barrow said, slowing down for a pedestrian pulling a set of suitcases through the airport crosswalk.

"I plan to make it up as I go along," Neil replied dryly. "Unless you have a better idea."

Barrow glanced over at him before pulling into an open space at the departures curb. "You could forget about all this and get on with your life. Maybe get Tracey back and settle down with a couple kids and grow too much zucchini in the backyard of a house in the suburbs."

Neil just looked at him and Barrow sighed and added, "Or you could go do what you think you have to do. Just be careful and don't do anything stupid."

"Like flying across the country on the off-chance it's the same guy?"

Barrow nodded. "Hold your temper until you have real evidence. Even if it is the same guy."

Neil frowned. "I had real evidence last time."

Barrow shrugged. "The judge said we didn't."

"The judge—" Neil bit off what he really thought of the judge. "I'll be good. I promise."

"I don't see why you can't investigate this from here. The Parkers couldn't have just dropped off the face of the earth."

"For all intents, they did." Neil should know. He'd spent every waking hour after the moving truck pulled away from the curb three years before trying to figure out where the Parkers had run. Where they'd started their new life, leaving anguish behind here in Seattle. "If you're rich enough, you can buy nearly anything, including a new start. I have to prove to myself it isn't Parker."

Barrow sighed heavily. "So when are you coming home, Neil?"

"When I'm finished, I guess. I had some vacation coming, so I took a few weeks off." Actually, he had more than a few weeks accrued. He hadn't taken a day off in almost three years.

If his LT hadn't allowed the leave, Neil had already planned to resign, which both Barrow and his LT would have classified as "stupid," but was consistent with how much he believed in what he was doing. Three years ago he'd made a promise to four dead girls who were denied justice due to a technicality, an error on the part of the Seattle police. His error.

Those four girls would get justice if it was the last thing he did.

"Take care, Neil," said Barrow and Neil forced a grin.

"Always do. Thanks for the ride."

Neil climbed from the car, his hanging bag swung over his shoulder, the handle of the locked case holding his service revolver clenched in his right fist. "Carolina, here I come," he murmured. "If you're William Parker, watch out. You won't get away again."

Raleigh, North Carolina, Sunday, October 2, 9:00 P.M. Eastern Time

He'd been frozen out, Steven thought, staring at the little peephole in Jenna's front door. By his aunt, his children, and now by the woman whose forgiveness he needed to secure before he'd be able to sleep another wink. He knocked again. "Jenna, please open the door. I know you're in there." He leaned his forehead against the cold steel. "Please let me explain." What he intended to say, he had no idea. He just knew he had to make this one thing right. If only this one thing.

He'd tried to let the whole situation just die down. He'd fixed himself a plate of turkey, which tasted like sawdust. But he'd eaten it, if for no other reason than to have some sense of normalcy. Then he'd looked up to find Nicky staring at him with those solemn brown eyes. "You shouldn't have yelled, Daddy," Nicky said. "She's a nice lady and she didn't know Aunt Helen invited her over on purpose." He'd raised both carrot-colored brows, his face looking so much older than seven. "You need to apologize, Daddy." Wiser than seven, too.

And if that weren't chastisement enough, Matt took his turn, extolling Jenna's virtues and frowning at his father as though he were mud. Helen was ignoring him and he didn't even try to talk to Brad. So he'd left, gotten in his car, and driven with no destination in mind, but was totally unsurprised to look up and find himself sitting in front of her apartment.

"Jenna, I saw you through your window. I won't stop knocking until you open the door."

"I'll call the police," she said through the door.

"I am the police," he reminded her. "Please."

"She's a stubborn one," a voice said behind him and he turned to find himself the subject of octogenarian scrutiny from a six-inch opening of the neighbor's front door. "I'm Mrs. Kasselbaum."

Ah, he thought. *The nosy neighbor. Perhaps she might be an ally.* He extended his hand. "I'm Special Agent Steven Thatcher of the State Bureau of Investigation," he said and watched her eyes go round as saucers. Antique saucers.

A gnarled arthritic hand appeared from the six-inch opening and shook his hand with a strong grip. "Is our Jenna in some kind of trouble?" she asked, dropping her voice to a loud whisper.

"No, ma'am. I got myself in trouble. I said something I shouldn't have and now she won't let me apologize. Do you have any suggestions?"

She pursed her lips, then said, "I've got a key." And it was Steven's turn to widen his eyes.

"You do? Jenna gave you one?"

Her expression fell. "No," she admitted. "The tenant before traveled a lot and I watered his plants and fed his cat. The landlord never changes the locks between tenants."

That had to be a violation of some kind, Steven thought and filed it away along with the intent to put a new lock on Jenna's door as soon as possible. "I couldn't use a key. Do you have any other suggestions?" He leaned closer. "She and I had a bit of a . . . spat. You know how it is."

She nodded. "My Harvey and I would have our spats from time to time. God rest his soul."

"I'm sorry, ma'am."

Mrs. Kasselbaum shrugged matter-of-factly. "He was

ninety-two. We had a May-December marriage, you see." She
batted her eyes and Steven bit back a grin. What a cutie-pie
she was.

"Well, I really want to apologize to Jenna." He sighed
sadly. "She and I promised we'd never let the sun go down on
our wrath."

Mrs. Kasselbaum nodded at the biblical reference as
Steven suspected she would. "Sensible. My Harvey and I had
the same arrangement. Step aside, young man." Steven did
and Mrs. Kasselbaum fully emerged from her apartment to
knock briskly on Jenna's door. "Jenna Marshall, open this
door this instant." Silence met their ears and she sighed. "I
don't want to do this, but you leave me no choice. I'll call the
landlord and tell him about the other dog."

The door snapped open and Steven had to grab Mrs. Kasselbaum to keep her from falling through. Jenna stood there,
arms crossed over her breasts, a German shepherd flanking
her on either side, her face full of righteous indignation. She
was magnificent, he thought, his mouth watering at the sight
of her. She glared down at the old lady. "You wouldn't."

Mrs. Kasselbaum looked up defiantly. "Will you let this
boy apologize?"

Jenna looked at Steven who gave her his best innocent
look. She snorted. "Oh, for heaven's sake. Come in and get it
over with." She bent down to stare Mrs. Kasselbaum square
in the eye as Steven slipped in the door. "If Seth gets wind of
this . . ."

Mrs. Kasselbaum straightened her body indignantly. "I'm
not a gossip, young woman."

"No, not you," Jenna answered sarcastically. "So, when
you do tell him, tell him I am not romantically involved, nor
do I have any intention of romantic involvement." She
straightened and shut the door hard, but didn't turn around to
look at him. After an uncomfortable pause, her shoulders

sagged and he clenched his fists at his sides to keep from turning her to face him. "Okay, Agent Thatcher," she said softly and he winced at the hurt in her voice. "You're sorry, you won't ever do it again. You've apologized. Now you can go."

He blew out a pent-up breath. "Jenna, please. I need to do something right today. My children aren't speaking to me."

She turned slowly and in her eyes he saw not anger, but grave disappointment. "As well they shouldn't. And not because of me."

Steven narrowed his eyes. That sounded like a rebuke. "Then why?"

"Steven, how many evenings have you been home this week?"

Now he knew where this was going. "You must already know if you ask the question," he answered tightly.

She just looked at him for a long moment, then limped to sit at her dining-room table where all her folders lay spread out. She patted the table. "Sit. Please."

She'd said please. So he sat.

"This isn't any of my business," she began.

"No, it really isn't."

She smiled and only God knew why that put him at ease. But it did. "I'm going to tell you anyway. You owe me, since you were rude to me today."

"You were rude to me on Friday," he countered. "So we should be even."

She raised a brow. "But you've already accepted my apology for that. Nice try, but no deal. While we were waiting for you to come home, I talked to your boys. Nicky told me you're never home. Matt said you'd offered to take him to a movie festival this weekend, but you got busy and forgot. And tonight, you're late again—and for a family dinner."

She was right, he knew. Still it annoyed him to have her

say it aloud. "And you are an expert on children, Dr. Marshall?"

"No," she said softly. "But I am an expert on the fragility of time. It passes, Steven. You can't stop it. You always think you're going to have another day to make things right, to say the things you should have said, to do the things you should have done. But sometimes time and life don't cooperate and another day never comes." She blinked, her eyes dry even though his had filled. "You know this, Steven. You almost lost Nicky last year. So why do you hide from your children? They love you."

Restless, Steven pushed to his feet and paced to the sliding-glass door that led to her balcony. She was right. He'd almost lost Nicky last year. So why did he work so much? Was he hiding from his children? He rubbed the stiff spot on the back of his neck. He'd deal with *that* after he dealt with *this*. "I came to apologize, Jenna. I'm sorry I became angry. I had a very bad day and thought my aunt had set me up on another one of her blind dates. I . . . I thought you were party to it. I'm sorry. I hope you'll forgive my rudeness as Brad so accurately labeled it."

"Accepted."

Steven wheeled around. "Accepted? Just like that?"

Jenna lifted one corner of her mouth in a wry smile. "Why not? You accepted mine on Friday as I recall. And I said you were an idiot."

"An incompetent idiot."

Jenna rolled her eyes. "Thank you for refreshing my memory. We seem to have gotten off to awkward starts both times we've met, Agent Thatcher. Perhaps we could begin again."

Steven rolled his shoulders, feeling the weight roll away. He approached, holding out his hand, feeling the grin split his face. "I'm Steven. I'm glad to meet you."

She took his hand and looked up, shyly he thought. "I'm Jenna. Would you like a drink?"

He looked down into her eyes and felt his heart turn over in his chest. Her lips moved but it was a few seconds before the whispered word sank in.

"Steven?"

He realized he still held her hand and hastily let it go. "Um, yeah. A drink would be great."

But she didn't get up. She just sat there staring up at him with those wide violet eyes and full red lips and the fantasy flashed right back. Her naked body in his bed, her black hair spread on his pillow, her violet eyes dazed with passion, her full lips moaning his name.

Her eyes dropped and when she lifted her eyes again he saw not compassion or ire or reproach, but heat. Want. Raw lust. Shuddering, Steven clenched his fists to keep from reaching out and cradling her face in his hands and finding out how soft her lips really were. "What's happening here?" she whispered.

I want you. Steven forced himself not to look lower than her face. Forced himself not to look down to her round breasts gently molded by the soft black sweater or to the tight jeans that showed off every curve. *God, I really want you.* He cleared his throat and lied. "I don't know."

She wet her lips and Steven's forehead broke out in a cold sweat. He needed to leave. Fast. Before he did something he was sure to regret. "I need to go." His voice was thick and hoarse. "I'll . . . I'll call you."

She nodded. "Okay," she murmured.

He made it to her front door when he stopped, his hand on the doorknob. He tried to ignore the throbbing of his body. It was no use. It was all he could do to stay where he stood and not go back and grind his mouth against hers until he found some relief from whatever madness wouldn't let him go.

"Your neighbors have keys to your apartment," he rasped out, feeling the words drag against his dry throat. "You should change your deadbolt. As soon as possible."

"Okay," she murmured.

Steven chanced a look back and immediately wished that he had not. She sat where he had left her, looking straight ahead at the wall, her expression stricken. Guilty. A thread of her conversation with her neighbor popped into the forefront of his mind, pricking at his tenuous composure. "Who is Seth, Jenna?" he asked.

She didn't move a muscle. "My fiancé's father."

Fiancé. Steven physically staggered backward against her front door. "You're *engaged*?"

Her head turned and he could see her face had grown pale. "My late fiancé. Adam died two years ago." Her lips twisted bitterly. "Two years ago next Saturday."

Now he understood her comment on the fragility of life. "I'm sorry, Jenna."

"Thank you," she whispered.

Steven shook himself into motion. "I'll replace your lock."

"Okay," she murmured.

"Matt has a soccer game tomorrow. It'll be Tuesday before I can come back."

She nodded. "Okay."

"Dinner?" The invitation was out of his mouth before he realized. But it was too late to back out now. Father Mike would be only too pleased.

For a moment he thought she'd say no. Half of him wished she would. The other half wanted her to say yes with a yearning that threatened to rip him in two. Then she nodded and his heart started beating again. "Okay."

Sunday, October 2, 10:00 P.M.

Casey found her in the same position an hour later.

"What are you doing here?" Casey thundered, letting herself in with her key. "I thought you were dead on the highway. In my truck! Why didn't you call me if you weren't coming?"

Jenna blinked. Casey stood in her living room, fists on her hips. "What are you talking about, Casey?"

"Dinner? New Italian place on Capitol? Cute friend of Ned's?" Casey crossed the room and tapped Jenna's head. "Ring any bells in there?"

Jenna sighed. "I'm sorry. I forgot." She pushed away from the table and rolled her shoulders. "Damn, I'm stiff. Serves me right for sitting here feeling sorry for myself. I'm starving. Do you want something to eat?"

Casey followed her into the kitchen. "Were you not listening to anything I said? I ate. New Italian place on Capitol." She poked Jenna's arm. "Without you."

Jenna opened the freezer door and frowned. "You didn't bring the Rocky Road last night like you promised. Now I'm out."

"I forgot." Casey peered under Jenna's arm. "Hey, there's some vanilla back there."

Jenna just looked at her. Vanilla wasn't even worth the trouble. She wasn't even sure how it got in her freezer.

Casey looked worried. "What's wrong, Jen? And why were you feeling sorry for yourself?"

Jenna stared into the freezer. She closed her eyes, feeling the cold air bathe her hot face. "Casey, have you ever cheated on Ned?"

Casey choked. "*What?* Where the hell did that come from?"

Jenna closed the freezer door. "Well?" she asked, urgency

making her voice shake. She looked over her shoulder to Casey's guilty face.

"No." Casey stepped back and shifted her weight to one foot. Her eye twitched. "Not exactly."

"Not *exactly*?" Jenna asked, knowing she sounded hysterical and not able to help herself. "What *exactly* is *not exactly*? You either cheat or you don't. It's like being *not exactly* pregnant." She pulled herself to an abrupt stop. Casey's mouth hung open in shock. Jenna blew out a controlled breath and hit her forehead against the freezer door. "I am so totally insane."

"Jen?" Casey asked in a tiny voice. "Do you have something you want to get off your chest?"

"I am insane."

"You said that already." She squeezed Jenna's arm. "You can't seriously expect me to believe you cheated on Adam. You barely left his side the whole year after he was diagnosed."

"Not then. Now. Tonight."

Casey tilted her head, puzzled and tentative. "Tonight?"

Jenna spun and flopped back against the refrigerator. "He was here."

Casey frowned. "What are you talking about? Who was here?"

"Steven Thatcher," Jenna snapped.

Casey's brows shot up. "Oh." Her eyes darted back toward Jenna's bedroom. "You aren't trying to tell me that you . . . and he . . . ? Jenna!"

Jenna limped back to the table. "For God's sake, Casey, of course not."

"Then I am confused. How did you cheat? Specifically now, Jenna. I need details."

"Steven was here. Long story." She massaged her temples. "He held my hand."

Casey was staring at her as if she were a french fry short of a happy meal. "And?"

Jenna closed her eyes, remembering the heat all over again. The almost-painful tingle that started at her fingertips and shot straight down to her core. "He looked at me." And she'd felt helpless to look away. She didn't want to look away. He'd wanted her. And God help her, she'd wanted him. She would have willingly kissed a man she'd barely met. And then what?

Jenna looked over to find Casey staring, her blue eyes rife with concern. Jenna looked away. "I held his hand and he looked at me and I think I would have done anything he asked. Anything."

Casey gently grabbed Jenna's chin and brought her face around. "And?"

"I wanted to . . . you know . . . just holding his hand, Case." Jenna looked into her best friend's eyes and made herself say the awful truth. "And I never felt that way with Adam. Never," she whispered.

Twelve

Monday, October 3, 7:35 A.M.

"JENNA," CASEY CALLED FROM THE DOORWAY of the faculty lounge, "wait up."

Jenna stopped, her head still pounding from sheer fury at

listening to Blackman's lecture a second time, practically commanding her to give "young Rudy" a passing grade.

Casey caught up, huffing and puffing. "Where's the fire, Marshall? Slow down. You've got twenty minutes till the first bell. Besides, doesn't that hurt your ankle, walking that fast?"

"Yes, but the throbbing in my ankle takes my mind off the throbbing in my head," Jenna answered curtly. "Keep up, Thumbelina," she added, her voice as sour as her disposition. "I'm in a really pissy mood this morning."

"No shit," Casey muttered, then was blessedly silent until they stopped in front of Jenna's closed classroom door. Casey leaned against a locker and looked up, her eyes worried and her forehead covered in a sheen of perspiration. "Look, Jen, I don't mind a morning run, but you could at least have let me change into my cleats." She stood on one foot and rubbed her ankle. "What's gotten into you this morning?"

"Nothing." Jenna dug in her purse, looking for the keys to her classroom. "I just didn't get much sleep last night and Blackman hit me with a guilt trip this morning about Rudy Lutz's grade."

"That's what I wanted to discuss," Casey said with an emphatic nod.

Jenna pulled the bag of dog biscuits from her purse and handed them to Casey. "What, Rudy Lutz's grade? I didn't know you had the pleasure of his highness's presence in your class this year. Anyway, I don't want to talk about that in the middle of the hallway. Where *are* my keys?"

Casey pursed her lips. "Not Rudy. I wanted to talk about why you couldn't sleep last night."

"I don't want to talk about that, either. Especially not here. Go away, Casey." She shoved her hand in her purse again and muttered a curse when something sharp poked her finger. She brought out a metal nail file and put it in Casey's outstretched palm. "Don't *tell* me I left my keys in Blackman's office. I don't want to go back there. Dammit to hell."

"Really, Jen. I've been thinking about Adam and . . . you know."

Jenna glanced up, totally annoyed. "What part of *not here* don't you understand?" she snarled.

Casey lowered her voice to a whisper. "Listen, Jen, you shouldn't even try to remember how things were between you and Adam. I don't even think you have rational memories of how he was before, so I'll remember for you. You were perfectly satisfied. You told me so."

Jenna went still. "I did?"

Casey's curls bobbed in a hard nod. "You did. I swear it." She grinned. "It was the night we were trying to discover the best recipe for Long Island Iced Tea. You gave all kinds of juicy details."

Jenna dropped her eyes to her purse, suddenly feeling worse even though she hadn't believed it possible. She remembered the night of the Long Island Iced Tea marathon. She remembered the juicy details and that she truly had been satisfied. That was the problem. What she'd felt just holding Steven Thatcher's hand had nothing to do with satisfaction.

It was greed. Pure, unadulterated craving. Throw-common-sense-to-the-wind desire. It was as different from any previous experience as . . . As Häagen-Dazs Rocky Road to store-brand vanilla. She swallowed the lump that had formed in her throat. Adam deserved a hell of a lot more than being store-brand vanilla. She felt like a dirty traitor even letting the comparison form in her mind. Her hand closed on her keys and she breathed a sigh of relief. "Here they are," she said thickly. "Casey, don't you have someplace to be?"

"Of course. I probably have thirty-two panting tenth graders looking for the dirty parts in the *Lady Chatterley's Lover* I left on my desk." She smirked. "They'll be surprised when they find out it's only the cover of *Lady Chatterley* on a copy of *The Iliad*." Her brows snapped together. "What?"

Jenna's body had gone still with dread. When she put her key to the lock, the door creaked open. It was already unlocked. With her fingertips she gave it a tiny push.

"Holy shit," Casey swore on a shocked hiss. "Jenna!"

Jenna was speechless. Her beautiful classroom was a shambles. Vandalized. A disaster area. She found her voice. "Call Blackman. Let's see what he says about his golden boy now."

Monday, October 3, 9:30 A.M.

The red-eye from Seattle had been uneventful. Neil landed in Newark at six in the morning where he'd reset his watch to Eastern time, grabbed a three-dollar bagel and a two-dollar cup of coffee. Then he'd changed planes and landed in Raleigh two hours later and five bucks poorer.

"Would you like a smoking or nonsmoking room, sir?" the man behind the motel counter asked politely and Neil wanted to scream "Smoking!" but didn't.

"Nonsmoking," he made himself say. He'd quit ten years ago, but there didn't pass a day that didn't have him fighting the craving. Especially stressful days, which was pretty much every day of his life. He signed the ledger and took the key.

The room was nondescript and mostly clean. He dropped his overnight bag on the bed, then pulled out an envelope. He drew out four photos and laid them on the dresser, edge to edge.

Four young girls. He didn't need to look at the neatly typed labels on the back of each photograph to remember their names. Laura Resnick. Trudy Valentine. Emily Barry. Gina Capetti. All sixteen years old. All cheerleaders. All brunettes.

All dead.

He studied each photo, seeing the girls as they'd been before meeting William Parker. Beautiful, vibrant smiles. Eyes shining with anticipation over their bright futures.

He didn't need to look at the "after" photos. He still saw their faces every time he closed his eyes. But he looked anyway, their eyes wide-open, blank, staring upward. Their heads shaved bald.

The photos blurred before his eyes, the smug smile and cold eyes of William Parker materializing in his mind, uninvited. The fatigue was catching up with him. He'd lie down for a little while, get over the jet lag. Then he'd find William Parker. It was time to honor his promise.

Monday, October 3, 12:15 P.M.

"Jenna, what is this word?"

Jenna tossed the putty knife to the lab table where some creative individual had superglued all of her glassware to the tabletop. She walked over to where Casey stood looking up at the spray-painted Periodic Table with a quizzical expression. Jenna looked up, squinted, and tilted her head.

"I don't know. But here"—Jenna pointed to the chart— "some Einstein connected the *Fe* in Iron, the *U* in Uranium, and the *C* in Cadmium. They missed the *K*, so I'd only give them partial credit."

"But you'd have to give them an *A* for coming up with a new swearword," Lucas said, sweeping up piles of broken glass. "*Feuc*. It sounds old-Englishy, like it could have come out of *Beowulf*."

Casey reached up and yanked one corner of the ruined ten-foot-wide Periodic Table from the wall. "So tell me again why Blackman didn't call the cops?"

"Because there's no indication of who did this," Jenna said, mimicking Blackman's nasal tone. She sighed. "At least there wasn't a threatening note this time."

Casey and Lucas stopped what they were doing. *"What threatening note?"* they said together.

Jenna bit her lip. "I didn't mean to say that. Must be the cleaning fluid making me dizzy."

Lucas dropped the broom, walked over, and grabbed her chin. "What threatening note, Jen?"

Jenna winced. "The one that was on my car windshield on Friday afternoon."

"Was there text included, or did they just make all those comic-strip cursing characters, like ampersands and asterisks?" Casey asked, tongue in cheek.

Jenna sighed again. "It said, 'Put him back on the team or you'll rue the day you were born.'"

Lucas squeezed her chin. "What else?"

She rolled her eyes. "'You bitch,'" she added. "They misspelled 'rue.' That's it, I swear. I didn't tell you because I didn't want you to worry. Steven gave it to the police and they took it in for prints, but Officer Pullman called me this morning and told me they didn't get a single print."

"Who's Officer Pullman?" Casey said.

"He took the report," Jenna said.

Lucas's eyebrows had shot to the top of his forehead. "Who's Steven?"

Jenna closed her eyes, feeling her cheeks heat. "He's Brad Thatcher's father."

"He's Rocky Road," Casey added slyly. "Yum, yum."

Lucas frowned at Casey. "Yum, yum?"

"Hey, I just call 'em like I see 'em," Casey said. "He looked pretty good to me on CNN."

"Hmm," Lucas mused. "So you're on a first-name basis with a parent. Interesting."

Jenna opened one eye. "Is it illegal?" She almost hoped it was, so she could have a decent excuse for canceling dinner on Tuesday night, which by turns she'd been dreading and anticipating with a furor that scared her.

"No. No. Perhaps a bit sticky, but a young Jedi like yourself can navigate." He let go of her chin and patted her head. "I have every confidence in you."

"Gee, thanks, Obi Wan," Jenna grumbled and went back to scraping glue from the tabletop.

Lucas looked at Casey. "She almost sounds like she wants it to be against the rules."

Casey looked disgusted. "She does. She—"

"Casey!" Jenna looked up in alarm. "Shut up."

Lucas looked hurt. "I thought I was one of the girls."

Casey leaned toward him and whispered, "Hormones. Approach with caution."

Lucas shot her a sympathetic glance. "What's wrong, honey?"

"Nothing. Lucas, it's really nothing."

Casey pulled the rest of the Periodic Table from the wall and scampered backward to keep from being covered when it fell. "It's not nothing. She's convinced she's being untrue to Adam's memory because she drools over Steven Thatcher."

Jenna scowled. "Last time I ever tell you anything."

"Hmm. Seems to me the situations are very different," Lucas said. "Adam and this Steven."

Jenna narrowed her eyes. "If you want to be one of the girls, you might as well jump in. Don't tell me it's different because Adam was sick. We had a very healthy sex life. I never drooled."

Lucas shrugged. "You women always blame men for your lack of orgasm."

Jenna choked while Casey laughed so hard she turned red.

Lucas, however, remained totally serious. "Seems to me, you're the one who's changed, Jen. I remember when Marianne turned thirty. *Rowl*," he growled in his throat and Jenna laughed too.

"You're impossible, Lucas."

"That's what Marianne *used* to say. Now she just says, '*Yes, yes, yes!*'"

Casey held her stomach, still chortling. "Stop, Lucas, you're hurting me."

"I think Jenna's increased sex drive is all her fault. The real tragedy is that Adam died before she fully matured." He backed up, then turned, startled. "Kelly. How long have you been there?"

Kelly Templeton's eyes were wide. "From yes, yes, yes. You said we could talk extra-credit on my test during lunch, Dr. Marshall."

Jenna covered her eyes, mortified. "Kelly, just go, and don't mention a word of this. Please."

"Eight points partial credit on my test?" Kelly asked, her tone smug.

Jenna frowned and peeked through her fingers. "I don't give unearned grades."

Kelly pursed her lips, then smiled. "*Yes, yes, yes.* I could make quite a cheer out of that."

Jenna sucked in a breath. "That's extortion."

Lucas chuckled. "Sounds like free commerce to me."

Jenna glared at Lucas, then considered Kelly. "Tell you what. I'll give you the *opportunity* for eight points extra credit on the next test. It'll all come out in the wash."

"Make it twelve points and you have a deal," said Kelly with confidence.

Jenna stuck out her hand. "Deal. Now go away. And never say *yes* to me again."

Kelly laughed as she turned for the door. "I never thought I'd be looking *forward* to thirty."

Casey sucked in both cheeks. "Whoa, that girl has a future."

Jenna shook her head. "As what I don't want to know."

"But the important thing is, will you partake of Rocky Road?" Casey wanted to know.

Jenna considered it. Maybe Adam had been Rocky Road all the time, but her taste buds were just too dull to appreciate him. Maybe she wasn't such a louse after all, just a slow bloomer.

Casey plunked her fists on her hips. "Well?"

Jenna sighed. "Maybe a taste. Just to see how it goes."

Casey patted her arm. "Good girl." Then she winked at Lucas. "I've never known Jenna to stop at one bite of Rocky Road."

Lucas chuckled and picked up his broom. "Some things are not made for moderation."

Monday, October 3, 12:45 P.M.

The Pineville Public Library looked like something out of colonial times. Neil just hoped they had Internet access. He needed to track down the Parker family. One Parker in particular.

He found the fifty-something librarian sitting at her desk, her hands neatly folded. Her nameplate said Miss Wells. "What can I do for you today?" she asked pleasantly.

"I'm visiting and I need Internet access. Can I use one of your computers for a few hours?"

"Of course you may," she said and he realized she'd corrected his grammar, probably through reflex. She stood and gestured him to follow, leading him to a large table with eight desktop computers. "Take your pick. They do have software that blocks access to certain sites."

Neil felt his lips twitch. "I'm not looking for porn, ma'am."

Miss Wells's face heated to the color of cherries. "I never . . . I mean . . ." she stuttered. "Well, please just take one. I'll sign you in. What is your name, please?"

"Neil Davies. D-a-v-i-e-s. It sounds like *Davis* so everyone forgets the *e*."

She gave a professional little nod. "Very well, Mr. Davies. Can I get you anything else?"

"How about local newspapers from the last two weeks?"

He watched her pleasant expression change. Harden. Her mouth thinned to a straight line. "Of course. I'm sure you'll find all the little tidbits you're so hungry for." She looked away. "Parasites."

"Excuse me?" Neil asked.

"Reporters," Miss Wells spat. She looked back, her eyes flashing. "We can't turn around anymore without running into one. Turning a tragedy into copy. Go right ahead," she added bitterly. "You won't be the only one."

"I'm not—" Neil started to say, then stopped. Perhaps being a reporter would be a decent cover. "I'm not going to write a story on the missing girls," he said earnestly and watched her eyes go from angry to merely suspicious. "I'm doing a piece on local families," he added, inspired.

Miss Wells nodded uncertainly. It didn't really matter if she believed him or not. The papers were public record, but he did prefer to be on good terms with the librarian.

"Very well," she finally said. "They're in the back room. I'll be right back."

Twenty minutes later, Miss Wells brought him a stack of the *Pineville Courier*. "We have the paper copies going back two months," she said. "Beyond that you'll be squinting at microfiche."

"Understood," Neil said, his fingers itching to begin. "Thank you."

Three hours later he was deep into the microfiche and still hadn't found the face he sought. Another man might have given up by now. Another man who didn't see the faces of four innocent girls crying for justice every time he closed his eyes. He blinked hard and gritted his teeth.

William Parker was in here somewhere. He knew it. He just had to find one picture. *One.*

Miss Wells sat in the seat next to him. "Perhaps if you told me what you're looking for," she murmured in her librarian voice. "I'd be happy to help you."

I'm looking for a monster, he wanted to say. But, of course, did not. Instead he made his mouth smile ruefully and said, "Thanks anyway, but I think this is an 'I'll know it when I see it' situation."

"Very well. But you might want to take a break. You're starting to develop a twitch."

A *twi-itch*, he thought with amusement. Only in the South could a one-syllable word become so elongated. Neil stretched. "That's a good idea, Miss Wells. I'll walk around your library."

She stood up with him and pointed to the far wall. "The high school has put together a collection of pictures of local events. Maybe you'll find what you're looking for there."

He wouldn't, he knew. But his back ached and his eyeballs felt like they'd been carved out with a melon-baller. He definitely needed a break.

Miss Wells resumed her post at the front desk and Neil walked to the far wall she'd indicated. The high school students had done a good job, capturing a number of different aspects of local life including agriculture—a dried tobacco leaf; commerce—an aerial view of the Research Triangle; society—the first high school dance of the season; and of course sports. He bent forward and stared at the photos gathered in collage fashion. And froze.

There, amid photos of farmers, white-collar professionals, babies and senior citizens, students, parents and teachers, was the one picture he was looking for. The only face that mattered.

William Parker. Smiling. It was the smile Neil had last seen from the window of a black Mercedes sedan on a cold drizzling day in Seattle. It was the smile he'd seen every day from across the courtroom where Parker sat at the defendant's table, tie knotted impeccably, hair neatly combed, eyes defiant. It was the smug, self-satisfied smile that had made Neil want to rip his face in two.

That still made Neil want to rip his face in two.

Gathering his wits, Neil walked back to the computer and brought up a search engine, typed in a few words and got the result he was looking for the first time out. It was amazing how simple a search was when you knew who you were looking for.

Then he cleaned up his area, thanked Miss Wells for her help, and left the Pineville Public Library, his gut churning in the absolute certainty that he had found William Parker and in the absolute belief beyond a shadow of a doubt that Parker was actively murdering once again.

The problem was, he had not a single shred of proof.

So go get some.

Monday, October 3, 5:15 P.M.

Steven pulled his Volvo into the very last parking place. Well, technically it wasn't a parking place, he thought, taking a fleeting backward glance as he jogged toward the soccer fields. It was a grassy area next to the Porta-John next to a sign that said NO PARKING. Technically he was in violation of the law. He was fifteen minutes late for his son's soccer game. The first one in which Matt started. First string.

Technically he'd royally screwed up.

"Don't miss it, Dad, okay?" Matt had asked quietly this morning over breakfast.

"Not for the world," he'd answered. Matt looked unconvinced, making Steven promise himself he wouldn't be late.

Well, damn. He was late. But he was here. He stopped at the sidelines where a group of parents stood cheering. "What's the score?" he asked one of the parents.

"Thatcher!" The man gave him a broad grin and a slap on the back. "Haven't seen you around in ages. Our boys are up one to nothing."

Oh, God, please don't let it have been Matt who scored. Please don't let me have missed that. Steven forced a smile. "Who scored the goal?"

The man drew up like a peacock. "Mine did." Steven breathed a sigh of relief. "But yours assisted," he added and Steven felt his heart sink.

He'd missed Matt's first assist. One game was all Matt had asked and he'd already missed the most important play.

Steven could see compassion flicker across the other dad's face. "I got it on video," he said kindly. "I can rewind it to show you at halftime."

"Thanks," Steven said, feeling his stomach pitch, knowing Matt must have looked for him, knowing his middle son must have been disappointed that his father hadn't been there to cheer.

He'd been late tonight for a very good reason. Kent had called with the results of the ketamine analysis of Lorraine Rush's body. Positive. So now they knew what they'd suspected. The same person was responsible for the abduction of both girls.

They had a serial killer on their hands.

And he'd missed his middle son's big play. Life sucked.

Have courage, Steven.

Steven easily found Matt among the running boys, his bright red head standing out like a torch. He waited until Matt looked his way and gave a tentative wave, afraid of the look of scorn Matt would probably give back. But his son surprised him. Matt's face broke into a huge grin and he waved back and pointed to the goal.

"I assisted," he shouted.

Steven felt his face break into a relieved grin. "I know," he shouted back. And then the ref blew the whistle resuming play and Matt turned back into the fray. Without taking his eyes from the dancing torch in knee pads, Steven reached in his pocket and turned off his phone. It was the first time the phone had been turned off since he'd bought the damn thing. *It's about time,* he thought.

He'd watched a full ten minutes of play before he heard the voice behind him. "Excuse me."

Steven looked over his shoulder to find a tall dark man in a denim jacket standing behind him. The man needed a shave and a new pair of shoelaces on his beat-up Nikes.

"I'm kind of occupied here," Steven said kindly. "Trying to watch the game, you know."

"It won't take long," the stranger said. "I want to talk to you about Lorraine Rush and Samantha Eggleston."

Steven huffed out a frustrated sigh. "No comment."

"But—"

Steven turned, keeping one eye on the field. "Look, you can call SBI headquarters and get a statement from the PR guys, but it won't be any different than what I've been telling you press guys all along. *No comment.* We have highly trained resources on this case. We'll let you know when we have something. Until then, no comment." A huge cheer went up and he turned his attention back to the field just in time to see Matt kick the ball into the goal.

"Yes!" Steven screamed at the top of his lungs, jumping a foot in the air and easily drowning out video-dad. And when Matt looked over this time, Steven gave his grinning son the thumbs-up. "Look, buddy," he said to the stranger behind him, "I have to get back to the game."

But when he glanced back over his shoulder, the stranger was gone. His eyes narrowing, Steven spied a teal Dodge Neon exiting the fields, now a hundred yards away. His hackles raised, Steven gave his attention back to the team who was high-fiving his son.

He pushed the feeling of trepidation to the side and moved closer to the field boundary line.

"Great goal, Matt!" he shouted.

Matt looked over, his face flushed with exertion and excitement. And his smile said it all.

Monday, October 3, 5:30 P.M.

"It's not like you've got a serial killer running around or anything," Neil muttered under his breath as he drove away, unimpressed with his first impression of Special Agent Steven Thatcher.

The leader of the investigation. The guy who didn't have

anything better to do than watch a group of kids play soccer.
Wonderful. These girls didn't have a fucking chance.

It would have to be up to him.

Grinding his teeth, Neil drove to the address he'd etched in
his brain. He pulled his rental car two houses down and . . .
spied. It was a nice house, he thought. Almost as nice as the
house they'd owned in Seattle. He wondered if they still had
the grand piano and the vases worth a year's salary. He wondered if they still had all the paintings and antiques.

He wondered if they were able to sleep at night. Knowing
what they'd done.

He hoped not, because he sure as hell couldn't. He wondered if he'd see William Parker coming and going. He wondered what he'd say, what he'd do when he saw the man
whose smug smile had haunted him for three years.

He knew what he wouldn't do. He wouldn't do anything
stupid. And he sure as hell wouldn't do anything to allow
some fucking defense attorney to have any evidence he gathered thrown out of court on a technicality.

This time he'd do it by the book. This time he'd do it right.

THIRTEEN

Tuesday, October 4, 8:03 A.M.

"GOOD MORNING," STEVEN SAID, QUELLING THE muttered
conversation around the table. Everyone was edgy this
morning. Harry and Sandra were squabbling, Kent looked

like he could use a fresh suit, Meg stood looking out the window, and Nancy was fussing over everyone, something she did a lot more when she was stressed. Nancy was like Helen without the matchmaking, he thought and looked up with gratitude as she refilled his coffee cup. "Thanks."

Nancy gave him her motherly smile and moved on to fill the next empty cup.

"So where are we?" Steven asked his team. "Sandra?"

Sandra shook her head. "None of my contacts on the street have a clue. I did, however, get three very interesting proposals, but none of them looked like relationship material so I said no."

Steven's lips twitched as he took the report Harry pushed across the table. "What, you want stability and morality? Get your head out of the clouds, Sandra."

"Hell, who wants stability? I'd just settle for a guy who wasn't on parole for something too sick for the prime-time news."

"You need to get out of the gutter, Sandra," Nancy clucked. "Find yourself a nice accountant."

Steven rolled his eyes. So much for Nancy not matchmaking. *You don't need a matchmaker anymore,* he thought. *You're having dinner with Jenna tonight.*

Drawing on every ounce of discipline he possessed, he put Jenna and her big violet, passion-dazed eyes out of his mind and looked down at Harry's report. "The ketamine supply," he said.

Harry nodded. "Got back answers from all but two of the vet supply houses I queried on ketamine orders and deliveries. Only a few new customers in a hundred-mile radius and none with any irregular ordering patterns. No one has any unaccounted-for ket."

Steven scanned the list. "When do you expect answers from the other two supply houses?"

"I'll call 'em again today, Steven."

Steven gave him back the list. "Keep it up, Harry. I want to know how our boy got the stuff."

"I'd still like to know what he's using it for," Meg said softly from her spot by the window. "There are a lot of ways to immobilize a victim. Why ketamine?"

"I guess we'll find out when we find him," Steven said grimly. "Nancy?"

She shook her head from where she stood by the coffeepot. "I didn't get any hits on the like perps when I cross-referenced against the ketamine," she said. "Lots of crack, pot, and heroin, but no ket."

Steven sighed. "I didn't think you would. And other than the fact the two girls were members of the same parish and were both cheerleaders, I can't find any other areas of commonality. The Rushes didn't even go to church that frequently. Samantha was there last week, but Lorraine hadn't been to church in months." He pinched the bridge of his nose, annoyed the headache was already there. "I've retraced their known steps, talked to all their friends, but nothing matches."

"What about the cheerleading angle?" Sandra asked. "They would have competed against each other, gone to cheerleading camps together."

Harry looked at her, delighted. "Don't tell me you were a high school cheerleader?"

Sandra's expression went sour. "Don't go there, Harry. It was part of my misspent youth. I'm sure if I dug hard enough I'd find a few things you'd prefer were left alone."

Harry was undaunted. "Did you wear a little skirt and *smile* and everything?"

Sandra narrowed her eyes at him, then looked back at Steven. "You want me to check the cheerleading circles?"

Steven threw a warning glance at Harry who was still

chuckling. "Beat the bushes, Sandra, see what you find. Kent? What about you?"

"Only that we found ketamine in Rush's tissue samples. But you knew that yesterday."

Steven's mind blinked back to yesterday and he remembered the man at the soccer match. The press. He suppressed a shudder at the thought. "Let's keep going, folks, we'll turn up something. And please, don't anyone talk to the press. Unfortunately that little jewel belongs to me."

Tuesday, October 4, 9:00 A.M.

"Well, you're early," Miss Wells said as she unlocked the library door.

Neil had been up since four A.M. pacing the floor of his tiny hotel room until he'd thought he would go insane. "I need to use your computer again."

"Well, help yourself," Miss Wells said. "Let me know if you need anything."

"I will," he promised. He sat down at one of the computers, brought up a search engine, and typed "Steven Thatcher and SBI." Then sat back to learn about the man who held the safety of Raleigh's young girls in his hands.

Tuesday, October 4, 5:00 P.M.

Jenna carefully closed the door of Adam's car, then walked around the car and stared at the gas cap, rage making her body clench and tremble. The twenty-minute drive from school had taken sixty as Adam's car bucked and kicked and sputtered and threatened to leave her stranded. And with every buck, every kick, every sputter, every minute that went by she got madder and madder.

She could take vandalism in her classroom two days in a row. She could even take slashed tires, because they hadn't touched what was important. Adam's car itself.

But this time they had. Hopefully it was only water in the gas tank, something she could fix with a bottle of STP. And if it wasn't . . . she didn't know what she'd do, but it would be very bad.

Adam's car. His pride and joy he'd lovingly restored with his own hands. She could see him in her mind's eye, running his hands over the car's curves, and suddenly realized the memories of Adam's hands on his car and his hands on her were intermeshed. But instead of making her feel soft and tender inside, the realization made her even angrier.

Stupid juvenile delinquents whose parents hadn't bothered to teach them right from wrong. Idiotic kids who had no respect for other people's property. Who would do anything that was a means to their end. Who she couldn't touch because she couldn't prove they had anything to do with anything. She'd call Officer Pullman. He'd dust for prints and probably wouldn't find any that didn't belong to her or Casey. There was nothing, nothing she could do.

Her nails dug into her hands and she wanted to hit something. She couldn't remember the last time she'd felt so close to the edge of violence. Yes, she could. It had been the day she'd realized Adam was really going to die and there wasn't a damn thing she could do to stop it. That was the day she'd run for miles and still felt the murderous rage burning inside her, so she'd called a friend, Mark. Adam's best friend to be exact. Mark was also her *sensei*, her karate master. They'd sparred and kicked and thrown each other to the mat until all the rage was gone. He'd understood her pain and her rage and let her work it out.

She'd call Mark now. It'd been almost a week since her last workout and she was due.

Tuesday, October 4, 6:30 P.M.

Rudy slumped down in the leather chair across from his desk. "You wanted to see me?"

Victor Lutz frowned. "I called Blackman today to make sure you'd be playing this week."

Rudy looked worried. "I will, won't I?"

Victor wanted to slap Rudy's perfect teeth to the other side of his head. "Probably not."

Rudy shot up in the chair. "Why? I thought you said Blackman was fixing it."

"Apparently that was before your friends destroyed about five thousand dollars of school property. You're lucky Blackman's afraid of me or you'd all be in jail, dammit," he hissed. "What the hell were you doing?"

Rudy looked affronted. "I didn't do anything. The guys did. Just like you said to do."

Victor slapped the desk. "I said, target the teacher's belongings, not school property, you idiot!"

Rudy's face blanked and Victor once again cursed Nora's stupid genes. The boy had the IQ of a damn turnip. Victor leaned across his desk, hoping his face showed every ounce of frustration he was feeling. "Her *belongings* means *things* that *belong* to *her.* Like her tires. Like the little clay figures she keeps on the balcony of her apartment." His lips thinned. "Like her dog."

Rudy's eyes widened. "You've been to her place?"

"I've driven by. That's all. Now tell your stupid, brain-less friends to stop vandalizing school property or you'll all be off the team."

Rudy raised a brow. "Kenny dumped water in her gas tank this afternoon."

Victor nodded. "That's closer. Too easily reparable, but closer. Now leave me alone and go make sure your friends understand what they need to do."

Dismissing his son, Victor resumed work on his ledgers when a pained cry split the air. Josh stood in the hall dou-bled over, his arms crossed over his gut. Rudy stood over him, flexing his fingers.

"He was listening. Again," Rudy muttered.

"Leave her alone," Josh moaned. "Dr. Marshall never hurt you."

Victor looked away. "Don't hit your brother, Rudy. You might damage your throwing hand."

Tuesday, October 4, 6:45 P.M.

"She's not still mad at you, is she?"

Steven jumped, startled that Mrs. Kasselbaum had got-ten the drop on him. He'd been deep in thought, standing in front of Jenna's door. Wondering how she'd look, how he'd get them past the awkwardness of their last meeting when he'd come so close to jerking her to her feet and—

"Well, is she?" Mrs. Kasselbaum demanded.

Steven turned to find the neighbor's door open the ex-pected six inches. "No, ma'am." He showed her the plastic bag he held in his hand. "I just came to put a new deadbolt on her door. It bothered me that she didn't know exactly who had keys to her apartment."

Mrs. Kasselbaum opened the door a few more inches and nodded once in approval. "That's very wise. I'll make sure I get a key when you're finished. But she's not home right now."

Steven stared. "What do you mean she's not home? Her car's out in the parking lot."

"Car trouble," Mrs. Kasselbaum confided in a lowered voice. "I heard her telling the man she left with that she barely made it home from school. Something about water in the gas line."

Rudy and his friends struck once again, Steven thought grimly. He'd heard about the vandalism in her classroom from Matt, who'd heard it from a soccer buddy, who'd heard it from his older brother who apparently shared the general opinion that Dr. Marshall was "hot."

Wait a minute. "What man she left with?" he asked sharply. "Was it Seth?"

Mrs. Kasselbaum shook her head, an unmistakable gleam in her old eyes. "Oh, no. This was one of her karate friends. Young, very nice-looking. A Marine with a tattoo on his right arm. He's a black belt, too. I always feel safe when Jenna leaves with him."

Steven tried to force back the jealousy that clawed at his gut. The thought of Jenna with another man made him want to punch the other guy's lights out, black belt or no. A ridiculous reaction considering he'd known the woman less than a week. She was free to see whomever she pleased. She was her own woman.

No she's not. *She's mine.*

The thought came from nowhere, shocking him with its clarity and force. He shook his head hard, trying to clear it from his brain. Totally inappropriate reaction. Looking for some diversion, he stared down at Mrs. Kasselbaum. "How do you know he has a tattoo on his right arm?"

Mrs. Kasselbaum batted her eyes. "I asked him to show it to me. Mercy, but that man has a wonderful body." She fanned her face. "Made me wish I was twenty years younger."

Under other circumstances Steven might have smiled at the flirtatious Mrs. Kasselbaum, but he couldn't make his lips curve even the slightest bit. He was too angry. And hurt, if he'd admit it. She'd forgotten about their dinner and gone off with some Marine with a tattoo. *So much for whatever electricity passed between them Sunday night.* His temper simmered. *So much for her so-called integrity.* He clenched his jaw. *So much for her being different than other women.* He looked down to find Mrs. Kasselbaum looking up with alarm and realized his face must have shown every spark of anger he'd been feeling.

He forced a smile for Mrs. Kasselbaum's benefit. "I need to be going."

Mrs. Kasselbaum's face fell. "Oh, no, dear boy, please don't leave. That karate man doesn't mean a thing to her, I know. He's—"

Anger bubbled up and overflowed and he could feel his cheeks heating. Pity was the one thing he absolutely couldn't stand. "It's okay, Mrs. Kasselbaum," Steven said stiffly. "She just forgot. Just tell her I came by and give her this deadbolt if you don't mind."

Just then the lobby door blew open. Steven looked over the railing at the black-haired, white-clad, sandal-footed figure rushing in, waving to a car at the curb. She looked up, her hair sliding away from her face. Even from three floors up Steven could see her eyes widen and her jaw drop.

Aware of Mrs. Kasselbaum watching every move, he waited to see how Jenna would try to explain. What lies she would concoct.

Jenna closed her eyes and quietly blew out a breath, all

the anxiety she'd worked out of her system returning with a vengeance. *She'd forgotten about him.*

After agonizing all day about what she'd wear, what he'd do, how she'd respond . . . Heat throbbed through her body, completely overriding the chill of the night. And she'd forgotten about him. She opened her eyes and lifted her gaze to where he stood, arms crossed tightly, staring down at her. Even from three floors down she could see he was angry.

She scrunched her brows together, searching his face. *More angry than he has a right to be over a missed dinner,* she thought, puzzled. Then Mrs. Kasselbaum appeared at his side looking decidedly guilty herself and it all became crystal clear.

Old biddy, she grimaced and started up the stairs two at a time, wincing every time her left foot took her weight. She'd wrapped it, but the pummeling she'd given poor Mark had made it throb almost as badly as when she first fell down. When she'd made it to her front door she threw a disgusted glance at Mrs. Kasselbaum who dropped her eyes to the floor.

"As you can see, I'm home safely, Mrs. Kasselbaum. You can go back to your stories now."

Mrs. Kasselbaum looked up, bristling. "I was watching the evening news. Not stories."

"Whatever. You've caused enough trouble." Jenna raised a brow. "Don't you agree?"

"I *tried* to tell him the karate man didn't mean anything."

Jenna bit her tongue. *Old biddy.* "Mrs. Kasselbaum. Please." Finding her key, she opened her front door to where Jim and Jean-Luc sat obediently, bodies quivering, awaiting her slightest command. *If only the whole world could be like dogs,* she thought. *Life would certainly be simpler.* Then she looked back to where Steven Thatcher still stood and her heart did a slow roll in her chest. *Simpler perhaps, but not nearly as interesting.* He still had his arms crossed over his chest. A plastic bag with the name of a local hardware store dangled from one of his big hands.

"Come in, Steven. Please."

Steven hesitated, looked over to where Mrs. Kasselbaum nodded vigorously, then back to where Jenna stood still.

She *had* said please. So he followed her into her apartment.

She shut her door and gestured to the dogs who in turn stood, nuzzled her hand, and went off to curl up on their dog beds in the corner. She met his eyes soberly.

"I'm sorry," she began without preamble. "Once again I've been rude."

His anger began to fizzle. "We never agreed on a time." He shrugged. "Maybe I'm early."

Her lips curved up. "Maybe you are. Can I explain what happened? It's not what you think."

"What do you think I think?" he countered.

She didn't look away and his anger fizzled a little more. "That I was off with someone else when I'd said I would go to dinner with you. That I'm unreliable and undependable and quite possibly a liar." She lifted a brow. "Am I close?"

Steven nodded. "Close," he admitted.

Jenna sighed. "Mrs. Kasselbaum told you she saw me leave with another man, right?"

"With a gorgeous body."

Jenna laughed softly. "I'm sure his wife thinks so."

"He's married?" Steven didn't know whether to be relieved or horrified.

"Very much so. I was a bridesmaid in their wedding." She walked over to the wall she'd covered with photographs and plucked one off. "Mark and Susan. Mark was my late fiancé's best friend. Our group of friends used to have so much fun," she said wistfully. "I don't see most of the old group anymore. But Mark is my *sensei*. My karate master," she added, "so I see him a few times a week." She took the snapshot and slipped it back on its nail on the wall.

When she turned around, a frown wrinkled her forehead. She paced by him to stare out the picture window to the parking lot below. "I've had a couple more bad days at school. Nothing too serious. Just a string of pranks. But tonight they did something to A—to my car. I was so . . . mad." She paced back, stopping to look up, concern in her eyes this time. "I'm glad none of those boys was around because I might have done something I'd truly be sorry for. I was so angry I needed to hit something. So I called Mark. I'd missed my workout on Saturday because of my ankle, so he picked me up for a sparring session."

Steven relaxed. "Did you win?"

Her mouth curved. "Against Mark? Of course not. But I got in my fair share and that's what I needed. I'm sorry I was late and forgot to call you."

"You wouldn't have gotten me anyway. I was out all day."

They each drew a breath and laughed awkwardly. Then the laughter pattered away, leaving the two of them staring at each other. Steven watched her eyes widen and dilate, her cheeks blush rose and her pulse flutter once again at the hollow of her throat. And once again his body responded, his erection hard and full against his zipper. She blinked then, the tip of her tongue stealing out to moisten her bottom lip and he bit back both the groan and the urge to let his own tongue follow the path hers had taken.

Jenna cleared her throat. "So . . . is my apology ac-

cepted?" she asked, her voice barely more than a breathy
murmur and he clenched his jaw.

She really wants this.

Steven, wait.

Shit. He hated when his conscience was right. Knowing
it was for the best, he forced a grin and shoved his hands in
his pockets. "Of course."

Jenna blinked. She'd been sure he was about to lean forward and kiss her. She'd all but lifted herself on her toes to
meet him halfway. "Just like that?" she asked, feeling more
than just a little bit vexed by his abrupt change of tone.

He nodded cheerfully and she wanted to smack him.
"Just like that," he said. "But you do realize that it's now
two to one. I'll have to apologize to even the score."

"I can think of a good one right now," Jenna muttered
under her breath.

He frowned and leaned an inch closer, close enough for
her to smell his aftershave. He smelled really good. "What
did you say?" he asked.

That you smell really good and why didn't you kiss me?
her brain shouted. "Nothing." She plucked at the sleeve of
her *gi*. "Look, I can be ready in fifteen minutes, if you still
want to go to dinner."

She watched his nostrils flare and his cheeks darken. His
brown eyes went from placid to smoldering in one hard
beat of her heart. So he was interested after all. "I still want
to go to dinner," he said and a shiver teased down her back
at the sudden huskiness of his voice.

Mesmerized, she could only look up into his face. "Then
I'll . . . just . . . go . . ." The words trailed off and she licked
her dry lips but her feet still hadn't moved an inch. His eyes
had grown even more intense and now a muscle ticked in
his jaw. He swallowed and drew his hand from his pocket.
Lifted it to her face and gently pushed a lock of hair behind

her ear. Brushed a fleeting caress against her cheek before burying his hand back in his pocket, leaving her cheek tingling.

She took a step back although what she really wanted was to jump up and wrap herself around his body.

"Take your time," he murmured and she all but groaned. "I'll wait."

Steven held his body rigid as he watched her back away. Releasing his pent-up breath did nothing to release the tension that wound him tighter than a spring.

She'd nearly set him on fire with a look and a few breathy words. Imagining what she'd be like writhing under him while he lost himself in her body . . .

He lifted his eyes to find two German shepherds regarding him with twin wary stares. Carefully he approached them, both to distract himself and to begin building a relationship with Jenna's animals. If this worked out he'd be seeing a lot of them.

He held out his hand and the one on the right sniffed him, then licked his fingers. The one on the left, not to be outdone, jumped up and licked his face. He guessed he was in. "Down, boy," he told the dog, whichever one it was, and amazingly it obeyed. He pulled at the dog's tag and frowned. "Captain," he read. He pulled the other's tag and found it said the same thing. "How come neither of you has a tag with your real names?" he asked them. Both dogs sat and wagged their tails. Apparently their training did not extend to articulation. "Well, at least you don't drool."

Steven took a look around him. Jenna kept a clean apartment, her taste running to rustic comfort. Her walls, however, were quite a different story. Nearly every square inch of wall space was covered and, as he discovered by taking a slow three-sixty turn, dedicated to a theme. One wall was covered in framed photographs, ranging in size from ten-by-thirteen portraits to snapshots. Another wall held awards and diplomas. The wall in her dining room was visually intriguing, bearing an assortment of colorfully painted masks. But the photo wall held the most appeal as he hoped it would provide some insight into the real Jenna Marshall.

She was, he discovered as he went from one photo to the next, a woman of diverse interests. There was the karate, of course. There were a half-dozen pictures of her teammates all lined up, sparring or board breaking. But she'd also played softball and volleyball, too. In fact, he saw, stooping down to see some photos closer to the floor, she'd coached a team of girls, a dozen grinning eight-year-olds wearing T-shirts from a local real estate office and proudly gathered around an impressive-looking trophy. And her volunteer efforts didn't stop there. He found five photos, one for each of the last five years, of Jenna with her arm around a kid under the sign proclaiming the Special Olympics. Admiration warmed him even as he heard the death knell of any last hope for a fleeting, no-strings affair.

She was a nice woman. A woman who formed attachments, supporting the same charities year after year. She was just too nice. Too nice to even think of proposing a no-strings relationship.

Steven stopped short at the next snapshot. And she fished. Damn. He leaned forward, squinting. The fish she proudly held up for the camera was a good sight bigger than anything he'd ever pulled in. She was a nice woman who fished and who was kind to children and puppies.

And who made him think of hot, sweaty sex every time he laid eyes on her. Who at this very moment was in the shower. He squeezed his eyes closed, able to imagine only all too well. He had to make this stop. It was ridiculous, not to mention humiliating, acting like a randy sixteen-year-old. He rapidly searched for a photo with a more . . . deflating theme.

And found it. Jenna in the arms of another man, standing in front of a Christmas tree. Her late fiancé, Steven supposed. He was a tall man with tousled dark hair and black wire-rimmed glasses. Kind of like a grown-up version of Harry Potter. Younger than she was now, Jenna looked up at the man with such unadulterated joy, Steven felt both jealous and wistful. To have a woman look up at him with such happiness in her eyes was something he'd never known, but that he'd always wanted. Something he'd never had, not even during the good years with Melissa.

He lifted the picture from the wall and brought it close enough to see the couple holding hands. The man held Jenna's hand up to the camera, showing off a modest diamond ring. The man wore a Celtic band on his right hand— the same ring Jenna now wore on her thumb. Another spear of jealousy pricked, followed closely by shame. He resented the ring on her thumb. But her fiancé was dead, unavailable. How low was he to feel jealous of a dead man?

Apparently pretty damn low.

"That was Adam."

Steven jerked guiltily, turning to find Jenna standing a few feet behind him. She'd done something with her hair, braided it up so that it looked old-fashioned and sexy at the same time—and left her neck completely bare. She'd changed into a simple black dress with tiny little buttons that ran throat to hem, sleeveless so that it showed off the definition in her arms. And unfortunately so long that it hid most of her incredible legs. Her stocking-clad legs. He wouldn't let his mind dwell on the fact that she was probably wearing real stockings with garters under that dress, instead, forcing his eyes to her feet on which she wore a pair of flats.

"No skyscraper heels tonight?" he asked, smiling.

She shook her head. "I seem to recall making a scout's honor promise, even though I didn't spit in my palm." She made a face. "That's just too gross."

They stared at each other for a long moment, then Steven cleared his throat, holding out the picture. "I'm sorry. I got curious."

She picked up the photo. Steven watched her face for any sign of residual passion, but she just smiled a little and wiped the dust from the glass with her fingertips. "This was Adam."

"Your fiancé."

"Um-hmm."

"You loved him." The words were out before he knew they were coming.

Her head snapped up, her violet eyes surprised. "Of course. He was a good man."

Steven felt his cheeks heat. "That's good to hear. I'm glad." Although a part of him wasn't and he wanted to squash that childish part like a bug. "Do you mind my asking what he died of?"

She met his eyes briefly before returning the photo to its nail on the wall. "Not at all. I've become something of a champion for the cause, although most men cringe to hear it. Adam died of testicular cancer." Steven winced and Jenna raised a knowing brow. "I told you that would be your reaction. But as the father of three boys, you have a responsibility for their health."

Steven felt his cheeks grow even warmer. He was fairly certain that testicles weren't on the list of approved first-date conversation. "I suppose so."

"Did you know that testicular cancer strikes young men between eighteen and thirty-five?"

He didn't. "No."

"And did you know that if caught early it is very easily treated?"

He didn't know that either. "No. So, Adam's wasn't caught early?"

Jenna's eyes flashed. "No, it wasn't, because he was too damn proud or scared to go to the doctor. His was an unusually fast-growing variety, but it still would have been treatable if they'd caught it earlier. But by the time he went to the doctor it had spread to his brain. We had ten months after that. *Ten damn months.*" She looked away and he could see her fighting for control. Finally she looked back, her eyes no longer turbulent, but not serene, either. "I'm sorry, Steven. It's a bit of a sore spot with me. I've tried to get the school to do more active education, but they refuse to corral the boys into a room and talk to them. I've brought pamphlets, but not a single boy wants to be seen taking one."

"I can kind of understand that," Steven said thoughtfully, taking another look at the woman standing before him. He could now add *crusader* to the growing list of her attributes. "Doesn't make it right, but I can understand it."

One side of her mouth tilted up. "Most men do. If you think of a way to get around it, let me know. I've got a box full of pamphlets in my closet, just waiting to be read. But enough about that. I'm starving." She pulled a jacket from the closet and shrugged into it. "Ready when you are."

He opened the door and breathed appreciatively when she passed through. She'd washed her hair with the coconut shampoo again and once again his mind ran through the connections—coconuts, suntan oil, beaches, *bikinis*. He let the door slam and said the first light-headed thing that came to his mind. "I'm up by two apologies now."

"No you're not," she returned and looked up into his face and grinned. "You apologized for your nosiness in there when you poked into my pictures. You're still only up by one."

Steven laughed out loud, the sound echoing in the empty apartment stairwell. "Jenna, you are incorrigible."

She nodded. "Thank you. I try very hard."

FOURTEEN

Tuesday, October 4, 8:00 P.M.

THE RIDE TO THE RESTAURANT HAD BEEN COMPLETED in what Jenna could only call contemplative silence. She wished she understood why he'd pulled back from the kiss in her apartment. He clearly wanted it as much as she had. He'd asked if she'd loved Adam. She wondered if he still loved the wife he'd lost, the mother of his sons.

She wished she knew what was going on inside his head. She sure as hell knew what was going on inside of hers. And if his thoughts were anywhere near as confused and . . . erotic as hers, well, this would certainly be an interesting evening. Wherever it led.

At the moment it was leading to dinner. He'd chosen the new Italian place on Capitol, ironically enough. Jenna took the chair he held for her, then met his eyes as he pulled his own chair to the table. His beautiful brown eyes that made her heart beat faster. That made her want to leap over the table, straddle him where he sat, and take the kiss from which he'd backed away.

Oh, for God's sake, Jen. Get it together here. You are not having sex with that man in this restaurant. So say something before he thinks you've lost your damn mind.

So she said, "This is nice. I haven't been here before."

"Neither have I, but one of my coworkers just raved about it last week." He ran his long fingers over the white paper covering the tablecloth, then pointed over to another table where some children were decorating their own white paper with crayons provided by the restaurant. "Looks like they provide pre-meal entertainment."

Jenna smiled at him simply because it felt right to do. "Nicky would like that, I think."

"I don't know," he said, his gaze still fixed on the giggling children. His shoulders sagged. "Nicky doesn't seem to enjoy much of anything anymore."

"I don't know about that, Steven. He got very excited about training Cindy Lou."

Steven looked back at her, his brow raised in dubious question. "You think you can train that blubbering, drooling pile of hair?"

"That eats your shoes?"

He grimaced. "Dumb dog."

"Nicky loves her."

His face softened. "Yeah, he does. It's the only reason she stays. So can you train Cindy Lou?"

Jenna grinned at him. "I don't think so. She's kind of a dumb dog."

And that made him smile. Which took her breath away. Which must have shown on her face because he got that same look that he'd had in her apartment right before he didn't kiss her. Once again she steeled herself against the overwhelming compulsion to jump the table and wrap her legs around his slim hips.

"Hi! My name is Amy and I'll be your server. How are you folks tonight?"

Jenna jerked her gaze up to the pretty young waitress who was bending over their table, entirely too close to Steven, writing her name upside down on the white paper with a handful of crayons.

Unfamiliar jealousy surged until she looked back at Steven and found his eyes fixed on her own face. He didn't even seem to notice the waitress was there. Just kept looking at her as if she were the only person in the room. As if maybe he was thinking about coming over the table for her.

As if maybe he wanted that kiss after all. The throbbing became a painful ache.

"We're . . . um . . . fine," Jenna managed, the inside of her mouth as dry as cotton. "Just fine."

"Well, good," Amy said cheerfully, and Jenna just wished the girl would go away. "Can I tell you about our specials this evening?"

Steven shook his head, his eyes still locked on hers, dark and intense. "I'll just have spaghetti," he said and held the menu up for Amy to take away. He'd never even opened it.

He just kept staring.

Jenna swallowed hard. *Oh, Lord.*

"Oh," said Amy, nonplussed. "With tomato or meat sauce?"

"Tomato. Jenna?"

Looking at the menu would mean looking away from his eyes which at the moment seemed impossible. "The same," Jenna murmured and handed the waitress her menu.

"Can I get you some wine?" Amy persisted.

Steven tightened his jaw and huffed an impatient sigh. "Jenna?"

"None for me, please." No way was she adding alcohol to

what felt like a fire ready to consume her from the inside out. "Just water."

"The same."

Then Amy was gone, leaving a few crayons on the table and the two of them quite alone. Unable to bear the intensity any longer, Jenna looked away, fixing her eyes on the bright white paper covering the table that was becoming wet as condensation dripped from her water glass.

Wet and dripping. Somehow the visual didn't help.

After a few beats, Steven broke the silence. "I didn't tell you that you looked very nice tonight," he said quietly. "I guess I'm out of practice."

Pleasure coursed through her at the simple words. "Thank you." She looked up to see that whatever spell had held him seemed to be broken. Gone was the intensity that had turned his brown eyes almost black. Disappointment mingled with relief. "Thank you."

He tilted his head to one side and frowned a little. "Mrs. Kasselbaum told me about the water in your gas lines. Are you all right?"

"I'm fine," she reassured him. "I've been doing what you said and parking close to the school and having someone walk me out after closing."

"Good. I heard about the vandalism in your class. Have they confronted the Lutz boy or any of his friends?"

"No, and I don't think they're going to." She lifted one shoulder in a half shrug. "Principal Blackman says we can't prove who did anything. They're trying to force my hand, but they'll find out I'm tougher than I look." She took a thoughtful look at him across the table. "What about you? How's your big case going?"

His face tightened. "Not well."

"I'm sorry. I saw you on CNN on Sunday morning. You looked . . . tired."

"I was. I still am. But we don't have anything definite to go on right now even though we're all pulling double shifts. It's small consolation for the Egglestons," he added bitterly, looking away.

Wanting to comfort him, she reached across the table to cover his hand with hers. The action was a reflexive one, a friend supporting a friend, but the feel of her skin on his was anything but friendly. The back of his hand was warm, rough, the reddish gold hairs coarse. Her palm . . . tingled. But her response was out of place at the moment so she swallowed it back. "I know you're doing all you can," she said softly.

His eyes snapped back to hers, then dropped to her hand resting on his. Suddenly feeling awkward she started to pull away, but he caught her, twining his fingers with hers and for a moment she could only stare at the sight. Her fingers and his. Together. It had been a long time since she'd held hands with a man. She hadn't realized until now just how much she'd missed it.

"Thank you," he said and she looked up to find him focused on her once again. And once again her heart raced. She opened her mouth to say something, but then his cell phone shrilled.

Jenna jumped while Steven swore. He pulled his phone from his pocket with one hand, still holding her hand with the other. "Thatcher," he barked, listened, then grew grim. Still one-handed he finished the call and dropped his phone back into his pocket.

"What's wrong?" Jenna asked.

"I have to go," he answered. "I'm sorry, but I have to go to the Egglestons' house. I can drop you off at your apartment on the way."

She stood up when he did because he still held her hand. "Will you be long?" she asked.

"I don't know. Why?"

Concern for him edged out the tingle of his hand on hers, the nearness of his body. "You need to eat, Steven. If you'd like I can make us something at my place after you're finished."

He looked down at her, worry in his eyes. "You don't mind?"

"Of course not."

He motioned to Amy the waitress who came hurrying over. "Cancel the order. We need to go." He let go of her hand only long enough to draw a bill from his wallet for the waitress's trouble. He tossed the money on the table, took her hand again, and led her to his car.

Tuesday, October 4, 8:45 P.M.

Sheriff Braden, Anna Eggleston's brother, met them at the Egglestons' front door and looked at Jenna, a question in his eyes.

"She's with me," Steven said. *With me,* his mind echoed and he liked the sound of it. Too damn much.

"I can wait in the car," Jenna offered and Braden shook his head.

"That's not necessary, ma'am. It's getting cold outside. Please make yourself comfortable." Braden gestured to a sofa covered with dainty little flowers, then turned to Steven. "Thanks for coming here to the house, Agent Thatcher. Anna didn't want to take Serena into the station."

Serena. Samantha's little sister. Steven's brain jogged to life. Four years old. The Egglestons had kept their youngest daughter far away from the investigation, shielding their baby from the ugliness of the situation, a response Steven certainly understood. But tonight Serena had burst into hysterical tears and her parents had been able to glean only that their littlest daughter knew something she should tell the police. What had the little girl heard that night? What did she know?

"Where is she?"

"In the kitchen." Braden looked at him helplessly. "She's just a baby, Thatcher."

Steven grasped Braden's upper arm and squeezed. "I know. Let's see what we can get without making this any worse than it is."

There was a crowd around the kitchen table. Marvin and Anna Eggleston sat on either side of Serena, creating a human protective wall around their daughter. Serena herself sat quietly, her little round face streaked with tears. She was a beautiful child, with large blue eyes and dark, dark hair that fell in damp baby ringlets around her shoulders.

Steven looked from the Egglestons huddled around their daughter to the older woman that sat on Anna's left. Anna's and Sheriff Braden's mother. Mrs. Braden looked at him defiantly, as if daring him to harm her granddaughter. Then someone stepped from the shadows of the back door.

Mike Leone looked at him with worry in his eyes.

Of course this family had called their priest. Of course it would be Mike.

Steven quickly looked back to the table where Serena stared up at him, her blue eyes huge and teary and terrified. He smiled as he sat down. "Hi, Serena. My name is Agent Thatcher."

The little girl sniffled. "I know."

Steven leaned forward, pressing his forearms into the table. "Serena, honey, can you tell me why I'm here?" he asked gently.

Serena's lips quivered. "Because I've been bad," she whispered. "I'm sorry."

"Now, Serena," he said softly, "there's nothing you did that could be that bad. The bad person is whoever took your sister. Samantha didn't do anything wrong and neither did you."

Serena was clearly unconvinced. Her lower lip thrust out and her delicate eyebrows bunched. But she said nothing.

"Serena, tell the officer what you heard," Anna said, her voice a shaky tremble. "Please."

Serena looked up at her mother, who forced a smile. Then she looked up at her father who put his arm around her tiny shoulders.

"It's okay, honey," Marvin said. "You're not in trouble. Just tell Mr. Thatcher what you know."

Serena turned her dark blue eyes to Steven and he smiled again, even more gently than before.

"See, honey? Your mom and dad aren't mad." Serena's lip quivered and Steven understood. At four years old, of course Serena would interpret her family's wild grief and anger to be her fault. It was normal. "Honey, I need you to listen to me. Can you do that?"

Serena nodded. "Yes, sir."

Steven ducked his head closer. "Good. Now I know you're a big girl, and a smart one. I want you to think about your friends. Do you have a best friend?"

Serena blinked, confusion in her eyes at the unexpected question. She nodded uncertainly.

"What's your best friend's name?"

"Carrie." Serena looked down, then back up. "We play dolls and video games."

"Good. You know who was my best friend when I was your age?" Serena shook her head and Steven winked at her. "Father Mike."

Her blue eyes grew round in disbelief. "Priests don't have friends."

From the corner of his eye Steven saw Mike hide a smile behind his hand. "No, it's true," Steven insisted. "When Fa-

ther Mike was a little boy we'd catch frogs in the creek behind the elementary school down the street from the church."

"I'll go to the element'ry school next year," Serena declared proudly, then narrowed her eyes. "If you and Father
Mike were friends, how come you're not a priest, too?"

Again Steven glanced at Mike from the corner of his eye.
"Busted," Mike mouthed silently.

"Well, I thought about it, but then I decided to be a policeman instead. What do you think priests and policemen have
in common, Serena?"

She thought a moment, chewing on her lower lip. "They
help people," she decided.

Steven nodded. "That's exactly right. See, I knew you
were a smart girl."

"I can count to twenty," Serena said with a decisive nod,
then shook her head in disgust. "Carrie can only count to ten."

"Well, I'm sure Carrie will catch up soon."

"I don't know." She shook her head and her damp ringlets
bounced. "She can only make it to level one on Sonic Two."

Steven was well acquainted with Sonic the Hedgehog, a
video game character who, although capable of racing at
sonic speeds, looked absolutely nothing like a hedgehog.
Sonic was one of Nicky's favorites. Had been anyway.

"So you're pretty good at Sonic?" Steven asked and Serena nodded hard. "You practice a lot?"

Serena's face abruptly changed. She looked down at the
table and said nothing.

And Steven thought he knew what had happened.

"Serena, are you allowed to play video games at night
when you're supposed to be in bed?"

Serena stared hard at the table and shook her head. Marvin
Eggleston opened his mouth to say something, but Mike
stepped forward and put a restraining hand on the man's
shoulder.

"But you were up playing Sonic the night Sammie disappeared, weren't you, honey?" Steven asked quietly.

Serena said nothing. Made not a single move.

Steven leaned closer and laid his fingertips against the little girl's cheek and she looked up, misery in her eyes. She blinked and fat tears rolled down her rosy cheeks. Steven felt his heart clench. What the public never seemed to realize is that crime happened to people. It wasn't sensational, it wasn't thrilling. Crime happened to people, to families, tore them apart. Made little four-year-old girls feel responsible and afraid. Made them cry.

He softened his voice. "Serena, honey, this is important. You will not get into trouble for playing video games. But, sweetheart, you need to tell me what you heard that night."

Her lips trembled and more tears flowed. "Sammie was on the phone," she whispered.

"Did she know you were there?"

Serena shook her head. "No."

"Do you know who Sammie was talking to, Serena?"

Again she shook her head. "No, sir."

Impatience simmered and he clapped a tight lid on it. "Did it sound like she was talking to one of her friends? JoLynn or Wanda, maybe?"

"No, sir."

Steven leaned closer still. "Was it a boy, honey?"

Serena looked up at him, her eyes filled with guilt. "Yes, sir," she whispered.

Anticipation sizzled across his skin. They were on to something. "Did she say his name?"

"No, sir."

"What were they talking about, Serena?"

She looked down at the table. "Kissing and stuff."

Steven glanced up to find Marvin's face pale and his body

trembling. Silently, Steven shook his head, then hooked his finger under Serena's chin and gently tipped up her face.

"What else, honey?"

Serena stared up at him and again his heart clenched at the misery he saw there. She was just a baby. No child should know this kind of devastation. "She didn't want to go," Serena whispered and Marvin and Anna looked sick.

"What do you mean, she didn't want to go? Go where, Serena?"

Serena lifted one thin shoulder. "To meet him. She kept saying, 'I don't know.' She knew Mommy and Daddy would be really mad." Tears rolled again. "But she finally said yes."

Anna swayed and her mother put her arm around her for support.

"Serena, I need you to think very hard," Steven said, his voice barely a whisper. "Did Sammie mention where she was meeting him?"

Serena nodded. "Behind the McDonald's."

Steven forced his voice to be very calm. His gut told him Serena was on the verge of remembering something critical. "Did she say which one?"

She frowned. "Behind the railroad tracks? I don't know." She looked up at her father, panicked. "I'm sorry, Daddy."

"It's okay, pumpkin," Marvin managed in an even voice and Steven respected him for the effort. His father's heart had to be shattering, visualizing what happened at the McDonald's behind the railroad tracks. "You're doing just . . . great." His voice broke on the last word and Mike put both hands on Marvin's shoulders. The big man managed a smile of encouragement for Serena, but his throat worked viciously as he struggled not to cry.

Steven touched Serena's hand lightly and she looked back at him. "Your daddy's absolutely right, Serena. You are doing fabulously. Now, can you remember anything else?"

Her feathery brows scrunched as she concentrated. Then she looked up sharply and Steven knew this was what he'd been waiting for. "Sammie told him he played a good game."

Steven tried not to let his excitement show. "Did she say what kind of game?"

"No." Her lower lip quivered again as more tears fell. "I'm sorry."

Steven cupped the child's face in his palm and gently wiped her tears with his thumb. "You did all the right things, Serena. You're a smart girl, and a brave one. Telling me took a lot of courage."

"Will Sammie come home now?" she asked and Steven heard Anna muffle a sob.

Serena was a smart child. He had no idea what her parents had told her, but he'd be damned if he'd tell this child anything other than the truth. "I don't know, honey. All us policemen are trying our hardest to find her."

Her eyes filled again. "I should have told before. If I'd told before you could find her faster."

Mike put his hand on Serena's shoulder. She looked up, biting her lower lip, and Steven felt his heart lurch. For the rest of her life this poor child would live with unearned guilt caused by a sadistic bastard that thrived on the misery and fear of others. Mike smoothed a lock of tear-drenched hair from Serena's cheek. "Serena, you know I would never lie to you, don't you?"

She nodded. "You're not allowed."

Mike smiled ruefully. "That's true. So I want you to believe me when I say there is nothing you could have done to make them find Serena faster. God is with her, wherever she is."

Serena nodded, then buried her face in Marvin's shoulder and Steven pushed back from the table. The little girl had been through quite enough tonight. He stood up and leaned

over the table, brushing his palm over the little girl's dark
curls.

Jenna's children would look like Serena Eggleston, he
thought, then physically jolted from the unexpectedness of the
idea. *Where had that come from?* he thought, almost panicked.

He cleared his throat and met Anna Eggleston's eyes as he
said to Serena, "You were wonderful, Serena. Your mommy
and daddy are very proud of you."

Anna jerked a nod, then put her arms around Serena and
together she and Marvin held on to the daughter they had left.

Steven looked at Anna's mother and the sheriff. Mrs.
Braden was crying and Sheriff Braden looked like he was
fighting not to. "She did great," Steven said quietly. "I'm
going to send a team over to the McDonald's to see what we
can find first thing in the morning."

Mrs. Braden bristled. "Why not now?" she demanded in a
hushed whisper. "What's wrong with right now?"

Sheriff Braden put his arms around his mother's shoulders.
"It's not a good idea to investigate a crime scene at night,
Mom," he told her. "They might miss something, or worse,
destroy it because it's too dark to see."

"I will make sure the area is roped off, Mrs. Braden,"
Steven assured her. "And I'll make sure nobody goes near it
until dawn."

Mrs. Braden jerked a nod, looking very much like her
daughter as she did so. "Thank you," she said, her voice
hoarse.

You're welcome seemed incredibly inadequate. "We're
doing everything we can, Mrs. Braden."

Her eyes filled. "I know." Then she stifled a sob and turned
to bury her face against the starched fabric of her son's uniform. Sheriff Braden looked at Steven, and once again he saw
helpless misery.

Steven squeezed Braden's shoulder. "I'll see myself out."

"I'll walk with you," Mike said behind him, then added to Braden, "I'll be right back."

Mike paused in the darkened hallway just outside the kitchen. "You did great, Steven," he said, and Steven heard pride in his old friend's voice. "That little girl was terrified, but you made it as easy as you could." He forced a grin and threw his arm around Steven's shoulders in a clumsy hug. "Y'done good, boy."

"Thanks." Steven looked back at the kitchen with a frown, then back at Mike. "You know Sammie's probably dead by now," he murmured.

Mike swallowed and his forced grin disappeared. "I know. So do they."

Steven sighed. "I need to go." He stepped from the darkened hallway into the light of the living room where Jenna stood next to the sofa covered in dainty little flowers, quietly waiting. The tortured look on her face told him she'd heard every word.

Beside him Mike stopped and Steven found his friend's face lit with a genuine smile. "Well, hello!" Mike drawled and Steven's face heated. "Do you plan to introduce us?"

"There are some times I wish you weren't a priest," Steven muttered.

"Steven, Steven, Steven," Mike said, quiet humor in his voice. "Five Hail Marys for just thinking what you just didn't say." He stepped forward, his hand outstretched. "I'm Father Mike Leone, an old friend of Steven's. You must be Jenna."

She shook Mike's hand. "That's right. But, um, Steven didn't mention you."

Mike laughed softly. "No, I don't suppose he would. It's very, very nice to meet you, Jenna Marshall." He held on to her hand, still smiling broadly.

Jenna frowned a little. "It's nice to meet you, too, Father Leone."

"Father Mike is fine. Yes, I've known Steven since he was knee-high to a grasshopper. Oh, the stories I could tell. Where do you want me to begin? Pick a year, any year."

Steven gritted his teeth. *You wouldn't,* he wanted to say. *Of course he would,* came the reply from his more pragmatic self.

Jenna glanced over at Steven with a look that seemed to say *don't worry,* then back at Mike with a raised brow as she discreetly disengaged her hand. "Well, I'm not Catholic, but what I would like to know is why all priests seem to be named Father Mike."

Steven felt a rush of appreciation. She'd felt his discomfort, but instead of exploiting it, she turned the focus to Mike.

"Probably because our mothers knew we'd be as heavenly as the archangel Michael himself," Mike declared reverently, looking up at the ceiling.

Jenna snorted in a delicate, ladylike way. "Your mothers had their hands full with little boys bringing home frogs from the creek in back of the school down the street from the church."

Mike looked impressed. "Wow, good memory."

"She has a Ph.D.," Steven replied, as if that explained everything. "Well, we need to be going. I have a lot of work to do."

Jenna frowned again. "You have dinner to eat," she said firmly and Steven didn't miss the satisfied gleam in Mike's eye. Meddling old fart. He'd have to make it six Hail Marys.

Mike looked back at the Egglestons' kitchen door, sobering. "I have to be getting back to the Egglestons. It was nice to meet you, Jenna. Make sure he takes care of himself, okay?"

She nodded. "I'll try, Father."

And Steven got the feeling she really meant it.

Tuesday, October 4, 10:45 P.M.

She'd put a frozen pizza in the oven. The aroma met Steven's nose as he closed her front door behind him for the second time. He patted the head of whichever dog he'd just walked and looked longingly at the soft brown sofa. He'd bet a week's pay he'd fall asleep as soon as he sat down on it.

He was bone-tired. It had been one hell of a long day.

The area behind McDonald's near the railroad tracks was sealed off, a patrol car assigned to assure no one further contaminated the scene. Steven honestly didn't believe they'd find anything in an open area after five days, but stranger things had happened.

There was almost no chance they'd find Samantha Eggleston alive. He could only hope they found her dead, so at least they could find any clues the sick bastard might have left behind.

The killer had left nothing behind at the clearing where they'd found Lorraine Rush. No hairs, no footprints. Nothing but an eviscerated body. And a fresh tattoo, half of which had been scavenged as the body lay out in the open, unprotected. The picture of Lorraine's mutilated body flashed in his mind and he wanted to close his eyes, but knew it would only make the picture clearer. More ghastly. More real. He shivered, suddenly cold.

Jenna stuck her head out from the kitchen, her smile a beacon in the darkness of his thoughts. "Supper's in the oven. Do you want something to drink?"

He stood still, just enjoying the warmth of her smile, which faltered when she saw his face. Sobering, she came all the way out of the kitchen. "Are you all right, Steven? You look like you've seen—" She broke off abruptly.

"A ghost?" he asked, a sardonic edge to his voice, remembering the expression Melissa's face would take when he came home late, tired, his mind full of images. Vile, inescapable images of what one Homo sapiens could do to another. At first Melissa's smile of welcome would falter, just like Jenna's had. Then, after one too many late nights, Melissa stopped smiling. Then came the frowning, followed by the sneering. Melissa hadn't had what it took to be the wife of a cop. He looked at Jenna's pensive expression. Maybe no woman did.

"Something like that." Jenna tilted her head. "What's wrong?"

Jenna watched his face change from tortured to carefully blank, watched the light in his eyes shut off, just as if he'd flipped off a switch. "Just the day catching up to me," he answered, then added abruptly, "Do you have any scotch?"

Jenna nodded, studying his face. He looked so incredibly tired. Worried. Consumed. She wanted to walk straight up to him and put her arms around him and just hold him until whatever images haunted him went away, but something told her that he wouldn't accept her concern at this moment. There was a sharpness to him, an edginess that went way beyond simple weariness. An anger, deep and intense. He reminded her of a caged cat even though he hadn't moved a muscle.

"Neat or on the rocks?" she asked.

"Neat," he answered and bent down to scratch Jean-Luc behind the ears. Jean-Luc responded by flipping to his back, presenting his belly for more scratching.

"Coming right up." She went back to the kitchen.

"Jenna, why do both your dogs have the same name tag?" he asked. He looked up when she approached him with his filled glass. "And why do both tags say 'Captain'?"

"You don't watch much television, do you?" Jenna responded, holding out his drink.

"Not anymore." He absently swished the scotch in the glass. "I used to enjoy old movies."

Jenna stowed that common interest away for a different day. "But not sci-fi?"

He looked appalled. "God, no."

Jenna chuckled. "Then I won't even ask if you're a *Star Trek* fan."

His mouth tipped up. "I admit I have watched a few reruns. I remember a green lady . . ."

Jenna tried to look severe. "The makeup artists must have used a year's supply of green paint on that woman," she said. "She showed an awful lot of green skin."

His smile went just a shade naughty and her heart skipped a beat. "Yeah," was all he said.

She hugged herself to keep from throwing her arms around him and narrowed her eyes in mock ire. "Forget about the green lady and think about the captain."

His brows bunched as he thought. "Jim, wasn't it?"

Jim perked up his ears.

"And, *Next Generation*?"

Steven shrugged.

"Counselor Troy, skintight uniforms?" she prompted and he grinned again.

"Matt *really* likes her," he said and she wanted to punch him.

"And her captain's name is . . . ?"

He snapped his fingers and both dogs sat up. He looked impressed. "That was pretty good."

"You should see what they do when I pop the bubble wrap at Christmas," she said wryly and he threw back his head and laughed. And once again took her breath away.

"The bald guy was the second captain, right? He must have been Jean-Luc."

Jean-Luc nuzzled his hand and Steven stroked the dog's

soft muzzle. "Sucker guess," she said, her voice coming out a little huskier than she'd expected and he chuckled, making her feel ridiculously clever for having made him laugh. For making the worry go away for just a little while.

"So much for the power of my honed deductive reasoning," he said mildly, sliding his hands into the pockets of his jacket. He cast his eyes aside, scanning the items covering her walls, and once again she felt the switch go *click*. He was gone again. She felt dismissed and wasn't sure if she should be taking it personally or not.

Maybe all cops did that. She wondered if he did that at home, flicking the switch, cutting off his kids. Then again, maybe it was just her. He'd been throwing mixed signals all night, by turns hot—she swallowed, remembering the restaurant—then . . . nothing. So maybe it was just her.

He was standing poised on the balls of his feet, hands in pockets, eyes looking everywhere but at her. She waited for him to "come back" or whatever it was he did when he flicked the switch back on, but there was only awkward silence.

She cleared her throat. "Can I take your coat, Steven?"

His eyes glanced toward her, then away again. "Sure. Thanks." He shrugged out of the tweed jacket and she wanted to groan. Yards of muscles stretched and moved and flexed under his crisp white shirt. *Take off your shirt, too,* was on the tip of her tongue.

She bit her tongue. *Don't be stupid, Jenna.* She hung his jacket on the back of a dining-room chair and returned to the kitchen without another word.

She hoped he'd follow her, but instead he released the clasp on his holster and draped it over his coat before wandering over to the wall where she kept her diplomas and awards. He shoved his hands in the pockets of his trousers. Camel trousers that clung to the nicest ass she'd ever seen.

"Duke for your bachelor's and UNC for your doctorate,"

he observed from the dining room. "And Maryland for your master's degree. Why did you go all the way up there for your master's?"

"My dad." The memory of her father put a chill on the heat. "My dad was sick and we lived in Maryland," she said, still remembering the day she got the call to come home. It was the worst day of her life. At the time. "He had a stroke shortly after I left for Duke. I wanted to come home then, but he wouldn't hear of it." She looked over her shoulder to find him still staring at the diploma, his hands still in his pockets. "I had a scholarship and Dad didn't want me to lose the opportunity. He had another stroke right before graduation, so one of my profs pulled some strings and I was able to get into Maryland's master's program at College Park at the last minute."

"What happened to him?" Steven asked, his voice softer, the edginess gone.

"He died before Christmas that year," she answered.

"I'm sorry," he said, and after a moment turned back to the frames cluttering her wall.

In the past she'd gone more for a tasteful print here and there, but when she'd moved into this apartment, days after Adam's death, the empty walls had mocked her. Cluttering the walls had made the place seem a little less empty. A little less . . . dead. At a minimum it provided distraction when she thought she would lose her mind from the loneliness. "Thank you."

"Who's Charlie?" Steven asked. He was looking at a certificate Charlie had made for her birthday the year Adam was sick and no one had known what to say. But then-eight-year-old Charlotte Anne had managed where all the grown-ups failed. *To the world's greatest aunt,* she'd penned in purple crayon. *I love you.*

"My niece. Well, actually she's Adam's niece, but I'm still

very close with his family. She's eleven. She made that for me when Adam was sick."

"So it's priceless," he said, and her heart clenched a little knowing he understood. He took a few steps to where her mounted patent awards hung. "You have patents," he said with surprise, changing the subject. He bent closer to read the fine print. "What did you do to get them?"

"Pharmaceutical research." She donned oven mitts and took the pizza out of the oven. "In a previous life," she added. Bending over, she searched her lower cupboard for a pizza cutter in the box of utensils she never used.

"I know it's down here somewhere," she muttered, clanging pots and pans. "Steven, this pizza is half supreme and half pepperoni," she said to the inside of the cupboard. "Which do you want?"

No answer met her ears. She put her hand on the pizza wheel and straightened, turning at the same time. "Stev—?"

The second syllable of his name evaporated from her tongue. He stood in the open doorway of the kitchen, filling it with the breadth of his shoulders. His chest heaved inside the starched white shirt as if every breath took superhuman effort.

Oh, my God.

He was . . . interested.

That look of his could melt solid steel. That look made her heart pound, her nipples hard, made every ounce of sensation pool between her thighs. One throbbing, aching mass of sensation.

He took a step forward and she met him halfway, taking the leap she'd wanted all evening, throwing her body against his, feeling every incredible inch of him pressed against her.

It was incredible. But it wasn't enough.

Then he was kissing her, finally kissing her, and she whimpered. His hands pulled her closer to him. His lips were hot and hard against her mouth.

Incredible, but not enough.

In one movement she opened her mouth beneath the pressure of his and slid her hands up his chest and around his neck. The oven mitt dropped to the floor behind him and she vaguely heard the clang of the pizza wheel against the linoleum as he thrust his tongue inside her mouth, seeking, finding a mate as she again met him halfway. Her fingers threaded through his hair, pulling him closer, still closer. Her tongue tangling with his. Exploring. Learning. Harder. Deeper.

Still not enough. *More. More. More.* The chant throbbed in time with the ache at her core and she lifted on her toes to get closer. Closer to the hard ridge that held the promise of satisfaction.

Not close enough.

Then his hands took a rapid slide down her back to flatten against her butt and pull her up into him. A wild little cry escaped from her throat and he ripped his mouth away to look down. His eyes dark and intense, pupils dilated, nostrils flared as he struggled to breathe.

He wants me.

I want him.

"Please." The single syllable was rusty, ripped from her throat. She had no idea what she was asking for, had no thought beyond *more*. More *something. Anything.* Anything was better than this terrible unmet need, the cavern that only he could fill.

In answer he took her mouth again, hotter, harder, and in two big steps backed her against the refrigerator, pressing hard between her thighs. Against the place that throbbed and wept for him. She thrust back, as hard as she could, leaning into the refrigerator for leverage.

It was a strangely erotic mix of sensations. Cold, hard machine at her back, hot, hard man at her front. Hard big hands against her, kneading, pulling her closer. Then one of his big hands freed its hold on her butt, and she wriggled against him in protest, making him groan, so deep she could feel the vibrations rattle against her breasts. But a moment later the groan was hers as he covered her breast with his hand.

But not enough. Not nearly enough.

His other hand left her butt, but instead of claiming the other breast that felt like it would burst, he pulled at her dress, straining the buttons. Some released. The others made a clatter as they rained to the floor. She pressed her head back against the refrigerator as his mouth moved from her bruised lips down her throat and his hands fumbled with the front clasp on her bra.

Yes. Please.

If she said the words aloud, she didn't hear them over the panting. Hers. His.

With a curse he gave another yank, tearing the delicate lace and her breasts fell free. Into his hands. And into his mouth.

The strangled cry was hers as he sucked, lashing the nipple with his tongue. All feeling clenched between her thighs and she felt her body tighten with need. Greed.

Oh, my God.

She was almost there and he hadn't even touched her yet. *There.* Hadn't slid his hand up her thigh and into the fragile lace panties that were now soaked with wanting him. Hadn't pressed his thumb against her clitoris or slid his finger up inside her. She was almost there and he hadn't done any of those things.

Not yet. Please.

Please.

More. More. More.

She looked down, the sight of his golden head at her breast more erotic than anything she'd ever seen. "Please," she whispered. "Steven."

He pulled back far enough to look up, his lips wet, his eyes almost black. Without saying a word he took the other breast in his mouth and his hand fell to her hip, ran down her thigh as she bent her knee, trying to get closer, her legs wider.

Closer.

His hand pushed at her dress, up her stocking to the bare inch of thigh between her garter and her soaked panties. Then his palm was on bare skin, cupping her ass and she cried out.

His hand froze on her butt and he pulled back from her breast, his eyes taking in the sight of her bare breasts, wet and swollen from his suckling mouth.

Then they lifted to her eyes and Jenna felt her body go cold in an instant.

He was angry.

His jaw clenched until a muscle in his cheek spasmed. He pulled his hand away and pushed at her thigh, straightening her leg, pulling her dress back in place.

"No," he ground out from behind clenched teeth and stepped away, leaving her trembling against the refrigerator, her legs barely supporting her weight, her breasts wet and cold.

Her senses frozen.

She said nothing as he marched into the dining room and grabbed his holster and coat from the back of the chair with jerky movements.

She flinched at the sound of the slamming front door.

Then unable to stand a moment longer on legs that felt like jelly, she pressed her back against the cold refrigerator and slid to the floor.

FIFTEEN

Wednesday, October 5, 12:15 A.M.

"NOW LET ME GET THIS STRAIGHT," Mike said, refilling Steven's empty jelly jar with iced tea he'd pulled from the refrigerator in the rectory. Steven scowled at the refrigerator. He'd never be able to look at a refrigerator the same way again.

Dammit all to hell.

"You kissed her," Mike said, sitting across from him and propping his chin on his folded hands. It was a very priestlike pose and should have completely quieted the lust that still throbbed in Steven's veins.

Should have.

Didn't.

"She kissed you back, maybe did a few things that you probably won't confess." He lifted a black, bushy brow. "Am I on target?"

You shouldn't have touched her, Thatcher, Steven thought fiercely. *Shouldn't have laid a hand on her. Shouldn't have turned from the wall. Should've kept your eyes on her diplomas and patents and "I love you, Aunt Jenna" certificates.*

But, nooo. He just *had* to look over into the kitchen. Had to watch her bend over looking for that damn pizza wheel. The sight of her black dress stretching over her incredible round ass . . . something had simply snapped, letting all the pent-up frustration come rushing out.

I shouldn't have touched her. But he had.

And it had been more incredible than he'd imagined. Dammit, he was *still* imagining.

So, was he angry he'd kissed her? Hell, yes. Was he angry she'd kissed him back?

She'd done a helluva lot more than kiss him back. But the fault was squarely his own. He'd started it. And dammit, he'd finished it, too. And with *such* sensitivity and regard for her feelings.

Thatcher, you are a dickhead.

Furious with himself and with Mike for being so right, Steven drained his glass and set it back on the table. Hard. Mike picked up the glass and checked the bottom to make sure it wasn't broken, which just made Steven angrier. "Yes," Steven hissed. "Right on target, as usual, Father Leone."

"Don't break my glassware," Mike cautioned. "Mrs. Hennesey gave me blackberry jam in that one and if I don't return the glass, I don't get any more jam."

"Dammit, Mike," Steven gritted and Mike pursed his lips.

"Mrs. Hennesey makes very good jam. And please don't swear." His lips twitched. "My son."

Steven just glared and Mike laughed. "I don't see the problem, Steven. She's beautiful. And she seems to like you, which I personally don't understand, but a basic understanding of women is unfortunately not taught at seminary. She has to be smart to have a Ph.D., although book learning does not necessarily equate to wisdom, which goes back to my not understanding why she likes you. She seems compassionate and articulate and has a sense of humor. She wanted to take care of you, for heaven's sake." He shrugged. "So you let things get out of hand tonight. Understandable, I suppose. Just don't let it happen again."

Steven looked away, focusing on the rosary that hung on the wall, wishing it would have the deflating effect he needed it to have. He'd been rock-hard since he'd stormed out of Jenna's apartment, an hour before, leaving her standing there shocked and openmouthed.

And bare-breasted. God, she was beautiful. Beautiful and passionate and . . . *Mine, mine, mine.*

His body throbbed painfully and he knew it was nothing less than he deserved.

Steven blew out a frustrated breath. "You just don't understand."

Mike spread his hands out wide, palms forward. "So enlighten me. Explain to me why you're so upset that a smart, pretty woman desires you. I may not have a Ph.D., but I do have wisdom, which, incidentally, *was* taught at seminary. Too bad *you* didn't go. Looks like a good dose of wisdom is what you need right now." He folded his hands and resettled his chin. "I'm listening. Go ahead. Explain."

Explain. How? How could he explain when he didn't even understand it himself? When he didn't understand why he was so angry. Why he'd left Jenna standing alone without a single word of explanation. She probably hated him by now and would never see him again, so he may have solved his problem by default.

Not a particularly cheering thought.

"I don't know, Mike." Steven slumped down in his chair and closed his eyes. "It's just too much. Too fast."

"Meaning your relationship with Miss Marshall isn't molding itself into the little space you've made for it." Mike gestured with his hands, forming a box in the air. "Not a tidy package. Can't put on the lid because it's a lousy fit. No ribbons or bows." Mike frowned. "You, Steven Thatcher, are a stupid control freak."

Steven's eyes flew open. "I am *not* a control freak."

"But you'll admit to stupid?"

Steven ground his teeth. "Yes."

"Well, that's some progress I suppose," Mike said thoughtfully. "You want my opinion?"

Steven narrowed his eyes. "I don't know."

Mike shrugged. "Tough beans, you came here, tore me away from *Sports Center,* so you'll listen to what I have to say."

Steven folded his arms across his chest. "Okay," he said, his agreement sounding belligerent even to his own ears. He sounded like one of the boys, for God's sake.

Mike rolled his eyes. "And I can see from your body language how *much* you value my opinion. No matter. As for Miss Marshall. You like her." He lifted a brow. "You *really* like her."

Steven rolled his eyes and felt his cheeks heat. "Thank you, Dr. Watson. Now tell me who killed Professor Plum in the study?"

Mike grinned. "Miss Peacock with the rope because she caught him cheating with Miss Scarlet in the study but that's not important now. Pay attention, Steven. You like her. A lot. She likes you. A lot. You want to get to know her better, so you ask her out to dinner. Just dinner, nothing else. You plan to work your way up to a physical relationship only a little at a time, because as soon as it gets physical, the floodgates open because it's been four years, and then you have to marry her. But you can't marry her until you prove to yourself that she's not another Melissa, but all this proving takes time. I bet you laid out a timetable that allowed you to kiss her when? Next month? On the fifteenth?"

"This month," Steven muttered, then looked away. "On the fifteenth."

Mike's laughter boomed. "Control freak. You always have been." Mike reached across the table and patted the table in front of Steven. "Look at me, Steven. I'm your best friend. I care about you." Steven looked at him and felt his heart squeeze. Gone was the laughter in Mike's dark eyes, replaced by a caring so fundamental . . .

"I'm listening."

Mike nodded. "Good. It's about time. Lose the timetable, Steven. Let life happen as it happens. Stop trying to make everything happen to your specification. Enjoy your life. Your children. The possibility of a woman who can complete you."

Steven swallowed. "It sounds like you're telling me to marry her tonight."

Mike sighed. "You know that's not true. Your problem . . . well, one of your many problems," he amended, "is that you only see life in black and white. Good, evil. Right, wrong."

"I have to. That's my job." Steven glared. "I thought it was yours, too."

Mike shook his head. "That's the point, Steven. Life is not black or white. One or two. Yes or no. On or off. Nothing is safe. Nothing is guaranteed. Only the essence of life itself is on or off. You either wake up in the morning or you don't. You're breathing or you're not. I feel sorry for you."

Steven felt his gut tighten. "Why?"

"You've forgotten what love is about. You are so afraid of losing it that you push it away."

Steven's eyes widened. "I do not."

"Yes. You do. Melissa left you, hurt your ego, made you choose to lie to your children, so you set up every possible barrier to avoid being hurt again. It's not abnormal, Steven. It's human nature. But it won't make you happy."

Steven picked up Mrs. Hennesey's jam jar and swished the melting ice around and around. "I don't even remember what that feels like," he murmured.

Mike sat back in his chair. "What? Being happy?"

Steven met his eyes and nodded. "Yeah."

Mike thinned his lips. "Then get off your butt and do something about it. You have a chance for happiness staring you in the face."

Steven sighed. "Your point. This time."

Mike looked amused. "My point every time, but sometimes I let you think it's yours."

Steven took an ice cube from the jam jar and tossed it in Mike's face. "You're so full of it." He ducked when Mike returned the lob, then sobered. "I don't know if she'll see me again. I left kind of abruptly tonight."

"Call her. The worst thing she can do is tell you what you deserve to hear."

Steven didn't have a thing to say to that, so he stood up and shrugged into his coat. "I'll give you a call."

Mike walked him to the door. "Steven, how close are you coming to catching the monster who stole our girls?"

Steven shook his head. "How close are you to taking a wife?"

Mike sighed. "I thought so. I'll pray."

"We're going to check out the McDonald's, but I doubt we'll find anything. It's been too long."

"If only Serena had come forward sooner," Mike said sadly.

"Pray for her, too, Mike. She's got a hard row ahead of her for the next eighty years or so."

Wednesday, October 5, 5:45 A.M.

They'd found out where he'd met Samantha. Dear, sweet Samantha. How pretty she'd been.

He frowned thoughtfully. Until he'd shaved her head. Women were decidedly unattractive without hair. Just one more way men were different from women he supposed, sipping coffee from the McDonald's cup he'd just picked up at the drive-through. Men could get away with being bald.

Women just looked revolting.

He considered the two uniformed policemen standing next to the bright yellow police tape. They were bent over the tape, looking into the grass. The sun was just coming up and the police car had been there all night, guarding the "crime scene."

Hell, it was no crime scene. Not *there* anyway. True, Samantha Eggleston had met him there, but no crime had been committed. She'd voluntarily climbed into the car with him.

Little slut. She'd deserved what she'd gotten. His only regret was that she'd . . . expired . . . before he was completely finished.

Next time. He'd do all he'd planned next time. With the next one.

He took another sip of coffee and grimaced. He hated coffee, but he hadn't wanted to call attention to himself by getting a Coke at six A.M. For now he was just another guy enjoying his cup of joe as the sun came up. Just another guy planning the next girl he'd lure from her bed. He hadn't yet figured out who she'd be, but he had a short list.

He watched as another car drove up. Out hopped Detective Steven Thatcher, resident Columbo. *Hah.* The man couldn't find his way out of a paper bag. Thatcher hadn't even found Samantha's body yet. He'd have to make another anonymous phone call to the police before the critters did to Samantha what they'd done to poor Lorraine.

Shame, that. The critters had eaten half of the perfectly good tattoo he'd applied himself.

Thatcher strode over to the two uniformed cops and began pointing. The cops nodded and Thatcher stood back, arms crossed over his chest as another, younger man in a trenchcoat approached and ducked under the yellow tape, a black bag under his arm.

He wasn't terribly worried. There would be no physical

evidence linking him to this place. The cops might find Samantha's hair or some such, but nothing from him.

He'd been careful.

He'd been smart.

Next time he'd be even smarter.

Wednesday, October 5, 7:40 A.M.

"Now let me get this straight," Casey said, her lips turned down in a frown as they hurried from the parking lot to the school. "You were making him dinner and he was being boring and then all of a sudden he became Mr. Frantic Hands? And then he left you in the lurch?"

Jenna nodded. She still felt numb. "He just . . ." She shrugged inside her jacket. "Walked away."

Casey pushed the door open and led the way in. "How rude."

Jenna's lips quirked up at the understatement. "That would be one word for it," she returned dryly. "I had a few others in mind."

Casey snickered. "Go, girl."

"But I of course didn't think of them until after he'd gone."

"Typical," Casey agreed, then muttered, "Look out, fearless leader at two o'clock."

Blackman. She couldn't take another brow-beating over Rudy Lutz this morning. "Maybe he didn't see me," Jenna whispered. But then he turned, met her eyes, and started walking toward her. "Shit. As if my life isn't already filled with too much fun." She stopped walking, Casey paused beside her as Blackman approached, his step faster than normal.

"Dr. Marshall," he said tightly and Jenna saw his mouth frown under his prim mustache.

"Dr. Blackman," she returned. She certainly wouldn't make it any easier for him.

"There's been another incident in your classroom."

Jenna sucked in her cheeks. "Now why does that not surprise me, Dr. Blackman?" she asked.

Blackman glared a moment. "This time it's worse, Dr. Marshall."

Jenna just looked at him. "How can it be worse? They've painted graffiti on every blackboard, white board, and blank wall, spray-painted my periodic table and my posters, and super-glued all the Erlenmeyer flasks to my lab tables. They've slashed my tires and poured water down my gas tank. What more can they possibly do?"

"Come with me," was all he said before turning on his heel and walking crisply up the stairs.

Jenna exchanged looks with Casey and followed him.

Five or six of her students gathered around her classroom door, held back by Lucas who looked angry enough to ... Jenna stared at him, her gut twisting. Mad enough to kill, as the saying went.

"What is it, Lucas?" she murmured.

"Don't touch anything," Lucas growled, then lifted his arm to let her through. Then held her shoulders to keep her upright.

"Oh, God." Immediate terror clutched her heart. "Lucas." The last was little more than a whimper. She lifted her hand to her mouth and ... stared. Up.

To where the carcass of ... something ... swung from a rope tied to a hook mounted in the ceiling tiles, a grotesque piñata.

Swinging.

Swinging.

It was almost hypnotic.

She felt Casey's arm go around her waist as she swallowed

back the breakfast that threatened to choke her. "What is it?" Jenna whispered, unable to tear her eyes from the horrific sight. The room swayed and Casey's arm tightened.

"Come on, honey," Casey murmured. "Let's get you out of here."

She let Casey turn her body around, but her eyes remained fixed to whatever the poor animal had been, her head craned like an owl's until her body ran into Lucas's. She turned her gaze then, lifting it to Lucas's familiar black eyes. Focusing on them while the swaying room came to a gradual halt. He took her chin firmly between his thumb and forefinger.

"You will not pass that boy," he whispered fiercely through clenched teeth. "No matter what Blackman says. You will not let them win."

Jenna shook her head, numb. "No, no I won't." She twisted, looking back at the swinging carcass over her shoulder. "Lucas—"

He grasped her chin again, making her look at him. "I'll set your classes up in the auditorium today. The kids can have study time until we clean this up." He turned to Blackman who looked decidedly grim. "Keith, you will call the police this time, or I will call them myself." He narrowed his eyes. "Then I'll call the press."

"I will call the police," Blackman responded evenly. "No need for threats, Lucas."

"And you will bring disciplinary action against Rudy Lutz and his *friends*." Lucas's mouth twisted around the word as if it left a bad taste in his mouth.

"If the police find evidence of those responsible, I will take appropriate action."

Jenna didn't blink. "That's a big if, Dr. Blackman. What happens when these boys take the game a notch higher?"

He flinched. "I don't believe they'll take it that far," he said thinly and Jenna felt her cork pop.

Pop and fly.

She took a step toward him, pulling free of Casey's steadying arm. "You don't believe," she said, her voice a low growl. "*You don't believe?*" Anger surged, blessed and raw, erasing the numbness, leaving fire in its place. She advanced another step, fists on her hips, staring down at him from atop her heels. He looked up, defiantly. Disbelievingly she shook her head. "Are you a fucking moron, Blackman?" she demanded and ignored how his mouth dropped open like a hooked fish. She pressed the tip of her finger to his scrawny chest. "Do you honestly believe these . . . these *animals* will stop on their own?" She jabbed. "Are you that unbelievably *stupid*?"

Blackman closed his mouth, pursed his lips. "You're out of line, Dr. Marshall. I'll forgive it this time because I understand you've had a shock, but—"

Red lights flashed in front of her eyes. "Didn't you listen to anything I *said*? I said they *won't stop*. They'll *continue*. Next time some*body* will get hurt instead of that poor animal, whatever it was." She flung her arm backward blindly, pointing to the swinging carcass. "And *then* what will you say, Blackman? Sorry? Forgive me? But we won the fucking *championship*?" Her voice rose until the last word was delivered in close to a screech.

Lucas grabbed her arm and lowered it to her side. "This is not the time, Jen. Don't worry. I'll make sure he does the right thing."

Blackman regarded the three of them, Jenna from her towering position and Lucas and Casey flanking her from behind. "We'll speak more on this topic later. I'll go and call the authorities."

"Call Al Pullman, Investigative Division," Jenna said, her voice trembling. "He's the one who wrote the report on my tires."

"If he's available," Blackman said crisply and turned on his heel.

"Blackman." Jenna again felt steadying hands on her shoulders. Lucas's. And a hand smoothing her back. Casey's. Blackman stopped, but didn't turn around. "Call Pullman. I'll know if you don't."

Blackman slowly turned his body, his face one big scowl. "Is that a threat, Dr. Marshall?"

Jenna stared, unmoving, then jerked her thumb over her shoulder at the swinging carcass. "No. That is."

Something flickered in his eyes and he looked over her shoulder at the . . . thing . . . before turning and leaving the room. Jenna took a breath and looked into the hallway, once again seeing the students gathered around, all thirty of them by this time.

She'd forgotten all about them. *Shit.*

She closed her eyes. They'd heard her call the principal a fucking moron. That was most probably against the rules in the teacher handbook. But he was a fucking moron. That really should come as no surprise to any of these kids.

But still . . . She'd said it. *Out loud.* She opened her eyes and looked around the group. Thirty pairs of concerned eyes looked back. No recriminations, no glee. Just concern.

No one said anything for a long moment. Then a pale Kelly Templeton said, "I'm sorry, Dr. Marshall. This isn't how the rest of us feel."

Murmurs of agreement rippled through the group and Lucas moved into the hall, herding the group toward the stairs. "Let's go, people. Let's give Dr. Marshall a chance to gather herself. You all get a break today. Miss Ryan, I'll get someone to cover your class this period so you can stay with Dr. Marshall until the police come." He took the lead, and one by one each teen followed him until the only one left was Josh Lutz. Josh, Rudy's quiet brother who sat on the back row of her first period class every day and took assiduous notes. Josh, who hadn't been able to meet her eyes since the vandalism had begun. Josh, whose face was paler than Kelly's had been. He looked down at his shoes, then back up. In his eyes she saw guilt mixed with mortification.

"I'm sorry, too, Dr. Marshall," he said quietly. "I wish there was something I could do."

Jenna made herself smile and tried not to wonder what life must be like for a gentle boy like Josh living with thugs like Rudy and their father. "Thanks, Josh. Just knowing you feel that way makes a difference."

He looked like he would say something more, then changed his mind. Shouldering his backpack, he set off in a loping jog to catch up with the class.

Casey tugged at her waist. "Come on, Jen. Let's go wait for Officer Pullman."

Jenna took one look back and wished she hadn't, knowing for a long time she'd see that poor creature whenever she closed her eyes.

Wednesday, October 5, 9:15 A.M.

Brad crept out of his bedroom. The coast was finally clear. Helen had gone shopping. Matt and Nicky were at school. His father wasn't home and hadn't been since the morning before.

Brad stopped by his father's bedroom door and looked in, his lips curling in contempt. His father hadn't come home last night. His lips thinned. His father had taken Dr. Marshall to dinner.

Dinner. What a joke. His father hadn't come home last night. Didn't take a Ph.D. to figure that one out. He'd thought more of Dr. Marshall than that. But his father . . . At this point he didn't know if there was anything his father wasn't capable of doing. Of saying. Anger pricked at him and he welcomed it. Nicky was up again last night, as he was every night, but his father was nowhere to be seen. Unavailable to soothe a little boy to sleep.

Because he was catting around. Selfishly seeing to his own needs while his children went without. No, not money, not food. Not any of those material things. But they went without just the same. Nicky and Matt especially.

He himself . . . He didn't need Special Agent Steven Thatcher. Not anymore. He—

The front door slammed and a few seconds later he was staring at his father across a ten-foot expanse of second-floor hallway carpet. Might as well have been a damn ocean.

His father narrowed his eyes. "What are you doing here?"

"I'm skipping school," he answered evenly. "I won't ask you what you're doing here as it's obvious you didn't sleep in your bed last night and those were the same clothes you wore yesterday. I have to assume your dinner with Dr. Marshall took a very long time."

He watched his father's eyes flash. "Brad, you cross the line. I was at work all night long."

Brad chuckled. Mirthlessly. "You must be getting old, Dad. I didn't think any guy referred to it as 'work.' Although I have to say about five hundred guys at Roosevelt would have loved to have been 'working' with you last night."

His father took a step forward, then another, until they were nose to nose. His father's eyes bored into him and a muscle twitched in his cheek. Brad's glance darted down to see fists at his father's sides and it occurred to him that he'd gone a step too far.

"How dare you?" his father hissed and Brad dismissed the small frisson of alarm that sizzled down his back. His father was a big man. Bigger than he was. But his father wouldn't hit him. And if he did, he'd just hit him back. That's what he'd do. And God help the old man because he had a lot of anger stored up. That would go a fair distance in closing the size gap.

"I call 'em like I see 'em," Brad said, preparing for the first blow.

That of course never came. Because on top of being a damn liar, his father was a coward.

"You can think what you like about me, Brad. But when you demean a woman like Jenna Marshall, you cross the line. I've tried to understand how to help you, but you've just shown me you're beyond my help. No son of mine would ever say anything like that about any woman."

"Then I guess I'm no son of yours," Brad said, making his voice cold, steady. Steady.

His father's chest heaved. Once, twice. "Get your books, you're going to school."

"No, I'm not."

His father took another step and towered over him and Brad felt another spear of fear.

"Yes, you will. Because I am your father and I say you will go to school. Get. Your. Books."

Brad took a step back. Fuming. Furious. Yeah, he'd get his books. He'd even go to school. Then he'd get the hell out of this house and everything that went with it.

He looked at his father and smiled. "Yes, sir."

Sixteen

Wednesday, October 5, 10:30 A.M.

"ANYTHING?" LENNIE ASKED.

Steven stared at the untouched paperwork on his desk, still ripped up from his fight with Brad. *I handled that badly,* he thought.

"Steven?"

Steven dragged his eyes up to Lennie's worried face. Steven pulled his brain to the topic at hand. Two girls. One dead, one missing. Lennie had a right to be worried. They didn't have shit.

Steven threw his pen on his desk. "We found a tire print that could have come from Samantha's bike, but the kids use that area as a stunt park, so there's a better than even chance that it didn't."

"So we have nothing."

"Pretty much." He handed Lennie a sheet of paper from his desk. "We brainstormed this morning on who could have been the ballplayer Serena overheard Sammie mention."

"All of these games were played the day Samantha disappeared?"

"Up to four days prior. Nancy has a bigger list of games for the week prior, but we figured it would have been within a few days."

Lennie scanned the page, then lowered it enough to see Steven over the top. "You've included pro games on this list."

"An adult sports figure with a yen for young girls would have an easy time attracting them."

"Pro games, college games, high school games . . . *church* leagues? That's just sick, Steven."

"But necessary."

With a sigh Lennie laid the paper on the desk. "That's why it's sick. How will you narrow down this list? You've got over a hundred games and each one will have twenty-plus participants."

"We eliminated college teams that played nontelevised away games. As for the pros, the only televised or home game in the last four days was hockey. The Hurricanes played last Wednesday."

"I know," Lennie said. "I had sixth row seats. Nearly caught a puck in my teeth."

"Which would have ruined your dazzling smile and ended your modeling career," Steven returned sarcastically and Lennie's lips curved. "Harry and Sandra are getting team rosters," Steven continued, "and Nancy's running background checks. We'll look for anybody with a prior."

"This will take weeks," Lennie said heavily.

"It can't." Steven's fists clenched on top of his desk. "Meg thinks he'll strike again soon."

Wednesday, October 5, 10:30 A.M.

"Do you have to do that?" Casey asked irritably as Jenna paced the length of the teachers' lounge for the hundredth time. "You're making me crazy."

Jenna shot her a hostile look. "Forgive me if I'm a bit preoccupied. It's not like the police are upstairs in my classroom or anything. How can you sit and grade papers like nothing happened?"

Casey scrawled a grade on the top of one theme paper and

plucked another from the pile that didn't seem to diminish over time. "Because if I don't get these *Crime and Punishment* themes graded by tomorrow, I can't get my quarter grades in early and I can't take off Friday. And if I can't take off Friday, Ned will be going to Myrtle Beach all by himself while my new bikini and I stay home." She looked up with a sideways grin. "And *that's* not gonna happen."

Friday. Jenna's brain kicked back into gear. It was a teacher in-service day where faculty prepared report cards and students got a day off. All in all, a really raw deal all the way around. "You still want to borrow my car for the trip?"

"Of course. Ned's salivating over it already."

Jenna winced. The thought of Ned driving Adam's car was not a pleasant one.

Casey's smile was wry. "Don't worry, Jenna. I'll drive." She frowned. "Unless you don't want me to take Adam's car. I know how attached you are to it."

Attached to a car of all things. It should be silly, a grown woman attached to a car. But Jenna remembered the raw fury she'd felt the night before when Rudy and his friends tampered with the gas tank. Of course she was attached. It had been Adam's. Still, it was just a car, she told herself. A grown-up toy to be enjoyed. Life was too short after all.

"Don't be silly," she said and watched Casey's frown relax. "Take the car and have fun. Besides, if you've got it, Rudy and his friends can't touch it, right? I need your truck this weekend anyway. I promised to take Steven's son Nicky to the park to teach his sheepdog how to sit."

Casey's frown snapped back into place. "You're going to entertain his son after last night?"

Jenna shrugged. What *had* Steven really done? When the steam cleared, what had he done? He'd kissed her and touched her and set her body on fire. Very nicely, she should add. Then he'd stopped. There really hadn't been a whole lot more to it than that. He'd made no promises, taken nothing she hadn't freely offered. Canceling on Nicky would be a hundred times worse because she *had* promised. "I made a promise to Nicky and that really has nothing to do with Steven."

She expected Casey to make some witty retort, but there was quiet at the table where Casey sat staring down at the theme paper she was grading, her pixie face troubled.

"What's wrong, Case?"

Casey glanced up, then back down at the paper. "This is the first unique theme I've read."

Jenna lifted her brows. "And that's a problem . . . why?"

Casey bit at her lip. "Because this student seems to identify with the story's main character a little too much."

Jenna rewound her brain. She'd been forced to read *Crime and Punishment* in high school, too.

"Wait a minute. Didn't the main character in *Crime and Punishment* kill an old woman?"

Casey nodded, still staring down at the theme with a troubled frown. "Because she annoyed him and because he wanted to know what it felt like to take another life."

Now frowning herself, Jenna walked over to where Casey sat. "Which kid is this?"

"Dr. Marshall?" Officer Pullman asked from the doorway and both Jenna and Casey whipped their heads around to see him.

"What did you find?" Jenna asked.

Pullman pulled a chair from the table. "Sit down, Dr. Marshall."

Her nerves jangled. "I'd really rather stand if you don't mind."

"Listen to the nice man with the shiny badge, Jen," Casey commanded sharply. "Sit your ass down in the chair." Casey looked over at Pullman with a sour grimace. "She's been driving me nuts with the pacing ever since you arrived."

Pullman's lips twitched as Jenna flopped into the chair he provided. He took the chair next to her and brought out his little notepad. "Well, the animal hanging from your ceiling was a possum at one time. It was most likely a roadkill somebody picked up from the side of the road this morning."

Relief shot through her. At least no one had purposely tortured the poor animal. "Did you find any evidence of who did this?"

Pullman shook his head, much as Jenna had expected him to. "Looks like whoever did this wore gloves. But it also looks like this isn't the only trouble you've had since your tires got slashed. I couldn't help but notice the artwork on your walls. I take it the QB hasn't brought up his grade?"

Jenna scowled. "The QB is waiting for me to fold."

"The QB will be waiting a good long time," Casey added darkly.

Pullman flipped his notepad closed. "Well, we dusted for prints, but I doubt we'll get anything concrete. You've just got too many people going in and out of your classroom." He stood up and looked down. "I'll tell you the same thing that I told you Friday night. Watch your back."

Wednesday, October 5, 3:45 P.M.

Harry threw his notebook on the conference-room table and dropped into the chair directly across from Steven's, disgust all over his face. Sandra took the chair next to Harry, looking tired.

"We've been checking perps with sex priors all day," Harry complained. "I need to bathe."

Sandra looked over at him with amused sympathy. Sex perps were her niche forte. *One hell of a niche forte,* Steven thought. Give him murderers any damn day of the week. "Don't worry, Harry," she said, "you'll develop a Teflon coating after a while. All the slime will just roll off."

Nancy rubbed her forehead with one hand while sliding her half-glasses off her nose with the other. "How long will that take? To develop the Teflon coating, I mean."

Sandra shrugged. "Five or six years."

Steven watched them all from his own chair. "But how about the vics, Sandra? How long before you develop a Teflon coating so that they don't stick in your mind?"

Sandra's face sobered. "Never."

Steven sighed. "Me either." He looked around. "Has anyone seen Kent or Meg?"

"Meg said she had an appointment," Nancy said. "Haven't seen Kent since this morning."

"Here I am," said Kent, huffing a little bit. He plopped into a chair. "Sorry I'm late."

"Well, let's get started, folks. Thanks for coming back this afternoon. We've got news."

"From the McDonald's search this morning?" Sandra asked, leaning forward.

"I wish," Steven replied grimly. He placed a sheet of paper on the center of the table. "Look."

His team gathered around the paper he'd already had analyzed six ways to Tuesday. "No prints, no identifying marks," he told them. "Just rather general directions on where to find Samantha Eggleston. It was dropped off with the mail this afternoon. I got it an hour ago."

"In the mail?" Harry asked sharply.

Steven shook his head. "Nope, just with it. No utilization of the U.S. Postal Service."

"Good," said Harry.

"I agree," said Steven. If their killer had used the U.S. Postal Service or even a fax they would have found themselves tangled ass-deep in Feds. "It's a printed sheet—came off a standard laser jet printer, just like the one in our office."

"And hundreds of other offices," Sandra muttered.

"'Find her before it's too late. If you can,'" Nancy read and looked up at Steven. "Too late for what, I wonder."

"I wondered the same thing," Steven said. "Either she's still alive, or—"

"Or she's dead and he wants us to find her before the animals do," Harry finished grimly.

"This is nowhere near the two other clearings," Sandra commented. "Is there a pattern? Like that nutcase who bombed mailboxes picking cities that made a happy face on the map?"

Steven winced. He hadn't considered that. He'd ask Meg if a map pattern like that matched the profile she'd created of their killer. "I marked them on the map. No pattern yet that I can see."

"But we only have three points," Harry said.

"Let's pray we don't have four," Steven returned. "I've sent some state uniforms over to secure the site and informed the local town sheriff. He's going to meet us there. He says the indicated area is huge, so we've got a long night ahead of us. Harry, I'd like you to come with me."

Harry sighed. "I'll grab some barf bags."

Steven almost smiled. "Sandra and Nancy, keep plugging away at the list of ballplayers."

"We've contacted ten of the players with priors so far," Sandra said. "They've all got alibis for Thursday night and the night Lorraine went missing."

"Keep going. When you've exhausted the list of priors, start in on the gentle folk." Steven looked over at Kent who hadn't taken his eyes from the note. "What, Kent?"

Kent glanced up, then reglued his eyes to the paper. "This, right here." He pointed to a small mark in the lower left corner of the page.

"I saw that," Steven said. "It's some kind of design. Why, does it mean something to you?"

Kent nodded and tilted his head to one side, taking in the design from a different angle. "This side of it, right here. This looks like it might match the tattoo on Lorraine Rush's scalp."

"The one that was mostly gone," Harry said thinly and Kent looked up with a nod.

"That's the one."

Steven got up and stood behind Kent, looking over the young man's shoulder. He squinted, trying to focus. "How can you tell, Kent? There wasn't a hell of a lot left of that tattoo."

"I had the ME take some photos and I had them blown up. Posted them above my desk and I've been looking at them every chance I get. I'm pretty sure, Steven. This is the mark." Kent turned in his chair so that he could meet Steven's eyes and once again Steven was impressed with the intelligence mixed with compassion he saw there. "And when you find Samantha's body—if you find it before it's scavenged—I'll bet you find this mark on her scalp, too."

Steven blew out a breath. "It'll be dark soon. Kent, come with me and Harry. If we find something I want you to be able to start on the scene before dark. Nancy, run that mark through your database. I want to know where it came from. Sandra, I guess you have enough perps to question so that if Nancy takes a break to run this design you won't be twiddling your thumbs."

"Unfortunately, I have plenty to do," Sandra said dryly and again Steven almost smiled.

"Then let's go, folks. Everyone be on call."

Everybody moved but Sandra who remained seated. As

the room cleared, her face clouded and Steven felt his gut twist. Twist more, anyway. She had something to say she didn't want the rest of the team to know. Yet. Steven watched her look anywhere but at him. What Sandra had to say would be personal, then.

His mind went to Brad, God help him, and for the first time he admitted that whatever was troubling his son could be more than emotional. It could be illegal.

But not like this. He looked up to the bulletin board where he'd pinned the photo of Lorraine Rush's body. He refused to believe whatever was troubling Brad could be anything like this.

When it was just the two of them, Sandra picked up her notebook and moved to the seat right next to him. "You want it sugar-coated or straight?" she asked.

"Just spit it out, Sandra," he said, his voice coming out harsher than he intended.

"Okay. When I looked at all the games that were played in the week before the disappearance and crossed it with people who had access to both victims one possibility popped up."

Steven swallowed. Brad didn't know either girl. Did he? Steven realized he hadn't even asked himself the question. *But why would he?* he asked himself defensively. "Who?"

Sandra sighed. "Father Mike Leone."

Shocked, Steven could only stare. "No."

Sandra shrugged. "I'm sorry, Steven, but it lines up. Both girls were part of his parish. And there'd been some kind of church league tag football game the weekend before. I asked Anna Eggleston if Samantha was involved and she said that Samantha didn't normally go to those games, but that last weekend she did because it was a special game. Father Leone was there."

The twisting in Steven's gut became full nausea. "He was *there*. He didn't *play a good game*."

Sandra looked as ripped up as he felt. "It was one of those special games, Steven. Old versus young. The priests and church faculty played the church's teen team. Father Leone played. And I understand from a few other teens who were there that he did play a pretty good game."

Steven looked away, not sure how to manage this latest stress. "Does Harry know you were looking at Father Leone?"

Sandra shook her head. "No. I thought you should know first. I asked everyone so that no one would know what I was really asking. If he's innocent—"

"You could ruin one of the best men that ever lived," Steven finished bitterly.

Sandra laid her hand on his arm. "I know, Steven," she said quietly. "But if he's guilty . . ."

"He's not," Steven insisted. "I know this man. He's simply not capable."

"But you'll let me investigate, won't you?" Sandra asked, just as quietly.

Steven fixed his eyes on the photos of Lorraine Rush. Before, beautiful and vibrant. After . . . Someone had done this to her, had robbed a vibrant girl of her very life. Violently. It wasn't Mike. Steven knew it deep down. But he also knew he had a responsibility to Lorraine and Samantha and their families. And crazy as it sounded, Mike would agree.

"Yes," he whispered, then cleared his throat. "Don't do anything without coming to me first."

Wednesday, October 5, 5:30 P.M.

Helen set the casserole dish on the table. Tuna casserole. One of the boys' favorites and one of the easiest things to make. She hated it worse than liver, but two outa three wasn't bad.

"Boys!" she yelled up the stairs. "Dinner!"

Footsteps pounded on the stairs and Matt appeared and plopped in his chair.

"I'm starving, Aunt Bea."

"You're always starving, Matthew. That's hardly earth-shattering news." She turned toward the open doorway. "Brad! Nicholas!"

"I'm here," Nicky said and slid into his chair. "Y' don't hafta yell."

"Sorry," Helen said, appropriately chastised. "Where's Brad?"

"Probably sulking in his room," Matt said cheerfully. "He's grounded for life, after all."

Helen frowned at him. "Your brother is not grounded for life. It's only for a week."

"Might as well be for life," Matt said, shoveling casserole on his plate.

"And you would know," Helen said dryly. "You, who have experienced the joys and woes of grounding for many weeks of your own life."

"Yep," Matt said, just as cheerfully, digging into his plate with a fork. "But not this week. I'm golden," he added, his mouth full.

"Put down the fork and go tell your brother it's time for dinner."

"Golly gee whiz, Aunt Bea," Matt whined and Helen lost control of her mouth and smiled.

"Go," she said, popping him on the head with her oven mitt. "Now."

Muttering, Matt complied and Helen turned to Nicky. "Well, how was your day, Nicky?"

Nicky shrugged. "Okay, I guess."

"Anything special happen?"

"No, ma'am." He looked up and brightened and Helen felt a tug at her heart. "This weekend Jenna said she'd take me and Cindy Lou to the park to teach her to sit."

"I remember," said Helen and told herself to call Jenna and remind her of her promise. There was no way she'd let Nicky become disappointed if she could help it. "Where are your brothers?" she demanded, craning her neck to see around the corner.

She heard footsteps on the stairs, heavier this time, and Matt reappeared, his freckles standing out against his pale face. "I found this on Brad's bed," he said, quietly holding out a note.

Helen scanned it and felt her heart stop. "Oh, Lord God. Your brother's run away."

Seventeen

Wednesday, October 5, 6:00 P.M.

IT GOT DARK TOO DAMN EARLY. WELL, TECHNICALLY it got dark the same time as it had the night before, Steven thought, but the night before they hadn't mobilized twenty cops, forty-odd volunteers, and a canine cadaver unit to search for what in all likelihood was a very dead teenaged girl.

"There's two hundred acres of wooded land inside the circle you drew," said the local sheriff, a big burly man named Rogers. Rogers tapped the map they'd laid out across the hood of Steven's car. "It'll take us three days to cover that much ground, even with the dogs. You sure you boys can't narrow the field a little bit?"

"We could call the killer and say pretty please, can you give us better directions," Harry said sarcastically. Sheriff Rogers glared and opened his mouth to say something uplifting, no doubt.

"Harry," Steven cautioned.

Harry made a face. "I'm sorry. I interviewed sex perverts all day and I'm no company for decent people."

Sheriff Rogers relaxed. "Who said I was decent people?" he asked kindly. "It would help if you boys could get a chopper in here. You could see the clearings, assumin' that's where he's put her."

"That's where he put the last one, and where he probably intended to put this one last Friday," Harry said. "Except he was interrupted by the old man's dog." He looked over at Kent who was staring at the map. "How is the dog, by the way?"

Kent looked up and pushed his glasses up his nose. "He'll pull through."

"You've been keeping tabs on the dog?" Steven asked, surprised.

"He's been keeping tabs on the lady vet that sewed up the dog," Harry corrected with a smirk and Steven watched Kent's cheeks redden. "Cute little thing, she is," Harry added with a sly wink and Kent's cheeks went even darker.

"Back off, Harry," Steven said mildly, although the tone of his voice belied the turbulence inside him. Harry's careless comment sent his brain flying to the mental picture of Jenna he couldn't erase from his mind. Was she okay? He'd planned to call her this evening, to see if he could stop by and discuss the night before . . . Heat spread through him despite the chill in the air. Just as heat had spread through him each time he thought her name. This was ridiculous.

So why couldn't he make it stop and concentrate? On his job? On Brad? On anything other than the kaleidoscope of emotions she made him feel? From undeniable want to a guilt that gnawed at him every time he remembered the hurt look on her face when he walked away last night.

He had to fix that. Make her bewildered hurt look go away. His mind flashed to the belligerent contempt he'd seen in Brad's eyes this morning. He had to make that go away, too.

Dammit, he had to fix *something* in his life.

He forced himself to focus on the map spread out on the hood of his car. Rogers was indeed correct. There was no way they'd search the entire area on foot in anything less than three days. "I'll call in a chopper at first light tomorrow morning," Steven said. "For now"—he pointed at the lower left corner of the circle on the map—"we keep searching here. Everybody's got flashlights. I've got a spotlight in my trunk, so when we find her, we can light up the area. We can at least keep the animals away until morning." He set his jaw. "If she's here, we need to find her."

"Before every wild animal in the forest does," Kent said.

Harry grimaced. "I—"

Steven's cell phone jangled and he pulled it from his pocket and checked the caller ID, motioning Harry toward the woods at the same time. "Check on those volunteers, Harry. I don't want them trampling anything important." He put the phone to his ear. "Hey, Helen. This really isn't a good time. Can I call you back later?"

"No, Steven," Helen said, her voice shaking. "This is important."

Dread had him standing straighter. "What? What's happened?"

"Brad's run away."

Steven sagged back against his car. "How do you know?"

"He left a note."

Like mother, like son. Another goddamned note. "Did he say where he was going?"

"No, no he didn't." Her voice wobbled and he knew she was crying. "Steven, I need you here."

He looked around and made a decision. Harry was ready for an increase in responsibility. And even if Harry wasn't, he'd have to become ready pretty damn quick. "I'll be home in half an hour."

Wednesday, October 5, 6:30 P.M.

Wednesday was meat loaf night at the Llewellyn house. Allison's meat loaf recipe had belonged to her mother. The dear, departed Mrs. Llewellyn must have been a god-awful cook too.

Jenna looked down at the generous helping of meat loaf topped with ketchup and felt her stomach roll. It looked a little too much like . . . dead possum roadkill. She swallowed hard and heard a snicker to her right.

Charlie nudged her. "Possum pie," she whispered with a grin.

Jenna swallowed again and frowned. "How do you know about that?"

"I heard about it from kids at school." She lifted a shoulder philosophically. "You know how gossip is. It was all the talk in the cafeteria." She grinned again, wider this time, the light from the chandelier glinting off her braces. "Especially since today the cafeteria ladies made goulash."

Jenna grimaced and pushed her plate away. "That's it. I'm done."

Allison frowned from across the table. "You haven't even started yet."

"I'm sorry, Allison. I just don't have a lot of appetite today." Jenna nudged Charlie less than gently when the little girl snickered again. "Shut up, Charlie," she gritted through clenched teeth.

Allison looked from Jenna to her daughter suspiciously, then set into her own meat loaf with fervor. "I suppose that's understandable, under the circumstances."

Jenna looked at Charlie who shook her head and shrugged. "What circumstances?"

"Well, Saturday, of course," said Allison impatiently, then true horror flooded her face when Jenna made no show of understanding. "You've forgotten about *Adam*? Jenna, how could you?"

Saturday. October eighth. The day of Adam's "passing." Jenna closed her eyes as guilt layered over all the other emotions churning in her gut. How could she, indeed? But somehow between the revulsion at the gift left swinging from her ceiling, frustration at all the antics of Rudy and his friends and Blackman's unwillingness to stop them, combined with a healthy shot of sexual frustration over Steven . . . she'd forgotten.

She heard the sound of Allison's fork clattering against her plate.

"I think it's just disgraceful," Allison said, anger tightening her voice.

"Allie," Seth started, but Allison cut him off.

"Disgraceful, Dad," Allison repeated with disgust. "Letting that man . . . that policeman she's only known a week—not even a week! Coming to her apartment, staying until midnight last night. She's let him make her forget about the man she was supposed to marry! I call that disgraceful."

Jenna's eyes flew open and immediately fixed on Seth's face. He looked very guilty.

"Mrs. Kasselbaum," Jenna said darkly. She could see the chain of events clearly now and it pissed her off. Temper flared and she was just too damn tired to clamp a lid on it.

"You know what a gossip she is," Seth said weakly.

"I know what a gossip *you* are," Jenna shot back, anger making her tongue loose, not caring when he flinched and hurt filled his eyes. She turned to Allison, fury making her body tremble. "And, Allison, even though it is absolutely none of your business, I made the man dinner last night."

Allison's lips thinned in disapproval. "At midnight?"

Jenna lurched to her feet, her palms narrowly missing her plate of meat loaf as she slapped them down on the table. "Yes, at midnight. As you so noted, he is a policeman. He got called to a case, so I made him dinner later so he wouldn't go hungry. Although if we'd screwed like weasels on Mrs. Kasselbaum's welcome mat it wouldn't have been any of your damn business."

Allison's mouth opened and closed like a fish out of water. Charlie's eyes widened. Garrett looked like he'd swallowed his fork.

"Jenna," Seth started and Jenna held up her hand to stop him.

"I'm not finished. You say you want me to get on with my life. But the first chance I get, I'm *disgraceful*," she sputtered, then pointed her finger at Seth. "I am *tired* of your gossip and meddling." She turned her finger to Allison. "I am *tired* of your bossiness." She felt a sob building in her chest and fruitlessly battled it. *"And I am tired of your damn Wednesday meat loaf.*" Leaving the table in stunned silence, she rushed out, managing to grab her purse as she barreled through the front door and down the steep driveway. She held off the tears until she got to Adam's car.

No, *not* Adam's car. Adam was dead. D-e-a-d, dead. Two years ago this Saturday. This was not Adam's car. *This is my car.* "My car," she gritted aloud. *My car. My life.* Her hands shook as she tried to put the key in the lock and the sob broke free. She leaned her forehead against the car and felt the waves of emotion crash in her head and the tears come. And come. And come.

My life. My totally out of control life.

A hand gently pulled the key from her fist and turned her body into his. Jenna felt Seth's arms wrap around her shoulders and his head pushing her cheek into his shoulder. And she cried.

Seth held her as she cried, rocking her, stroking her hair as her own father would have done. She cried over Adam, over the boys at school, over Steven. She even cried over the stupid meat loaf. And when her tears were spent, Seth held her a little longer, still stroking her hair.

"I understand you've had a rather taxing week, young lady," he said gently and she nodded, her cheek still pressed to his shoulder.

"My life sucks," she moaned and he chuckled. For some reason that made her feel better.

"You know, you've made me work pretty hard this week," he said and she pulled back to look at him. He pulled a cotton hankie from his pocket and she took it, mopping her wet face.

She sniffled. "What are you talking about?"

"Well, you told me about the tires and your ankle. But the rest I had to find out from Mrs. Kasselbaum and—" He closed his mouth. "And others," he added.

Her eyes narrowed. "What others?" she asked suspiciously.

His white brows lifted. "I don't disclose my sources," he said loftily, then he sobered. "Why didn't you tell us about the problems at school, Jenna?" he asked. "The vandalism to your classroom. The water in your gas tank. The possum. We're your family. Why didn't you tell us?"

Jenna dropped her eyes. "I didn't want to worry you."

"So instead you keep it all in until you explode all over Allison's meat loaf?" he asked, a smile in his voice, and her lips quivered.

"That was bad of me," she admitted. "You *are* a meddling gossip and Allison *is* bossy, but I shouldn't have let it come out like that. I'm sorry, Dad."

"Accepted." Then he grinned. "But I didn't hear an apology about the meat loaf."

"I couldn't pull that one off with a straight face," Jenna returned, her own grin wobbly.

"Come on back, Jenna. You have a family that's worried about you." He lifted her chin so that she looked up the driveway to where Allison, Garrett, and Charlie stood watching intently.

So she climbed the driveway to the people that cared about her. They were her family. Despite their eccentricities and terrible food.

"I'm sorry, Jenna," said Allison and Jenna felt tears well again. Allison had been crying, too.

"I'm sorry I called you bossy," Jenna said and hugged Allison tightly.

"What about the meat loaf?" Charlie asked and Jenna hiccuped a laugh.

"Shut up, Charlotte Anne," Jenna and Allison said in unison, then they both laughed and Jenna felt true peace for the first time in days.

And then, of course, the phone rang. Garrett answered it, his expression puzzled. "Yes, she's here." He cupped the phone. "Jenna, it's for you. It's a Father Leone and he says it's urgent."

The peace fizzled abruptly as she listened to Father Mike ask her to meet him at his parish.

Wednesday, October 5, 7:30 P.M.

"Where are we going?" Jenna asked after she'd strapped herself into Father Mike's car.

"Out past Shotwell Crossing," he answered, turning out of the rectory driveway. "We should just beat Steven and Brad there."

"So let me get this straight," Jenna said, holding up her hand. "Brad runs away." She ticked off one finger. "So Helen calls Steven who, thankfully, agrees to leave his job and come home." She ticked off another finger.

"So you've noticed Steven's propensity to work," Father Mike said, looking straight ahead.

"I've noticed Steven hides from his kids. I don't know why." Jenna studied Father Mike's profile. His perfect poker face. "And you're not going to tell me, are you? Even though you know."

"No."

Jenna sighed. "Okay, fine. So moving right along, Steven starts for home, but on his way Helen calls him back and tells him Brad's grandmother on his mother's side has called and Brad is there." She ticked off a third finger.

"Right so far."

"So Steven gets mad, surprise, surprise, and decides he'll go get Brad and teach him a lesson by, of all things, making him volunteer in the search for this missing teenager." She ticked off a fourth finger and frowned. "What is the man thinking?"

"That Brad needs to grow up and stop throwing childish tantrums," Father Mike responded.

"Hell of a way to grow up," Jenna said, then bit her tongue. "Sorry, Father. I just don't believe searching for a girl who's likely a corpse is the best way to effect maturity."

"And on that we agree," Father Mike said, maneuvering his car onto the highway.

"So wrapping things up"—she ticked off her thumb— "Helen gets upset and calls you. She tries to call me, thinking I have some magic wand I can wave to make Steven behave, and though I'm not home somehow she manages to figure out where I am. I still want to know how she tracked me down. And what possessed her to believe he'll listen to a blessed thing I have to say."

"He, Steven, or he, Brad?"

"Either. Both."

Father Mike glanced over. "Did you learn more than counting when you got your Ph.D.?"

Jenna smiled. "They taught me lots of stuff, but frankly, none of it of any great use lately."

"Your parents must be proud."

Jenna raised a brow. "If that's your way of inquiring into my past, you don't have to be so clever. I'll tell you what you want to know if you tell me how Helen tracked me down."

Father Mike grinned. "Fair enough. Where did you grow up?"

"Maryland suburbs outside D.C. Lower middle class. My dad worked for the government."

"Doing what?"

"Don't know."

Father Mike looked over in surprise. "What do you mean, you don't know?"

"I mean I don't know. Dad worked for the Department of Defense. He took an oath of silence or something. I know what building he worked in, but that was all."

"That must have made for an interesting childhood."

Jenna pursed her lips. "You could say that."

"So what about your mother?"

Jenna carefully considered her response. The man was a priest after all. "She didn't take an oath of silence," she finally answered.

"Hmm, I see," Father Mike said. "A tad dominant? Demanding?"

"A tad," Jenna said dryly.

"Made you an overachiever?"

Jenna didn't have to think back. She could hear her mother's voice in her mind as clearly as Father Mike's. Demanding straight *A*'s, saying her classes were too easy when she brought home perfect report cards. Critical. Always critical. "I was the valedictorian in high school, graduated top two percent from Duke, magna cum laude from Maryland, and with honors from UNC."

"And your mama never said she was proud of you."

Jenna was annoyed to feel a lump in her throat. She didn't like to think about her mother, much less feel wistful that she'd never gained her mother's approval. "No."

"And you were your daddy's girl?"

"Down to my Mary Janes."

"Which you could see your face in."

Jenna smiled ruefully. "If she weren't dearly deceased, I'd swear you'd met my mother."

"I've met enough mothers like her. And fathers too. Any brothers or sisters?"

"None that I know of," Jenna replied cheerfully. "Just little old me."

"Little old you that goes on to get a bunch of degrees, then goes to work teaching high school kids." He looked thoughtful. "I have to admit I haven't figured that one out yet."

Jenna shrugged. "No secret. I met a man in the doctoral program at UNC. Fell in love, got engaged. The two of us went to work doing pharmaceutical research. Then he got sick and died. I'd taken leave to care for him, but afterward, I didn't want to go back to research. It reminded me too much of him. My best friend is an English teacher at Roosevelt High and knew they needed another science teacher. Presto, chango, and voilà! I am now a science teacher."

"Who flunks quarterbacks."

Jenna's lips thinned. "Yep, that's me."

"And reaches out to bright kids that flunk chemistry."

Jenna softened. "Yep, that's me, too."

"Well, I'd say that was the reason Helen thought Brad would listen to you. I think you know why she thought Steven would listen to you."

Jenna thought of Steven's face as he walked away the night before, so angry. And only God knew why. Her eyes narrowed. Or maybe Steven's priest. "Shows how much you know," she muttered. "Exactly how much do you know?"

"Nothing," Father Mike replied. But she saw his jaw tighten.

"That's what I thought," Jenna said, then shrugged. "So how did Helen track me down?"

"You'd be much easier to find if you had a cell phone," Father Mike replied.

"No welching, Father. I kept my end of the bargain. How did she track me down?"

"Ready to count on your fingers again?" he asked with a grin. "Okay. Matt's best friend on his soccer team has a big brother at Roosevelt who has . . . noticed you. From afar of course."

Jenna felt her cheeks heat. She was aware of the stares of the adolescent boys, which was one of the reasons she always wore business suits—to be as unsexy as possible. That didn't extend to her underwear, though, which was the only place she could be truly feminine. Which nobody knew about. Except Steven. She cleared her throat. "Of course."

"Matt's friend's big brother told Helen your best friend was Miss Ryan, the English teacher."

"But Casey's unlisted."

"This is true. But enter Steven's trusty assistant Nancy, add one simple search of the Bureau of Motor Vehicles, and presto, chango, voilà! Miss Ryan tells us you routinely have Wednesday meat loaf with your former fiancé's family, who, incidentally, she finds 'totally weird.'" He punctuated the air. "Her words, not mine."

"It's a fair cop," Jenna said. "Except I didn't have meat loaf tonight."

"What did you have?"

"Nothing." To her surprise her stomach growled. "And I'm starving."

"Well, we're coming up to our exit and they have one of every fast-food joint there is. What's your pleasure, Dr. Marshall?"

The answer was simple. "Anything that doesn't look like possum roadkill."

Father Mike choked on a laugh. "I don't want to know. Truly do not want to know. You do realize that you've just eliminated nine out of ten of the fast-food places on the pike."

Jenna looked at the upcoming throng of neon arches and crowns. "At this point I'd be satisfied with loaves and fishes."

Father Mike grinned. "I like you, Jenna. I have no idea what you see in Steven, but I know what he sees in you.

There's a fish place about a mile from here that looks like a dump but has good fish and buttermilk biscuits to go."

"Then lead the way, good Father. My treat."

Wednesday, October 5, 8:00 P.M.

If looks could kill, they'd both be dead, Steven thought grimly, pulling the Volvo alongside Harry's Toyota. Brad sat sullenly staring ahead.

"Unbuckle and get out," Steven said, jerking at his own seat belt.

"Or what?" Brad asked, his voice sharp as a knife. "Or you'll lock me up?"

Steven twisted in his seat to study Brad's profile. The profile of a total stranger. "Do I have to? Do I have to lock you up to keep you from running away again?"

Brad turned to look at him, defiance in his eyes. "I'll be eighteen in four months."

Steven clenched his teeth. "I know when your birthday is, Brad."

Brad looked away. "Yeah, I guess you do," he muttered.

"What's that supposed to mean?" Steven asked sharply.

Once again his son met his eyes and this time Steven saw contempt mixed with the defiance. "Just that you should know my birthday. It's nine months to the day of your senior prom."

Steven felt the blood drain from his face. "Your mother and I never made any secret of the . . . circumstances of your . . . conception. You were free to figure it out from the day you learned how to add and subtract."

Brad's smile twisted. "The circumstances of my conception. I like that. Very good, Dad." He looked out the window. "You are such a damn hypocrite."

"Don't take that tone with me, Brad." Steven drew a breath and counted to ten. In Latin. Backward. "I don't know what your problem has been this last month or who the hell you think you are, but I have news for you, son. I am your father. And I will continue to be your father in the four months until you reach the sacred age of eighteen. And I demand respect for no other reason than *I am your father.*"

"Yeah, you brought me into this world, you can take me out," Brad said bitterly.

"I have never, *never* said that to you," Steven gritted. "In your seventeen years I have never, *never* laid a hand on you. Although at this moment, the idea holds considerable appeal." He reached over Brad, pulled the door handle, and pushed the door open, letting in the cool night air. "Now get your defiant *ass* out of this car or I may give in to my desire to whip the shit out of you."

"Why, so I can participate in the family business?" Brad asked with a sneer and Steven saw red.

"No, son. I don't need your help. I don't even want your help. What I do want is for you to take a look over there." Steven pointed at twenty bobbing lights in the distance. "Do you know what those volunteers are doing?"

"Looking for a body."

"Dammit, Brad, *no.* They are not looking for just a *body.* They are looking for a human *person.* They are giving of themselves. And that's something I haven't seen you do in weeks. Do you know who they're looking for? Do you even *care*?"

Brad's defiance faltered and Steven watched his son swallow hard. "A sixteen-year-old girl."

"Yes. A girl whose parents loved her. Who for some reason nobody may ever know left the safety of her bed in the middle of the night to find something. Excitement maybe. Who knows? Instead, we're looking for her with cadaver dogs, Brad. Do you know what that means?"

Brad swallowed again. "That she's probably dead."

Steven nodded, his heart in his throat. "So you get the Kewpie doll. I am sick and tired of watching you mope around. I am sick and tired of you not bathing or shaving or studying, but most of all I'm sick and tired of what you've done to our family."

Brad's jaw clenched. "What *I've* done to our family?" he asked softly, then laughed and the sound sent chills down Steven's spine. "You have one hell of a lot of nerve, Dad." He got out of the car. "I'll help those men search, because I want to. Not because I give a damn about you."

Clutching at the steering wheel, Steven watched his oldest son walk away, tall and slender. In every physical way totally the same as he'd been two months ago. In every other way, a total stranger. Brad reported to Sheriff Rogers who, after glancing over at Steven for an okay, handed him a flashlight and walkie-talkie and pointed him to the woods.

Steven closed his eyes and shuddered out a breath. Then breathed in again and knew he was hallucinating. Her perfume. As real as if she was sitting next to him.

"Steven."

His eyes flew open. She was sitting next to him. Dressed in a conservative suit with her hair down around her shoulders. Instantly he remembered the last time he'd seen her, not twenty-four hours before. The heat, the greed that hadn't yet subsided. It had been embers all day, embers that now fanned into a full-fledged flame. His body responded. Of course. His hands clenched the steering wheel harder to keep from grabbing her where she sat.

"What are you doing here?" he asked slowly, carefully.

She blinked those violet eyes, moistened her full red lips,

tucked a stray lock of black hair behind her ear. "To be honest, I'm not really sure. But your aunt and your priest believe I have some influence over your logic, which at the moment seems very flawed."

His aunt. He should have known.

His priest. Who Sandra was investigating at this very moment for possible murder.

God, his life really, truly sucked.

He shifted, stretching out his arm along the top of the steering wheel so he could see her face. "I have no idea what you're talking about," he said, the smoothness of his voice at odds with the temper he felt simmering inside, "but I have every confidence you will fill me in."

Jenna sighed. "Steven, when did you see your first dead body. On the job, that is?"

It was his turn to blink. It was not the question he'd expected. "My second day. It was a suicide. Guy ate his gun."

She winced. "And you still can see the picture in your mind," she said softly.

He could, as clearly as if it were before him at that moment. He could see it and smell it and taste it. Death. The terrible sight, stench, taste of death. He'd woken in a cold sweat for weeks.

"How you discipline your son is nobody's business but your own," she said and gingerly laid her fingertips on his arm. His muscles clenched and quivered at her touch. "But what would happen if Brad actually stumbles on that young girl's body? The first girl was stabbed, wasn't she?"

Steven nodded, the idiocy of his actions closing in. "Viciously."

Jenna swallowed hard. "Do you expect to find this girl stabbed as well?"

"Yes."

"Then is that an image you want in your son's mind for the rest of his life?"

Steven looked away. Dammit, she was right. He'd been totally wrong. He hated to be wrong.

"I'll go now," she murmured. "Should I take Brad with me?"

He jerked a nod and watched as she gracefully slipped from the seat and nodded to Mike, who'd been standing in the shadows. She hesitated, then leaned into the opening of the door. The dome lamp threw her face into shadow, but even in the muted light he could see the concern in her eyes.

"I'm sorry, Steven."

Once he'd welcomed her concern, but tonight it was a bitter pill.

"Just go," he said, his voice raspy. "Please, just leave me alone."

When she was gone, when she'd climbed into the car with Mike and Brad, he pulled himself out of the Volvo and approached Harry who'd been silently watching the entire exchange. "Well," Steven asked, silently daring Harry to say anything remotely funny or personal, "where are we?"

Harry looked subdued. "Same place as before. Nothing. We did chase away a reporter."

Steven's hackles went up. "Big guy? Dark hair, late thirties, denim jacket, teal Dodge Neon?"

Harry's eyes widened. "That's him."

"I don't suppose you got his license number."

"Actually, I did." Harry rattled it off. "I'll have Nancy run a check. Who is he?"

"I don't know," Steven said. "But I have a feeling that sooner or later I'm going to find out."

EIGHTEEN

Thursday, October 6, 1:30 A.M.

IT WAS GETTING COLD. HE HATED THAT ABOUT winters here. Too
damn cold. He jacked up the heat in his car. His clock said it
was one-thirty. She should be here any minute. Little miss
rah-rah.

Her name was Alev Rahrooh. She was Indian, from India.
He normally liked white girls, but he'd been attracted by all
that long, dark hair. It would look good in his collection. Besides, she was the only one available tonight. Available and
willing to sneak out of her house and meet him.

Here. He looked across the street at the golden arches
gleaming in the night. Thatcher hadn't found anything behind
the McDonald's, just like he'd known. He'd been careful.
He'd been smart.

So here he sat not a hundred feet from where he'd nabbed
pretty Samantha. If Thatcher ever figured it out he'd be kicking himself. Right under his fucking nose.

His pulse jumped at the shadow approaching. Oh, goodie.
Here she came. Alev walked. No bike. That was good. Meant
he didn't have to dispose of the bike afterward. He smoothed
back his hair and pulled his collar up around his face, then
leaned over and opened the door.

"Hi," he said. "Hop on in."

She slid in and pulled the door shut behind her. "I can't
stay long," she said. Shyly. How cute. "My mom and dad
can't know I'm gone."

They might have a cow, he thought, then laughed inside
his head at his own joke. Hindus. Cow. Good one. Outwardly,

though, he was silent. Waiting, saying nothing, just waiting for the moment she'd figure it out. That was one of the best parts. When they figured it out. And then, of course, it was way too late.

Alev was a lot slower on the draw than Sammie had been. Finally she peered closer into the darkness on his side of the car. "What—?"

Bingo! Her eyes grew wide and he could easily see the whites of her eyes against the darkness of her skin. "No! You're not—" He had to hand it to her. She tried to struggle. Actually tried to scratch his face with her fingernails, but pretty little Alev was no match for his strength. He grabbed her wrists in one hand and with the other covered her nose and mouth with the surgical mask he'd prepared with such care.

She continued to struggle, her head pitching back and forth, trying to escape the mask. He simply pressed harder against her face, patiently waiting until she drew a desperate breath.

Ten, nine, eight, seven, six . . .

Then she crumpled, gasping. Then she was still.

He pulled the surgical mask away and carefully folded it to keep the powder she hadn't inhaled from going all over his car seat. Wouldn't want to make a mess, after all.

He drove away. The night was still very, very young. He patted Alev's cheek. So was she.

Thursday, October 6, 5:45 A.M.

Sheriff Rogers put a large brown bag and a thermos on the hood of Steven's car. "My wife made nut bread," he said. "And coffee. Help yourself."

Steven looked at the burly man with as much of a smile as

he could muster on the fifteen minutes' sleep he'd had the night before. "Thanks, Sheriff," he said. "It smells great."

Rogers settled himself against the car and looked toward the horizon where the sun would start peeking up sometime in the next fifteen minutes. "Your boy get home all right last night?"

Steven felt his face heat and busied himself by pouring coffee into one of the foam cups provided by the thoughtful Mrs. Rogers. "Yeah. Thanks."

"I got a kid that age," Rogers said, still studying the horizon intently. "Pain in the ass."

"I know the feeling," Steven returned dryly.

"Wife keeps tellin' me he'll come around." Rogers's tone said he was clearly unconvinced.

"Women are optimistic souls," Steven said.

Rogers glanced over at him with a grimace. "Good thing they make good nut bread."

Steven's mouth quirked up. "How long have the two of you been married?"

"Twenty-five years next summer. And yourself?"

Steven took a large gulp of coffee, wincing as it scalded his throat. "I'm not married."

Rogers's brows went up in surprise. "Then who—" He looked away. "Sorry, not my business."

It really wasn't, but for some reason Steven didn't seem to mind. "It's okay. Truth is, I'm really not sure myself."

Rogers looked as if he were digesting this information along with his nut bread. "She seemed like a nice woman."

Steven took another gulp of coffee, this time knowing full well how much it would burn on its way down. Maybe it was a form of self-punishment, Mike's hair shirt and flogging strap, as it were. "Yes, she is. She really is."

Rogers chewed his nut bread contemplatively. "Nice

women who look that good in Wall Street business suits don't come along every day."

Sheriff Rogers appeared to be a master of understatement. "No, I don't suppose they do."

Rogers pushed himself away from the car, brushing the crumbs off his broad barrel chest. "My boys should be gettin' here any minute, now. I'll get the radios ready."

"Thanks, Sheriff," Steven murmured, looking up at the still-dark sky where the chopper would appear to take aerial photos as soon as day broke so that they could get on with their search for Samantha Eggleston. Trying to wipe from his mind the picture of Jenna's concerned face, her Wall Street business suit, and the sound of her voice whispering, "Have courage." Knowing he'd ultimately be unsuccessful. Jenna Marshall was in his mind to stay.

And his heart? She'd insinuated herself there, too. Down deep he knew it was true. What other woman would care enough to intercede on his behalf with Brad after being treated so callously? He'd left her Tuesday night without a word. And still she cared. Steven blew out a sigh.

So did he.

Thursday, October 6, 6:15 A.M.

Neil readjusted his body to fit inside the tiny Dodge Neon.

What had he been thinking, renting a soup can this small? He'd been trying to stretch his budget, that's what he'd been thinking. His salary had been sufficient when pooled with Tracey's. But without Tracey's salary and with the alimony . . . He shook his head and blindly reached for the cup of coffee that was growing cold in the cup holder. That alimony was a real kicker.

But, just like every time he thought of his ex-wife, he couldn't seem to dredge up any emotion other than regret. No malice, no hatred. She was a nice woman who just couldn't seem to deal with the fact her husband was a jerk obsessed with a mistake that had cost four young girls and their families justice. She couldn't deal with his sleeplessness, the dreams when he did manage to sleep. She couldn't deal with the fact that the man she'd married was changing before her very eyes.

So she left. It was really very simple. He couldn't say he blamed her. He couldn't say he even really missed her and he supposed that's why he felt no hatred or rage. Just regret.

Barrow never understood that. A loyal friend, Barrow usually had a few choice things to say about Tracey's lack of loyalty, but Neil could never find it in himself to agree. Then Barrow would make that harrumping noise of his and say, "Well, at least you two didn't have any kids."

Neil would always say, "Yeah, you're right." And he believed that. He'd make a lousy father with the hours and the "Parker obsession" as Tracey called it. So it was good he didn't have kids. He'd never really regretted that part. Not really.

Well, maybe sometimes. He would have enjoyed watching his kid play baseball. Or soccer. His mind went back to Monday night, to the look on Thatcher's face when his son made that goal. Thatcher was a good dad. Made his kids' soccer games. Cheered from the sidelines.

But it distracted Thatcher from his job. Neil thought about last night, when from his hiding spot in the trees he'd watched Thatcher leave the search area to get his kid, watched him hand the kid over to the woman with the long black hair. A different kid. Another distraction. He thought about the articles he'd read about the abduction of Thatcher's little boy and wondered if Thatcher worried it would happen again. Neil knew he couldn't live that way, always worrying if his kids were at risk. That would be the biggest distraction of all. So it was good he and Tracey hadn't had any kids. Thatcher would probably be a better cop if he didn't have any either.

A light came on in the Parkers' upstairs window. That would be Mrs. Parker's bedroom. Running true to style, she had her own room, just like she'd had in Seattle. He wondered if Mr. Parker was also running true to style. Back in Seattle, Parker kept a mistress in a posh apartment around the corner from his downtown office building. Convenient for the sonofabitch.

Another light came on, then another as the household roused itself for the day.

Neil shifted in the tiny little seat and prepared to wait. He'd wait until William emerged, then follow him again. Sooner or later William would choose his next victim. He'd have to leave his house to meet her. And Neil would be ready.

At that point, he'd call Thatcher and give him the damn road map showing him where to find his killer. There'd be an arrest and news media and fanfare. Thatcher might even get a promotion.

Neil smiled without feeling an ounce of mirth. Who knew? Maybe that's how he got the last one. Maybe they'd promote Thatcher to a desk job where he could go home to his kids and the woman with the long black hair every night at five.

And leave the real investigating to the guys who weren't so distracted.

Neil sipped at the coffee, now stone-cold. Although, he thought, watching the Parkers' downstairs lights come on one at a time, he wouldn't mind the distraction of Thatcher's woman. He frowned. With his binoculars he'd seen her face. She had a classic beauty, haunting somehow. For a moment he'd been simply mesmerized. And when he'd closed his eyes that night in the privacy of his hotel room, it was her face he'd seen. It had been a relief, a comfort, for it was the first time in a very long time he'd dreamed of someone other than the teenaged girls William Parker had robbed of life. Instead he'd dreamed of her, of Thatcher's woman. He could still see her face in his mind, even now as he sat, fully awake and waiting for Parker.

Neil sat up abruptly when the front door opened, then slumped back when Mrs. Parker appeared in a worn robe to grab the newspaper from the front porch. If today was like all the other days, William would be coming out any minute for his morning run.

Neil put the coffee cup aside. He could use a run himself. Sitting in this soup can was giving him a cramp in his ass. He—

He jumped at the bright light shining in his face, followed by a knock on the car window.

"Sir, please step out of the car. Keep your hands where we can see them."

And he knew even before he turned around that this was not the way to start the day.

"Shit," he muttered.

Thursday, October 6, 7:45 A.M.

Jenna paused, her hand trembling on her classroom door. "I'm afraid to look," she said.

"I'll look," said Lucas and pushed open the door. "No piñatas, at least," he said and Jenna peeked around him.

"No new graffiti," Jenna added.

"Check your desk," Casey cautioned, coming up from behind. "Maybe they booby-trapped the drawer or something."

But a thorough check showed no new activity through the night.

Breathing a sigh of relief, Jenna motioned to the students who'd been gathering at the door. "Come on in, guys. Let's learn some chemistry."

They filed in, each looking like they expected a nasty surprise to catch them unaware.

The muted sounds of scraping chairs and settling bodies was interrupted by Kelly Templeton. "Dr. Marshall, can we talk about the extra credit points on this quiz from Tuesday?"

Jenna rolled her eyes at the look of suppressed humor in the girl's eyes. At least it wasn't extortion this time. "Yes, Kelly, we can. Bring your paper on up and we'll take a look."

She watched her students' faces as Lucas and Casey took their leave. Most of the kids still wore the look of tentative caution, except for Kelly who smirked.

And Josh Lutz who looked very troubled. Troubled and torn. On one hand he looked to be on the verge of spilling his guts, but on the other, he looked ready to run at his first opportunity.

Jenna kept an eye on Josh, intending to talk to him when class was over, but when the bell rang he slipped away. She wondered what he knew. She wondered what he'd tell. She wondered, not for the first time, what went on behind the closed doors of the Lutz household.

Thursday, October 6, 9:45 A.M.

Steven glared at Assistant DA Liz Johnson as he walked into the reception area of Raleigh's first district. "This better be important." He'd come as soon as she'd called, once again leaving Harry point man at the search scene.

"What, were you actually doing the speed limit?" Liz asked sourly.

Steven grinned at her. "I can't afford any tickets on a cop's salary."

Liz grinned back like the old friend she was. "Like I can afford any on mine?" She sobered. "We're going to Interview Two," she said. "Lieutenant Chambers called me as soon as they brought the guy in. It seems he had some fascinating reading material Chambers thought we should see."

"Has he said anything yet?" Steven asked, falling into step beside her.

Liz shook her head. "Nope. He insists on talking to you. Who is this guy?"

"He's been hanging around," Steven answered. "I saw him at my son's soccer game Monday night and Harry said he was at the search scene last night. Looking for me. Told Harry he was a reporter. Harry was going to ask Nancy to run plates on him this morning."

They came to a stop in front of Interview Two where Lieutenant Chambers stood frowning at the glass. On the other side sat the dark-haired man from Matt's game, arms crossed over his chest. Chambers acknowledged them with a curt nod, handing Liz a thin folder.

"One of my patrol units picked him up this morning. A resident on Hook Street called with a complaint that this guy had been loitering there for a few days."

Liz took a thoughtful look at the stranger. "So they shine their light inside his car and find his photo collection in plain view." She handed the folder to Steven. "Four mutilated corpses."

Steven glanced through the photos. "Before and after," he murmured, looking at the pictures of the girls before they'd become mutilated corpses. "Pretty girls." He turned the pictures over to look at the names neatly printed on the back of each one. "Did you run these names?" he asked.

Chambers nodded. "All murdered in Seattle three years ago. All sixteen years old. All cheerleaders."

Steven sighed. "Damn. And his hair's just about the same shade as the hair we found in the clearing last Friday."

"So's mine," Liz said, her tone pointed. "That doesn't prove anything."

So's Mike's, Steven thought, then cursed himself. But that didn't prove anything either. There was absolutely no way Mike was involved. Mike had seen his son home without incident. Steven felt the prick of guilt. He knew because he'd called Helen to make sure Brad was all right. Mike had ensured Jenna got home safe and sound. The prick of guilt jabbed deeper. Steven knew that because he'd called Jenna's home number last night well after midnight, just to hear her answer sleepily. Just to know she'd gotten home all right. *Hell of a friend you are, Thatcher.*

He cleared his throat. "Lieutenant, did you get a rundown on the Seattle case? Was anyone arrested for those murders?"

"I've got a call in to the commander of the precinct that handled the case, but it's still early in Seattle. We checked the Internet archives of the local Seattle papers in the meantime. They say they arrested a William Parker, but there was no record of a conviction. We didn't touch this guy except to escort him in for questioning. We did see a rental car agreement out in plain view, so we looked at that. According to the rental contract he's Neil Davies of Seattle, Washington."

"When did he sign the contract?" Liz asked.

"Monday morning."

"Of this week?" Steven asked.

"Yep. So he wasn't here when either girl was abducted. Or he hadn't rented his car by that point," Chambers amended.

Steven looked at the man sitting in the chair inside the interview room. His face was hard, as if he were angry. But more than angry. More like he was poised to explode any minute. "Was he carrying any other ID, Lieutenant?"

"No. Said his wallet was in the gym bag in the backseat."

"And was it?" Liz asked.

"Haven't looked yet. We wanted to wait for you to make sure we didn't break any new search and seizure laws we hadn't heard about yet," Chambers grumbled and Liz scowled.

Steven smiled at Chambers's sarcasm. "Did you find anything else in his car?" he asked.

"Just the gym bag," Chambers answered. "We wanted to wait for Liz before we checked the trunk. My boys didn't want any trouble down the line."

"Well, we'll take a look after we've chatted with Mr. Davies," Steven said, then gestured to Liz. "Shall we?"

The man looked up when Steven and Liz entered the room, but made no move to rise.

Steven looked at him, tilting his head in an exaggerated fashion. "You were looking for me?"

The man's dark eyes narrowed. "I was looking for the detective in charge, yes."

Steven refused to be ruffled by the challenge in the man's voice. "Then you were looking for me. I'm Special Agent Steven Thatcher."

"Umm," the man said sarcastically. "North Carolina State Bureau of Investigation. Glad to see you could take a break from soccer games and the runaway roundup to take an interest in this case."

"I try to squeeze in an hour or two between golf and fishing," Steven said dryly, pushing back his temper. He pointed to Liz. "She's Assistant DA Johnson. So now that we've performed the social niceties and you know who we are, why don't you tell us who you are?"

"You have my ID."

"We have your rental car contract and your photo album." Steven dropped the folder on the table. The pictures slid out, the "after" pictures on top. Davies didn't flinch. Not one little bit.

Cold bastard, Steven thought. It was hard not to flinch at those pictures. "Your rental car contract says you're Neil Davies. From Seattle. As"—he pointed a careless finger at the pictures—"were these girls, surprisingly enough. So how long have you been in Raleigh, Mr. Davies?"

"It's pronounced Davis. Welsh name. Silent *e*. Since Monday morning."

"So says your rental car contact."

"So says my flight itinerary."

Steven pulled a chair from the table and sat down. "What line of work are you in, Mr. Davies?"

Davies sneered. "Are you truly as big an idiot as you appear to be?"

Steven blinked. Whatever this man's problem, he'd made it very personal. "I don't know who peed in your Wheaties today, but I don't think I like you, sir."

Davies bared his teeth in a parody of a smile. "Feeling's mutual. Did you run my ID?"

Steven shrugged. "I don't know. I just got here. Had to cut my doubles game short." He stood up and walked over to the window and tapped on it. "Let's take a look at the bag, Lieutenant."

Chambers brought it in and dropped it on the table with a thud that echoed off the cheaply painted walls. "There you go."

Steven pulled on a pair of plastic gloves before unzipping the bag and reaching in. "One pair of socks. One pair of running shoes." His brows went up. "One gun."

"Registered," Davies snapped. "If your computers are modern enough to check."

"They are," Steven said softly. He really, really didn't like this guy. "And one wallet." He opened the wallet with Liz looking over his shoulder. "Neil Davies. Good driver's license picture." He looked up at Liz. "Mine has me looking like a biker dude or a serial killer."

Liz smiled.

Davies rolled his eyes. "There's another wallet in there."

"Okay," Steven said, game. In went his hand and out came another wallet, and . . . he blinked.

"Terrific," Liz muttered.

"I'll be damned," Chambers said.

Slowly Steven opened up the wallet to reveal Davies's shiny detective shield. Seattle Police Department. Annoyance bubbled up and he didn't bother to push it back, especially when he saw the smirk on Davies's face. "And you'd planned to mention this when?" Steven asked, tossing Davies's shield to the table.

"When you asked," Davies said smoothly. "I tried to talk to you Monday night, but you were too busy cheering the home team."

Steven sat down again and stretched his legs out in front of him, feeling his cheeks heat and his temper boil. He bit back the words he really wanted to say. "Well, I can't help but notice you're a little out of your jurisdiction, what is it—Detective?" Davies nodded and Steven nodded back. "We also couldn't help but notice you carry pictures of other people's children in a folder, but you don't carry the normal complement of smiling children's portraits in your wallet."

"I don't have any children," Davies said, just as smoothly, but Steven detected resentment.

"Well, that's a shame. I happen to love mine. Because of soccer games and despite runaway roundups. Now, let's talk about these photos and the purpose for your visit to our fair town. I take it you suspect there's a link between your cheerleaders and ours."

Davies inclined his head, not quite a nod. "I do."

"So who was William Parker?"

Davies smirked. "So you do have a computer."

"We do."

Davies uncrossed his arms for the first time since Steven and Liz had arrived. He leaned forward and pushed the photos apart with one finger, lining up all the "after" pictures edge to edge. "William Parker did this."

"Then why isn't he in a Washington state prison?" Liz asked and Steven saw the first real emotion other than anger or sarcasm pass across Davies's face. It was pain.

"Because the SPD fucked up," Davies said, looking at the pictures as if imprinting them on his memory, although Steven suspected they already were. "Evidence wasn't handled correctly and the defense attorney petitioned it thrown out." He shrugged listlessly. "A judge agreed."

"You were primary?" Steven asked quietly, all posturing gone from the question.

Davies flicked a glance his way before returning to the pictures. "Yes, I was."

"And you want justice this time," Liz finished.

"Yes, I do."

Steven picked up one of the pictures by its corner, respectfully. "I have one of these. By noon I'll probably have two. The psychologist on my team believes he'll be on number three before the end of the week."

"He's escalated," Neil murmured.

"So how do I keep my bulletin board from being covered with pictures like these?" Steven asked. "You wouldn't have come across the country if you hadn't believed William Parker was here. Where is he?"

Davies took the picture from Steven's hands, just as respectfully. "Under your noses."

"I don't know any William Parkers." He looked at Chambers. "I assumed you ran a list."

Chambers nodded. "I did. We have ten William Parkers in the Raleigh-Durham area. Knowing a little more about him would be a big help," he added wryly.

Davies huffed a mirthless chuckle. "You know him, all right, but not as William Rudolf Parker." He reached into the pocket of the shirt he wore beneath his sweater and drew out another picture, this one a snapshot. "Here he is." He tossed the snapshot on the table where it landed on top of the photographs of the four mutilated corpses.

Steven's heart stopped as the face in the snapshot registered.

"Holy Mother of God," Chambers breathed. "Kid in a freaking candy store."

"Who is he?" Liz asked with a frown.

"You know him," Davies said to Steven. "Don't you?"

Steven's heart kicked back into motion. Into overdrive. He picked up the picture, his hand trembling. The face in the snapshot was younger, but he recognized the dark eyes, the surly mouth that even then wore a smug smile. He looked up at Davies and swallowed. "Yes, I do. And you're right, I don't know him as William Parker." He looked up at Liz. "This is Rudy Lutz. He's the quarterback at my son's high school." And the one directing all the malice against Jenna, he added to himself, a shiver of fear racing down his spine.

Liz sat down hard. "Shit," she said.

Thursday, October 6, 11:00 A.M.

After an hour they were able to pretty much piece together the checkered history of Rudy Lutz, a.k.a. William Rudolf Parker. The evidence the SPD had gathered had been strong. Davies swore no mistakes had been made. But something went wrong just the same.

"So his first victim was his girlfriend," Liz said thoughtfully.

"So much for puppy love," said Chambers, looking at the photo with distaste. The girl had been strangled, sexually assaulted, then stabbed. Repeatedly. "What a sick bastard. And he was only fifteen at the time?"

"He went for older women," Davies said dryly. "And apparently they went for him. Every girl he murdered met him away from her house so there was never any evidence of forced entry."

Liz pushed the folder away. "How'd you catch him, Neil?"

Davies's cheeks darkened under the black stubble of his beard. "After we found the last victim, a kid called in and said he'd heard Parker in the locker room the week before boasting that he'd fucked her."

"Gina Capetti," Liz said quietly.

Davies's lip curled and again Steven saw pain in the man's eyes. "We had forensic evidence from Laura Resnick, his first victim. Semen sample. We brought Parker in, he had an alibi, but it wasn't airtight. We found witnesses who'd seen him with Gina Capetti and were willing to testify. Judge ordered him to give a blood sample. DNA matched the semen found in Laura Resnick's body. We arrested him, but because he was fifteen, they let him be tried in family court."

Steven frowned. "Four vicious premeditated murders and he goes to family court?"

Davies shrugged. "He had a very . . . lenient judge."

"So you go to family court, what happens?" Lieutenant Chambers asked.

"Everything's set up, then the defense moves to have the semen evidence stricken."

"Because?" Liz prompted.

Davies's lips thinned. "Because they said the evidence had been stored inappropriately."

Nobody asked how or by whom. It didn't really matter at this stage.

"And without the semen evidence you had no case," Liz finished.

"We couldn't tie him to Laura Resnick, the first victim, so the whole case crumbled like a house of cards. Parker walks away, free as a bird. His whole record is sealed. But the community knew what he'd done. His parents had tried to keep his name out of the press, but it just wasn't going to happen. Crowds gathered, some threw bottles, most just picketed. Parker Senior's import business suffered. Nobody wanted to do business with the father of a monster like William. Senior had to declare Chapter Eleven, sell the house. They moved away, then just disappeared."

"It's hard for a whole family to just disappear," Liz observed.

"Mrs. Parker's father is a multimillionaire."

They all nodded, well aware of the power of cold, hard American cash.

"Lutz is the maiden name of Mrs. Parker's paternal grandmother." Davies looked frustrated. "I thought for a while they might have left the country. Gone to Switzerland or France."

"Not if they wanted their son to play football," Steven returned and Davies nodded.

"As I recall, that's what Parker Senior was maddest about," Davies mused. "He didn't care that four girls were dead. That every bit of evidence pointed to his son. He cared that William wouldn't get to play high school football and get picked up by the college scouts."

Steven sighed. "So his parents take him out of Seattle, then pop up as new residents to Raleigh-Durham, erase a year from Rudy's age, and have *'fourteen'*-year-old Rudy start high school all over again with a whole new set of girls to choose from," he said, punctuating the word in the air.

Lieutenant Chambers huffed his disapproval. "Like I said, kid in a freakin' candy store."

Liz rubbed her forehead. "You all do realize that none of this is proof Rudy had anything to do with Lorraine or Samantha."

"Not yet," Steven said grimly. "But now we have some place to look."

At that moment a uniformed officer came in with a note. "Agent Thatcher? Your admin assistant has been trying to get in touch with you all morning. She says it's urgent."

Steven looked at his cell phone, frowning. It was on, but the signal bars were down to one.

"You won't get any reception this deep in the building," Chambers said. "Pain in the ass."

Steven pointed to a phone in the corner of the room. "But that one works."

"If I remembered to pay the bill," Chambers said sarcastically.

Steven placed the call, listened to Nancy, then turned to the group with a sense of grim despair. "They found Samantha."

"In better shape than Lorraine?" Liz asked.

No one even assumed she'd still be alive. Correctly so.

"Marginally." Steven rubbed the back of his neck. "But that was the good news."

No one said anything, every one of the faces saying they knew what was coming.

"The bad news is that now we have a victim number three."

"Oh, God," Liz murmured.

"Who?" Chambers demanded.

Davies looked grim.

"Her name is Alev Rahrooh," Steven said. "Sixteen. Cheerleader. Went to yet a different high school. No sign of forced entry. Davies, I'll want to confirm your story with your LT in Seattle. Procedure of course."

Davies raised a brow. "Of course."

"Then we'll need to choose which site to see first. Door number two or door number three."

NINETEEN

Thursday, October 6, 4:15 P.M.

CASEY STOWED HER OVERNIGHT BAG IN THE XK 150's tiny trunk and slammed it closed. "I feel nervous about leaving you right now. I can cancel my trip if you want me to stay."

Jenna dangled her car keys from one finger. "I'll be fine. Tell her, Lucas. I'll be fine."

"She'll be fine," Lucas echoed obediently and Casey stuck her tongue out at him.

"Polly Parrott will say what you tell him. I say I have a bad feeling about this."

Jenna shrugged. "The way I see it, if you've got the car, they can't hurt it."

Casey pointed to the hood. "Your Jaguar thingy is missing."

The hood ornament. Adam had looked for a long time to find just the right one to complete his restoration. "It was gone yesterday morning before I left for school. I called Officer Pullman to report that, too." That the school hellions had invaded her home parking lot still left her blood cold. "Casey, go on now or you'll get stuck in rush-hour traffic."

They frowned at each other until Casey huffed a disgusted sigh. "Oh, all right." They traded keys and Casey got in the car, still looking worried. "Call me if you need me."

As she drove away, Lucas asked quietly, "How are you, Jen? I know yesterday was a shock."

"I'm fine. Really," she insisted when he looked unconvinced. "Although I am wondering why they took a day off. No problems in my classroom all day today."

"Maybe the surveillance camera deterred them."

Jenna's eyes widened. "You put up a camera? Where? When?"

"In the far corner of your classroom where you'll catch anyone coming in the door. Yesterday, after we'd gotten rid of your piñata. I've ordered a few outside models we can mount to the light posts here in the parking lot." He looked annoyed. "And you're welcome."

Jenna rolled her eyes. "Thank you, but you might have told me. Now I have to worry if anyone saw me picking my nose or straightening my nylons."

Lucas's teeth flashed in a grin. "I could sell either of those on video and get rich quick."

She smacked him in the arm. "Take that back or I'll tell Marianne."

"She'll just be mad she didn't get a starring role. You know what an exhibitionist Marianne is."

"No, I don't," Jenna answered primly, then met his eyes, sobering. "Thanks, Lucas."

He tucked a stray lock of hair behind her ear. "You're welcome. I'll see you tomorrow morning. Do not go into the school by yourself. Wait for me and I'll walk you to your classroom."

She swallowed hard. "Do you think they'll stop?"

His face darkened. "Is Rudy playing this weekend?"

"No," she whispered, shaking her head.

"Then they won't stop. That's why I put the camera in. I want hard evidence we can use to expel those juvenile delinquents and I'm tired of waiting for Blackman to be a man and do it himself."

"Thanks, Lucas. Go home and make dirty videos with your wife. This is Thursday, so I get to kick the crap out of whoever's unlucky enough to be my sparring partner tonight."

"I hope whoever is unlucky enough to be your sparring partner is wearing a heavy-duty cup."

"Stainless steel even." And she laughed out loud at his predictable wince. "Good night, Lucas."

Thursday, October 6, 6:25 P.M.

Steven sat alone in the conference room, staring at the board. A map held pushpins indicating the clearings where Lorraine's and Samantha's bodies had been found, the houses where the three missing girls had lived, the schools they'd attended. The churches in which they'd worshiped.

Mike's parish held only two pins. Steven had been relieved to push a third pin marking the location of a small house where the Rahroohs gathered to worship with other Hindu friends. Even if Davies hadn't surfaced with his picture of

Parker, Sandra's theory would have been put to rest. Mike hadn't known Alev Rahrooh. *Thank God,* he thought, tacking three new photos to the board.

Samantha Eggleston's body. Stabbed fifteen times, blade placement making a pattern very similar to the new tattoo on her bald scalp. Which Kent predicted they would find.

Alev Rahrooh, bright and smiling in her cheerleader picture. A copy of her picture, actually. Her parents hadn't wanted to give the original to Steven. It was the only recent photo they had, that they'd been able to afford. They'd given it only after Steven promised he would personally ensure its safekeeping. The original lay in an envelope on his desk. He'd return it to the Rahroohs tonight.

And finally, the third photo, Rudy Lutz, a.k.a. William Rudolf Parker.

"His hair color is similar to the sample from the Clary clearing," Sandra said from the doorway.

"Not good enough according to Liz," Steven said, turning to look at her. "We'll need a hell of a lot more to be able to support bringing him in, especially since we're not even supposed to know his sealed record exists. What's new, Sandra?"

Sandra didn't come any closer than the doorway. "Not a lot. Where's your new friend?"

"Davies? He's in a visitor's cubicle, making some calls back to the West Coast." He paused and asked again, "So what's new, Sandra?"

She looked up at the ceiling. "I checked into the . . . individual we discussed yesterday."

"And?"

She met his eyes. "And you were right. The night Lorraine went missing he was with twenty-five other priests at a seminar on church finances."

"And the night Samantha Eggleston was taken?"

"Giving last sacraments at Wake Medical Center. I'm sorry, Steven. I needed to check."

"I guess I should be grateful for death and taxes," Mike said dryly from behind Sandra and she jumped, turning red up to her hairline. Awkwardly, she turned to face him.

"Father Leone. I'm sorry. I didn't know you knew I was asking about you."

Mike gestured to the table. "These things tend to get out. After you?"

Sandra shook her head. "I was just leaving. I've got to get home to my kids." Still dismayed, Sandra looked from Steven to Mike. "Father, I tried to be discreet. I hope I haven't made any trouble for you."

Mike sat down. "Nothing I can't manage," he said, but his eyes didn't back up his words.

Sandra nodded stiffly and left, closing the door behind her.

"I was in the neighborhood," Mike said softly when she'd gone. "I hope I'm not intruding."

"No. Of course not." Steven took the tack out of Rudy's picture and slipped the photo into a folder. Mike was innocent, but Steven still needed to run a clean investigation, which meant keeping all leads confined to his team. "What brings you to my neighborhood?"

Mike regarded him soberly. "The Egglestons asked me to bless Samantha's body but the ME said he wasn't finished with her yet. We'll have to wait until her body's released."

Weariness hit Steven square in the chest and with it a sadness that was a palpable ache. "I don't want to imagine what her parents are going through," he said, joining Mike at the table. "But I am."

"You feel it for all of them, don't you? The sadness I see in your eyes right now."

Steven pinched the bridge of his nose. He'd had a headache all day. "I do. I don't want to. I try not to. But every

name in every folder that comes across my desk is a person
that belongs to somebody's family. It never seems to end. So,
how bad is it, Mike?"

Mike looked away. "How bad is what?"

Steven leaned forward to catch Mike's eye. "How badly
did we tarnish your reputation?"

"I'll live. I have a few people calling me, asking if it's true.
More are calling the bishop's office to ask if it's true. I'm not
blaming you, Steven."

Steven sighed. "Good. But you know I would have done it
anyway."

"I know. It's what makes you a good cop."

"That's special agent to you," Steven said, his heart mo-
mentarily lightened by the praise.

"That's why I came by," Mike said quietly. "To tell you I
would have been angry if you hadn't checked me out. I want
the man who killed those girls, Steven. I want him to . . ."
Mike's voice wobbled and he stopped. Cleared his throat. "I
want him to suffer for what he did." He closed his eyes. "I
never saw Lorraine's body, but I glimpsed Samantha's on the
ME's table. I'll never forget that sight as long as I live." He
opened his eyes and in them Steven saw anguish. "I have
never felt such hate," he whispered. "I want whoever did this
to suffer like Sammie suffered. Worse."

Like Alev's suffering right now, Steven thought, then
pushed the thought from his mind. "I don't know that there is
much worse, Mike."

"How do you stand it?"

"Like you stand all the suffering you see. One day at a
time. Sometimes an hour at a time."

Mike stood up, tugged on his robes. "Well, I need to go.
It's Thursday. All-you-can-eat night at Sal's Pizza. You want
to join me for a slice or two or twelve? The beer's cold."

Steven smiled wearily up at his best friend, grateful to

have him. "Will you believe me if I say I'd like nothing better? But I'd like to get home tonight. I haven't seen Nicky
since Monday night and I still haven't squared things with
Brad."

Something flickered in Mike's eyes at the mention of
Brad.

"What?" Steven asked, hearing alarm bells ring in his
head. "What do you know?"

Mike shook his head. "Go talk to your son, Steven. He
needs you."

Steven watched as he left the room, then turned back to the
board to look at the photo of Samantha Eggleston's mutilated
body. She'd needed him, too. Just like Alev needed him now.
Pretty soon he'd have to install one of those number machines
like they had at the deli counter.

He had to make it stop. He had to catch whoever was doing
this. God willing it was Rudy Lutz and they just had to make
sure they knew where he went, what he did. That would be the
only way they'd save Alev. And the countless other girls Rudy
Lutz had yet to victimize.

And there were his own kids, Steven thought. *I have to fix
my kids.* Hell, he had to *see* his kids.

And there was the small matter of Jenna Marshall. At this
point, he just hoped she'd still speak to him when he finally
got time to apologize. Whenever that would be.

Thursday, October 6, 7:30 P.M.

"You're not concentrating tonight, Jen."

Jenna picked herself off the floor and pulled at her *gi*. She
looked up at her *sensei* who stared down at her disapprov-
ingly. "I'm sorry, Mark. I've got a lot on my mind."

"Well, leave it outside. Your concerns have no place on the sparring mat. You'll get hurt."

Jenna rubbed her sore hip. "I already am. You caught me good."

"I caught you napping," Mark snapped. "You're supposed to be demonstrating technique, not volunteering to be the first-aid dummy."

Jenna looked at the rest of the students lined up behind them. Mark was right. She owed more to the students than she'd been giving tonight. Classroom vandalism, juvenile delinquents, Brad and Steven Thatcher aside. "Point taken." She held herself rigid. "I'm ready now."

Mark shook his head, his frown softening from frustrated to worried. "No, you're not. We'll try again later." He motioned to a boy standing at the end of the line. "Bill, you're up. Take five, Jen."

Chastised, Jenna walked to the water cooler and aimlessly she watched cars drive by until one pulled into their parking lot. Her stomach clenched. Lucas's car. *No.* Whatever it was . . . Just, *no*.

Dread made her immobile. She could only stand and watch as Lucas made his way across the parking lot, his normally bronzed face whiter than her *gi*. He pushed the door open and stood silently before her, his throat working frantically.

"Casey," he whispered and Jenna felt the room tilt. Blindly she lowered herself into a chair.

Lucas cleared his throat. "She lost control of your car and went off an embankment."

Bile rose in her throat, choking her. "She's . . . alive?"

He nodded. "Barely. Come with me."

Thursday, October 6, 8:45 P.M.

Steven and Davies's follow-up visit to the Rahroohs yielded nothing new. Their telephone records had shown a phone call at nine P.M. the night before. Mr. Rahrooh remembered taking the call. Tears ran down his face as he told them he almost had told the boy, no, it was too late to talk to his daughter. Past house rules for receiving phone calls. But she'd looked so eager. "So beautiful," he'd sobbed, completely breaking down, and Steven and Davies took their leave.

Steven buckled himself into the Volvo. "I'm done for the day," he said, completely drained.

Davies set his eyes on a point outside the car window. "Me, too. I'll need a ride back to the motel. You guys still have my rental car in the impound lot."

Steven chuckled. One very tired chuckle. "Sorry about that."

"Well, at least I can say I know how it feels to be on the other side of the mirror. I guess I'm glad the Parkers' neighbor took her civic duty so responsibly. I just wish she'd done it on Parker."

Steven steered in the direction of Davies's motel. "Speaking of which, how did Rudy get out of his house last night to meet Alev? She was in bed when her mother checked on her at eleven. What time were you watching the Lutzes' house?"

"After I left the search site last night I went back to my hotel room for a few hours sleep. I got to Parker's house about eleven. William got dropped off by some friends at about eleven-thirty—so I know he was home when Alev was still safe in her bed. I took a break around one or so to fill my coffee thermos and get a burrito from the all-night convenience store. Got back around one-thirty."

"So he had a half hour to get out of the house."

"Yeah, that's how I figured it. Damn coffee addiction," Davies said bitterly. "If I'd kept my station maybe that girl would be in her own bed tonight instead of where Parker's got her."

"And maybe if Mrs. Hitler had claimed a headache on the right night, Adolf would never have been born," Steven responded. "You can't change it."

"Yeah, I guess you're right," Davies muttered. "Doesn't make it any easier, though."

"No, it doesn't." The car got quiet as Steven mulled over the day. It was almost Nicky's bedtime. He punched the numbers into his cell phone and smiled when Nicky answered.

"Hey, Daddy."

"Hey, baby. How are you?"

"Fine." There was a beat of silence, then an upbeat, "Aunt Helen made pudding for dessert."

"Chocolate?"

"Tapioca."

"Mmmm. Did you save me any?"

Nicky giggled softly. "No, on account of you getting fat."

Steven smiled. If that was the shtick Nicky wanted to harp on, he'd go along for the ride. As long as he could hear his baby giggle. "I am *not* getting fat."

"Well, Aunt Helen says we've got to keep you fit so you can catch Jenna."

Steven coughed. "She said that?"

"Yessir. So when y'gonna catch her?"

Steven was speechless. "Honey, I don't know that I will." He skillfully guided the conversation elsewhere. "I do know, though, that I love you and wish I were home to kiss you good night."

"Will you see Jenna tonight, Daddy?"

So much for his skill. In more ways than one. He thought about the last two times he'd seen her. He'd be lucky if she ever wanted to see him again. "Probably not, honey. Good night, baby."

"Night, Daddy."

Steven punched END and rolled his eyes. He was going to tape Helen's mouth shut. But she'd probably find some other way to meddle. Sign language or semaphore or something. He'd slipped his phone in his pocket when it jangled. "Thatcher," he answered.

"Thatcher, this is Al Pullman. Investigative Division?"

Steven sat up straighter. "Yeah, sure, you took Dr. Marshall's statement on her slashed tires. Did you catch the boys that did it?" He could only hope. It would give them a way to get Rudy in for a DNA sample if he got arrested.

Hey. That was an angle.

"No," said Pullman, bringing him back. "But Dr. Marshall's had another incident with her car. I thought you might want to know since . . . well, since you two seemed . . . involved."

The hackles on Steven's neck had already started to rise. "What's happened?"

"Her car was vandalized again, but this time they cut her brake line."

Steven's heart jolted, as if struck by lightning. Then raced. "Is she hurt?"

"No, but her friend is. She'd let the friend borrow the car for a weekend outing. Her friend lost control going around a curve and went off the embankment. She's in critical condition."

Steven had to make himself think. Talk. Drive.

Think. She was okay. Jenna was okay. Alive. "Where is her friend?"

"Wake Medical Center," Pullman said. "Dr. Marshall is there with her. I didn't tell Dr. Marshall about the brakes yet. I thought you might want to."

"Thanks, Al. I will. I have an emergency," he said to Davies. "I'll drive you to your motel when I'm done at the hospital."

TWENTY

Thursday, October 6, 9:10 P.M.

LUCAS LEANED BACK INTO THE SOFA IN THE surgical waiting room. "I feel so helpless," he murmured. "When are her parents going to get here?"

Jenna looked across the room at Casey's boyfriend, Ned, who was standing in front of the television in the corner, a completely vacant look on his face. "Ned said their flight gets in at eleven or so. I offered to go pick them up at the airport, but he insisted on doing it himself."

Jenna stared at the man she'd previously thought to be adolescent and insensitive. And he may have been in the past, but he wasn't tonight. Ned had taken charge of the situation, signing forms, doing everything Casey needed him to do. But right now Ned's face was blank.

"He's gone into screen saver mode, I think," she murmured, memories of Adam rushing back. All those hours waiting in hospitals just like this one. Sometimes the mind simply couldn't function past the stress anymore. "I've been there."

Lucas took her hand and entwined their fingers. "I guess you have, honey."

A wave of reality unexpectedly bowled into her, leaving her shaky. Blinking away tears, she laid her head on Lucas's shoulder. "She might die, Lucas."

Lucas put his arm around her. "Sshh. Don't think it, Jen."

"I can't help it," she whispered. *She's all I have left.* "I couldn't stand to lose her, too."

Lucas said nothing, just pulled her closer and laid his cheek on top of her head.

A woman in green scrubs appeared in the doorway. "Casey Ryan's family? I'm Dr. Neuss."

Jenna and Lucas jumped up. Ned turned from the television, slowly, and Jenna saw the look in his eyes she instantly recognized. *He truly loves her,* she thought. *And he believes she will die.*

Lucas stepped forward. "We're her friends. Her family's on their way from out of state."

Ned stumbled toward them, looking nauseous. "Is she . . . ?"

The woman smiled kindly, but wearily. "She's alive."

Jenna felt her body sag, grateful for Lucas's strong arm. "Thank God."

The woman's expression became more businesslike. "She's alive right now. She came through the surgery, but not well. She lost a lot of blood. She has trauma to her head where her skull hit the steering wheel on impact." She looked from Jenna to Ned. "The air bag in her car didn't deploy?"

Jenna's stomach heaved. "It was a classic car," she heard herself whisper. "It didn't have an air bag." *Oh, God,* came the irrational yet very real realization. *This is my fault.*

Dr. Neuss looked philosophical. "Well, it might have prevented some of the damage, but then again, who knows? The car rolled down an embankment, so there is quite a bit the air bag wouldn't have protected her from. We had to intubate her during surgery. That means she's not breathing on her own right now," she added, again kindly. "She's a fighter, your friend. We had to resuscitate her twice, but she fought like a . . ."

"Like a mama tiger," Jenna whispered. The tears were coming and she didn't even try to stop them. "Oh, Casey."

"Like a mama tiger," Dr. Neuss repeated, then squeezed Jenna's arm. "Will you be okay?"

Jenna nodded. "I'm fine. I'll be fine." The words were rote. She may even have believed them.

Dr. Neuss slipped her hands in the pockets of her scrubs. "Well, she's stable for now. The next twenty-four to forty-eight hours will be critical."

"Can we see her?" Ned murmured.

Dr. Neuss shook her head. "She'll be in recovery for a few more hours. Once we get her a bed in ICU, one of the nurses will let you see her on a very limited basis."

"I understand," Ned murmured, but looking at his face, Jenna wondered if he really did.

"I'm on call tonight," Dr. Neuss finished. "Call if you have any questions. And try to get some sleep. The next few days will require you all to be strong."

The doctor walked away leaving them in silence.

Then a sob broke free. Ned's. Standing upright, the man just seemed to crumble inside. Without a thought, Jenna wrapped her arms around him and held him like Casey had held her all the times Adam's illness had become too much to bear. It only seemed right she support Ned now. She held on, rocking him, smoothing his hair, letting him cry. It helped, giving comfort to another. Gave her something to do, kept her own fear from choking her to death.

"Jenna," Lucas said urgently.

Jenna looked up and her eyes widened. There, not ten feet away, stood a pale Steven Thatcher next to a man she'd never seen before. A sense of relief coursed through her. Why? Just because he was here? *Yes, just because he's here. He came.*

Then Steven looked at Ned in her arms and his brown eyes flashed in—what? Anger? *It sure as hell better not be,* she thought. She hadn't done anything this time. Hurt? Unwarranted. Jealousy? Not acceptable considering she'd done nothing more than try to be Steven's friend.

Or more.

She cleared her throat as he turned to walk away while the mystery man remained planted in place, his dark eyes narrowed and alert.

"Steven, wait," she called and watched him stop. "Just wait." She turned Ned toward the chairs and gently pushed him into one and looked at his ravaged face. "I'll be right back. Do you want some water or anything?"

"Do you have any scotch?" Ned asked, leaning back and closing his eyes. "Scratch that, I've got to go to the airport for her folks in an hour. Water would be good."

"Have you eaten anything?" she asked and he grimaced.

"I don't think that's a good idea right now. Just water." Ned opened his eyes and met Jenna's even gaze. "Thanks, Jen. I know what you think of me, and I guess most of it's been true, but—"

Jenna put her fingers over his mouth. "No, Ned. You're here for Casey and that's enough for me. I'll go get your water. Lucas, you'll stay here with him?"

And with Lucas's nod she turned to find Steven still waiting, his expression more humble.

"Casey's boyfriend," Jenna said, looking up at him.

"How is she?" Steven murmured. His hands opened and closed like he wanted to touch her. She wished he would. She really, really wished he would.

Jenna shrugged. "Touch and go. Next forty-eight hours will tell." She closed her eyes. "If only she'd been in her own car. The air bag would have deployed and she'd be okay right now."

Steven looked at her, feeling a burst of relief that she was standing here on her own two feet. Alive. She could have been the one in critical condition right now. But she wasn't. She was alive. Wearing her karate *gi* and a pair of sandals, her face worn from worry, but she was alive. He needed to touch her, to prove to himself she was solid flesh and bone.

He just needed to touch her. But after the last time, would she let him?

It didn't matter. His hand was lifting to her cheek on its own. Then she turned her face into his palm and that was all he needed. He pulled her into his arms and she came willingly, sliding her arms around his waist beneath his jacket. He pressed a kiss to her temple and she shuddered.

He shuddered right along with her, but for a very different reason. Her best friend was clinging to life because somebody tried to kill her. Over a damn football game. How would she feel when she found out her life was worth less than a damn football game to Lutz and his hoodlum friends? And what if Davies was right and Lutz was capable of so much more? Anger clawed at his gut, but he kept his voice, his touch, gentle. He smoothed a hand over her shiny hair and lifted her chin so he could see her face. He brushed his thumb across her lower lip. "I came as soon as I heard."

Her dark brows snapped together, creating worry lines in her forehead he wanted to kiss away. "How did you know?"

This wasn't the time to tell her she'd been the target, Steven thought. He'd tell her when he got her alone. Where she could curse and cry in private. "The police called me," he said softly, still touching her face, still convincing himself she was okay. "You know how the rumor mill is. You visit me at a search site and half the force knows we're . . ." He shrugged. "Whatever we are."

She searched his face and his heart stumbled. "What are we?" she whispered.

You're mine, his mind answered. *Mine, mine, mine.* But he drew a breath and murmured instead, "I want to find out if you're still willing."

She blinked her violet eyes, then nodded. "I am."

A new wave of relief practically cut him at the knees. "Then will you wait for me here? I want to take you home, but I need to give someone a ride first. I'll be back to get you in an hour. Hour and a half, tops."

Jenna looked over his shoulder to where Davies still stood. "Who is he?"

Davies stepped forward, his hand outstretched. "I'm Detective Neil Davies. I'm working with Agent Thatcher on a case."

Steven looked at Davies and wanted to frown. There was a light in Davies's eyes, a light Steven recognized and didn't like one iota. It was the light that came on in a man's eyes when he saw a woman that he wanted. Steven was sure the same look had come into his eyes when he'd first seen Jenna.

Jenna pulled her arms from around his waist to shake Davies's hand, leaving Steven feeling bereft. And pissed at Davies. He'd let Davies on his professional turf because he knew the mind of their killer, but . . . *But stay away from my woman.*

"It's good to meet you, Detective," she said, giving him one of her beautiful smiles, and Steven felt irrational jealousy simmer. "I'm Jenna. I'm glad Steven has some support on this case. I know it's been consuming his time." She turned back to Steven with a sigh. "Thanks for offering to take me home tonight, but I think I'll stay here."

"No, she won't."

Surprise on her face, she turned around to where an older

man stood, looking determined. She frowned at him. "Yes, I will, Lucas."

The man named Lucas shook his head stubbornly. "You heard what the doctor said. We can't see her till she's stable. You might as well get some rest so you'll be strong tomorrow."

"He makes sense, Jenna," Steven said quietly.

Jenna sighed. "His logic is solid, this once. I'll wait for you here, Steven."

She's as beautiful up close as she was through binoculars, Neil thought. As beautiful as she'd been in his dreams. And now, having seen her up close, having heard the smoothness of her voice, he knew he'd never get Jenna Marshall out of his mind.

"So who is she?" Neil demanded without preamble as he and Thatcher pulled out of the parking garage ten minutes later. Thatcher had been wearing a self-satisfied smile since Jenna had promised to wait for him and Neil wanted to wipe it from Thatcher's face with a ferocity that shocked him.

Thatcher glanced over at him, his smile becoming a hard frown. "She's my son's teacher." Thatcher was no idiot, Neil mused. He knew another man on the hunt.

"Just your son's teacher?"

Thatcher clenched his teeth. "And my . . ."

If Thatcher didn't know, Neil figured Jenna Marshall was not his woman after all. "Friend, girlfriend, lover, betrothed?" he asked sardonically.

A muscle twitched in Thatcher's jaw. "Yes to one and two, not yet to three and four."

"I see."

"Make sure you do," Steven said with false mildness. It must be the way Southern men posture, Neil thought and was not impressed.

They were quiet for several miles until Thatcher said harshly, "That accident was no accident."

Neil turned in his seat, giving Thatcher his full attention. "What do you mean?"

"Jenna flunked one of the football players last week, suspending him from the team. The ballplayer and his friends have been making her life a living hell for the last week, slashing her tires, vandalizing her classroom. That call earlier was from the Raleigh PD. Her brakes were cut."

A new fury burned inside him. "Then Jenna was the target and her friend was just in the wrong place, wrong time."

"Yeah." Thatcher's voice shook when he said the word. "I'll tell her when I pick her up later. Oh, and three guesses as to who the football player is."

Neil shot upright in the seat. "No fucking way."

"Yes fucking way. Our own Rudy Lutz."

His heart began to race. Close. They were close. "Can you prove he's done the vandalism?"

"None of it so far," Thatcher said tightly. "We could bring him in for questioning, but we don't have enough to hold him. Certainly not enough to arrest him at this point. His father's fancy lawyers would have anything we gathered tossed out of court."

"But if we could arrest him—"

"We could get our own DNA sample to compare to the hair we found at the clearing." Thatcher nodded. "Yeah, I thought of that already."

"So what next?" Neil asked, practically vibrating, charged up and ready to pounce.

"See if we can't more closely link Rudy to the trouble at the school or Jenna's car tonight. Stay back for now, Davies. Let's let the locals do their job and see where we come out."

Neil bit his cheek. "I'll stay back for now." *From Parker*, he thought, *but not from Jenna.*

Thursday, October 6, 11:30 P.M.

"What do you know that you're not telling me?" Jenna asked when they'd stopped in front of her apartment. "You're too quiet. Too something. I don't know. Tell me what you know."

Steven braced himself. "Your brakes were cut, Jenna. Casey's accident was no accident."

Her face drained of all color leaving her white and trembling. "No," she whispered. "They wouldn't." He said nothing, but took her hand and let her squeeze the life out of his. She leaned back, her eyes shut, her lips a strange fluorescent purple in the glare of the parking lot lights. "I thought it, in the waiting room, but didn't want to believe it was true," she said, her voice harsh. "But it is." She clenched her teeth. "Steven, I need to run an errand. Will you drive me?"

"Where?" Steven asked warily.

"Just drive, please. I'll tell you where."

Thursday, October 6, 11:50 P.M.

After twenty minutes Steven stopped, looking up at their destination in a combination of disbelief and a strange feeling of karma. "This isn't a good idea, Jenna."

Her lips were set in mutinous determination. "You don't have to go in. I, however, do."

He guessed she did. He watched for a moment as she got out of the Volvo and marched up to the front door of the house, the whiteness of her karate *gi* making her look like she glowed in the dark. He caught up with her as she rang the doorbell.

Nobody answered. The house was dark.

"I think they're all asleep," he said mildly.

"Then let them wake *up*," she gritted and leaned into the doorbell, creating one continuous chime they could hear through the expensive stained-glass door.

Finally a light came on. The door opened revealing a tired-looking woman in a flannel nightgown. A god-awful ugly flannel nightgown. "What is this about?" she asked imperiously.

Jenna pushed the door open and stalked in, leaving the woman agape. "Mrs. Lutz, I'm Dr. Marshall and I want to talk to you and your husband. You might as well cooperate, unless you want to call the police. Then we'll have a nice conversation about what a saintly son you have."

Mrs. Lutz paled. "Get out."

Jenna stood her ground, nose to nose with Mrs. Lutz. "I will not. I will talk to you and your husband. Now."

"Nora, what's going on?"

Steven looked up to see Mr. Lutz coming down the stairs, tucking his shirt into his slacks. Jenna waited until he got to the base of the stairs before speaking.

"I have had enough of your terror tactics," she said coldly and Lutz had the nerve to look bored. *Big mistake*, Steven thought.

"I have no idea what you're talking about. *Miss* Marshall."

Jenna advanced until she was toe to toe with the hulking man and Steven poised himself to drag her away before it became physically confrontational. "It's *Dr.* Marshall, you sniveling little man," she said and Steven bit back a grin.

"Nora, call the police," Lutz said calmly.

"Go ahead, call the police," Jenna returned, now as calm as Lutz. On the surface only, Steven knew. "Call Al Pullman of the Investigative Division. I'm sure he'd like to talk with you."

Lutz scowled. "Get out. *Miss* Marshall."

"I will," she said evenly, "but not until I've said what I

came to say. You think you're clever. You think I'll give your son a grade he did not earn. But you're wrong. Not only will I ensure your son never graduates from my school, I will not rest until he's behind bars for what he's done."

Steven watched Lutz but didn't see a single flicker of fear. Either Davies was wrong and Rudy was not the infamous William Parker or Lutz was good. Steven preferred to believe the sonofabitch was good. Really good. But ultimately not good enough.

Lutz said nothing and Jenna shook her head in disbelief. "A few spray-painted epithets I can take. Slashed tires and water in my gas tank I can take. I can even take the dead possum your son hung in my classroom yesterday morning."

Steven straightened. He hadn't heard about that. Animal mutilation was inextricably linked to serial killers. Almost all of them had killed animals at one time or another.

"But," Jenna was continuing, "attempted murder I cannot take. Neither will the police."

Lutz raised a brow. "You're delusional."

Jenna's jaw went rigid. "No, I'm not delusional. I'm alive. But I may not have been and now my best friend's lying in ICU because she drove my car this afternoon. My brakes were cut today, Mr. Lutz. *That* is not adolescent vandalism. *That* is no longer a misdemeanor. *That* is a felony."

Lutz did pale at that. "What are you talking about?"

"I suggest you ask your son." Jenna turned away, then turned back for one more exchange. "One more thing, Mr. Lutz. You'd better be praying my friend pulls through or the charge will be murder. And *that* doesn't sit well with college scouts."

She turned on her heel and walked out the door. Steven followed her quietly, still mulling over the look of shock on Lutz's face. Of two things Steven was fairly certain. Lutz hadn't known about the brakes nor did he care for the idea of his son being charged with felony murder. Go figure.

TWENTY-ONE

Friday, October 7, 12:30 A.M.

JENNA DIDN'T SAY A WORD UNTIL THEY WERE in her apartment with the door closed.

"Son of a *bitch*," she muttered, jerking at the belt on her *gi*. Her fingers stilled and her shoulders sagged. "Dammit," she whispered and his heart sagged, too. A wave of tenderness washed over him, and with it, a fierce need to protect her.

"Here, let me," Steven said softly and went to work on the knot in her brown belt. He slipped the belt from around her waist and draped it over the soft arm of her sofa. Then he slipped the *gi* from her shoulders and laid it on top of the belt, leaving her in T-shirt and the *gi* bottoms.

And a bra, he thought, tenderness sliding over to make way for lust. He tried not to think about it. "Turn around," he ordered, his voice husky in the quiet of her apartment. She obeyed and he massaged her shoulders, trying not to let her soft groan distract him from his relatively innocent task.

To make her feel good. To take away her stress. *Be honest. To get your hands on her again.*

"That feels good," she said thickly, dropping her chin to her chest. He pushed her ponytail to one side and went to work on her neck. Tried to ignore the urge to kiss it. Tried to ignore the throbbing of his body. His erection was nothing new. He'd been stiff as a board since she'd given Lutz a piece of her mind. She'd been magnificent. But this was different. This was more.

He gave in and dipped his head, brushing his lips across the back of her neck, her sigh making his heart beat faster. Slipped his left arm around her, bracketing the underside of her breasts while his right hand massaged the long, lean line of her spine. Felt her heart beating hard against his arm. Felt her settle her incredible ass against his groin. He fought the urge to thrust, to bury himself deep inside her. He moved his arm, over and around so that her breast fell into his hand.

She drew a breath and he didn't move. Neither did she.

"Jenna," he whispered.

"What?" she whispered back.

I want you, his brain screamed. *I want to come inside you and pound and pound until everything else in the universe goes away.* "I want to kiss you."

She was quiet a moment, then drew another deep breath, pressing her breast into his hand, her nipple as hard as a diamond against his palm. "On one condition."

"Which is?" he breathed, ready to grant her anything.

"That you don't run away again," she whispered and he groaned.

He spun her around, pulling her into his arms, grinding his mouth against hers. Finding relief in the kiss even as the wanting built hotter and higher. Her arms came around his neck and she pressed against him, her breast to his chest. Her hips against his hips. Her soft mound against the hard ridge of his cock.

She was perfect. *And mine. Mine, mine, mine.* His hands slid down her back and under her waistband of her *gi*. Down until they touched lace. Until they covered her ass. Until they yanked, drawing her higher, closer, bringing him deeper into her softness. Making her moan his name.

His name. He pulled back, staring at her face. Her eyes, dilated and aroused. Her lips, full and pouty from their kiss. Her cheeks, slightly reddened from the scrape of his beard. "Say that again."

"Steven," she whispered again, but differently. Playfully. Flirtatiously. Her fingers dropped to his shirt, to the button in the middle of his chest. Nimbly she freed the buttons up until she reached his holster and down until she reached the waist of his pants. Then her hands were inside his shirt, splayed flat against his skin, her clever fingers tangling in the hair that covered his pecs. He shivered from the pleasure. Her hands felt so damn good. "Steven," she whispered huskily.

It was his turn to swallow. "What?"

Her fingers butted up against the barrier of his shoulder holster. "Take it off."

He was already shrugging out of his jacket. "Why?" he asked, catching a bit of her playfulness.

"Because it's in my way." She pushed at the holster again with her fingertips, from beneath his shirt. She looked up through her dark lashes, making him want to gobble her up in one bite. "I don't think you want to get in my way."

He unbuckled the clasp and blindly let the holster drop. "No, I don't think I do." He drew a startled breath, when her hands began to move again, her fingertips brushing against his nipples. His cock jumped against her and her eyes widened. His throat worked as he tried to make words come. Any words would do. Preferably words that would make her say "yes."

"I want you," he murmured. Direct. To the point. Honest as hell.

Her eyes on his, her fingertips still brushing his now painfully sensitive nipples she said, "Yes."

Steven blinked. "Yes, what?"

"Yes, I know." Her hands moved up to his shoulders and began to push his shirt off. "Yes, I want you, too."

Yes. She'd said yes. Wait. Steven shook his head and lightly grabbed her wrists. "Wait."

Her hands immobilized, Jenna leaned up on her toes and nuzzled his jaw. "For what?"

Her scent was in his head. He couldn't breathe. Couldn't think. He shook his head again, dropped her wrists, and stepped backward. "Wait."

Her pouty lips bent in a frown. "Are you planning to run away again?"

"Yes. No. Hell, I don't know."

"I like the no answer better."

"You would." Steven raked his fingers through his hair, frustrated. With himself, with her. But mostly with himself. "I'm sorry, Jenna, this is just too fast."

She huffed out a breath and looked up at the ceiling. "I don't believe this is happening." She turned and walked to the dining room, clutching the back of one of the chairs with a grip so tight Steven could see her knuckles whiten from ten feet away. "What's wrong, Steven? Is it me?"

He was across the room in less than a second, pulling her around to face him. "No, it is not you. Not the way you're asking anyway."

"Then in just which way?" she asked and he was appalled to see tears in her eyes.

Panic gripped his gut where lust had been only moments before. "Oh, God, Jenna, don't cry. Please." She jerked out of his arms and turned her back again, crossing her arms tightly across her breasts. *She's been through so much tonight,* he thought. That he'd made it worse wrenched at him. "Please, sweetheart, don't cry."

She sniffled and he knew it was too late. "I'll cry if I want to," she said, sounding very much like a little girl instead of the strong woman he knew her to be. "And you can't stop me."

He smiled, his own emotion swinging back to tenderness. "You sound like Nicky."

Her shoulders heaved and his smile disappeared. "I know," she muttered. "This sucks."

"What sucks?" he asked carefully.

"My whole life. Friends and family who won't rest until I'm married. Crazy teenagers trying to kill me, and now my best friend is in ICU." She wheeled around, tears streaking her face, still easily the most beautiful woman he'd ever seen. "And then there's you."

Steven tilted his head forward. Carefully. "Me?"

Jenna took a step toward him, her fingertip jabbing into his chest. "Yes, you. I'm happy with my life. I have dogs. I have sports. I have friends." She jabbed harder and he winced but said nothing. "I didn't want you," she went on, her voice gaining strength. "I would have been happy as a spinster with cats. But can I be happy as a spinster with cats now?"

Steven didn't answer. He didn't think he was supposed to. He was right.

"Nooo," she said, on an obvious roll. "And why not? Because *you* woke up my hormones and now all I think about is kissing you! When I'm not worrying about crazy teenagers of course."

"Of course."

She glared at him. "You think this is funny, don't you? You think it's funny that all I want right now is to throw you down on the floor and have sex with you. Right now."

Steven swallowed. Audibly. "No, I don't think that's funny at all. Believe me."

She looked slightly mollified. "Well, all right then. Now what'll we do?"

Steven ran his tongue over his teeth. "I'm sure I have no idea."

"I need to walk the dogs," she said wearily. "You can go if you want."

Steven grasped her shoulders firmly. "I'm not going anywhere. I'll walk the dogs. Why don't you get something to eat?"

"Okay," she murmured.

When he came back from walking the dogs, one at a time, he found her sitting at the table, wearing an oversized T-shirt and eating ice cream right out of the container with a big spoon.

"I actually had something more nutritious in mind," he said, patting Jim on the head. Or Jean-Luc.

Jenna looked at the spoon with a philosophical air. "It's Häagen-Dazs Rocky Road," she said.

"Sorry, didn't realize Häagen-Dazs Rocky Road had been elevated to one of the four major food groups." He pulled out a chair and sat down at her table. "Jenna, I think we need to talk."

She shrugged and looked away. "So talk," she said and shoved another spoonful of ice cream into her mouth. She waved the spoon at him. "Go ahead. I'm waiting."

He cleared his throat. "Truth of the matter is I'm flattered."

"Oh, God," she groaned. "Not the I'm-flattered speech."

Steven raised his brows. "You've heard this before?"

She shook her head and dug deeper into the ice cream container in disgust. "No, but I read."

Steven wanted to smile. "Well, I doubt you've heard it quite this way."

Jenna wanted to scream. Wanted to pull her hair and just scream. Instead she ate some more ice cream. "Whatever," she muttered, mentally preparing herself for more humiliation. "Just get it over with. I'm a nice woman and you like me, but you just want to be friends. Yadayadayada."

He took the spoon from her hand and stuck it back in the container. "Look at me. Please."

Jenna looked at him. At his beautiful brown eyes. At the body she still wanted. "I'm listening," she said.

He closed his eyes and she saw his cheeks heat. He was embarrassed, she thought, as was she. It was bad enough to throw yourself at a man, but to be refused . . . It was humiliating.

"The truth is, I want you more than I want to breathe," he said quietly.

Her eyes widened. "You do?"

He opened his eyes and glared. "I said I did."

She drew a breath. "Okay, I'm still listening."

"Good, because I don't think I can do this more than once," he said grumpily, which made her smile. He smiled then, too, and took her hand. "I have responsibilities, Jenna. Three of them. I can't just be bringing home a succession of girlfriends that my kids get attached to. When I get involved with a woman, I need her to be the one."

Jenna felt her throat close. The one. As in . . . the one. He couldn't make it any plainer. And that . . . one . . . wasn't her. "Okay, I understand. I'm sorry."

He shook his head, his brown eyes piercing. "I don't think you do. Jenna, I've known you a week. That's not long enough to know anything about you, or for you to know anything about me. I want to be honest with you. I like you. A hell of a lot. My kids could fall in love with you like that." He snapped his fingers. "Nicky already has. But this isn't a good time for either of us." He drew a deep breath. "Tonight I was so close to taking everything you offered."

"You were?"

He studied her soberly and her heart skipped a beat. "I was.

I still am." He squeezed her hand lightly. "I think I could fall in love with you, Jenna Marshall. You're beautiful and nice and kind. You're every man's dream. But if I'd taken what you offered tonight, it might have been taking advantage. You've had a shock. You've had as close to a near-death experience as I pray you ever get. Can you look me in the eye and tell me part of what's influenced you tonight wasn't that?"

She couldn't. Because he was right. "No," she whispered.

"I didn't think so. I want you to want me. For me. And I want you to know that if we go on, it's with the understanding that it's got to be very, very serious."

Jenna raised their joined hands to her lips and watched his beautiful brown eyes darken. He truly wanted her, but continued to control his own desires. For her. So as not to take advantage of her. *He thinks he could fall in love with me.* It was so unexpected. *He* was so unexpected. The way he'd turned her life upside down. She swallowed hard, yet her voice still came out as a husky whisper. "I think I could fall in love with you, too, Steven Thatcher. You're a good man. Strong and kind." She watched the muscle in his jaw twitch, his only movement. She thought about what it would be like with him, to be loved by him, and her heart raced. Then she allowed herself to think about his children, to imagine tucking Nicky in at night and hearing him call her "Mommy." And her heart sighed. "And if we go on it's with the understanding that I want your kids."

He seemed to relax before her eyes. "Good. Now I think it's your bedtime. I'll tuck you in."

And he did, just like her father used to. Then he turned out the lights and sat in the chair next to her bed. Within seconds her eyelids felt like sixteen-ton weights.

"Steven?" she yawned.

"Yes, Jenna." His voice rumbled in the darkness.

"You don't have to stay. I'll be fine."

"I know. I want to stay for me." His hand stroked her hair. "I almost lost you tonight," he murmured. "Before I ever got to have you."

"Umm." His hand on her hair felt wonderful. "Steven, can you call the hospital to see if Casey's all right?" She listened as he called, listened, then hung up.

His hand stroked her hair again. "She's stable, Jenna. Now go to sleep."

Friday, October 7, 6:00 A.M.

Steven expected to wake with a stiff neck from sleeping in the chair next to Jenna's bed. Instead he felt more refreshed than he had in days. So why wasn't his neck stiff and why didn't his back hurt? And why wasn't he in the chair next to Jenna's bed? He bolted upright, sending the frothy blanket to his waist, baring his shirtless chest. Because he was *in* Jenna's bed.

His heart caught. She was asleep in the chair. He reached over to shake her awake. "Jenna."

Her eyes opened. "Oh." She blinked hard and scrambled to sit up straight. "You're awake."

"I am. Why am I here and you there?"

Her lips curved. "I woke up in the night to check on Casey and you looked so uncomfortable in the chair. I pulled you onto the bed, thinking you'd just sleep. But, when I woke up again, your hands were . . . occupied. I didn't mind, but I thought you would so I bunked in the chair." Her eyes smiled as his face heated and she leaned over to trail the backs of her fingers against his cheek. "What time do you have to be to work?"

He captured her fingers and pressed them to his cheek, not wanting to let her go. Protectiveness welled from deep within and he didn't want to let her out of his sight. A group of crazed, angry teenagers had tried to kill her. It was difficult to keep the fury from his voice. "Seven-thirty."

"Then I should make you breakfast."

"And coffee?"

"If you're willing, I'll try."

Her eyes had grown smoky in the morning light. "Are we talking about coffee, Jenna?"

She gently pulled her fingers from his face. "We're talking about whatever you want. But right now, it's coffee." She stood up and covered his mouth with hers and it felt so right it hurt.

He watched her walk from the bedroom, then rolled to his stomach. He could smell her on the pillow and thought about what it would be like to see her face every morning for the rest of his life.

It would be heaven. Sheer heaven.

Breathing her perfume once again, he wondered exactly what more he needed to know before trusting her with his sons. *Nothing*, he decided. Absolutely nothing.

TWENTY-TWO

Friday, October 7, 8:00 A.M.

"GOOD MORNING, EVERYONE." STEVEN looked at his team. There were no cheery responses. "Please take a look at the new pictures on the board."

His team looked, their faces quietly contemplative. "Alev Rahrooh is missing. We can assume he has her and he'll kill her, unless we find him first. Okay, Harry, what have you found out about the sign he left next to Samantha's body?"

Harry blew his nose. He was allergic to pine trees. "Good quality plywood, paint available ad any hardware store. Dothing, Steven." He shook his head. "Doh fingerprints, doh dothing."

"Here." Meg slid a white pill across the table. "These work on my allergies."

"Pushing, Meg?" Sandra asked with a smile. "And in front of law enforcement officers?"

"I have connections," Meg said dryly. "I think I'm safe. So, our boy murders Samantha, then erects a sign next to the body with an arrow and the word 'Body.'"

"Deatly stenciled," Harry said. "Will this make me sleepy?" he asked, looking at the pill.

"No," said Meg. "Just take it. So we have a note, taunting you, Steven, and now a sign. It seems like our boy doesn't think too much of you."

"I figured that out," Steven said. "I don't think too much of him either. I'll have another press conference today. Should I taunt back?"

Meg chewed at her lower lip. "I think so, but carefully. He

thinks he's smart, and he is. I think the only way we'll catch him is to force him to make a sloppy mistake."

"Good. I hope you've all read the file Davies assembled on Parker. We need to find anything to help Liz get a court order so that we can get a sample of Rudy's DNA." He gave each team member a hard stare. "We need to be careful. William Parker's juvenile record is sealed. We aren't even supposed to know it exists. In no way do we do anything that will compromise this case once we catch the little bastard. I've got two unmarked cars watching the Lutz place on shifts. We'll know when Rudy leaves, where he goes, when he returns.

"Sandra, I want you to start really looking at all the high school boys. Anybody with a prior. Anybody who's fast with the girls. Get these kids to talk. They'll know who the big scorers are."

"High school locker rooms." Sandra shuddered. "I can hardly wait."

Steven smiled. "I know. Now you'll know how my bathroom at home smells. Just get a big enough group that will naturally net Rudy. I don't want anybody saying we only looked at him. Kent, where are you with the crime-scene analysis?"

Kent pulled out photos of Samantha Eggleston's body. "The ME got me the prelim last night. Cause of death was stab wounds. Heart, kidneys, lungs. He stabbed her fifteen times."

"That's how many times he stabbed the Seattle girls," Davies said. "We thought it was because he was fifteen years old before. He's a creature of habit."

"I'll buy the creature part," Kent muttered. "There was an important difference versus Lorraine. Samantha was not killed in the clearing. She was killed somewhere else and transported." He paused and stared at his notes. He swallowed hard, and Steven remembered this was Kent's first sexual homicide. "Samantha was sexually assaulted. No semen found. Multiple recent needle punctures on her inner arms. ME's testing for ketamine, but won't have results till later today."

"I have dews on the ketamine," Harry said, pulling an envelope from his pocket. "I found this in my box this morning. It's from one of the veterinary supply houses I'd inquired on ketamine sales. They've invoiced more than a hundred vets and farmers within a fifty-bile radius of the city in the last three months. They took a while to get back to me because they found an issue with one of their customers." He tossed the letter across the table to Steven. "George Richards ordered a twelve-vial box last August. He ordered adother twelve-vial box last week." Harry sniffled. "His dame came up when the supply house did an audit of unpaid invoices. Mr. Richards hadn't paid the August invoice, but because his account was in good standing they went ahead and filled the new order and enclosed a friendly reminder. Two days ago, they get an angry phone call."

"From?" Steven asked.

"From," Harry said, "an indignant Mrs. Richards. Her husband passed away six months ago."

"Interesting." Steven picked up the letter and scanned it. "Where was the ketamine delivered?"

"To the Richards's farmhouse. Mrs. Richards insisted she dever saw it."

"Pay her a visit today," Steven said thoughtfully. "Find out who knew her husband had an account with the vet supply company. And, *discreetly,* find out if her husband knew Rudy Lutz."

"Okay." Harry blew his nose again. "Anything to stay away from pine trees."

"Good work, Harry," Steven said. "Anything else, Kent?"

Kent was staring at the photo of Samantha Eggleston's

body. "Just that she was bald, like Lorraine. And she had the same tattoo, just like I thought."

Davies got up and walked to the bulletin board, staring with a frown at the Eggleston photo, identical to the one Kent held. "I've been trying to remember where I've seen that tattoo before."

"You've seen it before?" Steven asked, more than a little annoyed. "Why didn't you say anything when we were looking at the body yesterday?"

"Because I couldn't remember then and I can't remember now," Davies snapped. "He didn't tattoo our girls—that's a new little trick. But I've seen it before. I know I have. Do you have a tracing?"

Nancy pulled a sheet of paper from her folder, holding an enlargement of the symbol. "I've run this through every database I've got," she said. "Nothing."

Davies took the paper with a polite nod. "I'll send this to my old partner. He can pass it around, see if any of the other guys recognize it."

Steven raised his brows. "Discreetly."

Davies scowled. "Got it, Thatcher. I will be the soul of discretion."

"Good. Hit the road, guys, and remember the word of the day. Everybody, all together."

"Discretion," they all mumbled, grumbled, and muttered.

Friday October 7, 1:15 P.M.

Jenna was in the ICU waiting room when the press conference came on. Jumping to her feet, she rushed to stand in front of the murmuring television and strained to hear what Steven had to say.

He looked strong. Confident. And very tired.

"We must confirm reports of a third missing girl," he said when the media had become quiet. "We're withholding the name of the victim. All I can say is she is a sixteen-year-old female."

"Have all the girls been cheerleaders?" a reporter asked.

"Yes," Steven replied. "But all young women must be cautious. The danger is very real."

Jenna's stomach rolled over. Those poor girls. Poor Steven, having to watch it all happen.

"Do you have any suspects?" another reporter shouted.

"The investigation is ongoing," Steven replied. "I will say one thing. This vile perpetrator believes he is smart. I believe he's becoming a little too smug. He'll make a mistake and we'll catch him." He looked into the camera. "We *will* catch him." He turned back to the media. "That's all."

Needing to do something, Jenna went to Casey's room where Ned sat, staring at Casey's pale face. "Go get something to eat, Ned. I'll stay with her for a little while."

Ned shook his head. "I'm not hungry. But I could sure use the company."

So Jenna sat in the chair beside him and together they guarded Casey while Jenna thought about Steven guarding those young girls. And wondered how the world had become so screwed up.

Friday, October 7, 5:30 P.M.

Neil found Thatcher standing at the bulletin board, staring at the pictures of the girls. Grudgingly he admitted the man really cared. "I thought you'd be home by now," Neil said.

"I'll leave soon. I was just wondering if our boy has seen the press conference yet."

"And what he'll do when he does?" Neil asked.

Thatcher nodded. "Yeah. I want to push him, but I don't want another 'after' photo."

There wasn't a whole lot to say to that, so Neil left it alone. "Have you arranged for protection for Jenna?" he asked and watched Thatcher's spine go rigid.

"No need to tonight," he said. "She's staying at the hospital with Casey."

"I know, but what about tomorrow night? Assuming Rudy is Parker, Jenna could be in danger."

I know? Steven turned, eyes narrowed and pulse hammering. "I've thought of that," he said tightly. "What I want to know is how you know she's staying with Casey tonight."

Davies didn't look away. Smug bastard. "I dropped by the hospital today, just to see how her friend was doing." He lifted a brow. "Professional courtesy."

Steven gritted his teeth. Professional courtesy. Over his dead body. "Did you now?"

Davies nodded. "I did. I was concerned about how she was holding up."

Sonofabitch. Steven recognized the gleam in Davies's eye. He saw it every time he looked in the mirror. "So you're not only the soul of discretion but the *soul* of *beneficence* as well?"

Quick on the draw, Davies's jaw tightened. "I guess that was an intended slam on my parentage."

Steven shrugged. "Take it how you want. Just don't be paying Jenna any more visits."

Davies's eyes narrowed and it occurred to Steven that they stood poised for battle like those mountain goats who butted heads over pack leader rights. "Is that a command?" Davies said softly.

"Take it how you want. Just leave her alone."

"What about tomorrow night? How will you keep her safe?" Davies persisted and Steven thrust his fisted hands in his pockets.

"Don't trouble yourself about Jenna, Detective," Steven murmured, very quietly. "I'll make sure she stays safe without telling her about Rudy Lutz, so at the same time I can ensure the evidence I gather in *this* case isn't tainted in any way by a premature tipping of our hand."

Davies's dark eyes flickered in controlled rage, then he turned on his heel and left.

Friday, October 7, 6:10 P.M.

He switched off the television set with a snarl. He'd spent precious minutes away from pretty Alev in the barn this afternoon to come home and watch the press conference on television. He'd returned, just now, to watch the six o'clock news to see if that idiot Thatcher had anything new. Instead, he'd seen that idiot Thatcher try to make himself look smart. He'd known the police would posture, would try to stir him up, to make him angry, but the words still stung.

Smug. Thatcher had called him smug. "It's Thatcher that's smug," he muttered. "Arrogant bastard." Prancing around like he actually had a clue. Like he actually had any of this under control.

He opened his closet door where dozens of faces surrounded by long, dark hair smiled at him.

He focused in on *her* picture with a scowl. He'd thought she was different. More worthy than the others. Showed even a smart man could be fooled by a competent enough actress. He slipped his hand in his jacket pocket and fingered the silver Jaguar he'd carried since Tuesday night. Since he'd sat in the parking lot in front of her apartment and watched through her window as she kissed Thatcher like the slut he now knew her to be. He'd been so angry . . . One minute the hood ornament was on her car and the next, it was in his hand.

He twisted the warm metal in his fingers, wondering how it would feel when it was her warm skin between his fingers. When he held her hair in his hands. And he wondered just how smug Thatcher would be when he himself got the final prize.

TWENTY-THREE

Saturday, October 8, 12:55 P.M.

"NICKY, COME AWAY FROM THE WINDOW," Helen said. "She'll be here when she gets here."

Nicky looked back with his little boy frown. "She's late."

Matt ruffled Nicky's red hair. "She is not late. She said she'd be here at one. It's five till."

Nicky looked at Helen plaintively. "But she'll be here, right, Aunt Helen?"

She'd better be, Helen thought grimly. "She'll be here, honey. Go get Cindy Lou ready."

"Okay." Nicky raced to get Cindy Lou and Helen walked over to the window to take his place.

"She'll be here, Aunt Helen," Matt said, digging into a bag

of chips. He pointed to the street. "See, here she is. Punctual to the minute."

Helen felt the slightest bit guilty for not believing Jenna's promise. It's just that Nicky hadn't shown such excitement in . . . Since last spring.

Jenna lifted her hand to knock on the door, blinking in surprise when it opened under her knuckles. Helen stood there, a happy smile on her face. "Jenna, Jenna, come in."

Jenna almost stumbled as she was ushered into Steven's foyer.

"Told you she'd come," Matt muttered as he walked by, giving Helen a meaningful look. Helen glared back at Matt and Jenna knew they'd thought she wouldn't come.

"Nicky's had his nose pressed against the glass for the last two hours."

Jenna looked at her watch. "I'm sorry it took me so long. I spent the night at the hospital with a friend and I had to run home and shower." She looked longingly at Matt's bag of chips. "I've eaten hospital cafeteria food for the last day," she said, then grinned when Matt shoved the bag in her hands without a word. "Thanks."

"We were sorry to hear about Miss Ryan," Helen said.

"Yeah, will she be all right?" Matt asked.

Jenna nodded. "Yes, thank God. The doctors say she's out of the woods." The declaration had come this morning. "She'll be okay."

"Well, that's good news." Helen brought out a Nicky-sized jacket. "Nicky! Jenna's here."

With a yell, Nicky came racing through the kitchen, dragging poor Cindy Lou on a leash, stopping just short of Jenna's feet. For a moment he'd looked as if he'd planned to hug her, but pulled back at the last minute. "You came." His eyes were bright. "You really came."

Jenna tapped the end of his freckled nose. "I said I would,

didn't I? Do you think Cindy Lou's ready for her first obedience lesson?"

Nicky shrugged. Then he grinned. "I guess we'll find out."

Jenna laughed. "I guess we will. Come on, sweetie. Let's go."

Saturday, October 8, 6:15 P.M.

Steven came home on time for the first time in days, expecting a noisy house and a smiling welcome. Instead, it was dark and quiet met his ears as he shut his front door.

He flipped on the foyer lights overhead. "Anybody home?"

A beat of silence followed, then he heard Brad's voice from his office. "Just me, Dad. In here."

Steven stopped in the doorway to his office. Brad sat in the dark, watching a home video on the television in the corner. It was their family, on vacation at the beach. Brad and Matt were fishing from the shore. Melissa was lying on a blanket next to Nicky who was napping in the shade of the beach umbrella, wearing a diaper and nothing else. Nicky had been about a year old. He, himself, must have been the one filming because Melissa was giving him an evil glare and telling him not to take her picture. He remembered that day. Vividly. She'd almost refused to leave the hotel room, standing in front of the mirror and cursing her "baby fat." He remembered wondering if she cursed the baby, too, for ruining her figure. She'd started pushing him away then. Claiming headaches or that she simply wasn't in the mood. He wondered, now, as he watched the video, if she'd been cheating then, even though she wouldn't leave him for another two years.

Although it didn't really matter anymore. What mattered was the young man sitting in the chair, his eyes riveted to the scene. "Where is everyone?" Steven asked.

"Helen's with her canasta club. Nicky and Matt went to the park with Dr. Marshall," Brad answered, not looking away from the video. "The bluefish were running that day," he said softly.

Steven sat next to Brad. "I remember. Matt got so mad because you caught the biggest fish."

"And I got mad because he caught three more than I did."

Steven huffed a quiet chuckle. "You boys always were so competitive."

"Guess we must have got it from you," Brad said, not unkindly.

Steven searched in the darkness, the flickering light from the video providing the only illumination. Brad had shaved. Washed his hair. Was wearing clean clothes. Something was different. He remembered the look in Mike's eye Thursday evening when he told him to go home to his son, that Brad needed him. Something had happened when his best friend had driven his oldest son home from the search scene Wednesday night.

Steven cleared his throat. "It's hard for a parent to apologize," he said.

Brad turned his head and the two shared a sober glance. "For what?" Brad asked.

"I'm not sure, to be truthful. I don't know what I did to start all of this, Brad, and I don't know if I should even apologize, but I did hurt you Wednesday night. I'm sorry for that, son. I was wrong."

He watched Brad's throat work as his son fought to swallow. He knew how Brad felt. He was practically choking on the lump in his own throat. "So was I, Dad. I . . . didn't understand."

Steven frowned. "Didn't understand what, son?"

Brad shrugged. "Everything, I guess."

Steven had opened his mouth to press further, when the front door flew open. Barking filled the house accompanied by Nicky's shrill scolding. "No, Cindy Lou. Down, Cindy Lou!"

Then came the voice he'd been waiting to hear all day. "Nicky, I think Cindy Lou's had enough obedience training for one day," Jenna said soothingly. "Why don't you let her out in the backyard to run? I think she could use a break."

Steven found Jenna kneeling on the foyer floor, unzipping Nicky's jacket. Nicky was looking at her with nothing short of adoration. His youngest son was a very smart young man.

"Jim, too?" Nicky asked eagerly and Jenna smiled. And Steven felt his heart melt.

"Sure." She stood up when Nicky raced off and called after him, "Wash your hands for supper!"

"What's for supper?" Steven asked and his melting heart quickened at her brilliant smile.

"Fried chicken," she answered, licking her lips.

Steven's body quickened along with his heart and he could only hope his sons didn't notice. He wasn't in the mood to talk about the birds and the bees tonight. Unless it was with Jenna. And unless the talk included a little extracurricular tutoring. "Are you cooking?" Steven asked and had to grin when Jenna's smile went from brilliant to very naughty.

"Depends on who's asking," she said saucily.

"I'm asking," Brad said dryly, appearing at his side, and Steven choked back a laugh at the guilty expression on Jenna's face. Like she'd been caught with her hand in the cookie jar.

She opened her mouth, then closed it again when Matt breezed through the front door carrying four plastic bags bearing the Colonel's bearded face. "No, the Colonel is," she said, recovering admirably. "It's for the best, really. I'm not much of a cook."

Matt shook his head. "Then I say you're out of here. I will permit no potential stepmothers into this house without the appropriate culinary skill."

Steven watched Jenna's face go bright red and knew his had done the same.

"Then it's a good thing you're not dating her," Brad said and pushed past Steven to grab two of the plastic bags from Matt's arms. "Anything in here but bones?"

Matt straightened, affronted. "I didn't touch anything."

Brad looked at Jenna who appeared still on the verge of apoplexy. "Wouldn't let him, huh?"

Jenna shook her head. "Threatened him with loss of arcade privileges."

Brad looked amused. "I knew you were too smart for him," he murmured. "Come on, Matt."

Steven watched his sons walk away. "I wonder if he was talking about me or Matt."

Jenna looked up at him, her eyes smiling. "Does it matter? Brad's back. What happened?"

Steven shook his head. "No idea." He hesitated, then went with his gut and cradled the back of her head in the palm of his hand, threading his fingers through her silky hair. She seemed to unwind, right before his eyes. "How's Casey?" he asked and was relieved when she smiled.

"She's going to be all right. They took out the breathing tube this morning, so her throat was still too sore to talk. I gave her a pad and pen and I left her cussing a handwritten blue streak at how long it was going to take her to grow her fingernails back. She'll go to a regular room tomorrow."

"Good." He lowered his face a few inches. "Jenna," he murmured.

Her eyes smiled. "Yes?"

He came an inch closer. "Can I kiss you?"

"Are you planning to run home again?"

"Can't," he murmured against her lips. "I live here."

"Then in that case . . ." Her words drifted off when he kissed her in earnest and when he lifted his head she followed, lifting herself on her toes, prolonging the contact another moment longer.

A delicate "ahem" made them both turn. Matt stood behind them with a wide grin on his face. "I have been asked to inform you that the chicken is nearly gone. If you wish to partake, you'll need to move your butts. No offense meant, Jenna."

She chuckled. "None taken."

Steven slid his arm around her waist, amazed how easily she'd slid into his life. "I say we eat."

Saturday, October 8, 9:30 P.M.

Steven moved restlessly in the bench seat, bumping Jenna's head as he readjusted the arm he'd stretched out behind her. "I'll give Davies another fifteen minutes, then we can go."

Jenna relaxed, enjoying Steven's strong arm behind her neck as they sat in the booth of a sports bar. They were waiting for Detective Davies to show up with something Steven would only say was 'important.' "I'm fine, Steven. It actually feels good to just sit and relax like normal people."

He smiled at her and she felt herself go all gooey inside. "So now we're normal people?" he asked, one golden brow lifting in teasing question.

Jenna snuggled closer, rubbing her cheek against the solid muscle of his chest. He smelled so good. Felt so good, so healthy. "Yes. For right now we are two people on a date, having beer and hot wings. Casey's safe, we're safe, Helen's home with the kids who are safe. For right now there are no crazy teenagers or serial killers. Just us normal people having a normal date."

Normal people. God knew he wanted to believe her. Except he knew that there was indeed a serial killer who happened also to be a crazy teenager. That was the problem with the job. It never went away. But for right now he could pretend to believe her. It was the closest he'd get to being "normal people." He brushed his lips across her hair. "So we're on a date?"

She looked up at him, suddenly serious. "Yes. Do you have a problem with that?"

Emotion hit him right in the middle of his chest and he knew at that moment there was no other place he'd rather be. And that the place itself didn't matter. It was being with her. Wherever that might be. "No," he whispered, his voice husky. "Not a single one."

"Good. Because I decided that we will have dates."

He had to smile. "Dates? Plural? So we'll do this beer and hot wings thing again?"

She nodded firmly. "Many times. Because I decided it was time to get on with my life."

She wasn't teasing, he realized. "So when did you make this momentous decision?"

"At five o'clock this afternoon. I looked down at my watch and saw the date. Then I realized it was two years ago today that Adam died and I hadn't thought about him once. For a second I felt guilty, you know? Then Cindy Lou knocked Nicky down in some leaves and started licking his face. Nicky started to giggle and I started to laugh and then . . ." Her voice trailed off.

He grazed his knuckles along the line of her jaw. "And then?"

She looked him in the eye as if challenging him to disagree. "And then I decided I was tired of watching calendars and measuring time."

He realized he really knew very little about her ordeal. "Jenna, what happened with Adam?"

She shrugged. "You know how it is. Your wife died, too. You grieve. You cry. You swear at God. You say you're sorry to God so He doesn't take anybody else you love." She sighed. "I guess the hardest part was going back to our apartment after he was gone. Going through his things. Knowing he'd never use them again."

"Was that the apartment you live in now?"

"No, I moved into where I am now after I dealt with all his things." She downed a mouthful of beer. "Adam's sister wanted me to move in with her." She shuddered. "That was not a good idea."

He pushed a stray lock of hair behind her ear. "Did Adam die in the hospital?"

"No, he died in a hospice."

"The one you visit on Sundays? Nicky told me Jim is a therapy dog. He was very impressed."

"I only go once a month. I swear it's one of the hardest things I do."

But she did it. Here was a woman who didn't back down from adversity. He lifted up her chin and looked into her eyes. "I have to say I'm very impressed, too."

Her smile was wry. "Then you're as easy to con as Nicky," she said. "I'm not that special, I just did what I had to do. Just like you did when your wife left you with three kids. That had to be hard."

It was, but not the way she thought. The hardest part was pretending to grieve a woman he'd come to hate. To look at his boys and know if Melissa hadn't died, he'd be explaining why she hadn't loved any of them enough. Mike was right about most things, but he was wrong about telling his boys the truth. It wouldn't have helped anyone. "Yeah," he finally said. "That was hard." He took a drink of his own beer. "So tell me about these dates we're going to have," he said, looking to change the subject. "Where would you like to go?"

Jenna watched the shadows cross his face and wished she could make them go away. Forever. "I don't know," she said playfully. "Hawaii wouldn't be bad." His brows shot up in surprise. "I'm just kidding," she added hastily. "I'm actually a pretty cheap date. Beer and hot wings is fine."

"I've never been to Hawaii," he said thoughtfully.

Jenna rolled her eyes. "I'm not asking to go to Hawaii. Nobody can afford a trip like that."

Steven sipped at his beer. "I can."

She looked at him suspiciously. "What do you mean? Cops don't make that much money."

He grinned at her and his eyes crinkled at the corners and her heart flip-flopped. "I'm not an ordinary cop," he said. "I'm a special agent."

Jenna balled up a napkin and tossed it at his head. "So where did you get all this extra cash, Special Agent Man?"

He shrugged. "My wife was killed by a drunk driver. The insurance company was very interested in settling out of court. At any rate, I probably couldn't take off enough time to go to Hawaii."

"How long has it been since you had a vacation?"

His lips quirked up in a smile that wasn't really a smile. "We took the boys to the beach when Nicky was a baby."

Jenna frowned. "You haven't had a vacation in five years?"

"More like six."

Jenna stared up at the ceiling. "And you wonder why you're stressed." She looked back at him and decided. "One of our dates will be a vacation."

His eyes smiled. "It will?"

"Yes, it will. You remember me talking about my friend Mark?"

"Your karate master."

"Yes. He and his wife have a little beachhouse on the Outer Banks." She batted her eyelashes at him. "We'll go there when you've decided we're past the hand-holding and good-night kiss stage."

His eyes changed in a heartbeat, going hot, his face taking on the look that made her want to devour him. "Maybe I already have."

She swallowed, feeling the sexual tension spike and with it the skin-tingling rush of heat that made her nipples tight and her panties wet. She touched her tongue to her lips, noting his eyes watching her every move and that turned her on even more. "What made you change your mind?"

He dipped his head, covered her mouth, and although gentle, his kiss held the promise of more.

More was good.

He pulled away and rested his forehead against hers, his brown eyes so close she could see the flecks of gold surrounding his dilated pupils. "You made my baby laugh," he said.

It was a good answer. It was such a good answer it sucked all the air from her lungs. "Has it been fifteen minutes?" Jenna asked, her voice rusty. "Because if it has, I say we ditch Detective Davies and go back to my place."

"It's been fifteen minutes," Steven said.

She quickly calculated how long it would take them to get back to her apartment. Too damn long. But once they arrived, there would finally be relief from this awful yearning. Finally.

But then, of course, came a knock on their booth. "Sorry I'm late," Detective Davies said. "Hope I'm not interrupting anything."

Steven squeezed his eyes shut. A muscle spasmed in his cheek. "Shit."

In dazed disbelief Jenna lifted her eyes to see Davies wearing a smile that made her wonder if he didn't know darn well he was "interrupting something" and wasn't enjoying the fact that he was.

Neil stretched his legs beneath the table Jenna had been sharing with Thatcher. It felt good to stretch his legs after all the hours in that damn soup can they had the nerve to call a rental car. It felt better to savor the few minutes alone with Jenna Marshall. For days she'd haunted his thoughts and dreams. For days he'd been spared the nightmares of the past four years. For three years he'd dreamed of ghosts and demons. For the past four days he'd dreamed of her. For four straight nights he'd had peace. He'd decided peace was something he'd fight to keep.

He'd decided _she_ was someone he'd fight to keep. She'd have a choice, of course. So he'd have to ensure the lady had all the facts to make the right choice.

"So tell me a little about yourself, Jenna," he said as she glanced toward the front door where Thatcher had disappeared with his cell phone and the fax Neil had just received from Barrow in Seattle. He had to hand it to Thatcher. The man wasn't entirely inept. He'd taken one look at the fax and instantly understood the significance. Which was why Thatcher was in his car with his cell phone talking to ADA Liz Johnson at the moment.

"Not a whole lot to tell, Detective Davies," she said with a smile. A smile that said she wished him to perdition, Neil thought and made himself smile back. It didn't take a genius to recognize what he'd interrupted.

"Call me Neil. How's Casey?" he asked, and the light that came on in her eyes nearly took his breath away. She was a beautiful woman, but when her face lit up . . . she was unforgettable. And he damned Thatcher all over again.

"She's going to be fine," she said. "Thank you for asking."

"You're welcome. So I hear you're a teacher. What do you teach?"

"High school chemistry and general science." She looked over at the door again and Neil found himself becoming annoyed.

"He'll be back soon enough," he said irritably. "I take it your car was totaled in the wreck." And he watched her expression become angry and sad at the same time.

"It was."

"Well, your insurance should replace it."

Her eyes narrowed. "It was a 1960 Jaguar XK 150."

Neil winced. "Ouch."

She sighed. "It belonged to my fiancé who passed away two years ago."

"I'm sorry."

She gave a rueful wince. "Me, too. I still have to tell his family that I wrecked his car."

"But you didn't wreck it. It was sabotage."

"I don't think I'll mention the cut brakes," she said. "They worry about me enough as it is."

"They?"

"My fiancé's family. They're rather overprotective."

"So what will you tell them?" he asked, praying Thatcher stayed out in his car another ten minutes. Ten more minutes with Jenna. "I don't think this is something you'll be able to hide with a few cosmetic touch-ups."

She smiled ruefully. "I don't know. Do you have any ideas?"

He pretended to consider it. "You could tell them the car was stolen."

She shook her head. "No, then they'd staple 'lost' posters to every tree in Raleigh and take out an ad on a milk carton."

Neil threw back his head and laughed. "Well, how about telling them you sold it to passing gypsies for three magic beans?"

She smiled at him engagingly. "No gypsies would be safe from the Clan Llewellyn."

Neil cocked a brow. "Llewellyn is their name? My grandmother on my mother's side was a Llewellyn. My family came over from Wales about sixty years ago."

"You should talk to Seth. My fiancé's father, that is." She frowned. "My former fiancé."

"I understand," Neil said.

Her lips smiled but her eyes still frowned as if frustrated by her verbal slip. And it didn't take a very observant man to notice the man's ring she worried on the thumb of her right hand. He was sure it had belonged to her dead fiancé. When she was his, she'd put the ring away. She could keep it, just not on her finger.

"Anyway," she said, "Seth came over from Swansea when he was a boy." She leaned toward him and dropped her voice conspiratorially. "He'll carry on for hours about Wales to anyone foolish enough to step into his parlor. If he brings out the slide projector, run like hell."

Neil smiled back. "If I have time before I leave, I'd love to meet him. I have lots of questions about my grandparents' birthplace, which I don't think is far from Swansea. I—" He stopped when her facial expression froze and looked over to where she was staring.

Thatcher stood ten feet away, looking mad enough to chew nails.

Neil slid from the booth and approached him. "Plans in place?" he asked, but Thatcher didn't turn his way, just kept staring at Jenna with a furious look. Thatcher was jealous, an emotion Neil well understood.

"Liz says it's not enough," Thatcher gritted.

Neil frowned, glancing at Jenna from the corner of his eye. She was pale and he worried about the spot he'd put her in. But surely Thatcher wasn't a violent man, he thought, finding his protective instincts raised. Uneasily he turned his back on Jenna to stare at Thatcher. "What do you mean it's not enough? One of Parker's teachers signs an affidavit saying he threatened her with bodily harm if she didn't pass him out of her class? It's a direct link to the vandalism in Jenna's class. What more does your ADA want to bring Parker in for questioning?"

"Maybe you should go ask her. Now would be good," Thatcher responded through his teeth.

"Thatcher," he began, but Thatcher turned with his jaw clenched so hard it was a wonder the man didn't break every tooth in his head.

"I'll see you tomorrow, Davies."

Neil looked back to the table where Jenna sat chewing on her lower lip, her eyes now troubled. Not afraid, just troubled. And quite possibly more than just a little bit pissed. He remembered the brown belt she'd worn around her waist when he'd met her Thursday night and figured she was more than capable of taking care of herself. Even so, he'd check on her tomorrow. Just to make sure she was all right. A professional courtesy, as it were. "Tomorrow, then," he said to Thatcher, and against his better judgment, left the bar without looking back.

TWENTY-FOUR

Saturday, October 8, 10:15 P.M.

JENNA WAS OUT OF THE VOLVO AND HALFWAY UP the stairs to her apartment by the time he got the keys out of the ignition. Muttering a curse, he followed, catching up with her at her front door.

She looked up from searching her purse, her eyes accusing. "I think it's better for both of us if you just went home, Steven," she said softly, then turned to look behind her with a scowl. "I'm all *right*, Mrs. Kasselbaum. We just had a fight. If you'd care to come out in your hair curlers I'd be glad to tell you all about it."

The door clicked closed and Jenna gritted her teeth, dropping her eyes to search her purse again. Dismissing him.

"Jenna, we need to talk."

"I think you've said quite enough for one evening, don't you think?"

He blew out a breath. "I said I was sorry. Just open the door so we can discuss this in private, okay?"

She shook her purse in frustration. "I'd open the door if I could find my damn keys."

The door behind them opened and a gnarled old hand appeared with two keys connected with a bread bag twisty-tie. "Thank you, Mrs. Kasselbaum," Steven gritted and took the keys, remembering he still hadn't changed the deadbolt on Jenna's front door. He ignored Jenna's outstretched palm and unlocked the door himself, holding it open as she squeezed past him with a glare.

He closed the door and leaned against it. Watched her hang up her jacket and run a soothing hand over Jean-Luc's back before sending the dog back to his bed in the corner. The dog glared at him, able to read Jenna's mood.

So could Steven. She was upset. She had a right to be. He'd been jealous and curt and had embarrassed her in front of Davies. "I said I was sorry."

She nodded, her back to him. "Yes, you did. Now would you care to tell me why?"

"Why I'm sorry?"

"No, why you threw that little tantrum back at the bar."

He gritted his teeth at the trivialization. "It wasn't a tantrum."

She turned around, scorn on her face. "Then what was it, exactly, because I'm confused. I only know this is the second time you've jumped to the wrong conclusion when you've seen me talk to another man. Your track record leaves much to be desired, Agent Thatcher."

He shook his head. "What are you talking about?"

"Thursday night at the hospital—when you came in with Neil and I was with Ned and Lucas. You were angry then, too."

Steven locked his arms across his chest, remembering how he felt seeing her in the arms of another man. He hadn't been angry. He'd been hurt. But now he'd be damned before admitting that to her. "I was not angry. Surprised, maybe, but not angry."

She drew a deep breath and let it out slowly. "Fine." She lightly pushed him away from the front door and he let her do it. Opening the front door she gestured for him to leave. "I'd like to continue this when you're willing to talk to me," she said, in what he imagined to be her schoolteacher voice. It grated on him. "But it's late and I'm tired and I'd like you to go now."

He stared at her for a full minute. She meant it. She was throwing him out. "Davies wants you for himself," he heard himself say, then waited.

Her lips twisted in a humorless smile. "Well, Steven, you of all people should know we don't get everything we want. You actually thought I . . ." She let the thought trail away and shook her head. "If you could even think I could go with him not twenty minutes after talking about making love with you?" She swallowed hard. "Then we weren't talking about making love. We were only talking about having sex. And to borrow a trite phrase, I'm not that kind of a girl." She motioned to the hallway with a flourish. "Good night, Steven."

Uncertainly he stepped out into the hall and a second later was staring at the door she'd quietly closed in his face. Slowly he trudged down the stairs and to his car where he had an eagle's eye view of Jenna standing at her window, looking down at him.

She just stared down as he stared up, her expression so disappointed and grave. No hysterics or thrown pottery as Melissa would have done. And he heard Mike's voice in his head. "Not all women are Melissa." Steven knew that. He knew Jenna was nothing like Melissa. He'd known it from the very start. Yet at the first opportunity he'd allowed himself to believe the worst. He'd wounded her before she could wound him.

And he'd done a damn fine job.

He watched as she went into the kitchen, coming out with the container of ice cream she'd taken comfort in the night Casey got hurt. The night he'd told her he could fall in love with her. Because she was beautiful and kind. Every man's dream.

His dream. *So get your ass back up there and apologize*, his self told him severely. So he did.

"Jenna, open the door," he coaxed when she didn't answer. "Please." He'd leaned his forehead on her door when he heard a giant sigh behind him and turned to find Mrs. Kasselbaum in her robe and hair curlers looking as if she really wanted to take a switch to his hide.

"Do I have to do everything for you people?" she demanded in an exasperated voice. "I gave you the keys not ten minutes ago. Have you lost them already?"

Steven dug in his pocket and felt the twisty-tie prick his finger. "No, ma'am." He brought out the keys and showed them to her. "Here they are."

She rolled her eyes. "And there is the door. Do I have to draw you a map? Key, door. I swear, young man, if my safety is in your hands, I'm going to buy a gun."

Steven felt his lips twitch. "No, ma'am, don't do that. I'm sorry we woke you."

"Don't let this become a nightly occurrence," she snapped and stepped back into her apartment.

Jenna looked up, startled when her door swung open and Steven walked in as if he owned the place. She glared at him, wishing she had never let him into her heart. Wishing she'd never given him the power to hurt her so badly. Wishing Mrs. Kasselbaum didn't have a spare set of keys to her apartment. "I thought I told you to go away."

"I changed my mind."

"I didn't." Sensing her mood, Jean-Luc curled up at her feet and she could feel a low growl vibrating through his body.

"I'm sorry."

"Yeah, right," she said bitterly. "We seem to have had this conversation before."

He took another step closer and she could smell his cologne. He smelled so good. "I'm an idiot," he said, looking so good. So damn good. Her heart kicked up a notch and she felt her skin sizzle. And cursed the fact that she was so easy when it came to him.

She looked down into the ice cream, fighting the urge to forget his tantrum and throw herself into his arms, to simply take up where they'd left off before Davies spoiled everything. No, she corrected herself. Before Steven thought the worst of her. "I figured that out the day we first met."

"You were right then." He came closer until his hand closed over hers, sending the spoon back into the ice cream and a current straight down the middle of her body. "You were right tonight. I was a jealous jerk. I'm sorry."

She looked up at him and knew she'd be lucky to hold out for a reasonable explanation. She was a done duck. "Why are you a jealous jerk?"

He tugged on her hand and she let him pull her to her feet. "Because I never had a woman look at me the way you do," he said softly.

Damn. Slick words. "Save your rehearsed lines, Steven," she managed. "I'm not interested."

"They aren't rehearsed lines," he said sharply. "It's the truth." He closed his eyes and she watched his lips move as he counted backward from ten. When his eyes opened they were calm. And vulnerable. "I was hurt," he said. "I saw the way you looked at Davies and I . . ." He shrugged. "I guess I just wanted to be different." His lip quirked self-consciously. "Special." He rolled his eyes. "It sounds really stupid when I say it out loud like that."

Her heart touched, Jenna shook her head. "No, Steven, it doesn't. You are different." She reached up and rested her fingertips against his jaw. "Special," she whispered.

His brown eyes flashed. "How?" His whisper was fierce. "Tell me how I'm different."

In that flash of a moment Jenna remembered the Italian

place on Capitol and her own jealous feelings when the
waitress brushed too close to Steven's side. And the way he
just kept looking at her, Jenna, as if the waitress didn't even
exist. He was wrong about Neil, but now she understood his
pain. Something caught in her throat, making her voice
shaky. "Because of the way you look at me," she told him.
"Like I'm the only woman in the room."

His hands trembled as they gently framed her face. "You
are," he whispered, then all she saw was his brown eyes as
he came closer.

Then she closed her eyes and saw nothing at all. Just felt
his mouth on hers, gentle at first. Then he groaned and she
groaned and the kiss went wild and his hands were on her
breasts through her sweater, then under her sweater and
under her bra and finally on her bare skin. His fingertips
plucked at her nipples and she heard the sharp intake of her
own breath as she pulled her lips away from his. She looked
up at him, panting just as he was, sure her eyes were just as
aroused as his. But he was still holding back. She could
sense it.

"What do you want, Steven?"

He never blinked. "Everything."

"So take it," she challenged in a whisper and that
seemed to finally crack the hold of his control. Grabbing at
the hem of her sweater he pulled it over her head, taking
the bra with it. She could feel the burn of his eyes on her
bare breasts as he yanked off his jacket, his shoulder holster, his shirt. Until he stood before her naked from the
waist up.

His chest was covered with the coarse hair she'd only
felt, but never seen. Golden, it shimmered in the light,
beckoning her touch. Then he was kissing her again, hot
openmouthed kisses that stole her breath even as he flattened her hands on his chest, moving her palms back and

forth across the nipples that were almost hidden within the golden hair.

She wanted to feel the hairs on his chest against her own nipples so she slid her arms around his neck and pressed closer, her body drifting side to side, feeling the friction. It was wonderful. Absolutely wonderful. But not enough. But he took care of that, too, grabbing at her butt and pulling her higher until she wound her legs around his waist and felt him pulsing against her. Ripping her mouth away, she looked into his eyes, panted his name. "Steven."

"Which room?" he asked hoarsely, settling her legs around his waist.

"Back one on the left. Steven," she said as he took the hallway back to her room at a near jog.

"What?" he said, sounding slightly out of breath.

"I bought condoms." Her cheeks were red, but she didn't care. "A whole box."

"Good," he muttered and pushed open her bedroom door. Taking the three steps to the foot of her bed, he dropped her so that she lay sprawled before him. "I only brought one."

"So we'll do this more than once?" she asked, meaning to tease, but hearing the question come out as sexy foreplay.

Roughly he pulled at the snap on her jeans and in three seconds had her stripped to the skin. His eyes started at her face and explored every inch of her body, while the muscle in his cheek jerked and spasmed and she felt more erotic than she'd ever felt in her whole life.

"God, yes. As many times as you'll let me." His eyes returned to her face and she felt another rush of moist warm heat between her legs. "I dreamed of your silk stockings and garters," he said softly, his voice smoky with desire. "Next time I want you to wear those for me. Only those." Blindly, he pulled at his belt, dropping his pants, kicking off his shoes. The boxers went next leaving him naked before her eyes. His erection jerked and she could see how engorged it was. He was ready. For her.

Blindly she reached for the box of condoms in her nightstand, wishing too late that she'd taken off the plastic wrap. As she struggled with the box, Steven slid between her legs, sliding his body up along hers, then leaned forward, bracing one hand on either side of her head. And kissed her. Hotly, erotically, his tongue plunging in and out of her mouth in a prelude of what was to come. She ripped at the box and the plastic and cardboard came apart at once, sending a shower of condoms across the bed. She picked up one and tore the foil.

"Here," she said raggedly against his lips and unbelievably she felt him smile.

"Now?" He leaned back on one elbow and ran his hand down her body, over her breast, her stomach, his fingertips teasing against the juncture between her legs and she lurched up, a shiver making her hot and cold all at once. "What about foreplay?" He slid one finger up into her and she wanted to scream. Because she was close, so close. And because she wanted him inside her when she came, but her body moved against his hand of its own volition. She groaned and he shuddered.

"Now," she demanded, feeling the throbbing in her body, in her head. Everywhere. *"Now."*

Sobering, he raised up on his knees, looming over her, and she watched him slide the condom down his length. Slowly. Down his very long length.

"Steven!"

Then slowly he aligned his body with hers and whispered, "Now," and plunged, entering her fully in one stroke. She cried out and he groaned her name and then he was moving, in and out, harder and harder. She lifted her knees to bring him deeper, feeling her body tighten and climb higher and higher, rocking against him until she couldn't bear it another minute longer. Until she arched and came apart, flying, truly flying, his name on her lips even though her throat didn't make a sound. Gasping, trembling, she fell back against the bed, her eyes focusing on his face tight with unspent passion, on his eyes, filled with a myriad of emotions. She trailed her fingertips down his back, the only movement she had strength enough to do. With a feral growl he followed her path into oblivion, his body straining, his muscles quivering, his face a thing of beauty in his release.

He collapsed against her, shuddering as he buried his face in the pillow. She held him, stroked his hair while his finely honed body jerked from the aftershocks. She'd heard it called afterglow, but after such an earth-shattering experience, aftershock seemed a more appropriate term. Finally he lifted his head and kissed her, making them both shiver anew.

"You came," he murmured, as if unsure she would, and even after everything they'd just done together, Jenna found she could still blush.

"I did," she returned, unsure if she ever really had before. Certainly not quite like she had tonight. And if her first real orgasm was on the night of the second anniversary of Adam's death . . . She pushed the thought to the very back of her mind, resolving to deal with the guilt later.

He moved his lips down her neck and she stretched to one side to give him better access. "I'm glad," he murmured against her skin and she smiled.

"Me, too."

He lifted his head and kissed the side of her smiling mouth. "How do you feel about seconds?"

She ran her hands down his back, cupping the very taut

cheeks of his ass. He had an incredible body. "I don't know," she said and almost laughed at the disappointment in his eyes.

"Okay," he said although it was clear it was anything but.

"It's just that I don't know where we'll find any more . . . you know . . . protection."

His eyes gleamed and he reached out and grabbed a handful of foil packets and dumped them on her head. "I think we've got that covered, Jenna."

"Then yes, please. Seconds would be very nice. But I suppose we have to leave room for dessert. You owe me after all."

His brows snapped together. "How so?"

"You left my Rocky Road to melt all over the table."

His eyes crinkled at the edges. "I'll buy you another pint."

"Make it a gallon and we'll talk thirds and fourths."

"Jenna, are we talking about ice cream?"

She smiled up at him. "We're talking about anything you want."

TWENTY-FIVE

Sunday, October 9, 6:30 A.M.

THEY SNUCK INTO STEVEN'S HOUSE THROUGH the laundry room, holding hands like teenagers late for curfew. After the night they'd shared it was small wonder either of them could still walk. They'd made love twice more in the night, dozing until four A.M. or so. They planned to shower and get back to Steven's house so Jenna could get Jim and Casey's truck and be gone long before sunup.

Jenna squinted in the semidarkness. The sun had just started to come up. They were arriving home later than they'd planned, through no fault of her own. Steven had instigated the delay in the shower. She grinned to herself. She just helped. A lot. Her body still tingled from all the helping. She'd helped all night long. Altruism certainly had its benefits.

"What are you grinning at?" Steven murmured, looking down at her with a tender smile that made her heart do crazy things in her chest.

She lifted a brow and said nothing, which made him grin, too. "You're a pervert, Dr. Marshall."

She gave him her prim look. "And this is a problem how?"

He laughed softly. "Who said anything about a problem? Come on, let's find your dog and get you guys out of here before one of the boys discovers us. Or even worse, Helen."

"You're already trying to get rid of me," she grumbled playfully, following him through the door into the kitchen where she abruptly ran into his back. Because he'd abruptly stopped. Jenna peeked around his shoulder and immediately saw why.

"Oh, little boy," she murmured, experiencing a rush of something that felt suspiciously maternal. Nicky sat at the kitchen table, eyes closed, one freckled cheek plastered to the wood veneer, clutching something in his fist, next to his cheek. He was guarded by two hairy soldiers, Cindy Lou at his feet and Jim behind his chair. Jim lifted his head and Jenna swore the dog smiled.

Jenna took a tiptoed step closer to see what Nicky held in

his hand and frowned. It was a rubber worm. A fishing lure. She turned around to find Steven looking stricken.

"What's wrong?" she whispered.

"Last Friday I promised I'd try to take him fishing this weekend," Steven replied, his eyes glued to his little boy. He swallowed hard. "But I can't. I have a staff meeting at eight."

Jenna could practically touch the tension coming from him, and thought about all the responsibilities on his head. Three teenaged girls, two gone forever, one missing. A serial killer out there somewhere, still stalking his victims.

On the other hand, his own little boy was just starting to show sparks of life again after his own traumatic experience six months ago. His own little boy who he was going to have to disappoint. Feeling a bit like Solomon, Jenna put her arms around Steven's neck and hugged him hard. "Go to your staff meeting, Steven. Do what you need to do to keep our girls safe. I'll take Nicky fishing. When you're done you can come and meet us at the lake." She pulled back to find doubt written all over his face. "Don't worry, I am a very capable fisherman." She smiled up at him. "We might even catch something."

He shook his head. "Of that I have no doubt. There isn't much you can't do, Jenna. But are you sure you want to take an active boy fishing? You don't have to."

Jenna looked back to where Nicky sat sleeping. "I know I don't have to. I want to." Then a disturbing thought seized her. "But if you don't want me to, I'll understand. I know you're worried he'll get attached too fast."

Steven crooked his finger under her chin and pulled until she looked up at him and her disturbing line of thought was squashed by the look in his warm brown eyes. "He already is, Jen. So am I." He covered her mouth with his, so gently, so . . . lovingly, her heart clenched. A wave of wanting hit her, so intense she felt paralyzed in her tracks. Not sexual wanting. He'd more than satisfied her in that way. This was more, this was a wanting of everything he represented. The man, the children, the instant family.

A family who would need her as much as she needed them.

A family she could love. A real family of her very own.

She wanted it, wanted it all so intensely she could only stand there, her heart pounding as he kissed her in his kitchen, as if she belonged there. When he lifted his head, his eyes narrowed slightly in concern. "Are you all right?"

Jenna drew a trembling breath, feeling the literal earth moving under her feet. "I'm fine. I'll be fine." She made herself smile at him. "Go get ready for work. I'll make you breakfast."

Sunday, October 9, 8:05 A.M.

He should have been exhausted, Steven thought, but he wasn't. In fact, his skin still tingled from her good-bye kiss. There was certainly something to be said for the rejuvenating powers of sex. He felt like he hadn't felt . . . ever. But playtime was over. His team had assembled themselves together early on a Sunday morning to find a murderer and hopefully to keep him from raising their tally of dead teens to three. Steven wasn't sure how close they were to doing either. "Good morning," he said and the murmuring quieted. "What do we know?"

Harry opened his notebook with a yawn. He'd been responsible for following Rudy all night. "Well, Rudy had quite an evening. Three parties, none of them keggers." He looked up with a baleful glare. "I really wanted to arrest him for underage alcohol consumption."

"That would have been too simple," Steven said dryly.

Harry shot him an amused look. "He left the last party with a girl who looked a lot older than high school. They went to her place and Rudy didn't come out until three A.M. Looking very rested I might add. The girl dropped him off at his house just before four A.M. and he didn't leave again."

Steven looked over at Davies who looked frustrated but said nothing. "He's had Alev Rahrooh for two days now," Steven said thoughtfully. "He kept both Lorraine and Samantha just under a week. I doubt Alev's already dead, so he'll have to go to her sooner or later. That's still assuming Rudy's our man. Sandra, how far did you get with the list of athletes with priors?"

Davies now looked both agitated and frustrated but still said nothing.

"About three-quarters of the way," Sandra answered. "No obvious connections. But I did check the cheerleading schedules of each of the vics' high schools. All three played Roosevelt High *at* Roosevelt within a week of each girl's disappearance. That makes a pretty strong case for Lutz."

Davies's smile was just the tiniest bit smug. "It's him. I know it."

Steven pushed back from his chair and walked over to stare at the photos on the bulletin board feeling his own frustration grow. "Davies, any progress on the tattoo design?"

Davies's smug smile faded. "No. I've asked every cop I know. But I know it's him."

Steven gritted his teeth. "We have a prime suspect and we can't touch him. Dammit. I think we all need to take a break from the case," he said. "I know there's someplace I'd rather be today. See everybody tomorrow morning." Everyone filed out, Davies bringing up the rear, fidgeting with the change in his pocket.

"I called Jenna this morning to make sure she was all right after last night," Davies said.

Steven's defenses went straight up. "What about last night?"

"You were pretty angry when you left the bar. I wanted to be sure she was all right. That nothing happened. But she wasn't home."

Steven felt a smug smile of his own curve his lips and watched Davies's black eyes flash with fury. "Whatever did or didn't happen is none of your business," Steven said, "but if you must know, she's not home because she took my boys fishing. Which is just where I'm planning to go myself." He'd made it to the door when Davies spoke. Bitterly.

"Did she take her fiancé's ring off while you did it?"

Steven froze. She hadn't. He'd noticed. He'd also told himself she'd take off Adam's ring in her own time. Steven might be jealous of Davies, but he'd be pretty low to be jealous of a dead man. Making his feet move, he walked away without dignifying Davies with an answer.

He'd made it to the parking lot and was seconds from getting away when he heard someone clear his throat. He turned to find a holy man with a very worried expression on his face.

"Agent Thatcher? I'm Reverend Monsignor Brennan of the Raleigh Dioceses. I was wondering if you could take a few minutes to talk about Father Mike Leone."

Steven sighed. He'd figured this would be coming sooner or later. "Of course, Monsignor Brennan. Let's go up to my office." He didn't bother glancing at his watch. He figured it would be after noon before he got done clearing Mike's name. Fishing would have to wait.

Sunday, October 9, 8:25 P.M.

Weary beyond measure, Steven entered his house only to have Helen, Matt, and Brad lift their respective fingers to their lips and shush him. The three stood around the bottom of the steps and Helen pointed upward. "Jenna's putting Nicky to bed. Sshh."

"But I'm not tired," came Nicky's whine from upstairs and Steven's heart stuttered. Most parents hated that whining tone, but he hadn't heard it out of Nicky since before his abduction. His baby had obeyed automatically for so long that a whine about bedtime sounded like an angel's choir.

"Well, I am," Jenna was laughing. "You kept me busy, taking all those fish off your hook."

"I could have done it myself." Nicky sounded highly amused. "I'm good at that part."

"Well, *now* you tell me. Are you sure you want to sleep on that hard floor? It doesn't look very comfortable." There was a long pause and Steven met Helen's eyes and realized they were both praying for a minor miracle—for Nicky to sleep in his own bed for the first time in six months. "Well, suit yourself," Jenna said and Steven let out the breath he'd been holding. Rome wasn't built in a day, he thought. They'd get there with Nicky. They would. "Can I at least cover you up?" Jenna asked. There was quiet and then Nicky's voice.

"Could you sing?"

"Me?" Jenna's horrified response made them all smile. "You want *me* to sing to *you*?"

"You don't hafta." Steven looked at Helen who smiled at Nicky's dramatically mournful tone.

"Well, since I don't hafta, I won't," Jenna replied and Matt snickered softly. "Besides," she added, "we weren't much for lullabies in my house. My dad had an old drinking song he would sing when my mother wasn't around, but I suspect your dad might have a problem with that."

"Yeah, he prob'ly would," Nicky agreed thoughtfully. "But he's not here right now," he added in a bright voice and Steven choked back a laugh.

"Good night, Nicky," Jenna said firmly.

"Will you be here when I wake up tomorrow?" Nicky asked, so softly they all had to strain to hear him and Steven swallowed, trying to dislodge the lump that had formed in his throat.

"No, sweetheart, I have to go home. I have school tomorrow and Jean-Luc will be missing Jim. I think I'll see you in a few days. Now, go to sleep."

Jenna appeared at the top of the stairs, dressed in a pair of Steven's old sweats, her feet bare and her wet hair hanging down her back in a single braid. Steven felt his soul settle at the sight of her, even as she started in surprise. "I didn't know I had an audience," she said in a low voice when she got to the bottom where they waited. "Now I'm doubly glad I didn't sing."

"So are we," Matt said with a grin and she swatted him.

"Go get a shower, Matt. You're still covered in *yck*."

Steven took a look at his middle boy whose grin had become a scowl. Matt's jeans were covered in black slime up to his mid-calf. "Yes, you are. What'd you fall into, Matthew?"

"You don't want to know," Jenna answered for him and it was Brad's turn to snicker as Matt skulked up the stairs. "Don't you start," she said, turning to Brad. "Besides, I understand that you have some homework to catch up on." She looked his oldest in the eye, silently issuing a challenge.

Brad met her gaze for a long minute in which everybody held their breaths, then he nodded. "I understand that there's this really nice chemistry teacher who gives after-school tutoring."

Jenna sucked in her cheeks, considering his request. "It'll cost you. Standard tutoring fees."

Brad shrugged. "It's okay. My dad's good for it."

Jenna shook her head quickly. "Uh-uh. Cash comes from you or no deal."

Brad's eyes widened when he realized she was very serious. "Dad!"

Steven held up his hands. "I'm not involved in this negotiation. Plus, I agree with her."

"You would," Brad said in a disgusted tone. "I've got no cash."

Jenna raised her brows. "Then you'd best get a job." She looked at Helen. "Was there any pot roast left from dinner?"

Helen's expression was serene. "I already made you a plate."

Steven looked from one to the other. "Why didn't you eat with the others?"

"You don't want to know!" Matt yelled from up the stairs.

Jenna chuckled. "No, you really don't. Let's just say I hope I left some hot water for Matt after getting all the *yck* cleaned off of me and Nicky."

"I'm sorry I missed the fun," Steven said, with a pang of regret.

Jenna patted his arm. "Next time you can come. We'll just choose a different fishing hole."

"Brad, come," Helen instructed. "I have work for you to do to pay for those tutoring lessons."

"But—" Brad protested and Helen cut him off with a look. "Okay," he muttered and followed Helen, leaving Steven alone with Jenna in the relative privacy of his open foyer.

"Sounds like you all had an adventure today," he murmured, sliding his hands under the sweatshirt she wore, touching the warm, firm flesh of her back. Wishing they were more alone so he could touch the warm, firm flesh of her front.

"That it was." She linked her hands around his neck. "What about you? Any progress?"

He thought about his four-hour "deposition" with the monsignor. He thought of Mike's career and wondered once again if he'd ever fully repair the damage they'd done to a great man's name. He thought about the fact that Victor Lutz had finally detected the presence of the unmarked cars on his street and complained to the mayor and how Steven had to tell the mayor they were watching for school vandals because he wasn't supposed to know Rudy Lutz was really William Parker. He thought about how humiliating it had been to be scolded like a schoolboy for misuse of county resources. And how he'd defied orders and extended the patrol surveillance for one more day.

He considered the latest barrage of questions from the press, outraged at his team's inability to solve this crime in their allotted one hour of prime time. And he thought about the mountain of paperwork he'd scaled, knowing it would have grown back to its previous height by tomorrow morning. So had he made any progress? "No, not a whole hell of a lot," he answered.

"Don't do that," she said softly.

"Do what?"

"Click off with me. It's like you go somewhere else and leave me behind."

He stiffened. It was a very Melissa-like comment, but delivered without venom. Today. Who knew where they'd be in five years. Ten? "It's part of the job, Jen. It's part of who I am."

She digested this in silence, not breaking her eye contact. Then finally said, "All right."

"All right? Just all right?"

She smiled and he felt the knot in his gut loosen by slow degrees. "Just all right. I guess the trick on my end will be not getting hurt when you click off." She lifted on her toes and brushed a soft kiss across his mouth. "But the trick on your end will be not to click off that often. Or wait too long to click back on."

It was a proposal of sorts. "I can live with that. If you can."

"I can," she whispered, still a fraction of an inch from his mouth.

But for how long? he wanted to ask. But didn't. He didn't have any right to ask at this point. They'd known each other nearly two weeks. They'd never talked anything more long-term than the next day. Certainly never come close to uttering the word "love."

Yes, you did, Thatcher, his self told him. *You told her you could fall in love with her.*

Yes, I did. And maybe I have, he thought. *Maybe.*

"Steven, you look completely exhausted. Go eat dinner and go to bed."

Her words reminded his brain of how tired he really was. "I'm sorry, Jenna. I'm not much company tonight."

She slipped one hand from the back of his neck to put gentle pressure on his mouth. "Get some rest, Steven. Call me tomorrow and we can talk some more. I'm going home now."

Home. To her apartment. His brain kicked back into full throttle. Until they picked up Rudy Lutz and his friends, he didn't want her being alone at night. "Jenna, I've been thinking about that. I'd feel better if you stayed here tonight."

Her lips quirked. "I bet you would, but I don't believe you have it in you, Special Agent Man."

He chuckled, despite his exhaustion. "If that's a challenge, I'll declare you the winner right now. No, I'm talking about Lutz and his friends. Pullman hasn't found anything tying any of them to your car yet and I just want you to be safe. For dumb jocks who can't pass high school these guys have shown an amazing amount of planning and care."

Jenna chewed on her lower lip. "I don't want those thugs to keep me from living in my own apartment. I'll be careful and I've got the dogs. I'll be fine."

Sunday, October 9, 10:25 P.M.

She was home. Finally. Driving her friend's car. Shame about her Jag. Somebody spent a lot of time restoring that baby. *She could have been killed,* he thought, and huffed a chuckle. When he was done with her, she'd wish she'd been behind the wheel of that car instead of her friend.

He watched her jog up the two flights of stairs to her apartment. Studied the construction of the balconies jutting away from the building. They would easily hold his weight and the weight of his kit. He frowned a little. He'd be bulky tonight, but that was the price of a house call. He really didn't want to drag her off to the barn. She was a lot bigger than the others, a veritable Amazon compared to the petite Lorraine and Alev. Samantha had been taller, but so willowy. He smiled remembering how pretty she'd been. How pretty they'd all been.

No, house calls weren't nearly as much fun. He'd miss the extended play opportunities the barn offered. He'd just have to make this one night with Miss Marshall count. He'd been watching and waiting for this opportunity for days, even leaving Alev tonight, although Alev was just about gone. All used up. His heart quickened in anticipation. With her size and strength Miss Marshall would put up quite a struggle, so one night just might be enough.

He sat patiently as she walked her dog. Lifted his binoculars and watched her putter around her kitchen. Microwave her dinner and eat it at her dining-room table. From here he could just see the light glinting off the glass covering her diplomas and cursed the fact that from his vantage point in the parking lot he could only see both her and her apartment from above her waist. A lot of good stuff happened below the waist. He tingled just thinking about it.

And wondered if it felt any different killing a smart woman versus a stupid one.

Well, he'd find out tonight.

Twenty-six

Monday, October 10, 1:00 A.M.

THE BRIGHT LIGHT SHINING IN HER EYES lurched Jenna from deep sleep into instant awareness. The sharp bite of the knife at her throat made her flinch and obey the growled words.

"Don't move."

Quickly she fought past the mental confusion of deep sleep. "Who—"

"Shut up." And she heard the loud ripping sound of tape. Then her mouth was covered and she realized whoever this was either had use of both hands or wasn't alone. But when the light never wavered, she knew it was freestanding. That he had use of both hands. That he was alone. She also knew she owned no such light, which meant he'd come prepared. And that knowledge frightened her more than if he hadn't been alone.

He'd broken into her apartment. And gotten past the dogs. Jim and Jean-Luc. *Where were the dogs?* she wondered frantically, then forced herself to calm. Forced herself to draw deep even breaths through her nose. Forced herself to remember everything she'd been taught in self-defense. Clenched her fists under the blanket.

Which he ripped away like a magician with a tablecloth. "Now you'll pay, *Miss* Marshall."

Miss Marshall. Only one person called her *Miss* Marshall like that.

Victor Lutz. His image flashed before her, his huge hulking body, big hands. Cold, dark, threatening eyes.

Oh, my God. The panic bubbled up. *He's going to kill me. I never should have confronted him that way over Casey. Now he's going to kill me.*

Jenna, stop. Breathe. Think.

She stopped. Breathed. Tried to think.

She knew her physical capability. She'd never be able to overpower a man of Victor Lutz's size and strength, even with all her training in martial arts. But she might be able to surprise him long enough to get away. To get help.

Jenna stiffened her body, waiting for him to touch her, waiting for the slightest decrease in the pressure of the knife at her throat, the slightest indication he was distracted, knowing she'd have only one chance to surprise him and escape.

Instead, the pressure on the knife increased, ever so slightly. It hurt. A lot. A whimper built in her throat and with it, the panic.

He's going to kill me. Steven will find me, but it will be too late. I'll be dead.

Jenna, stop. Breathe. Think.

A heavy hand covered her breast through the worn T-shirt she wore to bed. Pinched her nipple hard. She jerked a breath through her nose. Couldn't contain the whimper this time.

"Do you like that?" he growled. He shoved her nightshirt up to her stomach and fingered her panties. She could hear his breathing grow harder. Faster. "Pretty."

She couldn't control the urge to close her legs, but he just laughed softly. His hand disappeared and she heard the soft scrape of leather? No. Plastic? Possibly. A bag? Maybe. No, she thought hearing a snap, click, snap, click. Metal buckles, opening up and hitting a plastic case. She captured each detail, knowing if she got away she'd need to tell the police everything she could.

Then she heard another sound, one that made her nearly sob with relief.

A soft growl, this one canine. *The dogs.*

Then a furor of barking, snarling.

Cursing. Vicious cursing. A sharp cry of pain. Human.

More cursing followed by a canine yelp, then nothing.

"Sonofabitch," he snarled.

Then everything happened at once.

There was knocking at her front door and Mrs. Kasselbaum's urgent voice asking if she was all right, did she need any help. There was the feel of the knife at her throat, pressing harder, then pulling back. And instinctively she rolled just as the knife came plunging into the mattress where she'd lain a split second before.

She heard another curse, then the sound of ripping fabric. Then the sound of him gathering his things and his footsteps as he ran, leaving the light behind.

Blinking from the bright light, Jenna lay still for a moment, unable to move. She put her hand to her throat and brought it away, sticky with her own blood.

She stared at her hand, at the blood. Disbelieving. She was bleeding. He'd cut her.

Then she heard the sound of her front door opening and another startled cry of pain. Mrs. Kasselbaum. *Oh, God.*

Got to get to her. Got to call for help. Jenna ripped the tape from her mouth, gulped a breath. She swung her legs over the side of the bed, flinching when her feet hit something hard and furry.

The dog. Which one?

He'd killed the dog. Which one?

Oh, God.

She grabbed the phone and punched 911 while she ran to the front of her apartment, stumbling, falling, crawling. She tried to pull herself up on one of the dining-room chairs, but it wobbled and fell, sending her sprawling again. She'd pushed herself back on her knees and crawled another few feet when the 911 voice answered. Jenna didn't wait for the woman to finish her question, just babbled. "Help. Please. A man . . . just came in."

"Is he still there, ma'am?"

Hearing the calm voice helped her breathe. Think. Speak. "No. No, he's gone." She shuddered, crawling closer to her open front door where another furry body lay just inside.

"Are you hurt, ma'am?"

Jenna felt a hysterical laugh fight its way up her throat. "I'm bleeding. He cut me. There's another woman hurt. My neighbor." She crawled past the dog and into the hall where another neighbor had appeared, a cordless phone to his ear. He was calling 911, too.

So she could hang up. She pushed herself to her knees next to Mrs. Kasselbaum's inert form. "Mrs. Kasselbaum." The tears were coming now as she realized she didn't even know the old woman's first name. She grasped a thin, scrawny shoulder and shook. "Mrs. Kasselbaum, please."

The other neighbor knelt down beside her and pulled her hand from the old woman. "Don't touch her," he said, panic in his own voice. "Wait for the paramedics. They're on their way." His name was Stan. His wife was Terri and they had a new baby named Bella. She knew all of this yet didn't know the first name of the old woman who might be dead because she cared too much.

Sobbing now, Jenna fell back against Mrs. Kasselbaum's closed door, reached for her own phone, and called the only other number in her brain.

"Steven, please, come."

Monday, October 10, 1:43 A.M.

Steven rushed up the steps of her apartment unit, flashing his badge as the paramedics were carrying a gurney down. He looked down at the gray face of Mrs. Kasselbaum, still in her hair curlers, then up at the paramedic's face. He shrugged. "Fifty-fifty," he said. "She's eighty-two."

"Where are you taking her?" Steven asked, knowing Jenna would want to know.

"Wake. Gotta go." They pushed past him and out the front door of the apartment building where a frightened, confused crowd of neighbors had gathered next to the flashing lights of the ambulance.

Steven took the rest of the stairs three at a time and stopped short at Jenna's threshold.

Two uniformed police stood back near her dining-room table where a chair lay on its side. The remnants of her dinner still sat on the table and Steven recognized one of his own plates. He looked down at his feet to where one of the dogs lay still. Then over to her sliding-glass door where a fist-sized circle had been cut neatly in the glass.

Jenna was lying on the sofa, a paramedic kneeling on the floor next to her. Her face was white in stark contrast to the black of her hair. She had a bandage at her throat.

Unholy rage started deep and boiled over. Sonofabitch. Coming into her home. *Hurting her.*

He swallowed hard, staring at her face, at the bandage on her throat. Someone had hurt her.

But she was alive. And she'd called *him.*

He crossed over the threshold only to be stopped by the uniforms. He flashed his badge.

One of the uniforms frowned his confusion. "Not your jurisdiction, Special Agent Thatcher," he said politely.

Steven clamped a lid on his temper. "*She's* my jurisdiction," he said through clenched teeth. "*She's mine.*"

The uniforms looked at one another, then stepped back without another word.

He dropped to his knees next to the paramedic. "Jenna."

Her eyes opened and in them he saw shock and tears and guilt. Her lips trembled and she blinked, sending tears down her white face. "I'm so sorry, Steven. I should have listened to you."

The paramedic looked at him sharply. "She's in shock, but she'll be okay."

From behind him one of the uniforms said, "She's said that a couple of times. That she's sorry and should have listened to you. What does she mean?"

Steven reached for her hand, ignored the suspicion in their innuendo. "She's been having trouble from some kids at the school where she teaches. A couple days ago, they cut the brakes on her car. I was afraid for her to be alone. Al Pullman, Investigative Division, has all the details."

"She's also asked about Jim and Jean-Luc," the paramedic added, packing up his things. "We assumed they were the dogs."

Steven looked over at the dog lying by the front door, then at the uniforms standing behind him. "Yeah. Are they alive?"

"Barely," Uniform One said. "I'd suspect poison for that

one. The one in the back tangled with her attacker. He's cut up pretty bad, but breathing."

Steven's mind flashed back to the clearing, to Pal and old Bud Clary. To what seemed like a day a hundred years ago. "I'll call a vet, but don't touch them. We'll want Forensics to check them for evidence." He'd no sooner punched Kent's number into his cell phone when the man himself appeared in Jenna's doorway with a woman Steven recognized as Kent's "lady-vet" at his side.

"Pullman called me," Kent said, "after Nancy called him, after you called her. Nancy told him you'd want me to check the scene and the dogs. Wendy was with me and offered to come along."

Steven chose not to comment on the fact that Wendy the "lady-vet" just happened to be with him in the middle of the night. "Thanks, Kent. Wendy, the dog in the back was stabbed."

She nodded. "Understood. I have a digital camera in my bag. We'll get pictures before I stitch him up."

Jenna struggled to sit up, pushing aside the well-meaning hands of the paramedic. "Jim's there by the door. Jean-Luc's in the back. Please help them. They saved my life."

Steven swallowed. And for that the dogs got beefsteak for the rest of their days. If they lived.

Wendy smiled at Jenna. "You worry about yourself. I'll worry about your boys."

Steven turned his attention back to Jenna, noticing the smears of blood on her worn Duke T-shirt. "Any other wounds?" he asked the paramedic.

The paramedic shook his head and snapped his case closed. "Only her throat. The blood on her shirt appears to be her own."

"We found bloody handprints on the carpet where she crawled from the bedroom," said Uniform Two.

Steven's gut seethed, picturing her scared and hurt and crawling through her own house like a wounded animal. For that alone, whoever did this to her would pay.

Kent reappeared, a question on his face. "Jenna, was there a blanket on your bed?"

She stared up at him dully and for a minute Steven didn't think she could answer. Then she licked her lips, chewed on her lower lip. "He pulled it off me. Onto the floor."

Steven's eyes flicked to the paramedic in a panic. "Did he—"

The paramedic shook his head. "She says no and I didn't see anything to the contrary."

"He started to," Jenna said unevenly. "He . . . touched me. He was wearing gloves. Then he stopped and opened a case." She paused and her eyes focused. "It sounded just like yours," she said, pointing to the paramedic's case. "The way you seated the buckle, then snapped it closed. Except he was opening his. Then Jean-Luc was there. They fought and he screamed. Then Jean-Luc . . ." She winced and looked away.

"If he can be saved, Wendy's the one who can do it," Kent said matter-of-factly and Jenna looked up at him, gratitude in her eyes.

"Thank you."

"There's no blanket there now, Steven," Kent said, dropping his voice. "I think the dog may have gotten him good enough to draw blood. He probably used the blanket to stem the flow. Wendy's checking the dog's teeth."

Unbelievably Steven felt his lips curve. "You'll be paying royalties to *Law and Order* before all this is over."

Kent grasped his shoulder and squeezed. "She's okay, Steven." He looked over at the paramedic who was now standing, watching with interest. "Does she need to go to the hospital?"

"No. I closed the wound and gave her an antibiotic injection. She should have it looked at by her doctor, but she can do that tomorrow morning."

Kent looked back at Steven. "Then take her home and have a drink to settle your nerves. Get some sleep. We can manage without you for one morning meeting."

Steven squeezed Jenna's hand. "I'll pack you a bag."

Monday, October 10, 8:00 A.M.

His team frowned when he came in the next morning. They started talking at once, his boss leading the pack. "We thought you'd be staying home today, Steven," Lennie said reproachfully.

"What the hell are you doing here, Steven?" Sandra demanded.

"Ste-*ven*," Nancy sighed.

"I told you we could manage," Kent said, looking a little hurt.

"You're an idiot, Steven," Harry muttered.

"You should be home," Liz declared.

Meg just looked at him, exasperated but unsurprised.

Davies sat at the end of the table watching.

Steven took his seat and looked at his team, his boss, his visiting "associate."

And thought about the night before. Jenna's terrified face, the blood on her shirt. Her two wounded animals. The blood on her bed. Next to the vicious rip in the mattress. He closed his eyes and shuddered. The rip that could have just as easily been in her. He would have lost her.

He opened his eyes to find everyone watching him, concerned. "I want him," he said simply. "I want him put away. I want to throw the key into the middle of the ocean so he never sees the light of day again." He looked at Liz. "Legally, of course."

She raised a brow. "Of course."

"So," he said, sitting back in his chair, "where are we, people?"

Monday, October 10, 8:00 A.M.

He eased himself into the only chair in the barn. "Damn dogs."

He winced as he pulled the watting from his leg and dabbed the torn flesh on his thigh with a ninety-nine-cent bottle of peroxide he'd bought at an all-night drugstore over the Virginia border. He couldn't waltz into a hospital with a bite like this. He simply wasn't willing to give Thatcher that big a handicap.

He knew from experience that he'd be all right in a week or so. Once, years ago, he'd been bitten by a dog he hadn't quite immobilized well enough before initiating a slice across his belly. He'd taken care of that bite himself, too, so he knew the drill. Key learnings from that experience had been to keep the wound clean, keep it dry, and use lots of antibiotic cream. And never, ever cut open a dog if he hadn't thoroughly tested the strength of his restraints.

After tonight he could add two more jewels of wisdom to the list. Never assume there is only one dog just because you've only seen one. And never, ever make house calls.

Next time, he'd bring Miss Marshall here. Where he had all his things about him.

He limped over to where pretty Alev lay huddled on his table in a fetal position. She was starting to get dehydrated and she hadn't eaten in a few days. She wouldn't last much longer, so he'd have to make the best of the time he had left.

He pushed aside the residual anger over the events at Miss Marshall's apartment.

Don't worry, he told himself. *Consider it a practice run. There's always next time.*

Monday, October 10, 8:15 A.M.

Steven massaged his throbbing temples. "Both Rudy *and* his father have alibis for last night?"

"By none other than our own unmarked cars," Lennie said dryly. "How's that for irony?"

"It sucks," Steven said. "So where does that leave us?"

"Somebody else was in Jenna's apartment last night," Harry said. "One of Lutz's football buddies most likely. We have the names Pullman questioned about the cut brakes. We'll pull 'em all in for questioning."

"Whoever it was will have a nasty dog bite," Kent said with satisfaction.

Steven looked over at him. "*Please* tell me you found something in Jean-Luc's teeth."

His eyes sparkling behind his thick lenses, Kent nodded. "Wendy took the swab and it's perfect. DNA lab says we'll get a good print."

Thank you, Steven prayed silently to heaven. To Kent he said, "Good work. Tell Wendy I said the same."

"But we're no closer to having enough to bring Lutz in for questioning on either angle," Lennie said, bringing them all back to the subject at hand.

Steven sighed. "Nope."

"And now Lutz knows we're watching him," Lennie added.

Steven cringed as he remembered the unpleasant conversation with the mayor the day before. And he was grateful he'd assigned the surveillance anyway. At least they knew who *hadn't* tried to kill Jenna seven hours before. "But for the cut brakes, he thinks," Steven said.

"And if I'm William Parker posing as Rudy Lutz, I'll think someone's on to me," Meg said thoughtfully. "It will change how he functions."

"How?" Davies said, uttering his first word of the day.

"Depends on how sure he is of himself. He'll either stop or turn up the heat a notch."

Davies rolled his eyes. "That's helpful."

Meg narrowed hers. "Well, he's your boy, Neil, why don't you offer some ideas?"

Davies stood up and walked to the bulletin board and stared at the photo of Samantha Eggleston. "Back in Seattle, when he was fifteen, he was different. He picked cheerleaders, shaved their heads, stabbed them fifteen times, but he didn't have the same sense of style."

"Style." Lennie repeated the word in annoyed bewilderment.

"Yeah, style. I mean, look at the way he's got her laid out. Hands tied together to look like they're folded in prayer. The tattoo." He smacked the bulletin board next to the photo. "The sign, for God's sake. He's playing a damn game. In Seattle, he didn't keep them for days on end. We found them within forty-eight hours of their going missing. The locations weren't forest clearings that you needed aerial photos to find. They were shopping mall parking lots and soccer fields."

"But he still wanted the victims to be found," Meg observed. "He still wanted everyone to know someone had killed them. But I see your point. Not only is he escalating in rate, he's escalating in panache. Not only does he want them to be found, but he's going to decide how and when. He sends a letter, leaves a sign. Harry, how did you feel when you found the sign?"

"Pissed off," Harry answered. "Like he was thumbing his nose at us."

"Or at me," Steven said. "He seems to have it in for me. Probably because of the press conferences."

"Then we should play up to that," Liz said. "We've got to draw this guy out in the open or he'll just keep on killing."

Steven checked his watch. "Nancy, schedule another press conference for two this afternoon. Meg, write me a script. I want him so mad he comes after *me*. Then we'll see if he can pick on someone besides little girls."

"The little girls might suffer, Steven," Meg said, looking doubtful.

"Then we fire with both barrels. Nancy, call all the high schools and set up assemblies for all students. Mandatory assemblies starting tomorrow morning. We'll each take as many schools as we have to get the message out to every young girl in the county."

Davies turned from his study of the bulletin board. "And the message is?"

"Don't get into cars with strangers and monsters don't always have fangs." Steven looked over at Meg. "Put that in the press conference script."

"Which part?" Meg asked with a smile. "About the assemblies or not all monsters have fangs?"

Steven's return smile was grim. "Both. And make sure I'm scheduled to speak at Rudy's school. I want the little sonofabitch to know exactly who I am so he knows who to target."

Monday, October 11, 1:50 P.M.

"So what do you think?" Jenna said, modeling her new sweater for Casey. "I'm normally not one for turtlenecks, but I wanted to hide the bandage when I went to Allison's for dinner on Wednesday." She'd stopped at the mall to buy the sweater on her way from the animal hospital, where Jim and Jean-Luc were not out of the woods, to the human hospital, where Mrs. Kasselbaum was stable and Casey was completely out of the woods.

Casey frowned from her hospital bed. "You mean you didn't tell the Llewellyns about the break-in?" she asked, her voice still rough from the removal of the breathing tube.

Jenna bit her lip. "I told them someone broke into my apartment. I just didn't tell them about the knife. So what about the sweater?"

"You're changing the subject. Whatever." Casey patted the bed. "Come, sit, tell me all about you and Special Agent Thatcher." Then she laughed, a strange little gravelly sound. "Is he as good as you thought he'd be?"

Jenna ran her tongue over her teeth. "Oh, yeah."

Casey grinned and clapped her hands. "Details, Jen, details." Then frowned at Jenna's yeah-right expression. "You're not going to tell me anything, are you?"

Jenna grinned. "Nope."

Casey grimaced. "Bitch." Then she brightened. "Can I be your maid of honor?"

Jenna rolled her eyes. "Casey, you're impossible."

"But now you'll think about it." Her blue eyes widened. "You *have* been thinking about it."

Jenna felt her face flame even hotter. The thought had only crossed her mind *briefly*. Many, many times, but each of them *briefly*. "Look, Casey, about your final grades for the quarter. Blackman asked me to ask you what else needed to be done."

"Nothing. I finished my themes and left my grades in an envelope on Blackman's desk."

"The *Crime and Punishment* themes, you mean."

Casey's brow crinkled at the mention of the book's title.

"What?" Jenna asked.

Casey looked troubled. "There's something important about those themes and I can't remember what it was." She bit her lip, then dismissed the thought. "It'll come to me. Anyway, I think I'd look good in blue. Satin. And if you pick a dress with a bow on the butt, you're toast."

Jenna barely heard the threat, her attention snared by the television. Where she'd heard only muted murmurs before, she heard Steven's voice. He was giving another press conference. She held her breath until she realized no more girls had been taken. She thought about the fact that he'd stayed up all night, holding her until her trembles finally stopped, then showered and went off to catch monsters of a different variety. "He looks tired, Casey. I'm worried about him."

Casey patted her hand and said nothing.

Monday, October 10, 2:20 P.M.

He frowned and stowed the bottle of peroxide in the closet with the rest of his darkroom chemicals. Nobody ever checked his darkroom and if they did, all brown bottles looked the same in the dark. Thatcher was upping the ante. And getting a bit personal. He bared his teeth in the mirror on the closet door, annoyed to find he sported no fangs.

He rolled his eyes. So monsters didn't always have fangs,

huh? What a lame attempt at a sound bite. He really had thought more of Thatcher.

He smiled sweetly at his own reflection. He didn't have fangs. He had really, really sharp knives that worked even better.

Monday, October 10, 3:00 P.M.

Her first name was Evelyn. "Kasselbaum, Evelyn" read the chart outside the room where Mrs. Kasselbaum lay, still unconscious but stable. Jenna drew a breath and pushed the door open. And stopped. Standing by the small window was Seth, his shoulders hunched.

He turned and his gaze focused in on her throat, covered in the turtleneck sweater. And in his eyes Jenna saw worry and fear. And hurt. He knew. About the knife. *I should have told him myself,* she thought.

"I'm okay, Dad," she whispered. "Really."

He said nothing. Just stood there and Jenna felt lower than a snake's belly.

"I'm sorry. I didn't want to worry you."

He still said nothing. But his throat worked like he wanted to cry and Jenna suddenly understood that she'd wounded him. And she knew it was time to come clean with the whole story.

"Adam's car is wrecked, Dad. Totaled. Last Thursday." He flinched, grew even paler. She drew an unsteady breath. "Casey was driving and went off an embankment. She nearly died." She held her back rigid. "The brakes were cut. I was the one who was supposed to be hurt."

Seth lowered himself into the chair next to Mrs. Kasselbaum's bed. Trembling visibly.

Jenna crossed the room, knelt by the chair. "I should have told you. I'm sorry. I didn't want—"

"To worry me?" Seth finished, his smile bitter and twisted. "I thought we'd settled that last week, Jenna. I thought you trusted me enough to tell me when you're in trouble."

Jenna opened her mouth. Closed it. Didn't know what to say.

Seth sighed. "You are so damn independent. You think you can handle everything and everyone yourself. You make decisions for people, Jen. And you have no right. You think you're a superwoman, that you can manipulate everything to be the way you want it to be." He closed his eyes. "And rob the rest of us of the privilege of caring about you."

Still she didn't know what to say.

"I made a promise to Adam," Seth went on, his throat swallowing convulsively, his eyes still closed. "He made me promise to take care of you. To make sure no one ever hurt you. He made me promise never to tell you, that you'd find some way of . . ." He faltered. "Of ducking me, he said. He said you were too accustomed to doing things for yourself. Of never trusting anyone to do things for you. Of taking care of you. Why is that, Jenna?"

Jenna shook her head. Adam had been right of course. "I don't know."

Seth opened his eyes and Jenna saw weariness mixed with the hurt. "He said it was because you never grew up with the love and trust of your parents. That you'd been on your own, essentially, since you were a little girl. That you didn't know how to really be a family."

Jenna's feathers ruffled. "My dad loved me."

"But not enough to make your mother stop criticizing you. Not enough to take care of you. Not enough to make sure you knew you didn't have to do everything all alone." He fluttered his hand in the air. "Never mind why. The fact remains that he was right. I can't fulfill my promise to my son, Jenna. You won't let me take care of you. You were almost killed last night and I had to get all the details from Evelyn's nurse."

Jenna let his words sink in and realized he was right, just as Adam had been right. Shaky, she laid her cheek against Seth's knee. And made herself allow him to care about her. Made herself allow him to share what she was feeling. "I was so scared, Dad. I thought he would kill me."

He stroked her hair and said nothing.

"He put the knife to my throat. He tried to cut me open, but I got away and he cut the mattress instead. Jean-Luc bit him and he ran. And knocked Evelyn down on his way out."

His hand on her head trembled, then resumed stroking. "Jenna, you're coming home with me."

Jenna looked up, not sure how he'd take her next words. "I stayed with Steven last night. He wants me to stay with him."

Seth studied her for a long moment. "He cares for you?"

She remembered the way Steven had held her the night before. Like rare china. "Yes."

Seth's eyes narrowed. "And he has a spare bedroom?"

Jenna felt her cheeks heat. "Dad!"

"Well, does he?"

Jenna nodded. "Yes." Then smiled. "And an aunt who doesn't make meat loaf on Wednesdays."

Seth smiled at her and she knew she was forgiven. "Can I come, too?"

TWENTY-SEVEN

Tuesday, October 11, 1:00 A.M.

JENNA COULDN'T SLEEP. PART OF IT WAS HER whacked-out sleep cycle. Part of it was knowing it was exactly this time the night before that she'd awakened with a knife at her throat and that the police had no suspects because Victor Lutz had an alibi. And certainly part of it was knowing Steven was sleeping in the next room. She told herself *most* of it was knowing Steven was sleeping in the next room and not an unreasonable twenty-four-hour anniversary fear.

She considered calling the twenty-four-hour emergency veterinary clinic that still had Jim and Jean-Luc, but figured their conditions hadn't changed in the last hour. Jim was improving but Jean-Luc still clung to life. Even though Kent's friend Wendy had done a superb job, Jean-Luc's stab wounds were deep and vicious. Knowing he'd taken them for her still made her ill.

"Both dogs were poisoned with strychnine," Wendy had told her and Steven earlier this evening when she and Kent had dropped by to give them an update. "Probably introduced to their system through the steak I found when I pumped their stomachs."

"So my intruder was very well prepared indeed," Jenna had remarked, feeling her skin grow cold. He'd brought his own lamp, his own plastic case. Poison for her dogs. Knives.

"Except," Wendy had returned, "neither dog had enough poison in his system to kill him outright, so he wasn't prepared all *that* well." Then she'd said Jenna could call the clinic anytime.

And Jenna had, but it didn't make sense to do it again so soon. She imagined the clinic staff did have other things to do besides calming her irrational nighttime fears.

So she pulled on her robe and set out for a snack, wishing she'd had the presence of mind to stop for Rocky Road on her way home, when a noise from Nicky's room caught her attention. Peeking in, she discovered him sitting in his sleeping bag on the floor, reading a comic book.

"Aren't you supposed to be asleep?" she whispered.

"Aren't you?" he whispered back.

Touché, little man, Jenna thought with a smile. "Can I come in?"

He shrugged and put the book aside. "Okay."

She settled herself cross-legged on the floor next to his sleeping bag. "Is the book any good?"

"It's okay."

She wondered how many nights he sat and read when he should have been sleeping. "I can't sleep," she confided in a low voice. "Any ideas on how I can fall asleep?"

"Aunt Helen says warm milk."

Jenna grimaced. "Sorry, but that sounds gross."

"It is. Matt says he counts ewes."

Jenna frowned. "U's? How would counting letters help?"

"No, ewes. Brad said he counted *sheep*, Matt said he counted *ewes*. They're *girl* sheep."

Jenna nodded, pursing her lips. "Oh."

"It meant something about sex because Brad smacked Matt upside the head when he said it."

Jenna coughed. "Excuse me?"

Nicky narrowed his eyes. "You know. Sex. You've got to know about sex."

Jenna swallowed hard. "I've heard of it, yes. I'm just surprised you have."

"Well, I am seven," he said.

"Okay." Wildly Jenna searched for something else to say. "Okay. So how often do you sit here reading—" She picked up the book he'd set aside. "*The Adventures of Captain Underpants*?"

"'Bout every night."

She set down the book in surprise. "Every night? Why, Nicky?"

He looked at her severely. "Because I can't sleep either. Not since the incident." Then his expression softened. "I heard Daddy and Aunt Helen talking about your incident. Don't worry," he said, patting her hand. "You'll get used to it."

Jenna blinked, not knowing how to respond to his matter-of-fact reference to his abduction. Her fingers moved to the bandage at her neck. "But I don't want to get used to it. I like to sleep."

"Then I'd try counting ewes," he said wisely.

Or perhaps sex, Jenna thought, but decided she'd keep that to herself. "Well, when I was a little girl and couldn't sleep my dad and I would play a game."

He looked interested. "Soccer?"

Jenna chuckled, just thinking of what her mother would have said if she and her father had played soccer in the house. In the middle of the night, no less. "No, it was a storytelling game. Dad would start the story, then I'd tell a little, then he'd tell a little, until it was done."

"Which story?"

"We'd make it up. You want to give it a try?"

He shrugged. "Sure, why not."

Jenna smiled at him. "You're funny, Nicky."

He perked up at that. "Really? Everybody always says Matt's funny, but never me."

"Well you are. Why don't we make up a funny story? I'll start. Once upon a time a man lived in a town called Walla

Walla, Washington." She leaned close to him. "That's a real place you know."

Nicky shook his head. "No, it's not."

"Is." She looked at him, suddenly inspired. "How much do you want to bet?"

"I can't bet. I don't have any money."

"Who said anything about money? Tomorrow, we'll look it up on-line. If I'm right—and I will be—you lie down in your bed tomorrow night. If I'm wrong, I'll sleep on the floor with you."

He considered it. "It's fair," he decided. "So the man had a llama. That's got two *l*'s, y'know."

"I know. One day his llama got sick and had to go to the doctor."

"And the doctor said he'd swallowed an alarm clock," Nicky said, snuggling into his pillow.

"Which made an awful racket every day at noon. The llama wasn't welcome anywhere . . ."

Ten minutes later Nicky had reduced the llama to selling kisses at the circus. And he was sound asleep. Rousing herself she left Nicky's room only to run into Steven's hard chest.

She swallowed. His hard, naked, hairy, naked, golden chest. "He's asleep," she whispered.

"So I see." His eyes twinkled and crinkled at the corners and she wanted to grab him and wrestle him to the carpet and have her way with him. "Kissing llamas, huh?"

She shrugged. "He's your kid." Then she frowned. "Your son knows about sex."

Steven grinned. "Well, he *is* seven."

She propped her fists on her hips. "Just how long were you standing there?"

"From the minute I heard you leave your room. I haven't slept a wink all night knowing you were in there asleep and not being able to touch you." He leaned closer until his forehead rested against hers. "I've heard of sex, too."

She had to bite her lips to keep from smiling. "Well, you are—how old are you, anyway?"

"Thirty-six." He tugged on her hand. "Old enough to know about sex, and how to do it, too."

Jenna was laughing softly as he closed his bedroom door behind them. "You don't say."

"Oh, I do. And I made a stop on my way home." He thumbed over his shoulder and her eyes widened at the sight of the three big boxes of condoms on his bed. "Think it will be enough?"

"Well, we'll just have to see, Special Agent Thatcher."

He kissed her gently. "And feel. And taste."

"Umm. Maybe you do know about this sex thing after all."

Tuesday, October 11, 8:00 A.M.

"We got a response." Steven tossed copies of his latest note from the killer on the conference-room table. "Special delivery to Special Agent in Charge Steven Thatcher."

Liz picked up a copy and studied it. "He promoted you."

"Yeah, don't tell Lennie." Steven sat down and rubbed his temples. "Harry, you'll need to get started at the search scene. I'll join you when I'm finished with the assembly at Roosevelt."

Meg stared at the page, a stricken look on her face. "I knew this would force his hand, but . . ."

"He was going to kill her regardless of what we did, Meg," Steven said wearily. "I've arranged for another chopper to take aerial shots of the coordinates in the note. He gave us a more specific range this time. We should be able to find Alev faster than we found Samantha."

"And once we have?" Harry asked.

Steven looked at the note that had no fingerprints. Not a single identifying factor. "Then we hope we've forced him to move more quickly than he'd planned and that he's made a mistake."

Tuesday, October 11, 7:30 P.M.

Steven pushed his front door shut, the desire to see Jenna's face the only thing that kept him on his feet. Shortly after leaving the Roosevelt High School assembly this morning he'd received word from Harry that they'd found Alev Rahrooh's body. Just where the killer's note said she'd be.

What he hadn't been prepared for was the scene that awaited him. Meg had thought the killer would either stop or kick it up a notch.

It had been the second one.

And Harry wasn't the only one to lose his breakfast this time, either. Steven still wasn't sure he could eat a bite, ten long hours later. But the worst part wasn't the body in the clearing. The worst part was having to pay the visit to the Rahroohs to tell them their daughter was dead. To try to prepare them for what they'd see when they arrived at the morgue to identify their daughter's body. That the beast had not only raped and murdered their precious child, but that he'd dismembered her.

Harry had not stumbled on one sign this time, but six. Head, Arm One, Arm Two, Torso, Leg One, and Leg Two. Lorraine Rush had not been the most horrific scene Steven had ever witnessed, but Alev Rahrooh . . . He could honestly say she was the worst in his career.

And to know he'd pushed the killer to commit such a vile act. Meg reminded him this evening of his own words from that morning, that the animal would have killed Alev regardless of what they'd done. But the words had been easier to believe before he'd seen that young girl's body. He sagged against his front door, emotionally drained. He closed his eyes when he heard Jenna's voice from his office, tried to rewrite her face over the carnage that seemed branded on his very soul.

"Now you remember our bet," she was saying. "Tell me what that says."

"Walla Walla, Washington," Nicky read in a grumpy voice. "You win."

"So where will you sleep?"

"In my own bed," he heard his son say morosely.

"So get to it," Jenna ordered crisply. "Go brush your teeth and I'll tuck you in."

"And we'll play the story game?"

"Sure, why not?"

They appeared and Steven forced himself to smile even though all he wanted was to drag her in his arms and bury his body in hers and pretend for just a little while that the world didn't exist.

That they were normal people.

That she didn't wear on her throat the evidence of some sick teenage band of thugs and that he hadn't seen an innocent life brutally ended, ravaged even after death.

"Hey, Nicky, how's my boy?" he asked, injecting a happy note into his voice, instantly seeing his son wasn't buying any of it. Nicky looked up at him, then looked up at Jenna, who'd sobered as soon as she'd seen him standing there. She tapped the end of Nicky's freckled nose.

"I think your dad's had a bad day. Maybe when he's had a chance to unwind he can come up and help us with our story. You go on up to bed and brush your teeth. I'll be there in a minute or two." When Nicky was upstairs Jenna turned to Steven and opened her arms.

Without a word he pulled her to him and buried his face in her hair. "You always smell like beaches and coconuts to me," he whispered.

She kissed his shoulder through the layers of his clothing. "You found her. The third girl."

He shuddered and her arms tightened around his waist.

"I'm so sorry, Steven," she murmured, lifting her face. "I'm so sorry."

He searched her face, looking for something he hadn't yet defined, but finding it in her eyes. He kissed her, taking from her whatever comfort she could provide, finding the well more than deep enough. His kiss grew desperate until she slid her hands into his hair and pulled his head back.

"Steven, what happened?"

He closed his eyes and shook his head. "I can't, Jenna. I just can't." *Can't talk about it. Can't stop thinking about it. Can't stop blaming myself.*

She pulled him close for a softer kiss. "Then stay here. I'll put Nicky to bed, then I'll be back."

As he watched her go up the stairs he realized more than anything in the world he wanted to hear about kissing llamas and any other silly tale Jenna and Nicky could concoct. He followed her up and waited outside Nicky's bedroom door.

"What if I wake up in the night and decide I don't want to be in bed?" Nicky was asking.

Steven peeked around the corner to see Jenna pulling the blanket over Nicky's small frame.

"Then you get out of bed and sleep in your sleeping bag," she said simply.

Nicky snuggled into the pillow and closed his eyes. "Once there was a man who lived in Kalamazoo." He opened one eye. "Aunt Helen has a friend there. It's in Michigan, y'know."

Jenna sat down on the edge of Nicky's bed and smoothed her hand over his hair. "I know. And this man had a kangaroo."

Nicky didn't say anything for a long time, so long Jenna whispered, "Are you asleep already?"

Nicky shook his head. "No. Jenna, I'm ready to get out of bed now."

Steven wanted to sigh, but Jenna just stood up and pulled his blanket back. "Okay."

He squinted up at her. "You're not mad?"

She shook her head. "No, you kept your end of the bargain. So into the bag." Nicky crawled into the sleeping bag and Jenna sat next to him, cross-legged on the floor. "So we have a kangaroo."

"From Kalamazoo."

"Whose shoes were new."

"Who liked to eat glue."

Jenna's lips twitched. "Until he got the flu."

"He had to stay in bed with the flu," Nicky said, abandoning the rhyme. "But one day a bad hunter came and stole him from his bed."

Jenna went still. "This isn't about the kangaroo from Kalamazoo anymore, is it, Nicky?"

Nicky lay motionless. Then he shook his head.

Jenna rubbed his back, making her touch soft against his small back. "Sunday night, when that man came into my apartment, I was so scared," she whispered. "I wasn't sure if I'd live or die. If I'd ever see you and your dad again. If I'd ever see Jim or Jean-Luc again."

Nicky didn't open his eyes. "But they'll be okay, won't they? Jim and Jean-Luc?"

She kept rubbing his back, keeping her strokes gentle. "I hope so. The vet says they ate a lot of poison then and Jean-Luc got stabbed." Her voice faltered and she steadied it. "For me."

"There was a lady who got hurt for me," Nicky offered in a whisper. "Her name was Caroline."

Jenna remembered reading the story in the newspaper six months earlier. Steven had been leading the investigation into a murder, only to find the victim had really escaped her abusive spouse. The woman had bravely started a new life with her young son, but had been found and dragged away by her husband. Her husband, who for God only knew what reason, decided taking little Nicky as a hostage would make Steven back off. "The lady was running away, wasn't she?"

His nod was almost imperceptible. "From the bad man. Winters," he added in a harsh mutter. "He tied us up and put us in a dirty cabin. He said he'd kill her. He said he'd kill me."

Her hand on his back faltered, then resumed the soothing strokes. "And you were afraid."

"Yes," came his barely audible reply.

Jenna swallowed and prayed for wisdom. "I know how you felt." She let the sentence sink in, then said, "I guess it was hard coming back to sleep in this room. In your bed."

His lips trembled. "Everybody thought I was a big baby."

Her heart cracked. "I'm sure they didn't, honey, even if it seemed like it at the time."

"They still do. Everybody comes to check on me at night, when they think I'm asleep," he continued as if she hadn't said a word. "They stand there and look at me."

"Why do you think they do that?" Jenna asked, very aware of Steven doing that very thing at that very moment. She could see the reflection of his stricken face in the mirror on Nicky's wall.

"Because they think I'm a baby."

"Well, *I'm* not a baby and I don't think I'm going to be too keen on going back to sleep in my bed either," Jenna said, inserting a tone of practicality into her voice. Anything to let this baby know that everything he'd felt, was feeling now, was so perfectly normal.

Nicky opened one eye. "You can't," he answered, just as practically. "The man sliced up your mattress with his knife."

Jenna flinched, her blood going cold at the memory of the knife at her throat, the sound of the mattress being torn to shreds. She cleared her throat. "Good point. But even if he hadn't, I'd have trouble sleeping in the same bed."

He didn't say anything and she mentally scrambled for a new angle. "Did you know I had a fiancé before I met your dad?"

He shook his head into the pillow.

"His name was Adam. He got very sick, and he died."

Nicky squirmed onto his back and his eyes opened. "Was he very old?"

"No, he was still a very young man. Anyway, when he died . . . I couldn't sleep in my bed. He'd slept there when he was sick and I . . . just . . . couldn't."

"So what did you do?"

"I got a new bed. How would you feel about a new bed?"

Outside, Steven kicked himself for not having suggested that months earlier. He'd replaced his own bed, for heaven's sake, after Melissa died. He couldn't even think of sleeping in the same bed he'd shared with the woman who'd betrayed them all. He leaned closer, listening for Nicky's reply.

"My friend Jon? He has a bed shaped like a *car*."

Jenna smiled at Nicky, watching Steven's face in the mirror from the corner of her eye. He was kicking himself, she knew. "It sounds pretty darn cool. I bet your dad'd go for that if you asked."

Nicky looked contemplative. "Maybe I will."

"Now about *everybody* checking on you." She made her voice overly dramatic and Nicky smiled. "I don't for one minute believe anyone thinks you are a baby. To escape like you did last spring took incredible courage. Not many boys Brad's age would have been so brave."

His smile faded. "Then why do they check on me every night?"

Jenna considered her answer carefully. "Well, you know my fiancé?"

He nodded soberly. "Adam."

"Yes, Adam. Well, I would check on him every night. Not because I thought he was a baby or about to do anything stupid, but because *I* needed to. For me."

His brows scrunched up. "Why?"

She sighed, searching for the right words. "Nicky, when someone you love is in danger, you worry. And when you get that person back, you still worry." She thought about the hurt on Seth's face and finally understood his pain. "It's like when you cut your finger. It stays sore for a few days, even after the bleeding's stopped. I know that's why everybody checks on you. In the night, when everything is quiet, that's when people realize just how close they came to losing you. They need to get up and make sure everything is still all right. And just because you're safe now—" She gave him a serious look. "And you *are* safe, Nicky. You know that man can never hurt you again."

He nodded, still sober. "I know. He died in jail."

And I hope it was painful for him, Jenna thought with vicious indignation, but kept the smile on her face. "Well, just because you're safe now, it doesn't take your dad's worry away." *Or Seth's,* she thought, glad she'd made things right this afternoon.

"He's worried now," Nicky said thoughtfully. "About the bad man that's killing the girls."

Jenna's brows shot up. "What do you know about that, honey?"

"I saw Daddy on TV talking about it."

She glanced to the mirror, saw Steven's face pale. "He doesn't want you worrying about that."

"Well, if he's worried about me, can't I worry about him?"

Jenna's heart squeezed and in the mirror she could see Steven's throat working. *Out of the mouths of babes,* she thought. "You know what I think he'd like even more than knowing you were worried?" she asked, bending down closer. "A hug."

Nicky's lips thinned. "Hugs are for babies."

Oh, so now it's clear, Jenna thought. Steven had told her Nicky wouldn't hug anyone. "First of all, that's not true. I hug your dad all the time."

"That's different. You're his girlfriend." His eyes went sly. "Aren't you?"

Jenna chuckled, feeling her cheeks heat. "I suppose I am. But, Nicky, grown men hug one another. I saw Father Mike hug your father just last week."

"That's different," he said, overly patient as if she were a dull student. "He's a priest."

"Fine, suit yourself. But you have my word that hugs are not for babies."

"Hmm," Nicky said, back to thoughtful from patient. "Well, if he wants one, he might as well come in." He looked at her pointedly. "He's been standing outside my door all this time."

Jenna didn't know what to say. "Steven," she called. "Your cover is blown."

Steven came in awkwardly rubbing his jaw. "I guess I need to practice that covert surveillance thing," he murmured and Jenna laughed. He dropped to his knees, grimacing as his joints creaked. "Nicky, I think we'll buy you a new bed as soon as possible. I'm too old to be sitting on the floor."

Nicky scrambled to sit up and Steven felt his heart hammer in anticipation. The one thing he'd missed above all others was the unfettered affection Nicky had always bestowed. He held out his arms and after a long moment's hesitation, Nicky crawled into them, his spindly arms straining to span Steven's back. Steven hugged him hard, drawing in a breath and letting the simple pleasure flow as the seconds ticked by. "I love you, Nicky," he whispered fiercely.

Again a moment's hesitation, then, "I love you, too, Daddy."

Steven looked over at Jenna whose fingertips pressed against her lips as her violet eyes filled with unapologetic tears. And in a flash of clarity, he knew he loved her, too.

Nicky struggled in his arms and Steven let go. "Ow," Nicky said comically and he and Jenna laughed, as Nicky wanted them to.

Steven rolled to his feet as Jenna fussed with Nicky's sleeping bag, covering him back up. Then he pulled her to her feet and slipped an arm around her waist. "Good night, Nicky," he said.

Nicky rolled over. "Night, Daddy. Night, Jenna."

Twenty-eight

Wednesday, October 12, 12:30 A.M.

IT WAS PAST MIDNIGHT WHEN STEVEN SLIPPED into the spare bedroom and closed the door behind his back. Jenna was sitting in bed reading and she jerked her head up, fear crossing her face in the instant before she realized it was him and she was still safe.

"Don't do that," she whispered, then relaxed. "Couldn't sleep either?"

He shook his head and sat next to her on the bed. "I was thinking about you. Wanting to touch you." He rubbed his hand along her forearm. "Needing to touch you."

"I'm all right," she said softly. "Really."

"I know. Mostly."

She took his hand and brought it up to her lips. "What happened today, Steven?"

He shook his head, wishing he could tell her all of it, and in so doing wipe the images from his mind. Knowing it was impossible to do so. He leaned his cheek into her hand, taking what comfort he could from her touch. "It was the worst I've ever seen," he whispered raggedly. "God, Jenna."

She caressed his cheek. "I'm so sorry, Steven. For you, for that girl's parents."

"For the next victim."

She shook her head. "You'll catch him. You have to."

He shook his head again, harder this time, trying to scramble all the pictures in his mind like a child's Etch-A-Sketch toy. It didn't work. He picked up her book, looking for a distraction, and found it. "*Captain Underpants*?" He laughed softly. "Why are you reading this?"

"Because I'm trying to sleep," she said ruefully. "But it doesn't help." She ran her fingertips over his lips. "Isn't there anything I can do to take your mind off your troubles, Steven?"

He leaned in and kissed her gently. "Yes, there is one thing."

"Name it."

"Make love with me."

"You don't have to ask," she said, but he shook his head and captured her face in his hands.

"No," he murmured and watched her eyes soften, heat. For him. "Tonight I want to make love to you. Slowly, like I haven't done before."

"Steven, I—"

"Sshh." He pulled her nightshirt over her head and dropped it off the side of the bed. "Just lay back and let me love you. Please. I need to love you."

He covered her lips with his, and pushed her gently to the pillows, following her down. Covering her body with his. Treasuring her mouth as if he had all night to just kiss her. She arched against him and he pressed her back down. "No, not fast. Not tonight."

He ran his lips down the side of her neck, pausing at the much smaller Band-Aid she now wore. He kissed her throat, an inch from where some crazed teenager had nearly taken her from him over a damned game. He kissed the swell of each breast, wishing he had a lifetime just to pleasure her there. He ran his tongue along the underside of one full breast, then the other, and she arched against him again. Minutes later she was writhing under him, her nipples wet and pitted hard from his suckling mouth. He looked up to find her staring at him, her violet eyes almost black.

"Steven," she began, but he cut her off.

"Sshh. Let me love you, Jenna."

He kissed his way down her stomach, gently, slowly, thoroughly until he got to her lace panties which he worried with his teeth.

"Steven, please," she gasped, then moaned, almost silently, when he lapped at her through the lace. She was already wet, which made him want to groan. Instead he kissed her there, softly. Promising. Her hands fisted in the blankets, twisting as she moaned again. He rolled away only long enough to slide the panties down her long, long legs and she was totally bared to him.

Totally vulnerable. Totally his. *Mine, mine, mine.*

He took his time, licking and lightly sucking until she whimpered, arching, pressing her softness closer to his seeking mouth. But he didn't want it to end. Not yet. Where before they'd shared explosive passion, tonight he wanted something more. He wanted . . . reverence. Gently he pressed her hips back into the mattress with his hands and held her there, imprisoned, and resumed until she drew in a tight breath, her body going taut, and waves of shudders racked her.

She cried out, muffling the sob of her passion with her hand.

He kissed her then, the soft folds that still quivered from the power of the orgasm he'd given her. Then he pushed himself up on his knees and watched her face relax by degrees as she came back to earth. To him. She was beautiful, and his.

Tonight. Forever.

Her breasts rose and fell as she struggled to breathe, one of her hands still clenching the blanket, the other lying slack on her pillow. Slowly she opened her eyes and he saw what he hadn't taken the time to see before. Wonder. Lust. And something much, much more.

He shuddered out a ragged breath of his own and pushed his sweatpants aside, then thrilled as her eyes slid lower and darkened as she took in the sight of him. He knew when her eyes reached his throbbing erection because she swallowed hard. Licked her lips.

Made him yearn. She reached out and took him in hand, her eyes rising to meet his.

"What do you want, Steven?"

"I want you to look at me in fifty years the way you're looking at me right now."

Her fingers teased his length, making every muscle in his body clench. "And how is that?"

"Like you'll never, ever get enough of me."

Her eyes flashed. "I won't. Please, Steven, I need you now."

She'd said please. So without taking his eyes from hers he sheathed himself, then entered her in one smooth stroke that made them one.

She shuddered, one hand still clutching the blanket. With the other she caressed his face.

"Steven," she whispered.

"I wish I could feel you against my skin," he whispered back and nearly convulsed at the power of the image. "I wish you were pregnant with my child."

Her eyes flared and she rocked up against him, tightening her muscles as she slid back, torturing him with the tight fist of her body. "I wish that, too," she said and he lost it.

Gone was the gentleness he'd intended, the consideration he'd planned. Instead he felt himself falling into rushing water, being drawn into the current, dragged under until he couldn't breathe. He rocked against her, into her, harder and faster until she moaned and convulsed around him and he knew he could no longer keep the words inside. They came in a torrent, matching the thrust of his hips as he sought to make her irrevocably his.

"I love you," he groaned and came so hard the world went black. He collapsed, hearing the thunder in his head, feeling his heart beat like he'd conquered the highest mountain. She was stroking his back, kissing his shoulder, the side of his neck, and he needed to say it again. "Love you, love you, love you." The words kept coming as his body quivered and shook. "Love you."

She waited until he was breathing again, saying nothing until he lifted his head and looked into her eyes. And saw her response before she uttered the words.

"I love you, too," she murmured.

He knew he'd found in her the strength to face anything.

Wednesday, October 12, 12:45 A.M.

She actually thought she had a choice. He sat outside her house in his car, so angry his hands shook. He'd almost had her. Almost had her in his clutches. But no. She had to listen to that idiot Thatcher's sermon at the school today. The SBI had been out in force, talking to every young girl in the county. Telling them all to stay home, to not even trust their own boyfriends until the killer was caught.

Like Thatcher had a prayer of catching him. Thatcher and his friends were probably still heaving up their breakfasts after stumbling across pretty little Alev. She wasn't so pretty anymore. And a good deal littler. Certainly more compact. It had felt so damn good, arranging the scene. Imagining Thatcher's distress. Wishing he'd be able to see it himself. He needed it again, that rush, the exhilaration of the kill. Of knowing he'd bested the famous Special Agent Thatcher. Before it had been a game, but now it was personal. He wanted Thatcher to pay, and pay he would.

He'd had a setback with *Miss* Marshall, but he would watch and wait for the next opportunity. He would get her, then Thatcher would experience his brand of terror truly first-hand.

He couldn't wait for the true fun to begin. But he had needs to fulfill in the meantime. He was hungry. And not for food. He scowled and gritted his teeth.

He'd almost had her in his clutches, the little cheerleader with the big smile. Too bad she turned out to have a brain, too. He'd called her, told her to meet him, like they'd planned. But at the last minute she refused.

Refused.

Not because she thought he was a killer, she'd said, no way. She was just being careful.

Careful.

Bullshit. *She knew.* He could hear it in her voice. And he couldn't leave any loose ends for Thatcher to trip over.

He'd have to break his own rule, just this once, and make another house call.

Wednesday, October 12, 8:00 A.M.

The team was waiting as Nancy came in, white as a ghost. Holding a single sheet of paper.

Steven shook his head, knowing even as he reached for the report what it would say. Read it and felt a fist squeeze his gut to water. "No." He looked up at Nancy's pale face, fury and memories of Alev making his hands tremble. "I can't believe this. Not another one."

There was silence around the table, then Sandra exploded.

"After all the assemblies? The warnings? Dammit, who's missing now? And what was she *thinking* to meet someone after dark?"

Steven stared at the report, his brain kicking into full gear. "She didn't meet him, Sandra. She didn't leave her house. Voluntarily."

Davies abruptly pushed his chair from the table and crossed to Steven's side, holding out his hand. Steven gave him the report and turned to the others. "She was ripped from her bed. He was there, in her bedroom." His hand closed into a fist. "He's finally popped."

"He's out in the open," Liz murmured. "Now we have to find him. Who is she? Who is the girl he ripped from her bed?"

Davies put down the report. "Kelly Templeton. Roosevelt High."

"Rudy's playground," Harry said from behind clenched teeth. He still looked shaken from the ordeal the day before. "God, I want that little sonofabitch to fry."

Steven rose to his feet, every muscle in his body taut. "To a crusty little crisp. Kent, let's get you and as many other Forensics as we can free up over to the Templeton house. He's left something there, I know it. And we'll find it if we have to rip up every damn floorboard and carpet fiber. Liz, can we bring him in now? *Please?*"

Liz nodded slowly. "As long as we bring in anyone else that knew her. As long as we don't single Rudy out."

"She was a cheerleader," Sandra said curtly. "She probably knew everyone in the school."

"Which may include Brad," Nancy reminded him and Steven felt his heart stutter and clench. Even though Brad seemed okay now, Steven still didn't know what had caused the rift.

But he knew Brad. Ultimately trusted his son. His heart

quieted to normal. "That's okay. He's a smart kid, maybe he can tell us something we don't already know." Then his mind prickled, a plan beginning to form. "You're right, Sandra, she probably knew the whole school, so we'll go to them. Nancy, call the principal and arrange to have any students who knew her brought to a closed room in groups of ten." He looked over at Liz. "I assume a videographer's out?"

"Without parental consent? You assume correctly."

Steven shook his head. "Damn Bill of Rights," he said and made Liz smile. "Sandra, special duty for you. You'll ensure our teens have liquid refreshment."

Sandra raised her brows. "And do I get tips for this?"

Steven grinned, feeling his adrenaline pumping. "No, you don't serve. You let the school serve from their supplies. You, my dear, just collect the trash. Label each cup carefully. I want Rudy and his friends to drink something. And I want you to carefully make sure the used cups are garbage they no longer want." They could search garbage without a warrant. He wished he'd thought of this before. "Got it?"

Sandra's lips curved. "Got it. We can get DNA from his cup."

"You'll have to get DNAs from all the cups," Liz cautioned and Steven shrugged.

"Hell, Diane's back from her cruise all rested. I think she can handle the job, don't you, Kent?"

Kent nodded with mock sobriety. "Absolutely."

"Plus, how we prioritize the evidence won't matter in the long run as long as we run and compare all the samples, right, Liz?"

Liz looked amused. "Right."

Steven turned to Harry and immediately gentled his voice. "Harry, can you handle another crime scene with Kent?"

Harry looked grim. "After yesterday, I can handle anything. How much worse can he get?"

The question took the wind from all their sails.

Steven saw yesterday in his mind once again, as clearly as if he were still standing amid the body parts and the signs. "I don't want to know. Let's not give him a chance to show us."

Wednesday, October 12, 8:50 A.M.

Jenna was reviewing the reading assignments the substitute had given her class when Lucas interrupted. "Dr. Marshall? Can I have a word with you?"

Glad to see him after the tumult of her weekend, Jenna turned from her blackboard with a smile—that immediately dissipated when she saw the look on his face. Lucas was frightened.

Her first thoughts flew to Casey as she dusted chalk dust from her hands. Still she injected humor into her voice. "Class, read section six again. You all missed the finer points the first time."

She walked to the back of her classroom amid teenaged groans, her heart wildly beating in her throat. Lucas followed her into the hall and pulled the door shut behind them.

"Casey?" Jenna asked immediately.

Lucas shook his head. "No." He looked into her classroom from the oblong window in the door. "There's been another girl abducted," he said quietly, still looking into her classroom.

Jenna frowned, then her heart rose into her throat again. Sixteen, cheerleader. One empty desk in the front row. The hallway blurred as she sagged back against the wall to keep from falling. "Kelly?" she whispered.

Lucas swallowed. "Yes."

She remembered the look on Steven's face the night before. The unspeakable horror he'd seen. Perpetrated by the monster that now held one of her innocent girls. *He had Kelly.* Nausea rolled through her stomach and she had to fight to keep from throwing up. "When?"

"Last night. The police want to talk to the students, ask them what they've seen. Groups of ten. I'm setting it up in the conference room. Since she was in your class, I want your kids to go first."

Jenna pushed her trembling body from the wall. "We're halfway into the period. Which kids do you want to go first, because you won't have time for them all."

Lucas turned from the window, his face wooden. "Pick ten. We'll get the others in their classes as the day goes on." He raked taut fingers through the silver hair at his temples. "I can't believe this is happening. Does Thatcher have any idea who's doing this?"

Jenna shook her head. "I don't know," she murmured, fighting a wave of nausea. *Dear God. The last girl had been the worst crime Steven had ever seen. And he had Kelly. Think, Jenna. Move.* "I'll send the first group down." She'd divide the class alphabetically, she thought, mentally running down her roster. The first ten would be last names A through H. Steeling herself, she went back into her classroom to break the news no one should ever have to hear.

Wednesday, October 12, 3:30 P.M.

Steven, Sandra, Liz, and Nancy had interviewed over a hundred teenagers. Most were shell-shocked, unbelieving that one of their own had fallen prey. Lucas Bondioli was their mainstay, guiding teens into the conference room, preparing lists of names of those they'd talked to, those they hadn't.

Bondioli sat in on every group, which seemed to put the students at ease. Steven was glad to have him, knowing he could pick up on expressions that were out of the ordinary for any given teen.

The football team was among the first questioned, but none of the boys would admit to knowing anything. They did have the pleasure of watching Rudy's friends squirm, if for no other reason than the fact the boys knew they were still under suspicion for Jenna's attack even though Rudy himself had been cleared by way of alibi.

Late morning, Steven had left Sandra in charge and taken a break, first going up to Jenna's classroom where she'd walked silently into his arms, oblivious to the goggle-eyed stares of her third period class. She'd been through hell but she was holding up just as he'd known she would. He satisfied himself with a brief embrace and a whispered "I love you." It seemed like a year since he'd said it, although it had been only a few hours before when he'd woken her up before dawn to make love. Just once more, he'd thought in the darkness, before returning to the horror he knew would be waiting at work. And she'd silently obliged, offering her body, holding him until he finally forced himself out of her arms. Out of her bed. Into the office where the hell had begun all over again.

Then he'd visited the Templeton house where Harry and Kent and Davies were literally combing every fiber and every floorboard. They'd found a handful of hair, yanked out by the root, but Kent was now too overwhelmed by the reality of their killer to be as excited as he'd been at the discovery of the partial hair at the Clary clearing twelve days before. They'd found white powder scattered on Kelly's pillow and on the carpet next to her bed. Grimly they'd bagged it. If it was ketamine in powder form, Kent told him, it meant the killer was not only injecting it intravenously, but forcing his victims to inhale it, rendering them completely helpless in under ten seconds.

They'd found a clump of sawdust in the carpet. *That* had excited Kent. He'd carefully tagged and bagged it. It was their first clue as to where Rudy was taking the girls.

They had Kelly's cell phone. She'd received a five-minute call just before midnight, no caller ID available. Like Steven expected there'd be one. For a boy who couldn't pass chemistry, Rudy Lutz seemed pretty damn smart.

They'd found a footprint in the soft dirt outside her window and Steven was grateful that Mrs. Templeton took such pride in her lawn and flowers. And that she was a conscientious water conserver. Her sprinklers were set to go off at eleven P.M. when water absorption into the soil was most efficient, meaning the ground would stay moist enough for a shoe print until about three A.M.

So they had a three-hour window when the kidnapping had taken place.

And they had a pair of wildly terrified parents, stunned by grief, unable to give Steven any more information than he already knew.

Beyond that, he thought, refocusing on the last group of teens just now filing out of the room, they had nothing. He rose and stretched. "That was fun."

Sandra glared at him balefully. "I want double overtime."

Steven's lips curved. "You're salaried. You don't get overtime. Besides, you have teenagers. You should be used to this by now."

Liz rubbed her forehead. "I'm so out of the loop. How can mothers let their daughters leave the house dressed that way? I haven't seen so many midriffs since the last time I tuned into MTV by accident. It's like a billboard for sex offenders."

Sandra shook her head, digging into the garbage for the cups the teens had thrown away. The school had set out a cup of each color before each group and she noted who'd picked up which color while the group was ongoing. "Sex offenders don't need billboards or midriffs, Liz. You know that."

Liz handed her labeled baggies one at a time. They'd developed a rhythm over the course of the day. "I know. I just hate to see these young girls displaying themselves so . . ."

"Sluttily?" Nancy supplied, then grimaced. "God, that isn't even a word. One day with these kids and I'm making up words."

"And we get to come back tomorrow," Steven declared with false cheer, then pretended to flinch when all three women turned on him menacingly. "Hey, at least we got the football team and soccer team and the basketball team today."

"You got part of them," Bondioli corrected, coming into the room, a marked-up roster in his hands. "You've still got about twenty athletes and another hundred kids in the junior class alone."

Sandra groaned. "We'll be at this all week."

"But we have to talk to all of them," Liz reminded her. "No favorites." Then closed her mouth abruptly when Bondioli's dark brows shot up like a rocket.

"You *do* have a suspect," he said. Then sat down in a chair, a stunned look on his face. "And it's one of our students. Dear God."

Steven sighed. "We never said that, Lucas."

Bondioli narrowed his eyes. "You didn't have to. Just tell me who."

Steven wondered if the man even knew he clenched his fists. "You know we couldn't do that even if we did have a suspect." He sat down next to Bondioli. "You want us to catch him, right?"

Bondioli nodded, looking completely miserable. "He's killed three girls. And now he has Kelly. I have a daughter her age. I just can't even imagine . . ."

"Nobody can," Steven told him, reaching for the roster in Bondioli's trembling hand. He ran down the list for the names they'd interviewed and the ones they had not. Then frowned.

"What?" Liz asked, dropping in the chair next to him.

Steven shook his head. "I just noticed that our resident flunkee Rudy has a brother. He never showed up on any of the lists of suspects for the vandalism in Jenna's classroom."

Bondioli leaned back in his chair and closed his eyes, weariness etched into his face. "He doesn't run with his brother's friends," he said. "Josh is a special needs student."

Steven stared at the name, wondering why Davies had never mentioned a brother. "What's his special need?"

"Josh is cognitively challenged. His IQ tests at about eighty-five. He's able to compete with the other kids on a re-medial academic level with special help."

"Then what's he doing in Jenna's beginning chemistry class?" Steven asked. "That is what she teaches first period, isn't it?"

Bondioli nodded. "Josh came to me early this year and begged to be put into 'normal' classes." He punctuated the air with his fingers. "Said he wanted to at least try. I think he wanted to show his father he could be as good at something as Rudy was. And given Rudy's propensity to fail classes for complete lack of effort, I think Josh has a pretty good chance of doing so. His grades are all in except for English and Chemistry. He's got mostly *C*s. A *D* in math." He opened his eyes and looked over at Steven. "He's in Casey's English class and of course Jenna's Chemistry class. Neither of them have been able to turn in their grades for the quarter."

"I suppose they've been otherwise occupied," Steven mur-mured, his mind racing, wondering if trying to trick informa-tion out of a cognitively challenged teen was as reprehensible as it felt and not caring one single iota. He'd interview Josh Lutz and he'd use every skill in his repertoire to get anything out of the boy he could. For now, though, he kept his voice even. "I'll be anxious to talk to him tomorrow. He knew Kelly, right?"

Bondioli's dark eyes flashed. "He *knows* her, yes. Have you already decided she's dead?"

Steven sighed. "I'm sorry, Lucas. That was an insensitive slip. I'm tired, I suppose."

"I guess I understand." Bondioli stood up. "You'll be seeing Jenna out tonight?"

"I will." *And every night until she's safe,* Steven thought.

Bondioli's eyes softened. "Good. She needs somebody to take care of her."

"I plan to," Steven answered, completely aware of the stares of his three female coworkers.

Bondioli's face lit in a slow grin. "Well now, that's good to hear. I can only hope she lets you."

Steven frowned. "She'd better."

"She will," Jenna said from the door. "I'm safe as I'll ever be with these fine people to guard me." She smiled at Steven and his heart did a slow roll in his chest. "Go home, Lucas. I'll be fine."

"I'm betting Steven will be, too," Nancy snickered and Liz and Sandra grinned knowingly while Jenna's cheeks heated to an attractive rose.

"So will Helen," Liz added. "Now maybe she can concentrate on finding somebody for me. I'm not picky. Tall, dark, handsome. Rich is good."

"Don't forget a good kisser," Sandra said. "And, uh, *undercover* skill doesn't hurt either."

Nancy's snicker became a full laugh. "Is he, Jenna?"

Jenna set her mouth in a prim line even as her violet eyes danced. "That would be telling."

Liz took Jenna's arm and led her from the room. "Which

is just what we had in mind. We have very sophisticated in-
terrogation techniques."

Sandra grabbed her purse with an amused backward
glance at Steven. "Yeah, it's called thirty-two-ounce margari-
tas at happy hour."

TWENTY-NINE

Thursday, October 13, 8:00 A.M.

"OKAY, BOYS AND GIRLS," STEVEN SAID loudly to bring his
team to order. "Tell us what you know."

Sandra rolled her eyes. "That you're *totally tubular* and
we're like, so *lucky,* y'know, to be like, your *helpers* and all."
She pretended to stick her finger down her throat. "Gag me."

Kent snickered and Steven felt his cheeks heat. "Thank
you, Sandra," he said dryly, "for that fascinating foray into
adolescent linguistics. Do we know anything more pertinent
to the matter at hand before venturing out into yet another day
with our teen interviewees?"

Sandra shuddered and Nancy looked pained. Liz just sat
there grinning.

"What?" he asked her. "What's so funny?"

Liz shook her head, her eyes twinkling. "Nothing. I was
just thinking how much a good night's rest agrees with you. I
expect Jenna is equally rested."

He knew his redheaded complexion was working overtime, but couldn't stop the grin that nearly broke his jaw any

more than he could erase from his mind the image of Jenna slipping into his room last night, her dark hair stark against her white silk kimono-style robe. Then the kimono slithered to the floor and there were only silk stockings, garters, and . . . skin. And Jenna.

Davies scowled, which made Steven feel inordinately pleased. That he'd had a rousing, satisfying night of sex must show. He could certainly think of nothing else short of blows to make the interest in Davies's eyes disappear. Because the man still was interested in Jenna. *His Jenna.*

Steven looked away from Davies and back to the group. "Okay, back to business. Kent?"

Kent sobered and opened his folder. "Alev's limbs were severed with a circular saw."

Everyone around the table became alert. "What?" Steven asked. "Can they tell what kind?"

"Diane's got one of her guys tracing the pattern of the saw." Kent looked slightly nauseous, then visibly shook himself back into focus. "The hairs we found in Kelly's room yesterday were microscopically similar to the hair from the Clary clearing. Same color, same everything."

"From the same guy?" Steven asked.

"Without DNA confirmation I can only testify that they are similar," Kent answered. "But between us, I'd have to say yes."

"What about the white powder?"

Kent frowned at that. "Ketamine, dried. This is a common way to treat the substance. Dissolve it in a solvent and let it crystallize on filter paper. The powder is commonly rolled into cigarette paper, lit up, and inhaled. Three puffs and the user's out. It's more uncommon to be directly inhaled. I found a fiber attached to one of the powder crystals." He pulled out an enlarged microscopic view. "This is at five hundred times magnification. See the fiber attached to the crystal? It's a specialty nonwoven, made for filtration."

Steven stared at the photo. "How special?"

Kent shook his head in disgust. "Not special enough. I called around and found three chemical supply houses that could FedEx it to me overnight. No questions asked, pay by credit card."

Steven pushed the photo aside. "Well, damn."

"But at least you know how he's overpowering the girls," Davies said thoughtfully. "It's a new piece of his MO. In Seattle, he just knocked them off with a pipe."

Nancy fidgeted with her glasses, her face worried. "Nancy?" Steven asked. "What's wrong?"

She bit her lip. "Well, yesterday I asked Dr. Bondioli at the school for the attendance rosters. I was thinking that all the known abductions have happened at night. Except for the day in the clearing. You figured that Pal, the Clary's dog, attacked the killer sometime between ten and noon."

"And whoever did it wouldn't have been in school that morning," Liz said slowly.

Steven's gut twisted. "Please tell me Rudy wasn't in school that day, Nancy."

Nancy sighed. "I wish I could, but I can't. He was there."

Davies paled. "Maybe he skipped a class and they just marked him present."

"I thought about that," Nancy said gently. "I checked the individual attendance records. He has Jenna between ten and noon. She marked him present and she of all people wouldn't lie."

"Could the attendance records have been changed?" Sandra asked. "Hacked?"

Nancy shrugged. "Sure. But teachers keep individual attendance records. It should be easy enough to check. I think he was in school that day, Steven. Which means—"

"He wasn't in the clearing," Steven finished grimly. "Which means the hair isn't his."

"Which means the hairs we found yesterday aren't his," Kent added, just as grimly.

Liz closed her eyes. "Which means all this time we've been looking at the wrong guy."

"Sonofabitch," Harry snarled softly.

"This can't be right," Davies said, sounding a little desperate. "It's him."

"We'll check Jenna's attendance records when we get to the school this morning," Steven said evenly. "If he was there, we have to eliminate him as a suspect." He looked away, furious with himself for allowing his team to become so easily sidetracked. He smacked the table with the flat of his hand. "*Dammit.*" Then he looked back at Nancy and made himself smile at her. "Good work, Nance. Really, really good work." He stood up and paced. "Let's review what we have. An athlete of some kind with dark hair. We still don't know what the tattoo means." He looked over at Davies who shook his head mutely. "We know Roosevelt High is a common factor, that the three dead girls all cheered at games their schools played against Roosevelt. We know our killer walked across sawdust and wears a size ten shoe and has access to a circular saw. We know someone ordered ketamine through Mr. Richards's account, strange because the old man is dead." He looked over at Harry. "Harry, see what more you can dig up on that while we question the rest of the kids."

"Okay, Steven," Harry said, his face dejected.

His whole team was dejected. Dammit all to hell. "Perk up, people. We've got him running. We just need to make him run faster, so we can make him trip."

When everyone filed out, only Steven and Liz remained. "Don't lecture me, Liz," he said sourly, looking away. "I'm kicking my own ass hard enough for both of us."

Liz put her hand on his arm and waited until he met her steady gaze. "Don't kick yourself, Steven. I thought Rudy was the one, too. I even went out on a legal limb." Her smile was wry. "I was going to surprise you with it this morning. I got William Parker's records unsealed."

Steven's jaw dropped. "You did *what*? *How*?"

Liz shrugged. "Friend of a friend from law school is now a judge on the Washington State Court of Appeals. I told him what we had and asked if he'd release Parker's DNA just so we could eliminate a suspect. I think he disagreed with the original ruling and pulled some strings to grant my request. The DNA prints should be here by courier by tomorrow afternoon at the latest."

"Are you in any trouble?" Steven asked and watched her eyes flicker.

"No," she answered slowly. "And if I am, I'll take copies of your photos to the Bar and see if anyone can blame me. Especially the ones of Alev Rahrooh." She stood up briskly. "Now let's get back to the school for more rousing interviews with teenaged girls who think you're totally tubular."

Steven followed her out the conference-room door. "Makes me sound fat," he grumbled.

Liz laughed and lightened his load for just a moment. "Steven, you are many, many things, but fat is not one of them."

He threw her a mock glare. "That didn't sound like a compliment."

She was still chortling as they walked to the parking lot. "It wasn't meant to be."

Thursday, October 13, 9:15 A.M.

Jenna was waiting for Steven in the conference room, drumming her fingers against the table. When he came in, she stood up. "I don't have a lot of time," she said without greeting or preamble.

Steven placed his briefcase on one of the chairs and looked at her, his brown eyes narrowed. "Good morning to you, too."

Jenna flushed. "I'm sorry, I really don't have a lot of time. I've got another teacher watching my class and I have to get back. Lucas says you plan to talk to Josh Lutz this morning."

Steven nodded, rather coolly she thought. "I do."

"Why?"

"Because he knew—knows Kelly," he said. "We're talking to everybody who knows her." His eyes softened and he trailed a finger across her jaw. "Why does this upset you?" he murmured and she felt her ire melt away.

"He's a gentle kid," she said quietly. "I think he gets knocked around at home. I don't want to see him get knocked around here at school."

Something flashed in Steven's eyes. "Nancy, scratch the rubber hose," he called behind him. "Jenna objects." Jenna looked over his shoulder to see Nancy busily labeling bags while Lucas set up cups and bottles of soda. The older woman looked away, but not before Jenna saw her smile.

"Okay," Jenna conceded. "You won't use the Dragnet technique. How will you talk to him?"

"Like everybody else," Steven said evenly and Jenna felt badly for even raising the subject.

"I'm sorry, Steven," she murmured. "I just hate to see him hurt. He's been ridiculed over all the things that have happened to me this last week. It's just not fair for him to be singled out because he has the misfortune to be Rudy's brother. He's a nice boy."

Steven sighed. "I promise we'll be gentle, Jenna. Now go to your class."

Thursday, October 13, 3:00 P.M.

"Steven, we have a problem," Lennie said.

Steven turned from the bulletin board, where he'd been staring at the pictures, hoping some wisdom would pop into his head. Rudy was not their killer. Josh Lutz had been absolutely no help at all, his eyes and manner confirming everything Lucas and Jenna had told him. Josh was at best slow, at worst abused by his brother and/or father.

He had no suspect. Kelly was still missing. And to ice the cake, Al Pullman had called an hour before to tell him none of Rudy's friends had any dog bites, so they were no closer to knowing who had attacked Jenna.

Steven raised a brow. "Only one?"

Lennie shook his head. "We have an appointment with the governor in thirty minutes. He wants to understand how we could have four missing girls and no suspects."

Steven gritted his teeth. "Because we took a little side trip to Seattle and back."

"Not a good answer."

Steven checked his watch. "I have to be at the school to pick up Jenna in an hour."

"I say there's a good chance you'll be late." Lennie gave him a sour look. "Have Davies pick her up. He's not doing anything special right now."

Steven's laugh was totally without mirth. "Does the phrase 'over my dead body' mean anything to you?"

Thursday, October 13, 4:30 P.M.

The school day had ended and Jenna was waiting for Steven, grading papers to keep her mind and hands occupied. She was trying very hard not to look at Kelly's empty chair or think about what horrors the young girl must be facing when a voice from her doorway startled her.

"Jenna, I need to borrow some silver nitrate. Do you have any?"

Jenna looked up to see Otto Bell, the faculty leader of the photography club, standing in her doorway. Otto tended to run out of developing chemicals often, so she kept several bottles on hand.

"I should have some, Otto," she answered, grabbing her key to the chemical closet. "Let's take a look. My inventory says I should have three bottles," she murmured, searching. "Here we are."

She pulled out the first dark brown bottle and smaller, empty bottle to fill for Otto. But when the crystals poured out, she and Otto both gasped. "That's not silver nitrate," Otto said.

That was overstating the obvious. What they had was a bottle of sand.

"Could someone have stolen it when they were ransacking your classroom?" he asked.

She looked over at him, biting her lip. "With all the vandalism, I've watched the chemical stores, but I haven't opened each bottle."

Otto lifted his bushy black brows that made her think of a great hairy giant. "I think it's time we did," he answered and, pulling out his cell phone, called his photography club and ordered them to join him. "More hands," he said. "We'll get an inventory in short order."

In the past she might have refused, but now Jenna nodded her thanks. "I appreciate it, Otto."

He clasped her shoulder. "I've wanted to do something to help all along. This is my chance. Have a seat, Jen. I'll bring out all the bottles while you take the inventory."

Thursday, October 13, 6:00 P.M.

Neil had been driving around for hours, aimlessly. Trying to accept the truth that Rudy Lutz had not been at the Clary clearing, that he was not their killer. Unable to. In his gut he *knew* Rudy Lutz was William Parker. He also knew the blood lust that drove a boy to kill three years ago would not simply die. William Parker wouldn't stop killing.

Neil slid his rental car into a parking place and looked up at the school. Roosevelt High. He'd stayed away before, not wanting to alert Rudy to the fact that he was here. That he was on to him. There didn't seem to be a lot to lose at this point. He got out of his car to see what he could see.

He'd lost Parker once. He didn't intend to let it happen again. Clearing or no clearing. Alibi or no. Parker was guilty and by God, this time Neil would see him pay.

Maybe then he himself would find peace.

Thursday, October 13, 6:00 P.M.

Jenna sat on the school's front steps, very annoyed. Steven was late. So late the security guys had locked the school. So late she needed to wait outside because he wouldn't be able to get into the building to find her. So late she'd had to call Mark and tell him she'd be missing their Thursday night karate class. I should have driven myself, she thought. She wouldn't wait around like this every night because Steven couldn't be depended on to be punctual.

But Steven would be there. He'd sent a message that he'd been called away that afternoon, but he'd get her as soon as he could. And at this point, she had more on her mind than Steven's whereabouts and missed sparring matches. She was missing chemicals. Quite a few chemicals.

Shivering from the wind, Jenna stared at the revised inventory list, trying to figure out why someone would steal these items. She was missing the silver nitrate plus bromine, chlorobenzonitrite, and propylamine. They were rather unusual chemicals to steal, she thought, her thoughts drifting back to her pharmaceutical days. The syntheses that used these ingredients were complex, so complex that to complete the synthesis, one needed a sophisticated lab. It certainly wasn't possible to complete such syntheses in her little high school lab.

"Jenna, you're still here."

Jenna looked up to find Neil Davies standing at the base of the school's steps. "Neil." She started to smile a welcome, but her eyes suddenly narrowed in concern. "Is Steven all right?"

Neil shrugged. "Don't know. Haven't seen him since this morning." He looked around. "Are you supposed to be here alone?"

Her patience snapped. "No, I'm not supposed to be here alone," she said testily, then watched his face fall and felt guilty. "I'm sorry, Neil. I've had a bad few days. I guess you all have, too."

He shook his head and leaned against the iron railing. "That's an understatement." He was quiet for a moment, then asked, "You tell your family about the wrecked car?"

Jenna nodded. "I finally told them the truth. They were not as upset as I thought they'd be."

Neil ventured a grin. "More worried about you, huh?"

Jenna nodded again, this time a small smile curving her lips. "Fancy that."

"I kind of hoped it would turn out that way."

"Mmm." When he didn't say anything, the silence grew awkward. "So, Neil, you never did tell me where you're from."

One corner of his mouth lifted and Jenna thought he was a very handsome man. Not as handsome as Steven by a long shot, but still the kind that made women swoon. "Wales," he said.

"More recently than sixty years ago."

He looked impressed. "Good memory."

"Umm-hmm. So where, Detective Davies?"

"Seattle," he said, surprising her.

"Really? What brings you all the way to little old Pineville, North Carolina?"

"I thought I could help on Steven's case," he said and she detected a touch of self-pity.

"But obviously you were wrong. Have a seat, Neil, and tell me a story."

And after a long look, he sat. "I thought I knew who was killing the girls. I was wrong."

"Mmm. So should I deduce that you've met this killer, or thought you'd met him, somewhere in the past? Say, Seattle?"

"I should have gone to Ph.D. school," he murmured ruefully. "I'd be a lot smarter than I am." He looked out into the darkness of the parking lot. "And Alev and Kelly might still be home with their parents," he added, his voice bitter.

Jenna digested this. "Steven believed your lead, didn't he? And then you realized you were wrong and the whole investigation was in the toilet."

"Right again."

"So what now?"

He turned his head to look at her and she saw he was lost. Totally lost. "I don't know."

"Will you go back to Seattle?"

He shrugged. "I don't know. Not a whole helluva lot left for me there."

"So I take it you're not married."

"Was. Not anymore." Neil looked down at his hands. "I kind of got obsessed with a case."

"A serial killer of young girls in Seattle?"

He nodded. "Yeah."

"You didn't catch him then. What happened?"

For a minute she thought he wasn't going to answer, then he shrugged. "The evidence I gathered had been tainted."

"Like O.J.'s glove?" she asked wryly and he looked up at the sky with another unwilling smile.

"Just like that. I gathered it right. I swear I did. By the rules. By the book. Just like I'd done a hundred times before. But something happened. The records showed I'd been in the evidence room the night critical semen samples disappeared—and then reappeared the following morning."

"They accused you of contaminating evidence."

He nodded morosely. "And even though I had a concrete alibi, a fucking judge let a killer go."

"And because you blame yourself for not catching him then, you come all this way, bent on catching him now, only you're wrong and quite possibly made everything worse. Am I on target?"

He nodded. "Right once again."

"So you punish yourself for something you should have done or shouldn't have done."

"That's me."

Jenna shook her head. "That's bullshit."

He darted a quick look her way and scowled. "What's that supposed to mean?"

"It means get a life, Neil. You goofed. Pick up and move on. Lots of people have."

"You mean like Steven."

Jenna heard the sneer in his voice as he said Steven's name. "Among others, yes. Why don't you like him, Neil? He's a good man."

Neil's laugh was hollow, launching warning bells in her head. He looked away, his jaw taut. "Do you know what it's like to lie awake and stare at the ceiling?" he asked, his voice hard.

"Yes," Jenna said unflinchingly.

"Night after night?" he pressed.

"Yes," Jenna answered.

"For years?"

"Yes." She could hear the edge in her voice. She was growing weary of his self-pity.

He fished in his pocket and brought out a pack of Winstons, still in the plastic. "I haven't smoked in years."

"So don't start again now," Jenna snapped.

The corner of Neil's mouth lifted. "If my wife had been more like you . . ." He shoved the cigarettes back in his pocket, unopened. "So do you still lie awake night after night?" he asked.

She thought about the enveloping warmth of Steven's body during the night, the utter safeness of his arms around her, and couldn't stop the satisfied smile that curved her lips. "Not anymore."

He turned his head, only his head, and she was startled by the way his dark eyes had hardened. "Because of him."

"Yes," she said, but it came out crackly. She cleared her throat. "And you? Can you sleep?"

He nodded, then pulled the cigarettes from his pocket. Nervously tapped the pack against his palm. "The first night I saw you I slept for the first time in three years." He closed his hand into a fist, crushing the cigarettes. "And dreamed of you."

Jenna blinked, unsure of what to say. "Neil, I—"

Neil lurched to his feet. "Stop. Let's just leave it alone, all right?" He strode toward the parking lot and she jumped to her feet to follow him.

"Neil, wait."

He looked up at the stars, then back at her. "You really love him, don't you?"

She nodded, again not knowing what to say. So she said the truth. "I really do."

He took her hand, squeezed it. "I'll probably go back on the first flight tomorrow."

And as she looked at him, she saw a very lonely man who truly cared about the girls he believed himself to have failed. Her heart squeezing in compassion, she leaned up and kissed his cheek. "I hope you find peace, Neil."

He grimaced. "I'd settle for a good night's sleep."

Her mouth curved up. "Try counting ewes."

"Ah. Girl sheep."

She rolled her eyes. "I knew it was a guy thing." And he laughed as she smiled. He stepped away backward until he got to a tiny little car.

"Good luck, Jenna. I hope Steven's the good man you believe him to be. If I had a woman like you waiting for me, I sure as hell wouldn't be late."

Jenna's smile faded. "Safe travels, Neil."

THIRTY

Thursday, October 13, 6:30 P.M.

NEIL WATCHED HER FROM HIS REARVIEW MIRROR as he drove away, cursing himself for once again being in the right place at the wrong time and Thatcher for having all the good fortune. Then a Volvo wagon zoomed past him on the right and exited the school's parking lot in a cloud of dust.

Thatcher's Volvo. Of course.

"Well, damn," he said softly, though only half of him could regret Thatcher misinterpreting what he'd seen. The other half was glad. Jenna didn't deserve a volcano ready to blow. She was also alone, waiting for a man who wasn't coming to get her. And she still had to worry about Lutz and his friends as the next football game drew nearer. Those thugs were more than desperate.

He'd nearly returned to the front of the school when he heard her scream. Senses on full alert, he jumped from the car and pulled his Glock from the waistband at his back. "*Jenna!*"

She screamed again. Running, following the sound of her scream, he rounded the corner of the school where four big figures were dragging her toward the football field.

And having a hard time of it, he noted as he drew his weapon. She managed to kick two of them away, but the other two shoved her against the brick wall. Her cry of pain ripped at his gut.

"Stop! Police!" he shouted, trying to see who was who in the dark, swearing he now saw five boys where just a moment before there had been only four. He pointed his gun upward and shot a warning round into the air when no one stepped away from her. "Police!"

There was cursing and scuffling and the two took final parting shots at her face before running. He took one quick look to make sure she was breathing before taking off after them. They were fast, he thought. Probably wide receivers. No tackle could run that fast. The tackles were probably the guys she'd dropped back in the scuffle. The two did some fancy maneuvering that took them around the bleachers and over a fence.

Neil stopped running, breathing hard. He hadn't had one good look at them. Sonsofbitches.

Hopefully Jenna had. Sprinting, he made it back to where she sat up against the wall, the fifth figure bending over her. So there *were* five. "Just step back from her, boy, and nobody gets hurt."

The fifth boy froze, then backed up slowly, straightening.

"Hands out where I can see them."

The boy's hands stuck out stiffly at his sides.

"Neil, it's okay." The cupped palm she held over her mouth was dripping blood.

"Shit, you're bleeding." He shrugged out of his jacket and unbuttoned his shirt with one hand while holding his weapon steadily on the boy with the other. He pulled off his shirt and threw it to her. "Here. Use that on the blood. It's clean. Mostly."

She held the shirt to her mouth. "Neil, put the gun down. Josh was helping, not hurting me."

Josh. Neil let his weapon drop to his side, his fingers still tight on the trigger. "Turn around, son." And waited while the big boy turned. And saw a face he hadn't seen in many years. Josh Parker. Josh Lutz. They hadn't bothered to change their other son's first name. Neil guessed the Parkers weren't as worried about the effect of a scandal on a boy of Josh's aptitude. Or lack thereof. There would be no college scouts watching their other son. No future to protect. Josh stood looking at him, his hands still out at his sides, that same vacant look in his eyes that he'd had years before. "Just back up, son. Back up and tell me what you were doing here."

If Josh recognized him, he gave no sign of it. One of the boys curled up on the ground moaned and cursed. Neil took a step back to see them clearly. "You two on the ground holding your dicks, put your faces in the dirt and your hands out to your sides." When they made no move to comply he shoved one of them with the toe of his shoe. "I said on your faces or I'll let the teacher here give you another kick." Immediately both rolled to their bellies, groaning pitifully, hands outstretched, like snow angels in reverse. "Next time you decide to fuck with a woman, make sure she doesn't have a fucking brown belt," Neil snarled and both boys made whiny whimpering sounds.

Josh Lutz glanced at the two on the ground. "They were hurting her. I had to do something."

"You did, Josh," Jenna said, her voice muffled by the shirt against her lip. "You did just fine."

Neil pulled his phone from his pocket, dialed 911, then tossed the phone to Jenna. "Tell them where we are."

Jenna gave the operator all the information, then stood up, his phone still in her hand. "I need to call Steven," she said.

Steven. Hah, Neil thought, sorry sonofabitch, caring more for his petty ego than the safety of this woman. "Good luck. He's probably halfway to Virginia by now."

Her hand stilled on the cell phone and she lowered it to her side. "What do you mean?"

He debated for a moment telling her, knowing it would hurt her, then told her anyway, knowing it was for her own good. "He passed me on my way out of here. Doing about eighty."

Even in the darkness he could see her pale. "He was here?"

"Yes."

"He saw us talking then." She paused. "He saw me kiss you good-bye."

Neil flicked a glance at Josh, then looked back at her. She was trembling now. Partly the shock of yet another attack. Partly the shock of knowing it wouldn't have happened had her volcano not blown. Mostly the shock of realizing Steven hadn't trusted her. "I'm sorry, Jenna."

"So am I," was all she said before turning back for the front of the school.

"Wait. Where are you going?"

She turned and he could see the lines cutting through the grime on her cheeks. Tears. Dammit, she was crying and there wasn't a damn thing he could do.

"I . . . don't know," she whispered.

"Well, sit down," Neil said irritably, mad at his own help-lessness. "Those other two are still somewhere around here. Just wait till the cops get here."

One of the boys on the ground twisted to look up at him, snarling. "You said you were a cop."

Neil bared his teeth. "Substitutes are a real bitch, you know? All the responsibility with none of the authority." He pressed his toe into the thug's back and if it was a bit harder than necessary, who was going to tell? Not Jenna, who stood in the same exact spot, looking like she'd lost her best friend. Not Josh, who stood looking like he was stuck sitting in the wrong movie but didn't have the means to get up and switch theaters. And certainly not himself. Hell, he'd do it again in a heartbeat.

Jenna cleared her throat from behind him. "On second thought, I think I will use your phone," she said, sounding almost like her old self again.

"You're not calling Thatcher, are you?" he asked, narrowing his eyes.

She smiled, grimly, then winced at the pain in her cut lip, using his shirt to dab at the flow of blood. "No, I'm not calling Steven." She dialed and listened. "Dad?" she said, starting out strong. Then her voice wobbled. "Can you come get me please? I'm at the school."

Thursday, October 13, 6:45 P.M.

Steven stopped a few miles away, pulled into a parking lot, and switched off the motor. Tried to force his heart to calm. The pain inside was . . . excruciating. Worse than Melissa. Much worse.

Jenna had said she loved him. Laid in his arms and said she loved him. Then twelve hours later she was kissing another man. And not just any other man.

Neil Davies. Steven's blood churned at the thought. The man disrupted his investigation, distracting his people from the real killer while two more girls were stolen. Then he had the nerve to move in on his woman.

But Jenna wasn't his woman. There was no way she could be his and kiss Davies. He leaned his forehead against the steering wheel, feeling his heart slog back to normal. Wishing his head and his gut would do the same. Right now it felt like a million sledgehammers were pounding away inside his skull while a million knives dug deep and ripped at his gut.

How could she? *Maybe she didn't.*

He lifted his head from the steering wheel and blinked. But she had. He'd seen them.

What did you see? Her. Kissing him.

She was kissing his cheek. Just like you've kissed Liz's. But it wasn't the same.

And why not? Because it's Neil Davies? Because you've felt wary of him since you've met? Because he looks at her, wanting her? Yes, that's why.

But has she ever looked at him the same way?

He bit his lip and stared at the night sky. No. In all fairness, no she had not. He glanced at the clock and felt his blood go cold once again. She was waiting for him, all alone. Vulnerable.

Oh, God. He'd left her there. All alone. He raced back to the school, faster than he'd raced away. And arrived just behind two squad cars and an ambulance, lights flashing.

Dread clutched at his heart and he made himself get out of the car. Made himself walk past the flashing lights of the empty ambulance. He almost collapsed with relief when he saw her sitting on the ground, cross-legged, her skirt hiked high on her thighs. Unhurt. Alive. He walked a few steps closer and stopped short. *She wasn't unhurt.* Her face was bleeding and her cheek was already starting to swell. Her clothes were torn and she had a dirty white rag bound around her right hand. One of the paramedics was unrolling it and Steven saw it was a shirt. A man's shirt.

He lifted his eyes to find Davies facing away, talking to the uniforms as they cuffed two teenagers. Then Davies turned and Steven saw the man wore no shirt under his jacket. It didn't take a damn detective to put the pieces together. While he'd been speeding away, Davies had come back and done *his* job.

Protected *his* woman.

Protected Jenna, who just now realized he was standing there. He didn't know what to say, didn't even hope Davies had kept his little tantrum secret. Because that's what it had been. A tantrum. She looked up at him. Then deliberately looked away.

He dropped to his knees next to her on the ground. "Jenna, I'm sorry."

She shook her head. And said nothing. Then she cleared her throat and said in as strong a voice as he'd ever heard her use, "Go away, Steven. Just go away."

"Jenna, honey, I'm here." They looked up to find a silver-haired man standing above them and she crumbled right before his eyes. The older man knelt beside her and held her while she cried.

The sound of her sobs tore at Steven, made him want to kick his own ass, and knew a kicking would never be enough. He reached out and touched her torn sleeve. She jerked her arm away.

"Jenna," Steven tried again. As soothingly as he could considering his heart was hammering right out of his chest, "Let me take you home."

She cried harder and shook her head. "Take me home, Dad. Please."

Dad. This was Seth. Seth met his eyes. Frowned. "Your apartment's not safe, honey."

"No, Dad. Take me *home*. Your home. And please tell *him* to go the hell away."

Seth's eyes narrowed, realizing Steven had hurt his girl. "You heard her. I'm taking her home."

Steven watched as Seth lifted Jenna to her feet and into his car. And drove away.

Someone stepped to his right and Steven knew it was Davies. "Thatcher, you're a fucking idiot," he said, his tone low.

Steven watched the taillights of Seth's car disappear, taking Jenna away. "I know."

THIRTY-ONE

Friday, October 14, 9:45 A.M.

HER HEAD ACHED, WORSE THAN ANY HANGOVER. And to make it worse, she had company. She winced at Allison's overly cheerful screech telling her to come downstairs. Coming home with Seth had seemed like a good idea last night, but now, in the light of day, she doubted its wisdom.

Neil stood in Allison's living room, holding a bunch of red roses. "I didn't know what you liked," he said, holding out the flowers. "I went for tradition."

She smiled, then winced when her split lip burned. "They're lovely, Neil. Have a seat." And when he did, she said, "I never got the chance to thank you for last night."

"I wish I'd gotten back sooner," he said, then blurted, "I told Thatcher he was a fucking idiot."

"That about sums it up."

"He's outside, sitting in his car," Neil added. "He was there when I got here."

"He's been there all morning," Allison said, sweeping in to get the flowers. "I've told him three times to leave, but he won't."

"He knows he fucked up," Neil said and Jenna lifted her brows.

"You're defending him? Last night . . ." Jenna faltered and shook her head. Then winced at the searing pain. "Never mind."

"Look, Thatcher's not number one on my hit parade, but I know what he looked like when you drove away. And I know how you looked when you said you loved him. At least hear what he has to say."

Jenna sighed. "Fine. Then everybody leaves so I can take these painkillers and go to sleep."

Neil went to the front door and gestured. "He's coming. I'll be going now."

Jenna squinted at the light of the open door. "I thought you were going back to Seattle today."

Neil frowned. "I changed my mind. Thatcher may have eliminated Rudy Lutz from his list of suspects, but my gut still tells me there's something there."

The room spun. "Rudy Lutz?"

Neil turned, still frowning. "I thought Thatcher would have told you."

She shook her head, every movement feeling like a thousand knives. "No. No, he didn't."

"Well, he was right not to," Neil said. "It would have contaminated the case."

Jenna felt like she was going to throw up. *Rudy Lutz?* Well, wasn't that just jiminy cricket? *Rudy Lutz?* He knew all this time. Damn him. Damn them both. She waited until Steven was in the living room before leveling both barrels at both men. "You didn't think it was important to tell me I had a *serial killer* after me? Did you think I was too *stupid* to understand?"

Steven looked at Neil with murder in his eyes.

Neil shrugged. "I thought you would have told her. Pillow talk."

"I run a clean investigation," Steven gritted. "No loopholes for overeager defense attorneys."

Neil scowled. "My investigation was every bit as clean as yours."

"*Shut up!*" Jenna pushed her fingertips against her temples. "Tell me, if you don't think I'm too feebleminded to comprehend, are there any strange chemicals at work in this case?"

Steven narrowed his eyes. "Why?"

"Yes or no, dammit," she snapped, then gobbled down the painkillers Allison silently put in front of her. "Thank you, Allison."

"You're welcome." Allison faced the two men. "Well, answer her question."

"For God's sake," Steven grumbled. "Yes, yes there are. Ketamine, if you must know. Why?"

"Because I found some chemicals missing from my storeroom yesterday. I had an inventory, but it got lost somewhere in the fighting. I know I was missing silver nitrate and some of the basic ingredients of ketamine. But your killer would have had to have access to sophisticated lab equipment. Not the kind in my classroom and certainly not the kind you'd assemble from a drugstore chemistry set. If the silver nitrate is involved, your killer is developing his own photographs. And for the record, there is no way under heaven that Rudy Lutz is smart enough to pull all of this off." She massaged her temples. "To pull any of this off. His father, maybe, but football boy? No way. That is all. Now please, both of you *go away*."

Neil gave Steven an intense look, then left.

"You too, Steven," she said. "I've had enough."

"You heard her," Allison said and Steven's face went red with anger.

"I will talk to her," he said softly, "and you will please leave."

"This is my house," Allison started, then Jenna waved her hand.

"Let him stay long enough to have his say." When they were alone, Jenna sat back and closed her eyes. "Let's get this over with."

"My wife left me for another man," he said and her eyes flew open.

"What?"

He was looking at her evenly. "The day my wife died I came home from work to find Brad watching Matt and Nicky. Brad was thirteen, Matt was nine, and Nicky was three. Melissa had gone to the mall, Brad said. Except I went to our bedroom and found a note lying on the bed. She'd said she left me for another man and that by the time I got the note she'd be halfway to Miami. She didn't love me, had never loved me, and was tired of chicken nuggets, soccer games, and diaper changes. The boys were mine and I was welcome to them." He was reciting the note in a monotone and Jenna knew he'd memorized every word. Stunned, she had no idea what to say to him.

"I sat there looking at the note for an hour, then figured I needed to tell the boys something. She wasn't coming home." He looked away. "I'd made it downstairs when the doorbell rang. It was a uniform from the third district, looking solemn, and I knew what he was going to say. She'd been in an accident on the way to the airport. She was in the car with another man. The married CEO of a Raleigh company, who had a blood alcohol level of point one eight. He lived, she died."

"The drunk driver whose insurance was so eager to settle with you," Jenna murmured and Steven shrugged callously.

"Why have scandal then? Melissa was dead and his wife, who was vacationing at Hilton Head, need never know. God knew I didn't want my kids to know."

Jenna's eyes widened. "So you told them she just died."

"On her way home from the mall," he said bitterly.

"Oh, Steven," she whispered. "All this time you've worried every woman would be like her."

"When I met you, I knew you weren't, but I was . . . afraid."

"But when you saw me with Neil last night, you believed the worst."

He leaned his head back against the sofa and studied the ceiling. "I did. And I'm sorry."

"So am I."

He looked at her then, truly looked at her. "None of this makes any difference, does it?"

"It makes every bit of difference." She looked away. "And none."

"Will you come home with me?" he asked.

She swallowed. "No."

"Why?"

"Because I know better than to love a man who can't trust me. You'll never trust me. You say you will, then the next time I'm friends with a man you'll do it all again and we'll be in the same place we are now." She felt tears on her own cheeks. "I'll resent you and then where will we be?"

He stood up and looked out the window. "You've got it all figured out, haven't you?"

"Just like you did," she returned, feeling angry and hurt.

"Then tell me you're ready to say good-bye." And he grabbed her and kissed her until the room spun and she clung to him. Lifting his head, he whispered harshly, "Tell me you don't want me."

She shook her head and pushed him away. "I won't lie to you. I want you. But I'm smart enough to know I can't have everything I want. What I want is a man who trusts me and who I can depend on. I had that once. I'll hold out for it again."

He held her shoulders tight. "What about Nicky, Jenna?" he demanded, facing her, anger visibly vibrating through him. "Can you walk away from him?"

Jenna flinched as if he'd struck her. "That's not fair."

His face spasmed in pain. "I don't give a damn about fair.

I don't give a damn about me, but you're hurting my son all over again."

She drew a breath and tried to be the logical one. "I'm sorry, Steven. I should have listened to you and not allowed Nicky to become so attached. But it still can't change anything. Continuing a relationship with Nicky knowing we're finished would be even more cruel long-term."

He looked at her for a long minute, his eyes so miserable and sad that she almost changed her mind. Almost. "I wanted to marry you," he said, so quietly she had to strain to hear him. "I was going to ask you in bed yesterday morning, but I wanted to have this case settled, so I waited. I guess my timing on a marriage proposal was the only thing I did right. I had a selfish wife once who didn't care about my children. I sure as hell don't need to go through it again."

Slamming the front door behind him, he was gone.

Allison put a box of tissues in her hand and Jenna snatched up a handful, mopped her face, then gave up and buried her face on Allison's shoulder. And cried her fool heart out.

"Thatcher, wait."

Steven stopped at the base of the Llewellyns' driveway thinking he was so close to the edge that just one of Davies's smug I-told-you-sos would push him over. "If you say I-told-you-so I swear . . ." He let the threat trail off, knowing he didn't have the emotional energy to follow through.

"I wanted to say I'm sorry for my part in this," Davies said quietly. "I honestly didn't go to the school to see her, but when I did, I didn't want to walk away."

Despair and rage battled, but in the end Steven was just too tired to give way to either. "This is supposed to make me feel better how, Davies?"

"It's not supposed to make you feel better," Davies snapped. "Any desire I had to make you feel better disappeared when I saw the bruises on her face this morning." He drew a deep breath. "But you mean something to her so I also didn't want to make it any worse," he said, his voice calm again. "I wanted you to know what happened. She said that she loved you," he finished quietly.

The quiet words cut deeper than any I-told-you-so ever could. She now wore bruises inside and out as testament to his lack of trust. He cleared his throat. "Thanks for doing what I should have done. For making sure those bastards didn't hurt her worse than they did."

"I went to the school to see if I could get a glimpse of your Rudy Lutz with his friends," Davies said. "I know the roster says he was in class, but my gut tells me something's wrong."

Steven sighed, so damn weary. "What do you want, Neil?"

"I want to take one more look around the Templeton place."

"I can't let you have Kent or anyone else from Forensics," Steven said, just wishing the man would go away so he could let go of the awful weight pressing against his chest.

"I understand. I'll call you if I find anything."

Then finally he was gone and Steven climbed in his car. Shut the door. And drove to work.

Friday, October 14, 11:30 A.M.

"You've got company," Allison said and with a groan Jenna pulled herself out of bed and down to the living room where Casey sat on Allison's sofa with her right arm and left leg in plaster casts. Ned stood behind her, his hands on her shoulders.

"Casey." Jenna hugged her lightly, for both their sakes. "When did you get out?"

"This morning." She frowned. "What happened to your face?"

"Long story. So how did you get up the driveway in that cast?"

Casey glowed. "Ned carried me. I wanted you to be the first to know." She held out her left hand and Jenna swallowed hard at the sight of the diamond on Casey's ring finger. She'd be damned if she let her own petty problems spoil Casey's moment.

So she smiled up at Ned, then at Casey. "I'm so happy for you both."

Then burst into noisy tears.

Casey didn't say anything for a moment, just reached out and patted her hand. Then said to Ned, "See if Allison has anything stronger than iced tea. And if she says no, ask Seth where he hides his stash."

Jenna sniffled. "I can't have alcohol. I'm taking pain medication."

"It's not for you," Casey said. "It's to calm me down so I don't go murder Steven Thatcher."

Friday, October 14, 3:30 P.M.

Neil stood in the middle of Kelly's bedroom, frustrated as hell. He'd spent hours covering every inch and found nothing new. *There had to be something,* he thought, walking to the window, looking at the neat circle of cut glass, visualizing how the killer would have come in. From the state of her blankets, Kelly would have struggled hard, but her attacker was much bigger and stronger. He would have put a mask over her face, made her breathe the ketamine powder that would have knocked her out in five to ten seconds. But in those seconds, she would have fought for her life.

She was young and had been a gymnast prior to her cheer-leading. Her ribbons and trophies were on the wall in the Templetons' living room. She'd been very good and to be that good, she had to have a great deal of physical strength and agility. But she was small, like her mother.

"Mrs. Templeton," he called and the worry-worn mother hurried in. "I need your help."

Warily, Mrs. Templeton regarded him. "What?"

"I want to reevaluate how your daughter would have strug-gled against her attacker. You're her same size. Would you reenact this with me?"

Mrs. Templeton's jaw squared. "Where should I stand?"

Neil smiled at her. "Right here, next to me." Gently he turned her around so her back was to him and put his hand over her mouth. "Now fight me. Fight hard." He winced when her elbow caught him unprepared and she abruptly stilled. "No, ma'am, fight harder." So she twisted in his arms, claw-ing at the front of his jacket until one of his buttons came off and flew across the room. He let her go and she turned around, her cheeks red and her breath coming in hard pants.

"Well?"

Neil opened his mouth, then closed it again as a furry shadow crept to the corner where his button had fallen. He put his finger to his lips to tell her to be quiet and together they watched the Templeton family cat pick the button up between his teeth.

Quietly they followed until the cat crawled under a chair in their unused spare bedroom. Neil picked up the chair, and the cat hissed, then ran. Leaving behind a pile of shiny buttons.

Mrs. Templeton's eyes were huge. "Do you think . . . ?"

"I'm praying, ma'am," Neil said and meant it. "Very, very hard."

Friday, October 14, 3:30 P.M.

"You have company," Seth said and Jenna groaned. Casey was gone and Jenna wanted to sleep.

"Go away, Dad. I don't want any company."

"You'll want this guy," Seth said and opened the door to her room, letting Jim bound in, tail wagging, tongue lolling, looking healthy and happy. Good as new. "Wendy said Jean-Luc had to stay for another few days until his sutures were healed more, but that Jim could come home."

Jenna took one look at Seth's happy face and Jim's wagging tail and burst into tears.

Friday, October 14, 3:30 P.M.

"Steven," Kent said and Steven lifted his eyes from his paperwork to Kent's excited face.

"What is it?" he demanded, rising to his feet. "What do you have?"

"New information," Kent said, the young man's tension almost palpable. Certainly catching. Kent laid two sheets holding DNA prints side by side on top of the clutter of Steven's desk. One was a bit faded and bore a bright yellow sticker declaring it confidential property of the State of Washington. The other was new.

"Liz's favor came in," Steven said and Kent nodded.

"This is William Parker's DNA from the sealed record in Seattle," Kent said, his voice crackling. "This is the DNA from the hair we found in the Clary clearing."

Steven leaned forward and squinted. "And?"

"They're not the same," Kent said triumphantly.

Steven looked at him in confusion. "So? We already knew

Rudy was in class that day. So he's either not William Parker or wasn't at the clearing or both."

"He could still be Parker," Kent said. "The Clary clearing DNA is not the same as Parker's, but it's dead close. Close enough so that the two came from blood relatives. And not a father/son because the sample from the Clary clearing came from mitochondrial DNA which only carries the maternal genetic print. William Parker wasn't in the Clary clearing, but a blood relative with the same mother was."

"That leaves the brother," Steven hissed. "The brother everyone said was too slow to notice."

Liz hurried in just then. "I came as soon as I got your call, Kent. What's happened?"

"It was the younger Lutz boy." Steven grimaced, slamming his fist against his desk. "The one everybody said was too slow to be involved. Dammit, Jenna even defended him. Poor boy, knocked around by his thug father."

"And he well might have been," Liz said, still breathless from running. She quickly looked at the DNA prints, Kent's neatly typed conclusion, and nodded her understanding. "But we won't let that stop us. You'll be wanting a search warrant on the Lutz place?"

"With a big red bow," Steven said from behind gritted teeth.

"I'm on it," Liz said. "Great work, Kent. Steven, call Neil. He'll want to know about this."

Friday, October 14, 3:45 P.M.

Neil spread the buttons out on the sheet of aluminum foil Mrs. Templeton had stretched across her kitchen table. One by one he separated each button from the pile with his gloved finger.

Then breathed a prayer of thanks both for Mr. Whiskers' consistent habit of button pilfering and for the sudden return of
his memory. He picked up a pewter button and held it up to
the light, watching the way the shadows bounced off every
turn of the design.

"You recognize it?" Mrs. Templeton asked hopefully and
he jerked his attention back to her.

"Yes, ma'am." He dropped the button back into the pile.
"Do you have a Ziploc bag—new and unused?" he asked,
then wrapped the buttons in the aluminum foil and dropped
the foil in the bag. "Close the bedroom door and don't go near
the area under the chair," he instructed. "Forensics will vac-
uum to make sure the cat didn't take anything else from your
daughter's bedroom."

Neil rushed to his car, his precious Ziploc bag of evidence
clutched in one hand. And prayed like he never had before.

THIRTY-TWO

Friday, October 14, 4:30 P.M.

CHARLIE STUCK HER HEAD IN JENNA'S ROOM. "Aunt
Jenna—"

Jenna sat up in bed snarling. "I know. I have company.
Send him home, whoever it is."

"I don't know, Aunt Jenna, I think you'll want to see him."

Jenna dragged herself out of bed, muttering all the way.
And stopped short at the sight of Brad Thatcher standing un-

easily in Allison's living room. He took a look at her face and closed his eyes.

"I'm sorry, Dr. Marshall."

"It's not as bad as it looks," she lied and sat on the sofa. "Sit, Brad. What's on your mind?"

He sat, blinking at her brusque tone. He licked his lips, opened his mouth. Closed it.

Jenna sighed. "Brad, do you have something to say or not?"

"It's about my dad," Brad said and stared down at his feet. "He was wrong last night, but you need to understand why."

Jenna frowned. "How do you know what happened last night?"

"Everybody knows, Dr. Marshall." He ventured a tiny grin. "None of the guys want to come near you anymore. They're all afraid they'll be singin' soprano."

Jenna huffed a single chuckle. "So what brings you way out here, Brad?"

Brad reached into his pocket and pulled out a ratty folded sheet, curled at the edges. "This."

She opened it and went still as the written words on the page jumped out at her. . . . *tired of chicken nuggets, soccer games, and diaper changes. The boys are yours and you're welcome to them* . . . She carefully put the note on the lamp table, her hands trembling. "You knew?"

Brad's brown eyes widened. "*You* knew?"

"Your father told me today. How did you know?"

Brad looked away. "I found the note."

Jenna's heart clenched at the thought of a boy reading those terrible, hateful words from his own mother. "When?" But she knew before he answered.

"Last month."

"Oh, Brad." She'd wanted to know how a boy could change overnight. Now she knew.

"So, if you knew about my mother, why didn't you come home?"

Jenna sighed again. "Oh, Brad. It's not that simple."

He glanced at her sharply before standing up to stare out the window, his hands in his pockets. And even though physically Brad resembled his mother, in that moment he looked so much like Steven that she wanted to start crying all over again. "Do you love him, Dr. Marshall?"

She wouldn't, couldn't lie. "Yes."

"Then it's simple."

"No, Brad, it's not. He doesn't trust me."

Brad made a frustrated noise. "Do you know how many people know about that note? Four. And I'm not even supposed to know. Father Mike knows because Dad told him early on. Then for four years he told no one. Until you." He turned from the window with a frown. "He trusted you with something he didn't even trust with his own family. That's how much he trusts you."

Brad's words echoed in her mind. *That's how much he trusts you.* But she shook her head, remembering last night. The pain of the boys' fists had been nothing compared to the knowledge that Steven had abandoned her. Because of something she hadn't even done. "It's not enough."

Brad's eyes flashed. "Last night he told Helen he wanted to marry you. She told him you'd come back. She's already planning her trip to the Serengeti." He stared at her with such authority, she wanted to back away. From a seventeen-year-old. "And what about Nicky?" he demanded.

She closed her eyes. And said nothing. What could she say?

"He already thinks of you as his mother," Brad said harshly. "Last night he was awake. Crying. Worrying about you."

Jenna felt the tears come, and damned each one. Her eyes

felt like they'd been pounded with a meat tenderizer. "Your father was right. It was wrong for me to let Nicky get too attached to me so fast. He was afraid if it didn't work out . . ." She let the thought trail away.

"So that's it?" Brad demanded. "You walk away without a word? At least *she* had the balls to leave a *note*." He pointed to the ragged page on the table. "I thought more of you, Dr. Marshall."

Jenna looked away. Brad was right. She was wrong about Nicky. But she was right about Steven, not to trust him. But how wrong she'd been to love him.

She drew an unsteady breath and handed him the note. "Then I guess we were both wrong."

Friday, October 14, 4:30 P.M.

Neil's cell phone started ringing as he rounded the corner, headed for Steven's office. Nancy pointed him to the conference room. "Davies," he said into the phone and skidded to a stop in the conference room where Thatcher held a phone in his hand. Thatcher rolled his eyes and hung up.

"It was me," he said. "Good timing."

Neil shook his head. "Uh-uh. Great timing. Look what I found."

Thatcher looked at the bag in his hand and raised a sarcastic brow. "Aluminum foil?"

His mood was too good to let Thatcher spoil it. "No, better." He slid on a pair of gloves and pulled the foil from the bag. "Buttons."

Thatcher looked positively grim. "Buttons."

"Yes. One in particular." He pulled out the pewter button and held it up. "Recognize it?"

Thatcher's eyes flashed. "The tattoo. Where did you find that?"

"The Templetons' cat had a stash of buttons under a chair in a spare room. The pattern on this button is the emblem of a prep school outside Seattle."

Thatcher pulled on his own gloves and held out his hand. An intensity buzzed around the man. Carefully Neil dropped the button into Thatcher's palm.

"I take it William Parker attended this prep school," Thatcher said evenly, staring at the button as if inspecting a diamond.

"He did."

"And did his brother go there too?" Thatcher asked. Dangerously, Neil thought.

"Yes, he did, but—"

"Don't tell me he was slow," Thatcher snapped. "It's the brother, Neil," he said, his voice biting. "Under our noses the whole fucking time."

Neil felt his pulse stutter. "No. He was never even a suspect."

"He is now," Thatcher said acidly, and pointed to the table, where two DNA prints lay edge to edge. One from Seattle, one from the Clary clearing. And next to them Kent Thompson's neatly typed conclusion. Not the same. Blood relatives.

Not the same. Not Parker. Not *William* Parker. Blood relatives. *Josh* Parker.

Neil looked down and his heart . . . just . . . sank. "Oh, my God," he heard himself whisper.

"And Nancy says the rosters show Josh as *absent* the day of the Clary clearing. We were after the wrong brother the whole time," Thatcher said, barely controlled fury in his voice. "Dammit!"

Neil couldn't take his eyes off the prints. He'd been chasing the wrong man. All this time.

"Steven."

Neil didn't look up at the voice at the door. Couldn't. He was frozen.

"Lucas," Steven said. "What a coincidence."

Lucas Bondioli, the high school guidance counselor. Neil made his body move, his brain function. Bondioli stood in the doorway, his face pale, holding a blue folder in his shaking hands.

"Steven, I found something today you need to see. Casey's substitute was going through all the themes Casey's class had written on *Crime and Punishment*. This one was written by Josh Lutz." He held out the folder, which shook like a leaf on a tree in a high wind. "Casey gave him an *A*."

Thatcher reached for the folder, his face still grim. "Pretty damn good for a kid with an eighty-five IQ, huh?" He skimmed the first few pages, then tossed the theme on the table in disgust. "Under our damn noses all along," he muttered. He marched to the bulletin board where all the girls' pictures were mounted side to side, Kelly Templeton's the newest. "Interesting point of view young Josh has of the killer in the book," Thatcher added, his voice tight. "That the killer was right. That those with superhuman intelligence are above the laws that bind normal men."

A picture flashed in Neil's mind from the night before. Josh Parker, standing over Jenna, then turning. Neil closed his eyes and his stomach seemed to implode. "He was missing a button last night," he said hoarsely.

"Who?" Steven asked, not turning from the board.

"Josh. He was with Jenna. He was there before I was, chasing off those boys before I got to her. I held my weapon on him, made him turn around. And he was missing a button."

Thatcher had gone pale. "Josh was there last night? With Jenna?"

Neil made himself nod. "He slipped away before the police came. Jenna said to let him go, that he'd helped her and she didn't want him scared by the police."

"Why was he there?" Thatcher asked, his voice now raspy, choking.

"He said he didn't want them to hurt her."

"But why was he *there*? At that particular moment?" Thatcher demanded, his voice shaking. Then he stilled. "Oh, dear God," he murmured. "Neil, look at these girls."

Neil moved on legs shakier than Thatcher's voice. Then he looked at their happy smiling faces. At their long dark hair. And with the exception of Alev Rahrooh, their big dark blue eyes.

"No," Neil whispered as their likeness sank in. He'd dreamed of Jenna and thought he'd escaped the dreams that haunted him. But he'd still been dreaming about the dead girls. He hadn't found peace. Dammit. He'd overlooked the vital link right in front of his eyes, awake and asleep. "*No.*"

Steven barely heard Neil's denial. His own heart was pounding so hard it filled his brain.

"They all look like Jenna," Steven whispered, remembering thinking that little Serena Eggleston could have been Jenna's daughter. Panic filled his throat. "Where's Kent?"

He didn't wait for an answer, just started running for Kent's office in the lab, barely conscious of Davies and Bondioli behind him. He found Kent hunched over his microscope, taking neat notes.

"Kent, where's the DNA print from the samples from Jenna's apartment?"

Kent looked up and blinked behind his thick lenses. "It isn't finished yet." He slid off his stool uncertainly. "I can call and see when it'll be back."

"Do that," Steven gritted, then grabbed one phone as Kent grabbed another. Kent called the lab and Steven called Liz to find out where the hell was his warrant. His next call would be to Jenna at the Llewellyn house to tell her not to move. Not to leave that house under any circumstances.

Friday, October 14, 5:00 P.M.

"Get in the car, Jen, we're going for a ride," Seth said.

Jenna turned from the window where she'd stood since Brad had driven away. She'd been thinking about Steven and Brad and Nicky. And Helen and the Serengeti, whatever the hell that had to do with anything. And Steven. And Nicky. And Steven. "Dad, please."

Seth shook his head. "Don't 'Dad, please' me. I said get in the car, we're going for a ride." He put her jacket around her shoulders and gave her a gentle shove out the door. "Go."

THIRTY-THREE

Friday, October 14, 5:30 P.M.

"HERE IT IS," KENT SAID, BREATHING HARD. "We got lucky. They'd just finished it." He pulled the newest DNA print from the envelope and held it side by side with the print from the Clary clearing. He swallowed and looked up and before he said a word Steven knew the truth.

"They're a match, aren't they, Kent?"

Kent nodded. "Whoever was in the Clary clearing was in Jenna's apartment that night."

Steven thought of the girls, all pretty, long-haired brunettes with eyes almost the shade of Jenna's. "She was his target all along," he whispered.

"Did she call back yet?" Davies asked.

Steven shook his head, worry and panic eating him up inside. "Allison says she and Seth left a half hour ago. Seth didn't say where they were going."

"Please tell me the man has a cell phone," Davies said grimly.

Steven felt a hysterical laugh bubbling up from his gut. "Oh, yes, he does, but he's got it turned off. Allison said he and Jenna were going to have a talk and he didn't want any interruptions."

Davies clenched his jaw. "If she's with Seth, she's all right. Try not to worry."

Steven's own cell phone jingled. "Thatcher... Thanks, Liz." He disconnected and looked at his team, now gathered around him. "We have a warrant. Let's go pay the Parkers a visit."

Friday, October 14, 5:45 P.M.

Seth stopped the car next to the grave Jenna hadn't seen in two years. "Get out, Jenna."

She glared at Seth from the corner of her eye, her temper simmering. "I will not. I will not sit on that little iron bench and talk to someone who's dead. Dead, Dad. D-e-a-d, dead."

Seth got out of the car and opened her door, then bent forward until they were nose to nose, and said firmly, "Then sit on the little iron bench and talk to me." He pulled her out of the car and onto the bench, looking at the marble gravestone.

"It's pretty," she said softly. *Adam Nathaniel Llewellyn,*

Beloved. Followed by the date of his death, which until recently she'd considered the worst day of her life. There were things almost as bad as dying, she was coming to realize. Hurting a little boy so that he stayed up all night crying was almost as bad. Leaving your husband and children with a surly note was worse. Not trusting the woman you claimed to love and leaving her to be beaten . . . On that one she wasn't sure.

Seth sighed. "So what are you going to do, girl?" He was on his knees next to Adam's grave, straightening the flowers someone had planted there. Most likely Seth or Allison.

"About what?"

He fussed with a hearty orange chrysanthemum. "Well, about your living quarters for starters."

Jenna lifted a brow, found it hurt to do so, and let it drop back down. "Are you evicting me?"

He glanced up at her, a twinkle in his eye. "Well, there is Wednesdays. I don't think I want to be at the table when you sit down to Allie's meat loaf again."

Jenna laughed, then surprised at the sound, let it trail away. "I love you, Dad."

"Of course you do. I also heard you tell that young man you love his father."

"You were listening!"

"Of course I was. You never tell me anything. I have to get creative if I want to know what's happening in your life. Evelyn's doing much better by the way," he added, jerking the thunder from her ire. "The doctor says she can come home tomorrow."

"Well . . . good," she mumbled. "Glad to hear it."

"Thought you would be." He sat back on his heels and surveyed his work. "Not bad."

Jenna looked at him, her heart softening. "It's the most beautiful grave in the cemetery, Dad."

He smiled. "Thank you. But this place still creeps you out, doesn't it?"

She choked on a chuckle. "Creeps me out? You been listening to Charlie's conversations, too?"

"Gotta know what's going on with my girls. So what will you do about Steven, Jenna? He hurt you and for that I want to make his face look worse than yours, but he didn't mean to, I could see it in his eyes. Will you throw away happiness for the pleasure of holding on to a grudge?"

She narrowed her eyes at him. "It's no pleasure, Dad."

He shook his head at that. "Sure it is. Not the same kind of pleasure as a gallon of Rocky Road or a night of really good sex—"

"Dad!"

"But it's a pleasure all the same," he went on as if she hadn't interrupted. "It's control, or the appearance of it, anyway. You, my dear, are a control freak."

She opened her mouth to utter a denial, then closed it. It was a fair cop. "So?"

"So you can't control everything. You, Jenna, really, really try, but you can't. You try to control your grief over my son here." He patted the headstone. "You've never really let him go."

"*What?* I'm not the one who visits his grave every weekend or serves his favorite dinner on his death day. *I've* let him go. *You're* the ones holding on. And *that's* what creeps me out."

"I have to admit, I don't like the memorial dinners either," Seth said, propping his chin atop the headstone. "My wife started them and Allie just kept it up. But those aren't because we can't let him go, Jen. We're just remembering him. You're the one still wearing his ring on your finger."

"I am not," she said, holding out her bare left hand, then realized she'd fisted her right. Her right hand where she still wore Adam's ring on her thumb. She held out her right hand and shifted it side to side, watching the waning light play on the Celtic curves. "I guess I am."

Seth lifted a white brow, then held out his hand, palm up. "So take it off." When she didn't move he dropped his hand. "I can imagine loving a woman with another man's ring on her finger would be pretty hard. Might even make him wonder down deep if she really cared about him or if she was still holding a torch for her lost love. Which are you, Jenna?"

"I . . ." She shook her head. "I don't know."

"Fair enough."

"But, Dad, it's not the same thing. Adam never would have thought the worst of me."

"Sure he would, and he did," Seth said firmly and stood up, brushing grass from his knees. "Why do you think he took up karate? He hated karate. I'll tell you why. He was jealous of Mark."

"Mark?" Jenna asked incredulously. "That's ridiculous. Mark was Adam's best friend. Mark and I were *only* friends."

"He knew that. He also knew you'd be true to him, but he wanted to be there, just be certain."

"That's just ridiculous," she repeated, then thought back. It made sense. It really did. Adam did hate karate, but he went, every single week. "Maybe it isn't so ridiculous," she amended.

"My son wasn't perfect, Jenna, but he loved you more than his own life. When he passed it was like losing the best part of me. But he left you behind and I love you like you were my own daughter. If you could make meat loaf worth a damn I might even love you more."

Jenna snickered, as he'd wanted her to.

"I never wanted you to come to Adam's grave and pine for him. I wanted you to go on and find someone who could make you even one-tenth as happy as my son would have."

He cleared his throat gruffly. "So say good-bye to my son and get on with the job of living. If it's with Steven, then put your grudge aside, because your excuse is a terrible one. If it's not him, then make it somebody else real soon. Dammit, girl, I want more grandchildren and I'm not getting any younger."

Jenna stood up and put her arms around him. "I love you, Dad."

"I know you do," he barked, then quieted. "Do you love Steven, Jenna?"

Jenna considered very hard, but the answer was amazingly simple. "Yes, yes I do."

"Then go to him and tell him so."

"I will, but I need to say something here, first. Would you give me a minute?"

He smiled. "I'll check the graves over there. Their families don't come often as they should."

And as Jenna watched him hike over the hill, she knew Seth Llewellyn did what he did out of respect and love, not out of a morbid eccentricity. She stared at Adam's headstone. "But Allison is eccentric, Adam. The memorial dinners creep me out and her meat loaf is like slimy cardboard. But they love you and they miss you." She tugged a stray weed Seth had missed. "And they've gone on, mostly. So now, I guess I will, too." She pulled off his ring and set it on top of the head-stone. "Seth can keep this or maybe give this to Charlie when she's older. I'll always love you and you were never store-brand vanilla. Maybe Heavenly Hash." She chuckled at the whimsical thought. "And Steven is rightly classified as Rocky Road." She ran her hand across the letters of his name lovingly. "We'll smooth out the rocks. Don't worry about me. I'm fine. I'm really fine."

"I don't think I'd go that far."

Jenna whirled around and held on to the headstone when

the world kept spinning. She blinked hard and brought a face into focus. And narrowed her eyes in confusion.

"Josh, what are you doing here?"

Friday, October 14, 6:15 P.M.

"You can't come in here!" Mrs. Lutz stood at her front door, clutching her collar to her throat.

"We can, ma'am, and we will. We have a warrant." Steven pulled it from his pocket and handed it to her. He pushed past her, looking around, knowing he had uniforms covering every exit of the house in case any of the Lutzes decided to bolt. "Where is Josh?"

She clutched her collar tighter around her throat. "He's not here."

"And Rudy?"

"He's not here either. I'm going to call my husband."

"You do that, ma'am," said Sandra, right behind Steven. "Any limits to the warrant, Steven?"

"None," Steven said with satisfaction. Liz had done an exemplary job.

"Good old Liz," Sandra said affectionately. "I'll take Rudy's room."

"And I'll take Josh's," Steven said, then turned when Mrs. Lutz screeched bloody murder. He was just in time to see the woman leap against Davies and pound her fists on his chest. Two uniforms pulled her away, wringing her hands. *Probably hurt her fists on Davies's Kevlar vest,* Steven thought, again with satisfaction.

"You!" Mrs. Lutz screamed. "You ruined our lives by setting my son up in Seattle!" She leapt again and the uniforms pulled her back as Davies just stood there, impassively.

"I never set up your son," Davies said calmly. "I simply targeted the wrong one."

She went white at that and tugged at the restraining hands of the officers. "You're lying. My Joshua would never do anything wrong. It's all that bitch teacher's fault. She's to blame."

"For what, Mrs. Parker?" Davies asked.

She spluttered, then seemed to calm before their eyes. "For failing my Rudy. Neither of my boys touched her. She's a conniving liar if she says they did."

"We're not investigating the school vandalism," Steven said mildly, his hand on the banister. "We're investigating serial murder." He had the unmitigated joy of watching Mrs. Lutz swoon.

Steven trotted up the stairs, Davies close behind him.

"Do you always make such devoted friends?" Steven asked.

Davies shrugged. "What can I say? I'm unforgettable."

They found Josh's room impeccably neat and clean. Davies walked right over to the nightstand and pulled a thick volume from the drawer.

"Please tell me that's not a Gideon *Bible*," Steven said dryly and Davies smiled.

"No, it's *I, Claudius*. You ever read it?"

Steven riffled through a drawer of socks. "Does it have comics like *Captain Underpants*?"

"No," said Davies. "Claudius was about twentieth in line for emperor of Rome. Everybody around him was being killed, so he played dumb so he wouldn't be perceived as a threat." He opened the book and flipped through the pages, then set it aside. "He outlived them all and became emperor. Ruler of the world."

Steven pulled a sketch pad from beneath neatly folded shirts and held it up so Davies could see the pages of sketches of the prep school emblem Josh had tattooed on his victims' heads. "Look."

"He was practicing," Davies commented, then pulled open the closet door and stopped. "Oh, my God. Thatcher."

Steven pushed the drawer shut and came to look.

And found the shrine to Jenna.

Friday, October 14, 6:15 P.M.

Josh took a step closer and Jenna noticed the blood on his hands. "Josh, what's wrong? Are you hurt? Did your father or Rudy hurt you?"

And then he smiled. "No." He lifted a brow and she knew something was different today. "Miss Marshall," he added.

It was his eyes. Not blank. Not downcast. No sign of mortification. Sharper, somehow.

It took her a minute. A full minute. Then she gasped. "*You*. It was you in my apartment."

"It was I," he said silkily and pulled something white from his pocket. "I'd thought to do this relatively painlessly, but you have really left me with no choice."

Jenna glanced from side to side, panicked, remembering the strength of the hands that held her down that night. The sound of the knife slicing into the mattress where she'd been sleeping just moments before. Then she realized Seth was not there and her heart stopped. *Seth.* The blood on his hands was Seth's. "You monster," she hissed, thinking fast about her options. Seth had the key to the car so she couldn't get away, unless it was on foot. She needed to get help back to Seth. If he was still alive. *Please, God, let him still be alive.* Her only hope was to run.

Now.

She took off toward the main road at a sprint and didn't look back. Then flew forward as something heavy hit her in the middle of her back. She hit the ground on all fours, a split second before she was pushed flat to the ground, his knee in her back. His hand came around to grab her chin, and her head was jerked back and she could hear his heavy breathing.

"Don't make me run, Miss Marshall," he said, his voice rough and . . . uncontrolled. It was different than the night in her apartment, because that night he'd had icy control. She could only hope she could use that fact to escape. To get help. *Seth. Oh, God, Seth. Please hang on.*

Then another face flashed in front of her eyes. *Steven. I never got a chance to tell you I'm sorry,* she thought just as Josh pressed something scratchy to her face and held her nose. She struggled, holding her breath until she could no longer, until her reflexes took over and she gulped a lungful of air through her mouth.

"That's the way," he said soothingly. "Ten, nine, eight," she heard him counting. "Five, four . . ."

Then nothing.

Friday, October 14, 6:25 P.M.

Steven pulled the string on the lightbulb and his gut clenched. The closet door was covered with photos, some cut from the Roosevelt yearbook. But most were snapshots of Jenna. Close-ups, above the shoulder shots with her apartment in the background. His blood ran cold realizing Josh Lutz had been stalking Jenna, watching her through her patio door. He thought about the neat hole cut in the glass. Josh had stalked her through that glass door, then came through it to try to kill her.

"Sonofabitch," he whispered.

Silently, Davies pushed back the clothing hanging in the closet to reveal more pictures.

"Lorraine, Samantha, Alev, and Kelly," Steven murmured. Before and after. The after shots were taken at various angles. The photos of Alev showed Josh had experimented to get just the right layout of body parts before leading them to the clearing. "He's developing his own pictures, just like Jenna said. I wonder where his darkroom is."

"*I* wonder where he's keeping his souvenirs. You know he's kept something to remember his victims by," Davies said, pulling the blanket from the bed and lifting the mattress up. "*Hello,*" he said. "What have we here?"

Pills, Steven saw. Hundreds of little pills. He held one up to the light. "Mellaril," he said softly, then looked at Davies. "Pretty powerful antipsychotic. When taken consistently it can suppress cognitive function, sometimes down to the level of an eighty-five IQ. But somebody hasn't been taking his meds. And I bet you somebody's mother thought her boy was under control. But he isn't. Maybe he was, but he sure as hell isn't now."

"That might explain why he took a sabbatical," Davies mused. "If he was on the pills during the years between Seattle and here."

"And this stash would certainly explain the fact that he's started again. He stops taking his pills and acts like he's still dull-witted to keep anyone from realizing he's changed."

"À la *I, Claudius,*" Davies said.

"But he must've gotten tired of pretending at some point," Steven said. "He wanted Casey to know he identified with the killer in *Crime and Punishment.* Sandra!" he called.

Sandra appeared, wearing a generally disgusted look on her face. "I haven't seen so much porn in one bedroom since my vice days," she said. "Too bad we can't arrest Rudy for that alone."

"Take a number, Sandra. For now, bring up our mother-of-the-year. I want to see the look on her face when she sees all her precious baby's unswallowed meds."

It was worth the wait. Mrs. Lutz's face went white with shock, then flamed red with rage when she saw the piles of unconsumed medication.

"You thought you had him under control, didn't you, Mrs. Lutz?" Steven asked smoothly. "Or do you prefer to be called Parker?"

"I am Mrs. Lutz," she said rigidly. "And I don't know what you're talking about. I have no idea who those pills belong to."

Steven lifted a brow. "And if we look hard, we won't find a prescription on file?"

She pursed her lips and said nothing, which said quite enough.

Steven leaned close. "Where is your son, Mrs. Lutz? Where is Josh?"

She stiffened. "I don't know."

"Mmm. That's a shame. Then you don't know where he is to warn him we're here, waiting for him? I really hope not, because I'd hate to have that happen, to spoil the surprise. You see, I want your boy behind bars and I really hate to be disappointed."

She straightened her body imperiously. "My son has done nothing wrong."

"Do you recognize these girls?" Davies asked softly, holding back the clothing hanging in the closet. "Maybe you've seen them on the news. Three are dead. Your son has pictures of their bodies, something we haven't released. And I'll bet we'll find pictures of four Seattle girls as well."

She opened her mouth, then closed it again. "I'll call my lawyer now."

Steven threw her a look of contempt. "You just do that. He'll need the time to prepare to defend your son against a death penalty sentence. Sandra, make sure Mrs. Lutz calls *only* her lawyer. I'm going to search for Josh's darkroom. Where's Kent?"

"I'm here." Kent stuck his head in the door.

"Good. I want everyone focused on finding out where he's taking his victims. He's had Kelly Templeton for almost three days. He kept Samantha and Alev longer than that so Kelly may still be alive. I don't want him hanging any more pictures in his closet."

Friday, October 14, 7:00 P.M.

Jenna woke with a horrific headache giving her the déjà vu feeling of waking up in Allison's spare bedroom bed all over again. Except the ropes tying her wrists and ankles were brand new.

And she was lying on a hard wood floor, not in Allison's spare-room bed.

She opened her eyes and looked up. She was in a barn with a high loft. Then she remembered. The graveyard. Seth. Adam. Josh. Running, falling. The blood. Seth. *Where was Seth?*

She jerked her head to one side and recoiled in horror. She felt the burn of bile as it rose from her stomach into her throat. Nailed to the wall was . . .

Hair. Human hair. Eight . . . heads of hair. All long and dark. Carefully braided and mounted below framed pictures of smiling girls. Four she recognized, four she did not. Then

Josh Lutz came into view, his cheerful whistle an unsettling contrast to the macabre scene. In one of his hands was a hammer, in the other was another framed picture. He looked over at her and she saw he had a nail between his lips. He saw her looking at him and grinned, the nail dark against the white of his teeth. He slipped the picture under his arm and took the nail out of his mouth.

"You're finally awake."

Jenna said nothing. Didn't move as reality began to seep into her brain. As she stared up at him from where she lay tied on the floor, she remembered bitter words to Steven and Neil that morning. No way it could be Rudy, maybe his father, but not Rudy. They'd all been wrong.

Josh Lutz was a killer. Not a nice boy. Not a victim of a dysfunctional family.

Josh was a killer. He'd already tried to kill *her* once. And this time he would succeed.

Stop that. You will escape. You must. People need you. Seth, Nicky, Steven. They need you.

Josh was grinning again as he pounded the nail into the barn wall. "I see you've noticed my decorating. I think it could use a woman's touch, don't you? You could help me spruce up the place. What do you think of my newest picture?" He held up the frame and Jenna's throat closed.

It was her in the park. Laughing. She recognized the sweater as the one she'd worn to the park the day she'd spent with Nicky and Cindy Lou. He'd seen her with Nicky.

Oh, God, no. Please don't let him touch Nicky.

"Good, I can see you like this one." He held the picture at arm's length and tilted his head. "You're very photogenic, Miss Marshall."

"Don't you touch that little boy," she heard herself say, her voice coarse and harsh.

He frowned. "I don't do little boys. I'm no pervert."

"You're insane."

He lifted a brow at that as if what she'd said amused him.

Amused him. Anger simmered and with it the frustration of helplessness.

"No, not really. Everybody thinks I am, but they're wrong." He chuckled and hung her picture on a nail. "So were you. Poor little Josh needs special help." He made a scoffing noise in his throat and hunkered down beside her, fingering the fabric of her shirt, just to one side of her breast. She pulled back, but he just grinned again. "I could *teach* your class, Miss Marshall. I don't need your special help." He bent his mouth in a thoughtful frown. "But I did get some decorating ideas from you. I really like the way you covered that one wall in your apartment with all those pictures."

"You were in my apartment."

He looked bored. "Of course I was. How else could I have held a knife to your throat?"

"You stabbed my dog."

His face changed, rage twisting his features. "I should have *killed* your damn dog. Or should I say *dogs*. Little miss goody-two-shoes, defying the rules, hiding two dogs in her apartment."

She narrowed her eyes. "You didn't know I had two. That's why you only put out enough poison for one."

"I put out enough poison for two," he hissed, "wishing to kill one with a great deal of pain."

"But Jean-Luc didn't get as much as Jim. He got you. Where did he bite you?" she taunted, not knowing if it would get her killed faster, but not wanting him to think he'd won. If she lay here silent, he would kill her anyway.

His eyes flashed. "Shut up." She cried out when his hand came crashing across her cheek, pain spearing her head where it banged against the wood floor. "I like you better asleep."

No. Not again. She didn't want to lose consciousness

again. *I might not wake up.* "So you'll make me inhale more of your ketamine?" she baited him, hoping to distract him. Anything.

He looked surprised, then philosophical. "Your boyfriend told you, huh?"

"I found the missing chemicals."

He stood up and walked toward the wall behind her, where she couldn't see him. "I know. I found your inventory last night. Stuffed it in my pocket. Didn't want anyone else to know."

"It's too late for that," she called, still not able to see him. "I told the police."

She heard his bored chuckle. "You told your boyfriend. That man is too stupid to tie his own shoes, much less find me. I had to draw him a damn map to find the girls. Right, Kelly?"

Jenna's body tightened. "Kelly?"

"Oh, yes," he said mildly, still behind her. "She's here, but I don't think she can talk right now."

"You killed her." Jenna felt a hysterical sob building, but shoved it back.

"I will, but I haven't. I'm not done with her yet. Besides, I think I'll have a little fun with you first, then let you watch me kill Kelly so you can see firsthand what will happen to you." He appeared over her, tall and grinning, a syringe in one hand. "Kind of like . . . foreshadowing. Yes, that's what Miss Ryan called it." He knelt beside her and laid the syringe to one side.

"Did you hurt Casey? Were you the one who cut my brakes?" she asked, trying to roll, to scoot, to get away, but he just held her down with one hand. Effortlessly.

"Don't be ridiculous. That's not my style at all. If I'd wanted to hurt you, you would have been hurt. My brother's friends cut your brakes, ineptly as usual."

"What's in the needle?" she asked, trying to make her

voice cocky, but failing miserably. She heard her own fear and so did he.

With a confident grin he grabbed her arm and with a pair of scissors cut her sleeve at the shoulder, then ripped it from her shirt. "You already guessed it, Miss Marshall. It's Special K."

"Why? Why the drugs, Josh?"

He tied a rubber band around her arm and tested her vein with his thumb. "You know, I've given that considerable thought myself. I think I just got so damn tired of doctors pumping me full of shit that I decided to have a little payback."

Jenna struggled, wildly now, and he frowned in irritation. "Hold still. I don't want to hurt you. Not yet anyway."

"No."

He grunted and held her down with his knee. "*Yes*. I'm in charge, dammit, and I say *yes*." He grabbed the syringe and slid it into her vein. "Now, Miss Marshall, settle down and I'll tell you a story. You're going to sleep soon, but when you wake up"—he lifted his brows, his dark eyes sparkling—"you'll be in . . . a forest. Yes, that's good. A forest, surrounded by wolves. I like that. It's very . . . apropos given your love for such beasts. Large, vicious wolves with fangs. Snarling, drooling fangs. And one by one, they'll creep up to you and . . . tear your flesh from your bones. And it will hurt. A lot."

Jenna stared up at him, feeling her body grow numb. "What . . . ?"

He sat down next to her, cross-legged, and carefully capped the syringe. "Ketamine has some pretty cool effects, Miss Marshall," he explained, now sounding incredibly like a teenager. "When you're going under you're suggestible and when you come out, you'll dream." He smiled. Satisfied.

"You'll dream whatever I tell you to dream. Because I'm in charge here."

Jenna struggled, but only in her mind now. Her body was frozen. "Sweet dreams, Miss Marshall," she heard him say. Then nothing.

Friday, October 14, 7:00 P.M.

The darkroom was in the small closet of an unused bedroom and what Steven found there chilled his blood. Pictures, hundreds of pictures in stacks, hanging from drying lines. He plucked one off the line and his heart plunged.

It was he and Jenna. Together. Shots above the waist, but they showed . . . He swallowed, remembering the night very well. He'd practically torn the sweater from her body in their passion and she'd wrapped herself around him, her arms around his neck, her legs around his waist, pressing her warm breasts into his chest. But he didn't have to rely on his memory. Josh Lutz had captured everything in full color.

"Steven." Sandra was behind him and she carefully took the pictures and placed them in a folder. "We'll take them as evidence, but I'll make sure no one sees them," she said softly.

Straightening, Steven rested his hands on his hips and blew out a sigh. "Thanks. I'm kind of glad he's not here right now," he said grimly. "I might kill him myself."

Sandra squeezed his arm and turned away to continue the search.

Steven picked up another stack and felt adrenaline kick even as his stomach turned over. "Sandra, look. He's taken pictures of the girls' bodies, but inside somewhere. It looks like a barn." He flipped through the photos quickly. "Here's one showing a table saw."

"The sawdust in Kelly's bedroom."

"Yeah. And circular saw patterns the ME found on Alev's arms and legs." Steven flipped through some more photos. "Here's one with a window in view. The sun's coming up."

"Or going down," Sandra said, her own voice tight with tension. "It faces a road. You can see a little bit of it through the trees here. Let me get this to the lab. Maybe they can get more detail."

"The negatives will be here somewhere," Steven said, putting aside a stack of pictures, only to have the stack slide sideways. "Dammit," he gritted, moving to straighten the stack. Then a single print jumped out at him and he froze. "Oh, God. Sandra," he whispered and heard her indrawn breath as she looked over his shoulder. "It's Nicky. With Jenna in the park."

"I'll get a cruiser over to your house right away."

Steven put the picture in Sandra's steady hands, wishing his were. "Thanks."

"Nicky's fine. He's with your aunt and we would have heard if there was any trouble."

He nodded. Tried to breathe. "You're right. I know you're right." Still he remembered how it felt to know his baby had been stolen. It couldn't happen again. He wouldn't let it.

"Go get some water, Steven," Sandra commanded. "You can't keel over on us now."

Steven forced a grin. "Yes, ma'am." Then his cell phone jangled and Sandra stopped, two steps from the door. Her face went white and he could see she was thinking the same thing he was. His hands shaking, he answered, "Thatcher."

"Steven." It was Nancy and her voice was frantic.

Steven sagged against a wall of the darkroom. "Not Nicky. Please."

"No, no, not Nicky. It's Jenna. She's gone."

THIRTY-FOUR

Friday, October 14, 7:45 P.M.

WOLVES. COMING. SHE TRIED TO RUN, but they chased her, drooling, fangs shimmering. She stumbled and fell and they were on her. *No, no.* The screams tore from her throat as sharp teeth sank into the back of her thigh. She pulled herself into a ball, but it did nothing to save her. Teeth ripped, tore. The pain, white-hot and excruciating . . . She tried to crawl away, but they descended . . .

"No!" she screamed, and woke up, huddled in a ball, drenched in sweat, her eyes clenched shut.

Clap, clap, clap. Applause.

"Not bad. Not bad at all. Sammie was better, but she was also in the drama club."

Jenna dragged in a breath. It was a dream. A dream. That was all. There was no pain, no ripped flesh. She opened her eyes. Only Josh Lutz standing over her with ropes in his hands.

He knelt and briskly tied her hands. "Next time I'll just have to think of something better. What are you afraid of, Miss Marshall? Samantha was afraid of snakes. Slithering silently. Coming closer. With fangs. *Sssss.*" His hands dropped to her legs. "So what are you afraid of?"

"Not you," Jenna spat, trying to wrench away, and Josh just chuckled and grabbed her ankles.

"Feisty. I'd hoped you would be." He pulled another rope from his back pocket and Jenna made her mind function. Made herself remember all the self-defense she'd learned, how to hold her feet to create the most give in the knot Josh was about to tie. Prayed she could pull it off.

He tied her ankles and she pretended to struggle, but in the end her ankles were placed exactly as she'd planned. She realized she could now see more of the barn. She could see the far wall, the table that held the plastic case he'd brought to her apartment that night. Her heart contracted. She could see the table that held Kelly's nude body. She strained to see if Kelly still breathed.

"She's still alive," Josh said. "But not for much longer."

Kelly was alive. *So am I.* But Kelly was nude and Jenna was still clothed. Why? Why had he not taken her clothes? Kelly was bald, her head shaved clean, her hair mounted on the wall. *But he hasn't done that to me yet. Why?*

Jenna kept her questions to herself in the unlikely event asking would trigger Josh to action. It was far more likely he had his own reasons for not proceeding. *Miss Marshall,* she thought. In school, he called her *Dr. Marshall,* but here, where he was in charge, it was *Miss.* A deliberate attempt to undermine her authority, learned from his dear old dad. But he didn't use her first name, so she still wasn't at the level of the other girls in his mind. She hoped to use it against him. She needed to search the walls she could see, looking for a way to escape. Because she had to. *She would.*

Friday, October 14, 9:00 P.M.

"What the hell is this all about?" Victor Lutz barreled into Interview One, where a tight-lipped Nora Lutz and her lawyer sat at the table with Liz. Lutz recognized Davies who sat in the corner, arms crossed, face hard, and Lutz's expression blanched as he and Davies played the staring game.

Karen Rose

Finally Lutz turned and Steven was gratified to see a flicker of fear in the man's eyes. "We settled this," Lutz said, considerably shaken. "My son had nothing to do with the vandalism."

Steven wanted to strangle the man here and now. Instead, he calmed his knocking heart and smoothed his voice. "We're not talking about vandalism. We're talking about murder."

"The English teacher is fine," Lutz insisted. "She was released from the hospital this morning."

Steven raised a brow. "Worried about Miss Ryan, were you? I suppose you had cause to be considering it was your prompting that incited your son's friends to cut Dr. Marshall's brakes." Steven held up his hand when Lutz would have denied it. "Save it for your indictment, Mr. Lutz. Detective Pullman has two young men who've sworn out affidavits implicating you. I'm not talking about attempted murder. I'm talking about serial murder. Four young girls four years ago in Seattle. Four young girls in the last month here in Raleigh. Ring a bell?"

Lutz's gaze flicked to Davies sitting in the corner, then back at Steven. "He is insane, so determined to ruin my family that he comes all this way to spread his lies. Rudy was exonerated."

Steven pursed his lips. "I'm not talking about Rudy. I'm talking about Josh."

Lutz's face blanked. Then he laughed. "Josh? You're crazier than he is. Josh is a half-wit."

"Shut up, Victor," Nora snapped and jerked her arm away when her lawyer tried to silence her. "For years you've told my son he's stupid and unworthy. And for years you've been wrong."

Lutz frowned at her outburst. "Nora, you know as well as I do that Josh is retarded."

"I don't think so, Mr. Lutz, and I'm not prepared to give

you all the wherefores and therefores right now," Steven said, abandoning his patient routine. "Your son's kidnapped four girls, killed three of them, and three hours ago Dr. Marshall was abducted." He drew on the scattered remnants of his calm, doing his best not to think about Jenna at the hands of Lutz's sick bastard son. Tried not to think about the frantic cell phone call Allison made when she discovered her unconscious father at the cemetery. Steven slipped his hand in his pocket and fingered the silver Celtic ring Jenna left behind on Adam's headstone. Allison had insisted he take it, as if knowing she'd said good-bye to Adam would make him search for her harder.

He clenched his fist, feeling the edges of Adam Llewellyn's ring cut into his palm. Like he could be looking any harder. He'd turned the Parker house upside down, but found nothing.

There was absolutely no clue to where Josh had taken his victims and if Nora Lutz knew, she wasn't saying. She just sat next to her lawyer, unconcerned about Jenna, Kelly . . . Any of the senseless tragedy her son had caused . . . It made him want to scream, to throw something. To put his hands around her neck and shake her until she at least showed some remorse. Some regret. Something beyond the arrogant, self-absorbed concern over her precious, demented spawn of Satan.

Lutz was staring at his wife as if she were a complete stranger. "Josh is just not capable."

Steven gritted his teeth. "I'm not interested in your denials. *I just want to know where he is.*"

Lutz turned his disbelieving eyes from his wife to Steven, then shook his head. "I don't know."

"Where would he go? Where would he hide? Where could he take, kill, and dismember four young teenaged girls?" Steven smacked the table and Mrs. Lutz flinched, then straightened, making Steven think of a very dowdy queen.

"My Joshua is innocent," she said coldly. "And this conversation is over."

"Are my clients being held?" the Lutzes' lawyer asked mildly. "Or are they free to go?"

Steven looked at Liz who shook her head. "We can't hold them, Agent Thatcher."

"Then they're free to go," Steven said bitterly and watched them leave. Free as birds while their son held Jenna. He closed his mind, not allowing himself to think about what could be happening to her at that moment. To Kelly, should she still be alive. Not allowing himself to remember the horror of Alev's mutilated body. Or Samantha's. Or Lorraine's. He knew Neil had tacked four more names onto the list of victims he wasn't allowing himself to remember.

But of course they remembered. Josh had made sure they knew exactly what he could do. Because Josh knew that made the terror that much worse.

He waited until the Lutzes were gone before finding Sandra. "Follow them," he said through his teeth. "I want to know how many squares of toilet paper they use to wipe their asses until we find Jenna and Kelly." He looked around, irritably. "Where's Harry? I haven't seen him all day."

Nancy slid her arm around his waist. "He called a few hours ago. He's got a lead on the Richards man, the dead farmer who supposedly bought the ketamine. Harry said he'd call again when he had something. Steven, I want you to go home. Brad's called for you twice. Your kids need you at home." She hugged him to her. "Have courage, Steven. It will be all right. I know it."

Steven dragged his palms down his face, feeling numb. *Have courage, Steven.* "She said that to me, the first day we met. Jenna did."

Nancy hugged him again and shoved him toward the door. "Then listen to her, Steven."

Friday, October 14, 10:00 P.M.

Helen met him with open arms. Nicky stood in the foyer, stoic and wise. Mike stood behind him, hands on Nicky's shoulders, Nicky's red hair bright against the black of Mike's robes. Matt's eyes were red-rimmed and swollen. Brad stood beside him, his arm around Matt's shoulders.

No one said a word until Nicky spoke up, his little boy voice strong. "She'll come home, Daddy," he said. "You'll bring her home just like you brought me home."

Matt stifled a sob that he tried to hide.

Steven's throat closed. He dropped his chin to his chest, clenched his eyes shut, and battled to keep it all inside just a little longer. Just until he got alone, away from the boys, where they couldn't see him cry. He'd nearly shoved it all back down when two little arms wrapped around his waist and hugged tight. He opened his eyes to see Nicky's red head burrowed into his stomach. His chest heaved as his breath came shuddering out. He brushed his hands over Nicky's hair, then hoisted his little boy into his arms and hugged him with a ferocity that made Nicky protest.

"Daddy."

Steven loosened his hold, burying his face in Nicky's shoulder. "Sorry, buddy."

Nicky patted his back. "It's okay."

Mike stepped forward and took Nicky from his arms. "I think your dad needs some space, boys," he said, shepherding everyone into the kitchen. "Let's fix him some dinner."

Only Brad remained, looking at him with serious eyes. Steven cleared his throat, refusing to be embarrassed. "Nancy said you've been trying to reach me all day. I'm sorry I didn't call you back."

Brad shook his head. "It's okay, Dad. I didn't know what

was happening. I never would have bothered you if I'd known."

Steven made his mouth curve. "Well, now I'm home. So tell me what's on your mind."

Brad didn't smile back. "Can we go in your office? There's something I need to say."

So they went, Steven's stomach heavy as lead. *What next? What now?*

Brad shut the door and leaned back against it. "I'm only going to tell you now because I know Dr. Marshall would want me to. I went to see her today."

Steven's eyes widened. "Why?"

"To try to get her to come back to you. To show her this." He reached into his pocket and pulled out a folded sheet of paper Steven instantly recognized. His eyes shot up to Brad's.

"When did you find it?" he asked quietly.

Brad shrugged. "Labor Day. I was looking in the top drawer of your bureau for a picture of all of us together because I wanted to have it made into a calendar for Grandma. Then I found this."

Steven took the ragged paper and stared at it for a moment. "You blamed me."

"For lying to me," Brad said. "And for making her leave," he added, looking away.

"You thought she'd left because I cheated?"

Brad shrugged. "I didn't know. I guess it was easier to blame you because you were here. And you hadn't told the truth from the beginning."

"You want the truth now?" Steven said and Brad met his eyes and nodded. "I was never unfaithful to your mother. In the thirteen years we were married I never touched another woman."

Brad looked up. "I believe you."

Steven exhaled, relieved. "Your mother wasn't happy,

Brad. So she decided to leave. I had no idea it was coming to that."

"What would you have done if you'd known?"

"I honestly don't know, Brad. I don't even know if there's anything I could have done. But I don't regret not telling you the truth. I would have done anything to spare you this pain."

"So you took it all on yourself."

"I did."

"Did you think we might have been able to help, Dad?" Brad asked, his voice wavering. "Did you think maybe we could have supported you through it?"

"No," Steven answered truthfully. "I didn't. I didn't want to hurt you."

"It hurt more knowing you didn't trust me." He looked away. "I'm sorry. I didn't mean to . . ."

"It's okay, son. I know I should have trusted Jenna, too, but I didn't and now she's gone."

"She'll be back, Dad. I know it." Brad hesitated, then put his hand on Steven's shoulder. "And when you get her back, she'll come back to you."

Steven swallowed, slipped his hand in his pocket, and fingered Adam Llewellyn's ring, hoping against hope his son was right on both counts. "You seem sure."

Brad's expression became intense. "She cares about you. Anybody that has eyes can see it. You hurt me, too, by not trusting me about Mom, but here I am. I came back. Because . . . because I love you, Dad. She'll be back, just like I came back."

Steven struggled, then gave up and let the emotion come, choking on a sob when Brad's arms circled him, holding him, patting his back as the tears came. "I'm so afraid," Steven whispered. "I'm so afraid he'll hurt her. That he'll kill her like all the others."

Brad held on. "You'll get her back, Dad. We have to believe that."

Steven sucked in a deep breath and straightened, pulling his palms over his face to dry his eyes. "We have to have courage."

Friday, October 14, 11:30 P.M.

He'd cut her hair.

She was still weak from the last round of dreams, populated by hundreds of hissing, striking snakes. She woke, screaming and gasping, but still tied up. It wasn't until she'd caught her breath and come back down to earth that she realized her hair was gone.

Her hair was gone. All but a quarter inch he'd left all around. As her vision focused, he'd shown her the razor he'd use to finish the job, to make her smoothly bald. But now he was . . . playing with her hair.

Jenna watched as Josh laid her hair out on his worktable and braided it. Almost lovingly.

"Why, Josh?" she asked from the floor, trying to sound as teacherlike, as authoritarian as she was able. "Why do you take our hair?"

Josh looked over and shrugged. "It's a little embarrassing, actually. Kind of a Freudian thing."

Jenna had to fight not to show the revulsion she felt. "You like your mother's hair?"

"Oh, yes. My mother has absolutely beautiful hair. I've heard my father tell her that it's her best feature. She used to brush it every night. One hundred strokes." He ran his hand over the braid he'd created from Jenna's hair. "I used to love to watch her braid her hair. That's what I first liked about you, in fact. Your hair. I wished I could braid it, sitting there in your class. I'd planned to brush it and braid it when I finally got you."

"When you finally got me," Jenna repeated. "But now you've got me and you cut my hair."

He frowned at her. "That's your doing, not mine. I'd planned to take you away after graduation, to make you happy. You'd earned it. You weren't like the others. But then you spent the night with Thatcher," he said bitterly, "and I knew you were no better than any of these others, willing to crawl into a car with a man they barely know. So you lose your hair, Miss Marshall. Just like you'll lose your life." He took Jenna's braid and mounted it under her picture. "There. But I get ahead of myself. I'm not supposed to mount the hair until I've finished and I'm behind schedule." He turned with a grin. "It's Friday night, Miss Marshall. Time for a show."

Thirty-five

Saturday, October 15, 1:00 A.M.

STEVEN ANSWERED THE PHONE ON THE first ring. "Thatcher."

"It's Harry."

"Where are you?"

"In Pembroke, Virginia. The widow of George Richards is here, visiting her sister. It took me all day to track her down, but when I did I had her go through yearbooks from every high school in the county. I didn't want anyone saying we directed Mrs. Richards unfairly."

"And? Dammit, Harry, *tell me*."

"She identified Josh Lutz as the boy who used to help her husband chop wood and do errands a few years back. It was some program for troubled kids. You know, back to nature, fresh air. Mrs. Richards said Josh seemed harmless as a lamb, except when it was slaughter-time. Then he seemed to enjoy his job a little too much. Her husband let him go. Josh's mother even came to ask Richards to give him another chance, but the old man was firm."

"So that's how he got the ketamine. Well, that explains a lot."

"There's more. Mrs. Richards said her husband had a woodworking shop in a barn on the farm."

Steven's knees went weak and he sat down. Sawdust. *Jenna*. "Where? Exactly where, Harry?" He listened, memorized the location. Then ran from the house, dialing for backup.

Saturday, October 15, 1:30 A.M.

Jenna swallowed back terror as Josh placed an assortment of very large carving tools on the table where he'd tied Kelly. From across the barn Jenna could see Kelly struggle, although the girl's movements were pathetically weak.

He was going to kill her now, kill Kelly. *I need to get him away from Kelly.*

Stall, she thought, *do anything*. Sooner or later the police would come looking for her. Steven would find her. Jenna wanted to cry, just thinking Steven's name, but she knew she needed to keep her voice firm. She pulled on her teacher's cloak of authority. "So help me understand, Josh. You had nothing to do with the vandalism in my class, or the dead possum."

Josh rolled his eyes. "Really, Miss Marshall. That possum was a roadkill one of my brother's friends found on the road. They're bullies, not sadists." He held up a curved knife so that she could see it. "Nice, isn't it? It's always rewarding to work with quality tools. Old Mr. Richards always had great taste in tools. Now I, on the other hand, am a sadist. If I'd wanted to leave you a gift, it wouldn't have been a roadkill." He smiled mockingly. "Roadkill's so off-the-shelf. I do made-to-order. Rudy's friends have no style. They haven't a shred of creativity."

"But you do," she said archly.

"I do," he answered. "Watch and learn, Miss Marshall." He pulled out a laminated page covered with a design she'd never seen before. "My old school. Fond memories." He looked over and winked. "Figured out I needed to laminate it after the first time. It was all covered in blood." He pulled out a smaller syringe and a bottle of something dark blue. "Art class, creativity at its most enjoyable. Today, Miss Marshall, I'll teach you the art of tattooing. Got this idea from Lorraine. She had a peace symbol tattooed to her ass. Such poor quality workmanship."

"And you can do better."

He shook the bottle and chose a needle. "Oh, yes. I find there's very, very little I cannot do."

The sight of the needle made her stomach roil and Jenna desperately scrambled for another distraction. "Why cheerleaders, Josh?"

Josh smiled easily as he measured and mixed the dark blue fluid. "Oh, I guess I could have picked anybody, but picking from cheerleaders helped narrow the pool to the prettiest of the girls from the get-go. No sense in picking an ugly girl when the pretty ones are so eager to please."

Jenna wiggled her feet in the ropes. "But how did you get them to go with *you*?" she asked, then too late realized she shouldn't have. The blatant disbelief in her voice was a slap at his ego.

His cheeks went brick red and his fingers tightened on the bottle. "Be quiet, Miss Marshall."

She knew she'd succeeded in rattling him and, glancing over at the knives next to Kelly, realized rattling him further was the best strategy to delay his hand. *But you could make it worse,* she thought, then thought of the third missing girl and Steven's ravaged face. It had been the worst crime scene of his career. That's what Josh Lutz was capable of. So anything she did couldn't make anything worse. Faster, maybe. But not worse.

"They wouldn't go with you, would they?" she asked. "So how did you make them meet you in the middle of the night? I doubt it was on the force of your winning personality."

Josh's jaw clenched. "For a woman claiming an advanced degree, you are very foolish."

"You're going to kill me anyway," she said evenly. "What do I have to lose?"

A scowl furrowed his forehead, then smoothed. "Sensible, actually."

He'd calmed. She needed to stir him up again. "You lied to them, didn't you?"

He drew dye into the syringe. "I told them what they wanted to hear," he said reasonably. "They all wanted to date a popular jock. It was pathetically easy." He picked up the needle.

Jenna's gut churned. *Stall.* "You told them you were Rudy," she said, keeping her voice steady.

Josh huffed an impatient sigh. "Of course I did. Now be quiet. I want this tattoo perfect."

Jenna searched her brain again. "So you failed in your initial synthesis of ketamine," she blurted and watched his hand wobble, then steady.

"No," he said carefully. "I quickly realized I needed a lab more well equipped than my own."

"That's what I figured. That's what I told the police. I told them you were incapable of synthesizing ketamine all by yourself, that it was beyond the limits of your intellect."

His hand clenched around the syringe and a few drops of blue dye spilled on the table. "I said, my laboratory was insufficient," he gritted.

"You couldn't have done it even if you had a well-stocked lab. You're not trained to do so. I, on the other hand, am trained to do so. You overrate your own skill."

He turned and she could see his eyes glittering. "Be quiet, Miss Marshall."

"It's Dr. Marshall," she said crisply and watched him flinch. "It's *Dr.* because I earned my degree. Which makes me a great deal smarter than you. So did you steal it?" she asked, pressing forward, now that she had him off-kilter. Anything to keep him from touching Kelly. Even if he turned the syringe and carving tools on her. "Did you resort to common theft to get the ketamine?"

"No. Now be quiet or I'll tape your damn mouth shut." He bent down over Kelly's head, the syringe once again steady in his hand, and Jenna worked her ankles in the knotted rope, loosening the knot with every movement.

"What about Seattle, Joshua?" she asked, grabbing for any detail. "Did you kill girls there?"

He jerked, his jaw clenched. "Shut. Up." She saw blue ink spurt from the syringe, covering Kelly's bald scalp. With a curse Josh wiped the ink from Kelly's head and threw the towel in a trash can. "Now look what you've made me do," he snarled, then visibly got hold of himself.

"Did you? Those four girls on the wall, are they the ones you killed in Seattle? You know that's why Detective Davies is here, don't you? He knows it's you." She wasn't sure Neil knew any such thing, but prayed Neil and Steven would figure it out.

"Davies is another cop that can't tell his ass from a hole in the wall," he gritted. "Davies thinks Rudy is the killer," Josh continued, his voice laced with sarcasm. "I even gave him Rudy on a silver platter back in Seattle, but Davies screwed it up. Mishandled evidence. And Rudy went free."

"So Rudy was innocent the whole time."

Josh laughed, tapping the bubbles from the syringe. "Rudy is incapable of the thought required to be a killer. Rudy is good for one thing only. Football. And thanks to you he doesn't even have that." He looked up, one brow cocked. "Thank you for that, by the way."

She'd actually opened her mouth to say "you're welcome," but said instead, "You hate Rudy."

"And you have a Ph.D.," Josh drawled. "Of course I hate Rudy. Everybody hates Rudy."

"Not true," Jenna corrected and saw his spine snap. "Everyone likes Rudy. Especially girls."

"Stupid whores. All of 'em," Josh muttered. "Shut up and let me work."

"Davies had a semen sample on the Seattle killer. If Davies thought Rudy was the killer, it must have been Rudy's. Now that took work—making it look like it was his when it was yours."

Josh looked across the barn with narrowed eyes. "If you want to know how I killed those girls and made it look like Rudy did it, just ask."

"So how did you, Joshua?" Jenna asked, making him

scowl. He didn't like to be called Joshua. "How did Rudy's semen get in your murder victim?"

"The old-fashioned way," Josh snarled. "He fucked her."

"And you wanted to," Jenna guessed, "but she liked Rudy better."

"She was mine," he said coldly. "He stole her from me."

"So you killed her."

"Oh, yes."

"And the second? What about her? Was she Rudy's girl also?"

Josh stopped, then looked up with an easy smile that chilled her more than the snarl. He was back in control. "Not bad, Miss Marshall. Got me to say a little more than I'd planned. Well, I'll tell you how it was." He put down the tattoo needle and picked up one of the large knives. "I killed the first one and didn't really mean to. I wanted her and wanted her to want me, you know?"

Jenna swallowed and watched him walk around the table, deliberately, the knife clutched in his hand. So this would be it, she thought. Steven would find her stabbed, bald corpse, just like the others. But her feet were nearly free. A few more wiggles and she'd have worked a space big enough to slide her foot through. So she'd stall. For just a few more moments.

"But she didn't want you," she made herself answer. "She thought you weren't as good as Rudy. You weren't as handsome. Weren't as smart."

His step hitched and he stumbled, wincing, grabbing at his upper thigh. Jean-Luc had bitten him on the thigh. He resumed walking toward her, slowly but steadily. "I was smart," he snarled, "right up until those doctors doped me up so I couldn't think. I was smarter than all of them and they couldn't stand that. They drugged me, every damn day, until I didn't know who I was or what I was doing."

"Until your IQ was eighty-five and they put you in special classes," Jenna gibed. "That hurt."

"What will hurt is when I cut you, like I cut all the others." He grabbed her by the collar and pointed the knife at her throat. "I killed the first girl without meaning to. But you know what? I found out it was fun. It was damn exhilarating. It was pure pleasure."

"It was control," Jenna whispered, watching his eyes, inches from her own. They flickered. Then narrowed.

"It was control," he repeated. "Maybe you did deserve that Ph.D. after all," he mocked and pressed the knife closer. She wanted to swallow, but fought it. If she swallowed, the knife would cut deeper. "I missed out on killing you the first time, Miss Marshall. Now I have another chance and I intend to make the most of it."

This is it. He'll kill me. Then he'll kill Kelly. Her brain froze, then blessed anger surged, loosening her tongue. *No. I'm not ready to die yet.* "You won't, Joshua. You can't. I am your teacher. I am in charge here."

His eyes flickered wildly. "You are not in charge. You're tied up. I am in charge."

She didn't think then, just acted, planting both her feet against his gut and shoving.

Caught off guard he grunted and stumbled, giving her the precious seconds she needed to work her feet, loosening the knot the millimeter she needed. Then she slipped her foot free and kicked him with all her might.

Stunned, he staggered back and she kicked his thigh where he'd held it. Where her dog had bitten him in a frantic attempt to save her life. His cry of pain told her the kick had been well placed and she jumped from the table and ran. Ran toward the barn door, away from Kelly and prayed he'd follow her. She paused at the barn door, looked right, then left.

Then stopped as moonlight glinted off the shiny barrel of the gun pointed straight at her face.

Saturday, October 15, 2:15 A.M.

Steven stared at the small barn, seeing the muted light through the only window. *She was in there.* That's where the bastard held her. If she was still alive. *Don't even think that.*

He pulled his weapon from his shoulder holster. "I know you want him to stand trial in Seattle, Davies, and so do I, but if I have to kill him to get Jenna away, I will."

Davies drew his own weapon. "Understood." Then his eyes narrowed and he pointed to the far corner of the barn. "Thatcher, look. She did know where he was. That bitch."

Steven watched the slim shadow creeping toward the door, a grim satisfaction settling over him. "Harry said Nora asked the farmer to give Josh another chance. She must have known where this barn was all along." Then the satisfaction evaporated when a loud crash came from the barn.

The thin dark shadow ran for the barn door and too late Steven saw the glint of silver.

"Shit, she's got a gun." Steven held his radio to his lips, his feet already moving. "Lennie, keep everyone on standby. We're going in."

Then he cursed again when he looked to his side and saw Davies was no longer there.

THIRTY-SIX

Saturday, October 15, 2:20 A.M.

THE GUN WAS SHINY, ALMOST TOO PERFECT to be real. But it was very real. And pointed in her face.

"You've caused enough trouble for my son, Miss Marshall. It's time to go."

Jenna looked down the barrel of the gun to the face of the woman she'd last seen wearing a god-awful nightgown. "Mrs. Lutz."

"*Mother,*" Josh said from behind her, angry.

Jenna heard hysterical laughter and vaguely realized it came from inside her own throat. "You're going to help him," she said, incredulous.

"I am his mother. That's what mothers do. Not being a mother, you wouldn't understand. Joshua, take the path to the car. We pulled off as the main road has been closed by the police."

Police, Jenna thought, her knees going weak with relief. *Steven.*

Mrs. Lutz was frowning at Josh, who hadn't moved. "Run along, son. I'll take care of her."

Jenna shook her head, hardly able to process what she'd heard. "*You're* going to kill me now?"

"Without fanfare. A simple bullet in the head and both my sons' problems will be solved."

Jenna looked into Nora Lutz's eyes, realizing she was seeing true insanity. "Like you solved all the problems in Seattle?"

Mrs. Lutz's lips bent in a tight smile. "My Rudy was innocent. Any jury would have said so."

"Any jury didn't have a chance. You paid someone to set Neil Davies up, didn't you?"

She lifted a shoulder in a half shrug. "My Rudy was innocent."

"Because your Josh is guilty as hell," Jenna returned, enraged and helpless.

"My Joshua is a sick boy who will get help. You are a bothersome insect who will be a bother no longer. Into the barn, please."

Jenna stared. "You've got to be kidding. If you're going to shoot me, it will be right here. You're insane. Simply insane."

Mrs. Lutz cocked the trigger. "I am armed," she corrected in a calm, genteel voice. "Simply armed. And if I have to shoot you here, I will."

Jenna watched as Mrs. Lutz's arm rose steadily, as if in slow motion. *She's going to kill me. Right now. Steven will find me dead. It's too late.*

Mrs. Lutz's arm had reached the top of her arc when she flicked her eyes sideways, the gun following. There was a flash of light, two deafening blasts in rapid succession. Then the sick thud of a body hitting the ground. A big body. *Steven. No.*

With a hoarse cry Jenna spun around, only to see the body on the ground was Neil's. A sick combination of relief and panic coursed through her and she took a stumbling step, falling to her knees next to Neil. But with her hands still tied behind her she was unable to help him. Unable to stem the dark stain spreading on his thigh. He lay bent at the waist and writhing, his face contorted in agony. He clutched one hand with the other and Jenna could see another stream of blood gushing from his right hand. He'd been shot twice, leg and hand. But he was alive.

"That felt remarkably cathartic," Mrs. Lutz said from behind her, her voice dry. "Get up, Miss Marshall, or the next one will go between his eyes. And I promise you I'm a very good shot."

Neil looked up at her, his eyes glazed with pain. "Do it, Jenna. Do what she says."

"Oh, to hear those words from your throat after all this time," Mrs. Lutz said, her tone now amused. "Get up, Miss Marshall. Now."

Jenna pushed herself to her feet, trembling from a combination of shock, fear, rage, and utter helplessness. Kelly lay dying inside and Neil lay at her feet, his blood spilling onto the ground.

"That's very wise, Miss Marshall. Now, Josh, go to the car. Dr. Nelson is waiting for you."

"No, Mother. I won't."

You go, Josh, Jenna thought, another hysterical laugh threatening to break free.

Mrs. Lutz heaved an impatient sigh. "Joshua, I found the pills under your mattress. I know you haven't been taking them for months. Now go to the car and let Dr. Nelson help you."

"He'll dope you up so you can't think, Josh." Jenna said desperately. "He'll dope you up so you won't be smart anymore."

Mrs. Lutz shoved the gun against her head. "In the barn, Miss Marshall. Joshua, in the car."

Jenna stumbled, the gun at her temple, trying to think of something, anything she could do. Then she heard another click and the voice she'd feared she'd never hear again.

"Put the gun down, Mrs. Lutz," Steven said calmly, "and Josh will not get hurt."

Pure relief coursed through her, leaving her shaken. "*Steven*," Jenna said, wishing she could say everything else that rushed to her lips, but Mrs. Lutz shoved the gun harder into her temple.

"You won't shoot my son," Mrs. Lutz said evenly. "You'll just take him to jail and I'll get him out. I, on the other hand, will shoot *her* with very little compunction. So what will it be, Agent Thatcher? My son or this woman? Decide quickly. I have very little time and very little to lose."

Jenna held her breath, knowing Steven was behind her, knowing he wouldn't, couldn't let a killer go. Knowing Kelly lay inside the barn, her life in the balance. "Steven, Kelly's inside," Jenna said, knowing he needed the full score. "She's alive."

"I have more than one bullet, Agent Thatcher," Mrs. Lutz said, with that same eerie calm. "And I will do anything to save my son. Drop your gun and kick it over to me."

After a pregnant pause, Jenna flinched at the sound of gunfire as Steven released his round.

Into the air. Followed by the soft thud of a blunt object hitting the ground. Mrs. Lutz's gun left her temple and she heard the rustle of clothing as the insane woman retrieved Steven's weapon.

"Take your son," Steven said. "But let the women go."

Jenna cried, "Steven, no—" and stopped when the gun ground into her head once again.

"Into the barn, Dr. Marshall," Mrs. Lutz commanded.

"But you said—" Jenna's protest was cut off when Mrs. Lutz pushed her. Jenna stumbled and fell into the barn, scraping her face on the wood floor, unable to break her own fall. Fueled by sheer instinct, Jenna rolled and Mrs. Lutz's shot narrowly missed her head.

Shaking her head clear, Jenna saw Steven rush forward, only for Josh to grab Steven around the neck and pull him backward, away from the barn. Jenna scrambled to her feet as Mrs. Lutz took aim and again Jenna let her instincts rule. Her leg shot out and around and the gun flew, landing harmlessly against the far wall. She came down on the balls of her feet and kicked again, this time striking Mrs. Lutz mid-torso, hearing a crack as Josh's mother's skull hit the floor, seeing the woman lay there, stunned.

Breathing hard, Jenna looked over to where Josh had Steven pinned to the ground, straddling his chest, his hands around Steven's throat. Steven's hands were around Josh's wrists, the two engaged in silent struggle. Steven was strong, but Josh had the advantage of youth and the strength of insanity. Josh was killing Steven.

Not today, Jenna thought. *I need my hands.* She ran to the table where Kelly lay tied, her eyes open, but unfocused. Jenna fumbled for one of the knives with her tied hands and slid the handle under Kelly's body as the girl blinked and struggled to speak.

"Just lean on it, honey," Jenna begged. "Don't let it slide."

Jenna leaned back against the sharp edge of the knife and tried to cut her bonds.

And felt the knife slide, the sharp tip nicking her own wrist. Pain pricked and blood flowed and Steven and Josh still struggled. So Jenna repositioned the knife and tried again, leaning backward to work the blade against the rope.

And this time the blade stayed put as Kelly somehow summoned enough energy to lean on the knife. "Good girl, Kelly." A few jerks and another deep nick and Jenna's hands were free. She grabbed a mask, knowing it was filled with the powder that would make Josh powerless in less time than it took to count backward from ten.

She ran to where Steven was still locked in struggle with Josh, his brown eyes wide, his face mottled red from exertion and lack of oxygen. Standing behind Josh, Jenna wrapped the mask around his face and pulled like hell. *Ten, nine, eight . . .* Just a few seconds more.

But Josh fought hard, dropping his hands from Steven's throat and grabbing at Jenna's hands behind his head. She hung on and counted as Steven pulled Josh's hands from hers.

"*Seven, six, five . . .*" she muttered, then cried out when Josh dug his fingernails into her wrists, ripping at her already abraded skin. Just when she thought Josh would break free, an arm reached around her and pressed the mask across Josh's mouth. *Neil*. His hand dripped blood, but still he used the flat of his arm to hold the mask in place, forcing Josh to breathe the ketamine.

"*Four, three . . .*" Jenna whispered and Josh slumped to the ground. Steven rolled onto his side, drawing in great gasps of air, and Neil collapsed behind her with a weak groan.

For a moment no one said anything, their labored breathing the only sound.

Steven pushed himself to his knees and looked at her through the sweat pouring in his eyes, his heart beating so hard he thought it would break free from his chest. Her hair was gone, she had a new purple bruise covering the side of her face and her wrists were smeared with blood. But she was alive. And still the most beautiful woman he'd ever seen.

"Are you okay?" he rasped out, choking on each breath he forced down his sore throat.

She nodded. "You?"

"I've had worse." He grabbed his radio. "Officer down. Neil's been hit."

"What about Jenna?" came Lennie's crackling voice. "And Kelly Templeton?"

"I'm fine," Jenna said. "Kelly needs an ambulance and quickly."

Steven lurched to his feet. "Three ambulances." He stumbled into the barn doorway and saw Nora Lutz's unconscious body sprawled on the floor. "Make it four."

His radio rattled. "Steven, it's Liz. Where's Josh Lutz?"

Steven looked at Lutz's motionless body with disgust. "He's alive. We can Mirandize him when he comes to." He dropped to one knee and cuffed Nora Lutz, thinking it ironic how the silver of the cuffs clashed with the diamond bracelets she wore on both wrists. *Let's see what your money will buy you this time, rich bitch,* he thought, then rolled to his feet when Jenna limped into the barn.

Jenna grabbed his arm, her hands smearing blood on his sleeve, her eyes frantic. "Seth?"

"He's alive," Steven assured her and watched her relax. "Allison figured he'd taken you to the cemetery to talk. She found him unconscious and called 911. He has a headache, but he's alive. You need to sit," he said, wanting to take her face in his hands but was afraid he'd hurt her.

She shook her shorn head. "I want to cover Kelly before the paramedics come."

She wanted Kelly to maintain some semblance of dignity, he understood, so he shrugged out of his jacket, tossing it on the ground, then unsnapped his holster and unbuttoned his shirt. "My shirt will be softer than my coat," he said, then refastened his holster against his bare skin.

Jenna hesitated, clutching his shirt in her bloody hands. "I have so much to say to you," she whispered. "I don't know where to start."

Steven took her face in his hands, as gently as he could. He had to prove to himself she was whole. He placed a kiss on her forehead, a half inch from where the stubble that had been her beautiful black hair began and felt her shudder. He looked down into her incredible eyes, so very grateful she was still alive. Nothing else seemed to matter. "Do what you need to do for Kelly." He cocked his head, hearing approaching footsteps. "Hurry and cover her and I'll tend to Neil. The cavalry's here."

THIRTY-SEVEN

Sunday, October 16, 10:00 A.M.

CASEY RAN A SHAKY HAND OVER JENNA'S stubbled scalp.
"Well, we could take it down to the skin and you could go as
Sinead O'Connor for Halloween," Casey said, trying for a
cheerful tone but her voice wobbled and Jenna knew she was
close to tears.

Jenna made herself smile for the benefit of her friends and
family who'd gathered in the hospital waiting room to make
sure she was truly all right. "Won't Father Mike be pleased?"

"I don't think he'll mind," said Father Mike from his seat
against the wall. His had been the first face she'd seen when
the ambulance brought her into the ER, smiling but terribly
worried.

Her first words had been questions about Kelly's and
Neil's condition. He'd told her Neil was in surgery and that
Kelly's family was with her in ICU but wanted to talk to
Jenna.

Six hours later Neil was still in surgery to repair the shattered bones in his thigh and hand.

Kelly's family had found Jenna in the ER, their expressions a wild combination of gratitude, relief, and grief.

Now, hours later, Jenna was numb. She expected to feel
the jitters and the panic later. For now she was taking refuge
in the faces of the people who loved her most.

Seth was there, of course, sporting his own bandage, com-
pliments of Josh Lutz. Allison sat very quietly, clinging to her
father's hand, knowing how close they'd come to losing him.
Seth was blustery and tried to joke, but in the end he'd broken

down, holding Jenna, rocking her, which she understood was purely for his own peace. If there was anything she'd learned in the last weeks it was that people needed to care for those they loved and to deny their care was to deny their love.

Lucas came and joked about Casey and Jenna setting up permanent residence in the hospital, which the nurses had not found amusing. Casey had apparently been a less than ideal patient.

But Charlie was the one to truly break the tension, walking boldly into the hushed waiting room, a baseball cap in her hand. "Some people have attractive bald heads, Aunt Jenna," she'd said. "You are not one of them." And she slapped the cap on Jenna's head with a great flourish.

Helen had arrived with the boys about an hour before, Nicky giving her a hug that nearly broke her ribs, reminding her that she and Steven were no closer to resolution. They'd been through fire, saved each other's lives, but had no closure on the very basic issue of "them." Still she'd held Nicky, laughing in all the right places when he told her about a rhino from Ohio who yodeled in the Alps.

Steven was the one person she hadn't seen that morning, her last look at him being from the back of the ambulance at about three A.M. He'd looked scared, as if he still couldn't believe it was over and she was safe. He'd gone into SBI headquarters, insisting he follow the arrest of Josh and his mother to the end and Jenna supposed that's where he still was.

She wasn't sure what she'd say when she saw him. *Thank you,* seemed inadequate. *I love you,* would be true, but awkward considering where they'd left things. She'd start with *I've missed you* and *Hold me.*

Then, as if conjured from her thoughts, she heard his voice behind her. "Jenna."

She turned, conscious of everyone watching her. She stared at him, at his face that was bruised from Josh's fists, at the marks around his neck from Josh's strangling hands. At the look in his beautiful brown eyes that seemed to say everything that was racing through her mind.

Thank you. I love you. I'm sorry. I've missed you. Please hold me.

She wasn't sure who moved first, just that she was in his arms and he was holding her, finally. Then he was kissing her, there in the hospital waiting room with all their friends and family looking on.

Jenna rested her forehead against his chin. "I was going to say I've missed you and ask you to hold me," she murmured. "But you already are."

He kissed her forehead. "Back at the barn you said you had things to say to me," he whispered.

Thank you, I'm sorry, I love you. The words sang through her mind. "I do, but I was hoping for a place a little more private to say them," she whispered back, now very aware of the curious eyes behind them. "How about some coffee?"

"I was going to suggest Rocky Road."

"Then what are we waiting for? Let's go."

They were sitting in the Volvo, parked in front of the convenience store, and Jenna was just finishing the Rocky Road. She'd hung back, saying she didn't want to be seen in public, and his stomach clenched. Despite the bruises and the cuts and the shorn head she was still beautiful and now, as he sat next to her, he desperately wished he had the words to make her believe that.

"Jenna, I don't know where to start."

"Thank you," she said abruptly, then sighed. "That was on my list of things to say."

He looked out the car window, unable to look at her. "For what? Putting bruises on your face?"

She sighed. "No, for saving my life. You never touched

me, Steven. These bruises have nothing to do with you." She paused. "Well, the ones from Thursday night do," she amended.

"Thanks," he muttered bitterly.

"Well, they do. You want to know what the other two things were I wanted to say?"

"Sure, why not?"

"I'm sorry."

He jerked around to meet her eyes. "For what?"

She shrugged uneasily. "I think mostly for holding you to an unfair standard. I was comparing you to Adam from the beginning and that wasn't fair. I'm also sorry for not considering the hurt I'd do to the boys by being so stubborn. They're part of you, so they're part of me, too."

Steven swallowed hard. "Thank you." He dug in his pocket and pulled out Adam Llewellyn's ring. "This belongs to you."

Her eyes widened. "Where did you get that? I left it on Adam's headstone yesterday."

"Allison gave it to me. She hoped the ring would bring me luck in finding you, I think."

She just looked at the ring, making no attempt to take it. "You never said anything about me wearing it all this time. I usually forgot I had it on."

Steven shrugged. "I figured you'd put it aside in your own time."

She closed his hand over the ring, enclosing his fist in her hands. "It's time to give it back to Seth," she said. "I don't need it anymore."

He brought their hands to his lips. "I'm sorry, Jenna," he whispered. "I'm so sorry I didn't trust you. Once I'd calmed down I knew you'd never be a betrayer."

She looked at him, yearning in her eyes. "I know. What I want to know is what will happen next time before you calm down? What if we're married? What if we have children together?"

His heart stumbled, then kicked. "I want that more than anything."

"So do I," she said and for a moment he felt such elation . . . Then she added, "But not if I have to worry about every man I see, I smile at, or say hello to. I have to know you trust me, or this isn't going to work. I don't want to build a life with you only to resent you years from now."

He hung his head. "I can't make promises like that, Jenna. I want to, but I can't. I can't promise I won't see you with another man and wonder or even get mad. I may falter and fall because I'm human. I can promise to make it the thing I work hardest on in my life. But *I* need to know you won't walk away from me. I couldn't take that again."

"I love you," she said and his head jerked up. She smiled at the surprise on his face. "That was the last thing I wanted to say to you. I think if you'd made a rash promise to never get jealous again just to keep me I probably would have asked you to take me back to Seth. But you didn't, because you're a man of integrity. I love that about you. I respect that about you."

He was almost afraid to ask. "Jenna, will you come home with me?"

She put her finger over his lips. "No, and let me tell you why. Do you remember the night I tried to seduce you? The night Casey was hurt? That night you said you had responsibilities? Three of them? You still do, Steven. We leapt into this whole relationship so fast. Partly because we'd both been lonely and partly because of all the craziness around us. We played house this week and it was wonderful. I tucked your son into bed and pretended he was mine. I want him to be mine. But I want him to understand how normal people do things."

His lips quirked up against her finger. "I thought we'd abandoned all hope of normalcy."

Her eyes smiled at him. "Pretend with me, Steven. We'll have dates. You'll pick me up at my place and take me out for beer and hot wings. Sometimes, if I'm at your house, I'll tuck in your son. We'll grow together. Then, soon, we'll grow into a family." She swallowed and brought his hand to her lips again. "I was so afraid I'd die last night, Steven, and never have you as my own. Never have a family with you. But I don't want that fear to make us leap so fast we miss the important growth along the way.

"You've given this a lot of thought."

Her smile was wry. "I had some free time last night."

"I love you, Jenna. I'd ask you to marry me today if I thought you'd say yes."

"I would say yes," she said. "So don't ask. Not yet. Give us the time to become a family. Then ask me and I'll still say yes."

"Jenna?" He leaned forward and pushed the baseball cap off her head, grabbing it when she would have pulled it back on. "Stop. I want to see your eyes and I can't with this hat on your head." She put her hands in her lap and he could see her worry her thumb, where Adam's ring had been. *Old habits die hard,* he thought. "Look at me, please?"

She did, and the look in her eyes made him kiss her again. "Just don't take too long, okay? I need you in my life. I'm not a normal guy. I won't have time for beer and hot wings all the time. I have soccer games and bedtime stories and I need you to have those things with me."

His plea pulled at Jenna's heart and she was so tempted to give in and go home with him today. The picture he painted was everything she ever wanted. But they did need the time to get to know each other. To ensure they'd be a functioning family unit once they took that irrevocable next step. "Let's give ourselves till Christmas," she said. "Then we can decide what to do next."

"Christmas it is," he whispered, cupping the back of her head, reminding her—as if she could forget—that she had no hair. But he honestly didn't seem to care so she tried not to either. He grazed her lips with his. "We don't have to wait for everything, do we?" he murmured. "I mean, we can still . . ."

"I should think so," she whispered. "We've still got two unopened boxes."

He groaned and kissed her. "I was hoping you'd see it that way."

THIRTY-EIGHT

Friday, October 28, 9:00 A.M.

STEVEN WALKED INTO THE HOSPITAL ROOM, wishing he had better news for Neil Davies.

Davies was sitting up in bed, looking grim, and Steven knew he'd already heard.

"How are you?" he said and Davies scowled.

"My ass hurts and the whole sponge-bath thing is a damn myth."

Steven's lips quirked up. "You're feeling better then."

Davies grunted. "Yeah. I guess so. How's Jenna?"

"She went to karate last night, looking very scary in her *gi* with that hair. Like an extra in a very bad Jackie Chan flick."

Davies grunted again, but this time with the ghost of a

smile. "Grace Jones watch out," he said, then sobered. "And Kelly?"

"She's been released from the hospital into the care of a therapist. Her parents are talking about moving to another town. Getting a new start."

"Sometimes that's the way to do it," Davies said.

"Are you going back to Seattle?"

Davies smiled. "And don't you just wish I were?" But it was said without antagonism.

"Honestly, yeah. But if you stay you know you're always welcome in my home."

Davies chuckled. "I knew I hated you," he said companionably. "I try to steal your woman and you invite me home for supper."

Steven raised a brow. "Of course I have heard Seattle is pretty this time of year."

Davies shook his head. "Actually, I was thinking about going down to Florida. My brother owns a charter boat and he's asked me to come and give him a hand with the fishing excursions."

"I can think of worse places to recuperate," Steven said.

Neither of them said anything for a full minute, then Steven handed Davies the newspaper he'd brought. "You heard, I take it."

"Yeah, I saw it on CNN. '*Mother of serial killer kills family, killer, then self,*'" Davies read, then looked up. "Chilling courtroom drama," he said dryly. "Sorry I missed it."

"Nora hid the needle in her lipstick. She apparently went to the ladies' room just before the arraignment and assembled the syringe. Then when the judge banged his gavel, she jumped up, hysterical. Hugging Josh. Then ten seconds later Josh hit the deck and everybody scrambled. She'd stabbed the needle in his heart and hit the plunger. The ME said there was enough tranq in that syringe to take down an elephant." He sighed. "The bailiff was trying to make Josh stand up—he didn't realize he was dead already. Nora grabs his gun. Eats it. The end."

"And they all lived happily ever after," Davies said dryly. "In hell."

Davies looked down at the paper. "She shot the other two before she left the house."

Steven rubbed the back of his neck. The sight had been a grisly one. "Rudy was in his bed. Didn't look like he suffered. Her husband was on the toilet, of all places." Steven thought of the shots to Victor Lutz's head, heart, and groin, the latter probably for all his unfaithfulness over the years. "I think he did. Suffer, that is."

"Couldn't have happened to a nicer guy."

"I'd have to agree with you there."

"I can understand the husband, but not the kids," Davies said. "Why'd she do it?"

"Nora left a note. Said she couldn't bear the thought of her son in jail, that he was sick, needed help, et cetera, et cetera. If he couldn't get help it was better to die than to rot in prison for the rest of his life. She couldn't live without Josh and she didn't want Rudy to have to survive without them all. After Rudy's arrest in Seattle she took Josh to a psychiatrist without Victor's knowledge. She suspected then that it was Josh, not Rudy, who'd done the crimes. Apparently she'd caught Josh doing some pretty sick things to the neighbor's dog and knew her kid wasn't right. Anyway, she paid someone to tamper with your evidence, then had the shrinks dope Josh up. To control him. His psychiatrist from Seattle called me yesterday after he heard Josh was dead. Told me his doctor/client no longer applied and he filled in a few more blanks. He said that Josh and Rudy were twins but that Nora pulled Josh out of school for a year after Seattle for treatment. That's why he was a year behind Rudy." One corner of Steven's mouth lifted. "Told me that in his clinical opinion Josh Lutz was one sick bastard, but that Nora might have been worse."

Davies folded the paper. "Guess the apple didn't fall too far from that tree."

Steven pushed away from the wall he'd been leaning against. "Like you said, couldn't have happened to a nicer family." He turned for the door, hesitated, then turned back. "Neil, thanks."

Davies looked away. "I still hate your guts."

Steven's smile was more rueful than anything else. "Just so we're square. Drop by before you head south. I know Jen will want to say good-bye."

He'd made it to the door when he heard, "Thatcher."

Not looking back, he said, "What?"

"You're welcome. Don't fuck up again 'cause I don't plan to be as benevolent next time."

Steven sucked in his cheeks. "You're a real prince, Davies. See you around." He walked to the end of the hospital corridor where he punched the down button on the elevator, a definite spring in his step.

Tonight he had a date with Jenna. Beer and hot wings. And afterward he was planning to get very, very lucky.

Epilogue

Sunday, December 25, 10:30 A.M.

"IS IT ALWAYS LIKE THIS?" JENNA ASKED, humored exhaustion in her voice. She and Steven sat on the sofa looking out at the sea of wrapping paper covering the living room.

Steven put his arm around her shoulders and pulled her closer to him, enjoying the scent of coconuts and the feel of her breast pushed against his side. "Sure. This was actually pretty tame."

At that moment Cindy Lou tore out of the kitchen through the living room sending wrapping paper everywhere. Nicky ran after her, Jim and Jean-Luc at his heels. His boy was happy, laughing. And sleeping through the night in his new bed shaped like a car.

Brad had sent out his college applications and now his only reason to frown was over which school he would choose when he was accepted.

Matt . . . was Matt. And Steven was awfully glad it was so. No traumas, not yet anyway, except Matt had brought a girl to the Christmas party they'd had the weekend before. Scary.

Jenna snuggled closer against him. "I saw the postcard you got from Helen."

"The one with the naked natives?" Steven asked wryly.

Jenna choked. "No. I saw the one of the safari truck on the Serengeti plain." She looked up at him with a naughty grin. "Where'd you hide the one with the naked natives?"

"For you to find later." He kissed her and she settled into him like warm honey. "How'd you like your presents?"

Her eyes softened. "I thought I was going to cry."

She was thinking about Nicky's gift then, not the one he'd given her. That fact made him love her even more. What kind of woman would get excited over a seven-year-old's hand-made storybook populated with kissing llamas, yodeling rhinos, and glue-eating kangaroos?

A mother would, that's who. She leaned forward and plucked the book from the top of her small pile of gifts and opened it once again to the last page where Nicky had scrawled in purple crayon, *To Jenna, From Nicky* and below in very small letters, *I love you.* She traced her fingertip over the three little words and sniffled.

Steven pulled her close again and kissed the top of her head where her hair had grown just long enough to be considered very stylish. "If I'd known you were that easy to please I'd have made the plane tickets with crayon myself."

She looked back up at him and her eyes sparkled. "I can't believe it. You're really going to take off two whole weeks to go to Hawaii with me?"

I'd do anything for you, he thought. "Um-hmm. But there's kind of a catch."

Her violet eyes narrowed. "What catch? Kent and Harry are not coming."

He drew a breath, then spit it out. "I want it to be our honeymoon trip." Her eyes widened.

"Your logic appears to be flawed, Special Agent Man," she said lightly. "We can't go on a honeymoon unless we've had a wedding first."

He didn't take his eyes off hers and in two long beats of his heart, all teasing fled and her eyes heated. "Marry me, Jenna. Be my family."

"Yes," she whispered. "It's all I've ever wanted. You're all I've ever wanted. I love you."

He fumbled in his pocket for the simple but elegant diamond ring that had been all but burning his skin all morning, brought it out, slid it on her finger. "I love you, too." But she didn't look at the ring, just kept looking into his eyes. As if she couldn't get enough of him. And he knew that this time, with this woman, he'd done it right.

THE HEARTBREAKER

Carly Phillips

It takes a very special woman to catch a Chandler man . . .

Meet the Chandlers – a trio of sexy brothers and the most eligible guys in town . . . until their mother falls ill. As her three sons gather at her side, she makes two desperate demands: "Get married!" and "Give me grandchildren!"

Journalist Chase Chandler is single and loving it . . . until a tantalizing redhead catches the eye of the eldest Chandler brother. A senator's daughter who refuses to play the Washington game, Sloane Carlisle has come to Yorkshire Falls to solve a family mystery that's already making headlines. All Chase has to do for an exclusive is keep her out of harm's way. It's bad enough playing bodyguard to a woman who has "settle down" written all over her – does she have to be irresistible, too? Suddenly a lifelong loner with a reputation for breaking hearts is starting to think about getting hitched and raising a family. What will it take to get Sloane to say the two words that will turn the town's most eligible bachelor into the world's sexiest husband?

'Carly Phillips, publishing's newest, brightest star, shines'
– Fern Michaels, *New York Times* bestselling author

'A seriously sexy story!' – Romantic Times Bookclub

'Carly Phillips writes sexy stories packed with fast-paced fun' – Stella Cameron, *New York Times* bestselling author

Other bestselling Warner Forever titles available by mail: